VANDELLA
RESILIENCE

VANDELLA
RESILIENCE

M.CH.LANDA

LANDA PUBLISHINGS

Edited by Kelly Schaub and Lara Kennedy

Dear reader, thank you for purchasing a copy of *Vandella: Resilience*. As an artist, your economic support, honest reviews, and sincere recommendation to your close ones are what allow me to continue this writing venture.

That's why, as a token of gratitude, I want to share with you the short story **"The Courier,"** intended to be read before this novel. Please visit my webpage, **www.mchlanda.com**, and subscribe to my newsletter to download it for **FREE**.

Thank you again, and I hope you enjoy it.

Sincerely,
M. Ch. Landa

For my late mother,
for your resilience and dedication

Boundary with Netherlands
Journey
Nijmegen
House
Kleve
Groesbeek
Rhine River
Kranenburg
Wesel
Reckli
Weeze
Meuse River
Dinslaken
Gladbeck
Knikkerdorp
Oberhausen
Essen
Nederland
Deutschland
Duisburg

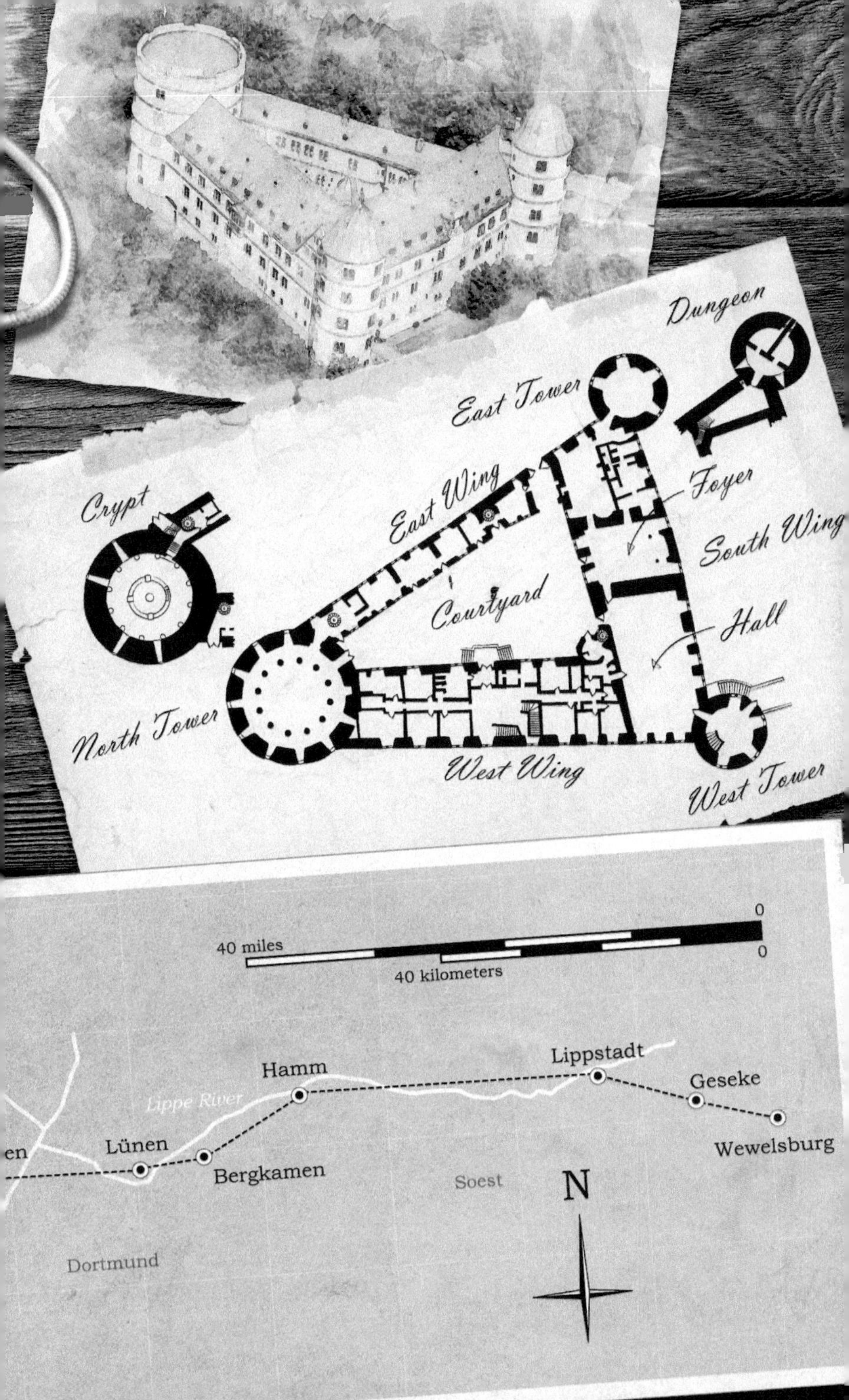
East Tower
Dungeon
East Wing
Foyer
Crypt
South Wing
Courtyard
Hall
North Tower
West Wing
West Tower
40 miles
40 kilometers
0
0
Lippstadt
Hamm
Geseke
Lippe River
Lünen
Wewelsburg
Bergkamen
Soest
Dortmund
N

PROLOGUE

DESPITE HAVING ONLY BEEN GONE FOR A FEW DAYS, I was a stranger in my own house. Without Gran, it felt huge, cold, and lifeless.

"Maia, are you sure about this?" Shelly stood at the doorjamb. "You can stay at my house until you feel better… We can have girls' night every day!"

I smiled briefly, remembering all the silly things we'd done wearing pajamas. "Thanks, Shelly, but… I want— I need to be here." My heart sank at the sight of the vacant chair where my gran used to sit every morning to drink her coffee.

"I know." Shelly squeezed my shoulder. "I'll leave this in your room." She lifted the backpack containing my clothes and the manila envelope Bill had given me at the graveyard.

"You can leave them on the table."

"But the stairs—"

"Don't worry, Shelly. I'll manage. Crutches are temporary." I hugged her. "Thank you for everything you've done for me."

"That's what friends are for."

I nodded, and we both grinned.

"Please call me if you need something."

"I will."

Shelly closed the door.

Alone, I sighed, looking around. "What am I supposed to do now?"

I somehow still expected the always-wise response of my gran, but the empty house did not answer.

I grabbed the manila envelope and sat on the armchair. I dumped its contents over the coffee table, including the mysterious ancient, leather hardcover book. I brushed my fingertips around the outline of the word carved into the cover: *Resilience*. The word transmitted the despair of the hand that had engraved it. I browsed through. The first third of the book was missing, the remains of the torn pages still stuck to the binding. The first available page contained a dedication from my gran, so I assumed the discarded pages were unimportant. I read it aloud.

"'My dearest Maia'…" My voice broke at the thought of hearing her voice. "'By the time you read this, you will be clouded with questions, many of which not even I have an answer for. Sorry, I should have told you this before, but I lacked the courage. I kept silent, hoping my past would never haunt you, that you would not inherit my curse. But watching you lying prostrate in the hospital bed, my little Ruddy Bear, is what encouraged me to write this, heartbroken. Because you have the right to know the truth. The secret buried in my chest for so long. Maia, you must know how I met the Harbinger of Death…'"

CHAPTER 1

THAT MORNING I WOKE UP like a trained soldier, before my *Kienzle* alarm clock could ring. I blew out the candle on my nightstand as the first ray of light shone through the dew-tarnished windows. As a person afraid of sleeping in the dark, growing up during a time when keeping a light at night could pinpoint the target of a bombardier was challenging. Yet every night I dared to kindle a candlelight. It was a muffled cry of protest at war, when light and darkness were not a perfect metaphor for good and evil. There was too much evil happening in broad daylight, but also kindness blooming in the darkness.

I put on a white top, tucked this into my shorts, tied the laces of my shoes, and fastened my unruly frizzies with a headband, following the apparel of the woman depicted in the poster hanging on my bedroom wall. A beautiful, strong, and heroic woman crossing the finishing line, with the Nazi flag waving behind her. I sighed, envisioning myself like her, winning gold at the Olympics. I heiled, reading the phrase written at the top, *"Im Bund Deutscher Mädel,"* longing to reunite with my friends Gerda and Ania and all the other *BDM* girls. Because what was the point of belonging to a Band of German Maidens if we could not be together? Bonding, friendship, and belonging were all my eyes could see in that image. As a teenager, you didn't dare to question your allegiance. *Our cause is just,* we were told. Taught. Indoctrinated. So, they sent us off to wander a ruptured world, blindfolded by our naivete.

I grabbed my coat and sneaked out of my room, tiptoeing all the way down the stairs to avoid waking up my mother. In the kitchen, Frau Weber was already preparing breakfast. She smiled in collusion, her stubby finger pressed against her pursed lips. She sliced a bulky loaf of wheat bread and smeared it with marmalade—true strawberry marmalade, farmed and preserved by her, not the chemically colored jam distributed in those days in Berlin. It was one of the few advantages of living in the countryside. "*Danke,*" I whispered and headed outside.

The early sunbeams tinted the cloud canopy, and the spruces and pines topping the mountains radiated a halo of holiness. Chilly September wind blew my hair as I devoured my bread and went on stretching. "Up, right, down, left, up…" I touched my feet and the soil at each flex. I trotted back and forth across the earthen driveway several times, my heart pumping warm blood to my limbs, until my coat became unnecessary.

A figure loomed in the driveway. It was Herr Huber pulling his mule. "You rose earlier than the sun today, Peach!" he said, removing his hat.

"We leave for Wewelsburg after my class. My dear friend Gerda is marrying."

"*Ja,* your mother told me about it. Let me take old *Schwein* to the barn," he said, petting his mule. "I'll fetch your equipment before starting my day." Herr Huber was the first farm worker hired by my grandpa, and after fifty years was the sole remaining. "*Too old to remarry, too old to fight in the war,*" he used to say, after the passing of his wife by pneumonia and losing his son during the Great War. "*Plowing the fields is the only thing I have left.*"

Herr Huber came out of the barn carrying the wood frames he had helped me to assemble when I moved to the farm. We spaced the hurdles proportionally along the eighty meters of my makeshift track, and I jogged to the starting line. I knelt, hands behind the lime line and feet gripped tightly to the soil. Herr Huber held his handkerchief aloft, pocket watch in hand. When he gave the signal, I ran.

Sprinting a hurdle race relied on precision as much as speed, to calculate the exact moment to jump, having body and mind perfectly synchronized. After endless hours of training, your body acts instinctively, feeling almost magical. As I approached the finish line, I saw neither Herr Huber nor the farm. My mind had transported to the *Olympiastadion* in Berlin, surrounded by a crowd of thousands of cheering attendees. I raised my arms at crossing the finish line, imagining myself climbing to the summit of the podium, everybody cheering my triumph.

"Less than fifteen seconds, Peach!" Herr Huber said excitedly. "You broke your previous record."

"Yay!" I cavorted at the thought of being closer to materializing my dream. But my joy was short-lived.

"Emma!" My mother appeared at the door, arms akimbo. "How many times must I tell you not to play outside while it is still dark?"

I gulped. "I was training, not playing," I retorted.

"And you think the bombardiers will make a distinction?"

I sighed.

"Emma, we're at war."

"I know," I said, disheartened, remembering the air raids that broke Berlin's peace starting the summer of '40. Those countless nightmarish nights we'd had to sleep in the cellar had become unbearable for my mother by autumn of last year, 1943. "But that's why we moved to the quiet of the countryside, right? To live at peace. No bombings." I echoed her own words when justifying to my father.

My mother frowned and grunted.

"Frau Niemeyer, please, I'm sorry, it's my fault—" Herr Huber tried to intercede for me.

"Don't apologize on her behalf, Herr Huber. I know my daughter. She's a professional at dragging everyone into her mess."

But for me, that "mess" was something the skeptical eyes of my mother could not see. Without school or BDM and having only paper friends—Ania's letters weren't half as funny as real Ania was—my dream of becoming an athlete like Trebisonda Valla was all I had left. My mother always complained, *"Why not as Anni Steuer?"* one of our best German athletes, but Trebisonda was the Italian who had robbed the gold from Anni in a hurdle race in '36. And I wanted to be the best, to win gold, and as the *Führer* said, *"If you win, you need not to have to explain."*

Unfortunately, my mother never pictured me as an athlete but as a housewife like her. "What honorable man will marry you if he sees you romping like that, Emma?" But despite her efforts, I could not see marriage at my finish line. "I hope your father loves to see his daughter all grubby and smelly." My mother pushed the door open. "Now, get inside!"

"I'll bathe before my class with Herr Günther." He was the tutor my father had hired to continue my studies.

"Bad news for you, maiden, there will be no class today. Our transport will pick us up early, so you better finish your breakfast and wash yourself, now!"

"But first I need to clean up my mess, as you taught me, right?"

My mother's jaw dropped at being outsmarted, while Frau Weber battled to contain her laughter under the scrutiny of my mother.

"Did you see, Herr Huber?" I asked, helping him to carry the wood frames back to the barn. "At each jump, I felt like I could almost fly."

"My eyes could not believe it. You flew as gracefully as a swan."

I grinned. "But my knee grazed the sixth hurdle."

"Don't worry, I'm sure you will do it perfectly next time."

We heaped the frames behind a haystack. Schwein greeted us by regurgitating his meal, making a sound like an oink—hence his nickname, "Pig."

"Before you leave." Herr Huber rummaged through his bag and pulled out a letter. "Despite being addressed to me, it seems it's really intended for you."

"You don't know a Jacques DuBois from Paris?" I asked, reading the name of the sender.

Herr Huber shook his head. "Flip it over."

Written on the back, the word *For* could be read beside a colored-pencil drawing of a peach with a smiling face. "'For Peach'… Could it be from… Anton?"

Herr Huber smiled knowingly, and my heart raced at the thought that my brother could be behind the sender's identity. I struggled to believe it, considering Anton had passed a year ago, meaning this might be the last letter he'd penned before his death.

"Emma!" my mother shouted in the distance.

"You better go," Herr Huber advised.

"*Danke*, Herr Huber."

I held the letter against my chest as if it were my lifeline and sprinted back, imagining that if I ran fast enough, I could find my brother waiting for me at the house. To challenge myself, I used the posts of the fence running parallel to the road as marks to erect mental hurdles that I jumped as if they were real obstacles. But upon my arrival, somebody else welcomed me instead.

"From whom are you running away?" a young man asked from the driveway. His gray uniform flaunted oak-leaf badges on his collar and braided shoulder boards, but what called my attention were his polished jackboots, impeccable, just like my father's. He had arrived in a car while I was in the barn, a shimmering black Horch with protruding, chrome-plated headlights.

I hid the envelope behind me, startled. "Pardon me?"

"I'm sorry." He removed his cap and held it under his left armpit. The top of his silken hair glistened under the sun, contrasted with his close-cropped sides. "I saw you running all the way here. Quite impressive." His darting, sterling-gray eyes rendered me speechless, and I blushed, realizing he had watched me jumping. "You must be Emma, right?"

"Emma, I told you—" My mother came out reprimanding me, but she composed herself at noticing our visitor. "Oh! I'm sorry."

"*Sieg Heil!* Frau Niemeyer."

"Sieg Heil," my mother replied. "I thought Hermann would drive us."

"I'm sorry, Frau Niemeyer. Your husband and Hermann had an urgent matter to attend to, so *Obergruppenführer* Von Schroeder instructed me and Otto to come for you, and not to delay your arrival to Wewelsburg."

Otto emerged from the wheel of the car wearing the same uniform. "Sieg Heil." He saluted and adjusted his thick, rounded spectacles, emphasized by his bushy brows but at least helping to dissimulate his hooked nose.

"I'm sorry…" My mother beckoned, looking for his name.

"*Brigadeführer* Ghislain Fleischer."

"Oh!" My mother's voice turned melodious at hearing his name and rank. "My apologies, Brigadeführer Fleischer, but as you can see, my rebellious daughter is not yet ready. So I'm afraid we will have to delay our departure."

Ghislain turned to Otto, who fished a gilded watch from his jacket pocket. Otto held it carefully, and using the knuckle of his index finger, he knocked the lid three times, as on a door, before opening it. He observed the clock for a moment and nodded to

Ghislain.

"We'll wait until your daughter is ready, Frau Niemeyer." Ghislain smiled agreeably, with his perfectly aligned teeth. "Your daughter's commitment in sports is what the *Reich* needs the most."

"Emma, your bath awaits," my mother urged me with a half grin. "Gentlemen, can I offer you a cup of tea to alleviate the wait?"

"Splendid," Otto replied, and both men walked inside after me.

I hurried upstairs, not least concerned about washing myself. Once alone in my room, I opened the letter. At first glimpse, I confirmed it was Anton's handwriting. I struggled to contain my sobbing, to avoid being heard downstairs. I put the unread letter away and slid inside the bathtub to wash off my tears, hoping water could also carry away the image of Anton resting inside the casket. The mortuary paleness of his stiff skin, the coldness of his perfectly intertwined fingers, and the hollowness of his wide, shut eyes. I scrubbed my skin vigorously, as if the memories of his funeral were dirt I couldn't remove.

Once the water had quieted my nerves, I climbed out of the tub and dried myself.

Then, I dared to read the letter.

Dear Peach:

If you're holding this letter, it means two things. First, the letter outwitted the intelligence agencies all the way from Paris. But it also means I'm already dead.

People will say many things after my demise. Some will remember me as a hero and others as a traitor. Truth is, neither those who praised nor those who condemned me really knew me. Only you know the man your brother really was.

Peach, I did terrible things that haunt me in my sleep. But once I discovered the truth, I could not turn away from it. I wish I could explain to you, but that would put you in peril. It's enough to say that many secrets hide behind Wewelsburg's walls.

Don't divulge the contents of this letter to anyone, not even our parents. Please look after Mother for me. She'll need you more than ever. When war knocks at your door, stay close to Father and everything will be fine.

I send you my congratulations in advance for all your birthdays I'm going to miss.

Don't miss me, because after what I've seen, I assure you, we will meet again.

Don't rush through life, no matter how slow time passes. Clock hands always circle around.

Don't despair, because in the place where I'm heading, no days pass by.

Be true to yourself, because I'll only recognize you if you don't forget who you really are.

Traitor?… Terrible things?… Secrets in Wewelsburg Castle? I sighed, disheartened, wondering about the unknowns surrounding my brother's death. "Wewelsburg…" I whispered, convincing myself I could find the truth behind his murder at that castle.

Be brave, because bravery is what you'll need the most… were Anton's last words before his pen trailed off.

"Is what the *Reich* needs the most," I repeated Ghislain's words that echoed my brother's. Fueled with determination, I wore my BDM uniform: a full blue skirt, brown lace-up shoes with gray stockings, a white blouse with a dark neckerchief, and on top, a velvety golden-brown, four-pocket jacket. Finally, I wore my cap, cocked, with my curls sprouting below.

"Emma!" my mother shouted from downstairs. "Hurry! We're leaving!"

"I'm coming!" But before leaving, I hid the letter behind the poster on my wall, and I collected my orbed locket necklace from the nightstand. It contained Anton's photo as a cadet on one side and a photo of my parents on the other. I kissed it before closing it and hung it around my neck, hiding it carefully inside my blouse— remembering no jewelry should be displayed with the uniform.

I rushed downstairs, suitcase in hand, but halted midway at finding Ghislain waiting for me at the bottom. He climbed the last set of steps to meet me. "You okay?" He extended a gentle hand. "Eyes always betray the silence of a broken heart. You are far too young to cry for a man." His eyes became brighter, illuminated by the sunbeams filtering through the window at my back.

"Not all women's tears are attributed to men," I answered, and offered my suitcase instead, which he politely grabbed with a smile and carried to the trunk of the car.

"Your mother waits for you in the car," Frau Weber informed me, squeezing me with her plump arms.

"We'll be back soon."

Before departing, I waved at Herr Huber, who was feeding the pigs, thinking about the improvements we could make to the wooden hurdles next time I would see him.

CHAPTER 2

ONCE WE ABANDONED THE SAFETY of Grandpa's farm and the car headed west, the war-torn landscape became palpable for me again after my yearlong seclusion from the world. We crossed military checkpoints, bypassing cargo convoys and marching troops that extended the duration of our trip. But unfortunately for me, my mother would make sure nobody got bored, with her endless chatter. I was still trying to digest the contents of my deceased brother's letter, but my mother's awkward questioning prevented this.

"You seem so young to be an accomplished brigadeführer," she complimented Ghislain.

"No age is too young to serve the fatherland."

"Right. It's not an obligation but a birthright, and so should be taught to the children… But tell me, are you married?"

Ghislain half turned back from the passenger seat, puzzled by the question. "No, I'm afraid not—yet." He grinned. "I'm still looking for the right woman."

"I understand," my mother said with genuine empathy. "It's so difficult to find the right person nowadays. Youth have lost interest in the traditional mores. Women don't respect themselves anymore. All this—*relaxation*—comes with a price. Divorces and broken marriages. Don't you agree, Brigadeführer Fleischer?"

"Indeed…" Ghislain replied abruptly, caught unprepared. He paused, and his disoriented eyes betrayed him as he elaborated his response. "The—the strength of the Reich emerges from the values of our families."

"That's what I tell Emma all the time."

Oh no. I rolled my eyes at hearing my name.

"Marriage is the sole path to happiness," she said. "But a gentleman will never fall for a libertine."

The silence in the car turned uncomfortable. Ghislain and Otto exchanged looks, but that didn't dissuade my mother from continuing her monologue.

"I lie awake at night worrying about how Emma will find a decent man to marry amid the war."

I wanted to object, but experience had taught me the outcome would only be worse. So I refrained myself and remained quiet.

"No reason to worry, Frau Niemeyer," Ghislain said with a conciliatory tone. "She has the finest example in her mother. I'm certain your daughter will marry a decent man, and maybe one day, the Führer will award the Cross of Honor of the German Mother to her."

"I hope…" my mother said with an air of resentment, since she could not herself attain the award. For the bronze cross, you were eligible if you had four or five children, a silver cross for six or seven, and a gold cross for eight or more. But my mother had had three miscarriages before me, and the rules stipulated only healthy and genetically fit children. No abortions, stillbirths, or miscarriages. After a risky pregnancy with me, she'd had to give up the idea of having a big family, by doctor's recommendation. "That would bring such a joy to this family," she said, caressing my shoulder.

But I refused the idea of accomplishing her unfulfilled dreams. As a teenager, I was incapable of visualizing myself as a mother, and besides, I was interested in a different medal—Olympic gold. "Bear eight children just to have a secure seat on the bus or the best cut of meat at the butcher's shop?" I retorted, considering the benefits given to the decorated mothers unappealing. "I want to do something more." Shame prevented me from sharing my Olympic dream with strangers, so I replied by the book. "I want to serve my country."

"There is nothing more serviceable than motherhood." Otto

eyed me through the rearview mirror. "Carrying this nation's soldiers in your womb is nothing if not heroic."

Otto's words triggered something inside my mother. Her eyes got lost in the scenery framed by the window, her hand squeezing her gloves. "Where are we?" she asked when she had returned to herself.

"At Kassel," replied Ghislain.

While we were absorbed in our conversation, the rural landscape had turned urban.

"What happened?" I pointed at the columns of smoke snaking over the city. Before anybody could answer, a fire truck sped by our side, blaring its sirens as it headed toward the fires. "Bombings…" I replied, hypnotized by the glaring flames exhaling nebulous torrents of smoke.

"It seems they targeted the *Henschel* industrial complex," Otto explained, steering wide to avoid the rubble.

"Not just the factories…" my mother said gloomily, as fire surged from the windows of suburban houses in the vicinity. The ash-covered survivors crawled through the debris in search of their loved ones.

"Carpet-bombing," Otto added.

"Carpet?" I repeated, puzzled.

"Indiscriminate bombing," he clarified.

A small girl wearing a bloodstained nightgown cried uncontrollably at the top of a pile of rubble, what presumably had been her home. She seemed unnoticeable to everybody running around her, instinctively absorbed in surviving their own hell. The collection of horrors that still haunted my sleep resurfaced: the terrifying air-raid sirens, the deafening *bong* of explosions, the crunching of the scorching houses, the fire sparks reddening the clouded sky, the haunting screams of the wounded, and the echoed weeping of the survivors. When my attention returned to the girl, she was not alone anymore. A man dressed in black stood behind the girl, resting a comforting hand on her shoulder to put an end to her weeping. She raised her troubled eyes to meet the man's gaze and regained calm, as if she had found a missing relative. The man glanced at me; our eyes briefly met, until the car left them behind.

"Why have these people not evacuated the city? It's destroyed," my mother said with a cracking voice.

"They refuse to," Ghislain explained. "Germans are resilient folk."

"Last October, Kassel endured a raid of over five hundred bombers," Otto recounted the happenings as he navigated the maze of unroofed, dilapidated walls. "In a single night, the British dropped thousands of bombs, along with magnesium incendiary fire sticks, literally setting the entire city ablaze."

"The fires lasted for a week," Ghislain added. "I was returning from Frankfurt when I found myself in the middle of the chaos…" He paused as if he were searching for the words buried somewhere in the debris by the road. "Fire twisters rose in the middle of houses… My eyes could not believe such things could even form." Otto eyed Ghislain briefly, as if they were previously unheard remarks for him as well. "Amid the destruction, I found an old man digging up canned food from a collapsed house. I urged him to escape, but with the same calmness as he unearthed the goods, he replied, 'My family has lived in Kassel for four generations… and I hail from here,' as if his eyes could still see a home underneath the ash and dust."

"These people are the true heroes," I concluded, observing the people on the streets trying to conduct a "normal" life despite the tragedy.

"Brigadeführer Fleischer, is it true?… About France?" My mother said after an overwhelming silence.

Ghislain's eyes deviated to Otto with nervousness. "Yes." He cleared his throat. "We have… em… lost France. But don't worry. Plans are already in motion to repel the American invasion."

My mother received the news with troubled eyes. She couldn't care less about France's invasion, but since my brother Anton had been found dead in a room in Paris a year ago, she felt like France had robbed her of happiness, or rather taken it away, as she cried over his casket, *"Paris gave me my son, and Paris took him away."* My parents had conceived my brother during their honeymoon in Paris.

Anton's passing weighed like an anvil inside my mother's heart. How could it not? He was her favorite. I could not complain about my mother favoring my brother above me, because I was his favorite. Seven years older than me, Anton was not just a brother but also, considering our father's long absences from home, a paternal figure to me. Anton's concern for me, his amusing games and silly jokes, had attenuated the absence of our father.

My mother used to say that Anton had come into this world

struck by luck. Life always appeared to rearrange in his favor. After excelling at school and sports, he started a brilliant career in the *Schutzstaffel* that not even the shade cast by our prominent father could overshadow. Anton quickly drew the attention of all SS high-ranking officers, and a position in the *Sicherheitsdienst*—SD for short—was offered to him. His new job for the security service had turned Anton hermetic, but what I resented more was that he became distant with me. In his last "official" letter sent from the Slovak State, Anton had blamed the war for his change in demeanor. *So much the war has changed you, Anton?* I'd questioned him in my reply, feeling as if his letter had been penned by a different man. Now, considering the posthumous letter I'd just received, my suspicions about a forgery intensified. *But who could benefit from impersonating my brother just for the sake of writing to his family?* Anton was found dead resting in his bed, poisoned by his wine, according to the autopsy conducted by SD. His murder was attributed to the French Resistance.

With my brother's death, the Reich lost a hero, but my mother lost her sunshine. Beneath the pride of a German mother whose son had died aggrandizing the fatherland lurked the uneasiness of an unfair trade-off.

Every time I watched my mother submerged in her silent agony, I wondered if she would prefer that it was my body filling the casket instead of Anton's.

Many times, I had thought yes.

CHAPTER 3

BY THE TIME WE ARRIVED AT WEWELSBURG Village, northeast of Büren, the sun was about to set. The castle silhouette crowned a hill tucked into a robe of oaks, pines, and spruces that cropped the orange pastel sky with furrowed clouds. A view worthy of a Renaissance painting.

The castle was imposing, an immensity the pictures my father had brought home could not convey. "Look, it's like in the fairy tales you like to read," my father had illustrated to a six-year-old me, sitting by his side in total awe. "A castle like the one King Arthur and the Knights of the Round Table lived in, remember?"

"Are you a Knight of the Round Table, Papa?" I had asked naively. "Then where are your shining armor and sword?"

My father laughed. "We are not fighters, but researchers."

"What do you look for?"

"We…" My father turned serious. "We look for the Holy Grail, as King Arthur did."

Wewelsburg Castle had once indeed been a medieval fortress, but used against Hungarians—instead of Saxons, like King Arthur fought—and later was rebuilt to house lords during the early 1600s. Finally, in 1934, Heinrich Himmler leased it to house not only the headquarters, but the heart and soul of the SS.

As the car ascended the sloped road by the south side of the hill, having Anton's words spinning in my head, I wondered if the story of *Reichsführer* Heinrich Himmler and his Knights of the Schutzstaffel would be a fairy tale, as my father had implied.

Once on the summit, we cleared the guard post. Otto drove the Horch parallel to a perimeter wall erected around the castle garden and continued to the guardhouse, a three-story building with non-plastered stone walls and a blue-tiled, gabled roof, matching the architecture of the castle. As the car turned left, the castle became visible in its entire splendor. Wewelsburg Castle had three buildings, arranged in a triangular layout connected by three round towers acting as vertices. The triangle was isosceles, like an arrowhead pointing north, with a wider tower as its tip.

The car approached the eastern wing, crossed the moat through a stone bridge, and entered the gate leading into the inner courtyard. "Welcome to Wewelsburg," Ghislain said with relief once the Horch stopped.

"Finally!" my mother exclaimed.

I descended from the car and spun around, admiring the castle with amazement. The east and west towers had pointy domes, contrasting the flatness of the north tower, but the diameter of the latter was twice the size of the other two. From the inner courtyard, you could access the east, west, and south wings and the north tower, but east and west towers were reachable only through the buildings. To facilitate the access to upper or lower levels of the buildings from the courtyard, a spiral staircase was housed inside a thinner tower embedded in the intersection between west and south wings.

"Emma!" my father called from behind me.

"Papa!" I rushed to his embrace and hugged him with the effusiveness of long months of separation, but found no correspondence to my affection.

"I'm glad you're here," he said half-heartedly, patting my back with a mild smile.

I'd grown accustomed to my father's sporadic demonstrations of affection, hidden behind his facade of formality and diligence, but as the war progressed, his staidness had turned to iciness. His—now—absentminded eyes transmitted a feeling of hollowness. And his hollowness was not only psychological but now also physical, as my arms corroborated when I squeezed his loose attire. He had lost enough weight to make his cap fit deeper than usual. I sensed his discomfort about my probing inspection, and his gaze wandered to my mother.

"Frieda." My father extended his hand to find hers. The two stretched arms formed a long bridge that neither dared cross.

"Hans." My mother and he stared at each other with nostalgic smiles in the moment their fingers remained intertwined, until my father resumed his role.

"Thank you, Ghislain, and Otto, for any inconveniences this might have generated."

"It is our duty, Obergruppenführer Niemeyer," Ghislain replied ceremoniously.

"Hermann, please show them their rooms," my father instructed the man standing behind him. "Unfortunately, I have other matters to attend to." Hermann was my father's assistant and personal driver. I had met him before when my father visited us. He was a reserved man, only speaking when asked by my father, to such an extreme that I didn't even dare to say hi. I'd been happy to know he was not driving us to Wewelsburg.

"Understood, Obergruppenführer." Hermann clicked his heels.

"Make yourselves comfortable, and rest from the strenuous trip," my father said to us. "But, please, be ready for dinner."

Hermann tried to collect my suitcase from Ghislain, but he refused. "I'll carry this one." A gesture not questioned by my parents.

"Please follow me." Hermann led us to the west wing.

The west wing was a five-story building, including the underground (moat) level and the attic, dedicated mainly to lodging. Contrary to the raw exterior, the interior walls were plastered and painted in white, with details in oak wood. Oil paintings of German landscapes decorated the walls of the foyer. Swastikas and runes—especially the jagged SS, like twin stylized lightning—were the main motifs.

We climbed the stairs to the second floor. "Frau Niemeyer, in Obergruppenführer Niemeyer's room," Hermann announced, pointing to opposite sections of the aisle. "And *Fräulein* Niemeyer will stay in the room—"

"I'll lead Fräulein Niemeyer." Ghislain snatched the key from Hermann's hand.

"Please don't be late for dinner, Emma," my mother reminded me before our parting.

The silence stretched as we paced the many-doored hallway. Ghislain turned briefly now and then to glance at me from the corner of his eye. A door slightly ajar caught my attention. Inside, a young SS cadet browsed through books.

"Wewelsburg Castle was supposed to host the SS school," Ghislain explained, noticing my interest.

"What happened?"

"War turns schoolboys into soldiers."

"But do they study when they're not fighting? My father told me there are study rooms and even a scientific library in this castle."

"Of course." Ghislain halted in front of the door at the end of the hallway. "There is always room within these walls for indoctrination." He unlocked the door and motioned me in.

I expected the lodgings of the castle to be lugubrious and humid, like a medieval inn, but to my surprise, the room was quite cozy, bathed in sunset light through a huge picture window with oak casement composed of four hinged windows in an array of two by two. The walls of the castle were astonishingly thick, allowing the long windowsill to function as a bench. The furniture comprised two wooden bunk beds at either side of the room, a two-door mahogany wardrobe, and a small table.

"Am I sharing the room with somebody else? My BDM friends are staying with me?"

"No… a man," Ghislain said casually, and I didn't know how to answer. "Don't worry, he's a brave and handsome gentleman, the kind women adore."

Unsure whether it was a joke, I played along. "How do I know he's brave?"

"He wears one of these." He pointed to the Iron Cross hanging from his neck, a recognition granted by the Führer himself as a sign of bravery in battle.

"And handsome?"

"He has a pervasive gaze and iron-willed features." Ghislain smirked, his gray eyes tinted ocher by the sunset. "Would you accept an invitation to stroll through the gardens of the castle on the arm of such a fine gentleman?"

"Maybe." I rocked on my heels. "But first, I would like to meet this mysterious suitor."

"Actually, I have a photo."

I turned serious, puzzled from believing the entire time he was referring to himself. Ghislain pointed to a poster pasted on the wall portraying the Führer, Adolf Hitler, with a right fist resting on his hip, standing before a crowd, with the legend *Wir Folgen Dir.*

"'We follow you,'" I read.

"You will share the room with him. The Führer himself will oversee your sleep."

I giggled, realizing my naivete.

"What a gorgeous smile you have. And to think you deprived us of your smile during the entire journey. It would certainly have eased the trip." Ghislain stepped closer to me. "Please don't tell your mother," he whispered, and winked.

Something about Ghislain reminded me of my brother, something beyond the features, the uniform, or his age. Perhaps the capacity to amuse me by converting a triviality into something special.

"Peach!" A familiar voice broke the silence, and I unwittingly stepped back, making the scene look even more incriminating.

Ania's bright eyes peeped through the cracked door. "I just heard of your arrival." My best friend walked into the room wearing a dark blouse with sleeves rolled up and a knee-length skirt. Her hair, arranged in twin braids, fell over her shoulders.

"Ania!" I hugged her with excitement and the affection of a sister.

"Peach, look at you, you've grown so much!" Ania's bucktoothed smile seemed permanently carved on her face. It never abandoned her, not even when she cried. I'd always admired her for that—and envied her in equal degree.

"You think?" I was skeptical of how much difference a year could make, but for a teenager, it was a great deal, I supposed.

"Please, come with me. We have so much to catch up on since your last letter." Ania turned to Ghislain. "Oh, I'm sorry, Brigadeführer."

"I was just escorting Fräulein Niemeyer to her room," he said solemnly.

"Where are we going?" I asked as Ania dragged me outside.

"With Gerda."

"Fräulein Niemeyer." Ghislain halted our escape and handed me the room key. "Please be ready for dinner."

"Sure, I will," I said as Ania pulled me down the hallway.

"He's dapper," Ania declared, but I hushed her, fearing Ghislain—who was walking ten steps behind—could hear us.

"Where are you staying?"

"There." Ania pointed to a room next to the staircase.

"Is Gerda staying with you?"

"She received a special suite as the bride-to-be. I'm sharing with Olga and Mitzi from BDM, remember them? I'm not the daughter of a renowned SS official, to have the privilege of being escorted by a brigade leader to my exclusive room."

"Ania!" I reprimanded her, squeezing her arm as we descended the stairway. "I'm not alone. The Führer is watching me."

"The Führer watches us all," Ania jested in a cryptic tone, and we laughed. "Come, I want to show you something."

I followed her into the courtyard, where a group of young men in singlets were offloading supplies from a truck and carrying them to the kitchen. We scuttled past their prying looks and entered the south wing through a door next to the staircase tower. The castle hall constituted an entire half of the south wing's first floor. The finishes followed the line of my room, white walls with huge oak windows framing views of the castle gardens, but the decoration was extensive: shining medieval suits of armor stood around the periphery, pennants hung on the walls displaying the SS runes and swastika, and a huge portrait of Hitler hung at the center, with a smaller one of the SS leader, Heinrich Himmler—my father's superior—by his side. Ring-shaped chandeliers hung in chains from the tall, oak-beamed ceiling, and iron torch holders bolted to the walls illuminated the place. Three women vigorously mopped the square-layout stone floor, with all the furniture stacked at the end of the room.

"They are preparing everything for the wedding. Isn't it beautiful?" Ania held her breath. "This hall will host the reception."

"Yes, beautiful," I repeated, but I was praising the view of the garden instead.

"Marrying in a castle, a true castle!" Ania sighed, romanticizing the idea of the fairy-tale wedding. "Let's go outside."

I followed Ania through a door that led into the foyer of the west tower, and we continued our way out, passing the guards at the gate. Outside, a narrow stone bridge continued over the moat, which was, in fact, a natural slump of the terrain, with a trail to walk around the castle, passing below the arched bridges.

"Peach, look, it's Gerda!" Ania pointed down at the garden. Gerda ambled gallantly, wearing a dark blue dress with an azalea pattern, arm-in-arm with Brigadeführer Bruno Unger, just as Ghislain had described in his proposal. "Come! Let's go." We descended the stairs, running parallel to the outside wall of the castle.

"Gerda! Gerda! Look who's here!" Ania waved her hand as we approached.

"Emma!" Gerda hugged me. "I'm so glad you're here to accompany us. Have you met my husband-to-be?"

I nodded. My father was his superior, and in his words, Bruno was a trustworthy man.

"Little Niemeyer." Bruno shook my hand. "It has been a long time."

"A year." My smile faded, remembering the last time had been during Anton's funeral.

"Certainly," Bruno acknowledged with visible remorse at bringing the painful memory back. "Damsels, I'll leave you. I assume you have a lot to catch up on." Bruno held Gerda's hand and kissed it. "Dear." He bowed and donned his cap. "I'll see you at dinner."

"There goes the love of your life," Ania said idyllically, more excited than Gerda herself.

"Gerda, I'm glad you're marrying Bruno. He is a trustworthy man," I echoed the words of my father, lacking any better compliment.

"Since I met him, Bruno has been nothing but kind." Gerda turned to me. "During hardship, there's nothing like being with someone who makes you feel it's worthwhile to wake up the next day."

Gerda had a lovely but melancholic face, granting her a mother-esque air. Her doleful eyes had witnessed so much sorrow. After she abandoned BDM at eighteen, the military had recruited Gerda as a searchlight operator to identify bombers amid the night sky. She'd witnessed the shelling of Berlin firsthand. One day, Gerda overslept. In her hurry to arrive on time for her shift, she'd jaywalked, and a car almost ran her over. The driver was Bruno.

"A true love story." Ania sighed, but I was unsure if the sparkle in Gerda's eyes was true love or just admiration.

"'Marry only for love' says the eighth commandment for the German woman," Gerda declared, as if she were spying on my thoughts. "I learned it in the *Reichsbräuteschulen.*" A couple of months after announcing the engagement, Gerda had abandoned the service and joined the Reichsbräuteschulen, or Reich bride school, to prepare herself to be the perfect bride.

"How was it?" Ania inquired, genuinely interested.

"Not much different from the BDM, but we did more cooking, ironing, and gardening and less exercise."

"That sounds terrible," I said, considering track-and-field events were my favorite activity.

"Classes on animal husbandry and childcare are the substitutes for sports."

"Perfect, because I want to bear eight children, to receive a Gold Cross of Honor of the German Mother and not have to wait in line when boarding the streetcar," I said sardonically.

Gerda and Ania laughed.

"'You should want to have as many children as possible.' It's the tenth commandment, so you'd better get used to the idea," Gerda informed us.

I rolled my eyes. "Nothing about winning an Olympic gold medal?"

"*Kinder, küche, und kirche,*" Gerda said. "'Children, kitchen, and church' is the motto, nothing about Olympics, sorry."

"Attending was not among my plans anyway," I said, relieved.

"I don't think you have an option," Gerda said in her terribly honest, bordering on baneful, tone. "With your father being a prominent SS leader, I assume he will want you to attend a bride's school to marry a distinguished SS officer."

"And Peach already has a handsome brigadeführer suitor." Ania nudged me, and I blushed. "Maybe in a few years it will be us attending your *SS-Eheweihen.*" An SS-Eheweihen was an SS marriage consecration, not Catholic. Gerda's was my first to attend.

"I-I don't know," I said half-heartedly, thinking about my not-so-promising future.

"Shake off the gloomy face, Emma," Gerda instructed. "It's not as bad as it sounds. I truly enjoyed the six-week course. We played, learned songs, and even read legends and fairy tales."

"It's not that. It's just… the idea of marrying— I-I would like to do something else. Something big… for my country."

"Are you planning on joining the service, Peach?" Ania questioned my judgment.

I went mute.

"There is no need to prove yourself to anyone, Emma, not even to your parents," Gerda said, holding my hand. "You are not your brother. You can't compete to fill the void he left. It's not fair."

Gerda's words hit me like a bucket of ice water. *Am I subconsciously trying to replace my brother? Or deep down is that what I really want, and it just transpires in the outside world?* Maybe it was my personal war for being noticed, to be taken care of and to be loved.

"I-I—" I fell short of words, trying to explain myself.

"You don't have to join the service, Emma, nor press yourself on competing for the Olympics." She squeezed my hand. "As women, we have a higher obligation to our country. We need to keep our bodies pure. Mind and spirit. The fatherland expects us to become supportive wives and mothers who uphold the racial values in our family." Gerda said this as if she were reading a text from the teachings of the bride school. "Just follow the commandments, and you will marry a handsome man, Emma. I'm certain about that."

"Oh my God! It's so late." Ania broke the unsettling silence. "I need to prepare myself for dinner."

"Nonsense, you look lovely," Gerda said.

"There's no such thing as too much. Who knows? Maybe I will bump into the love of my life in the castle corridors." Ania winked before leaving.

"I wish I had half her enthusiasm," I said as we observed Ania hurrying upstairs. "She daydreams about attending the bride's school and having her own SS-Eheweihen."

Gerda turned serious. "Unfortunately, she never will."

"Why so?"

"The SS Race and Settlement Office will never allow it."

"She is German."

"Her father died of tuberculosis."

"But she is perfectly healthy and beautiful," I retorted with frustration.

"No matter how beautiful, Ania carries her father's genes, and health is a precondition of beauty."

Gerda's comment made me feel small, powerless, as if everything in life had been preconditioned from birth, engraved in the stars, and nothing could be done to change it.

As we returned to the castle, I turned my face to the sky. I noticed a man standing on the balcony on the top floor of the south wing. I could not recognize his facial features at that distance.

But I harbored no doubt that he was looking at us.

CHAPTER 4

WHEN I ARRIVED AT THE DINING HALL, the deprecating gaze of my mother made sure I knew I was late. "Good evening," I murmured apologetically as I sat in a vacant chair between Ania and my mother.

"My daughter, Emma," my father announced, drawing the attention of all diners toward me. "Do you remember her, Eric?" he asked his fellow obergruppenführer. His face was familiar, but it had become difficult for me to identify by name the hundreds of faces of uniformed men recorded in my memory.

"Yes, two years ago, if I remember correctly, during the Führer's birthday celebration," Eric said. "It might seem like a long time, but for old men like us, Hans, it was like yesterday, eh?"

My father concurred, "In the past, humanity measured years with crops. Now, time has become relativistic."

"Where were you?" Ania murmured.

"Unpacking," I said, unable to admit that my five-minute nap had gotten out of control.

"Something to drink?" a maid offered.

"Just water," I responded, and the maid poured a glass from a porcelain pitcher.

Ghislain, who was sitting in front of me, said, "I hope you enjoyed your stroll around the castle grounds."

"We certainly did," Ania responded. "Right, Peach?"

I was about to answer when two more men entered the hall. At their appearance, Ghislain and Otto stood and clicked their heels with the usual formality.

"At ease. Please remain seated," the older of the two said, removing his hat and placing it on the table, flaunting the *Totenkopf* insignia: the skull and crossbones. "Tonight, we can spare the formalities." He grinned, and I could not avoid noticing two tiny holes above his eyebrows an inch apart from the center of his face, too oddly symmetrical to be caused by an accident. He sat at the head of the table, flanked by his colleagues, my father and Eric, and his younger companion sat between Ghislain and Eric, in front of my mother.

"This is a celebration," he continued. "If you could serve us." He motioned to the line of maids standing behind us. "I can't remember how long it has been since the last time Wewelsburg was this alive. So much young blood." He emphasized this as if he were an elder. His sharp features and the expression lines stressed around his prominent cheekbones made him look older than my father, but his recently shaved face transmitted a younger feeling compared with a bearded, old Herr Huber—too recently shaved, since multiple raw wounds were still visible across his face. I wondered if his skin was sensitive, since he was old enough to be comfortable with a razor.

"You should thank our visitors." Eric turned to us.

"Allow me to do the introductions," my father said. "My daughter, Emma, her friend Ania Klein, and, of course, the bride-to-be, Gerda Lange. The three are close friends from BDM."

"A pleasure," the three of us replied in unison.

"The pleasure is all mine, ladies. I'm Obergruppenführer Wolfrick Von Schroeder, and this is my *gruppenführer*, Reinhard Schmidt." Von Schroeder waved his hand at his younger companion, a man probably in his late thirties. "I assume you already know the two brigadeführers, Ghislain and Otto, who serve under his command." Von Schroeder had clarified the chain of command; in the army, the equivalent would be from lieutenant general down to major general and finally brigadier general, meaning Reinhard was Ghislain's superior.

"The rumors were truth," Reinhard said, sight cast down, fingers toying with the silverware, his right thumb running along the serrated side of the knife. Then he turned to Gerda, squinting through a tuft of hair falling across his face. He smiled widely, flirtatiously. "Bruno's fiancée is indeed beautiful."

"A true German beauty indeed," Von Schroeder said. "Congratulations, Bruno."

Bruno thanked him, a little embarrassed. "I could not be happier about marrying such a beautiful and smart woman as Gerda." He held Gerda's hand. "My daisy."

"Nor could I," Gerda replied modestly.

"*Hochzeitssuppe*," a maid said, filling my rune-decorated bowl with soup. "Wedding soup."

I turned briefly to Ghislain, who hadn't removed his eyes from me as I sliced my meatballs.

"Isn't it cute?" my mother asked. "True love is always childish."

"That's why I believe it's better to leave romance in the dominion of women." Eric winked, raising his glass of wine.

"That's because nobody understands children better than women," my mother replied.

"You are right, Frau Niemeyer," Von Schroeder conceded. "There is a child concealed in every man." He turned to Gerda. "Go now, you woman, go discover the child in the man."

"What inspiring words, Obergruppenführer—"

"*Thus Spoke Zarathustra*," Reinhard said with a guttural voice, interrupting my mother.

"What?" I said, too late to contain my question in the realm of my thoughts.

Reinhard's avid eyes rested on me. "*Thus Spoke Zarathustra*," he repeated, this time softer.

"It's a quote from a book," Otto explained.

"*Thus Spoke Zarathustra* is a philosophical novel by German philosopher Friedrich Nietzsche," my father elaborated.

"Did nobody in the BDM teach you about Nietzsche?" Von Schroeder inquired, clasping his leather-gloved hands and resting his elbows on the table.

"I-I don't know…" I turned, puzzled, to Ania and Gerda. "Not that I can remember."

"I told you. We can't delegate indoctrination to the mediocre," Reinhard said with displeasure, meticulously dissecting his food.

"Can you hear it?" Von Schroeder said calmly. We all exchanged looks, hearing nothing, insulated as we were inside Wewelsburg's walls. "Don't you hear the hammering of the cannons? The thumping of bombs or the wind gusts caused by bullets?"

"We are—fortunately—too far away for that, Wolfrick," Eric said lightly, trying to ease the mood.

"Precisely, Eric; we are at war, yet not all Germans know the reason. Only a few can identify our enemy." Von Schroeder turned to me. "Fräulein Niemeyer, could you say who our enemy is?"

All eyes sat on me. My lips pursed, my palms perspired, and the heel of my right foot pecked the floor. *The British? Americans? Russians? Jews?* My mind wandered, trying to figure out the right answer.

"What do you think you would see across the battlefield?" Von Schroeder added.

Uniformed figures were the sole image in mind. "Men?" I said, feeling stupid.

"In fact," Von Schroeder responded, to my surprise. "But not any men. Lesser men."

"I've seen them in battle. They are just a painful embarrassment," Reinhard interjected. "Chimpanzees waging war."

"We wage war against the ignorant man who cannot dream," Von Schroeder continued, disregarding Reinhard's comments. "The one who made his way from worm to human simply to earn a living and work all day just to keep warm. The one who negates the supreme for the mediocre, the underman. The world is plagued by undermen, uninterested in the salvation of mankind. But humanity should thrive and become better, even if the means to attain the end might seem evil. Only great pain is the ultimate liberator of the spirit."

"But the pain endured by the German folk is not enough?" I dared to question, under the astonished looks of everybody, especially my mother, but the scenery we had witnessed in Kassel was still fresh on my mind.

"The decimation of men is precisely the driving force that breeds a stronger race, a master race. This war is just a bridge, not an end; a bridge between the underman and the Übermensch, the Overman. A superior being conscious of its own strength, not humble but delighted in its own abilities."

Ghislain listened solemnly to Von Schroeder's words, the way one listens to the homily of a priest.

"Could you imagine it?" Von Schroeder asked rhetorically. "A being with superior strength and reflexes, with outstanding psychic abilities, capable of bending the trajectory of a bullet in battle or manipulating the vital signs of his enemy and forcing him to surrender. Just imagine the possibilities of having the capacity to control the elements or simply to possess a foe's mind to exert control over their body. There would be no more wars. Such could be the power of the Overman."

"Possessing somebody else's body? That sounds like demonic possession," Ania whispered to me, but apparently loud enough to be heard across the table.

"What did you say, Fräulein Klein?" Von Schroeder leaned over the table to take a better look at her.

"Um, nothing." Ania shrank back in her chair.

"Demonic possessions might sound like stories to frighten children at night," Von Schroeder continued. "But this very castle has witnessed such events. In 1631, the Holy Inquisition conducted two trials in the dungeon in the basement of the west tower. The first to judge the infamous Witch of Fedelm, or the Bony Duana, as she is referred to in the folktales, for her gaunt limbs longer than the height of a man, and for being fleshless, her skin adhered to the bone and torn at the joints. Tales said she feigned being a hunchbacked old lady, but hidden below her robe, her crooked limbs could make her stand taller than a man mounted upon a horse.

"The Witch of Fedelm roamed the roads near the woods at dusk, cat-yowling, and if she heard the crying of a newborn, she would snatch it from the crib, carry it with her in a womb made of cobwebs, and would never be seen again. Across centuries, folk undertook endless witch hunts after the disappearance of the newly born to bring the Bony Duana to holy justice, but all failed. Tales said her hood hid a deformed skull with three pairs of eyes: a pair to see the present, a pair for the past, and one more to see the future. So, she was all-wise and could not be fooled by men."

The story gave me the chills, yet I dared to ask, "If she could not be fooled, how was she captured?"

"The Witch of Fedelm was brought to justice by her own kind, another witch, or rather a warlock, the famous Gaulish kidnapper called *Ravisseur*. But the price to pay was high, since he was wanted by the Inquisition as well. The eccentric warlock was sentenced to death on counts of satanic rites and witchcraft, listing among his vices 'feasting naked on the blood of virgins.' Myths of the time asserted that Ravisseur could control the minds of women, but more demystifying versions pointed out he was simply an attractive man and skillful seducer. It was also said Ravisseur boasted about possessing Charlemagne's magical sword, which had a blade that could turn invisible; however, at the moment of his detention, he carried no weapon.

"At the end, both died, Ravisseur killed by his executioner inside the torture room, and the Witch of Fedelm burned alive in a furnace at the outskirts of Wewelsburg Village. The reason for Ravisseur to confront the Witch of Fedelm, risking his own life, remains unclear. Some argue that the Bony Duana possessed the knowledge for everlasting life, but her death at the hands of the Inquisition refutes such argument. It's worth mentioning that reports state her public burning lasted for three entire days, since villagers claimed her screams could still be heard from the interior of the kiln on the third day. They also reported hearing cats yowling during the three nights—quite unusual, considering all cats in town had been previously slain."

The dining hall was dead silent. Even the clinking of cutlery had ceased after the bone-chilling story. Pieces of meat hung from forks, waiting to be devoured by gaping mouths, or remained half-chewed, resting behind pursed lips. Nobody dared to break the spell that had converted all diners into living statues.

"Just like you said, Wolfrick," my father finally said. "Tales to frighten children." His tone was conciliatory, but he fixed stern eyes on Von Schroeder.

Von Schroeder exchanged irritated looks with my father, but after a moment of growing tension, a smile finally erupted on his face. "Oh yes… Nothing but the chains and shackles remains from those dreadful times, bolted to the stones of the dungeon of this castle, ancient like the folktales." Two drops of blood seeped from the tiny holes above his eyebrows, running down past his eyes like blood tears. He grabbed his handkerchief and dabbed his face. "I'm sorry. I inherited the disease of the kings." He chuckled. "Hemophilia." Everyone knew this condition impaired the body's ability to create blood clots.

Von Schroeder fished a watch from his pocket and, just like Otto had, knocked three times on the lid before opening it. He contemplated it for a moment and furrowed his brow before closing the lid. "My apologies, but you will have to excuse me. Ur-

gent matters require my attention." He stood and donned his cap.
"Please enjoy the dinner."

Von Schroeder walked away, and Reinhard followed. "Ladies."
He bowed without removing his eyes from me and combed back
the tuft of his hair with one hand.

CHAPTER 5

I WOKE AT NIGHT TO THE PITTER-PATTER of rain against the window. The candle I had lit to avert the darkness was out, but a stripe of light running across the floor from a door ajar made me jump from my bed. *I closed it before going to bed.* I was certain. No one was inside my room, but when I peeked outside, a child passed by, rushing inside a door a few rooms away from mine.

"Hello?" I approached the gloomy dormitory he had entered, but nobody replied. I could not remember seeing a child in Wewelsburg before, and so ventured inside. My toes shrank, sensing the cold floor. The windows facing the castle's courtyard were open, and apparently had been like that for a while. A puddle of rainwater had gathered on the floor. A cold gust of wind passed by, so I embraced myself to keep my nightgown warm. No belongings sat on the desk, and the beds were made. The room was vacant.

A figure stood at the door, casting an elongated shadow, and I turned to confront the person. A child stood there, probably six or seven years old. It was hard to tell with the backlighting.

"Hey—" I said.

He interrupted, "Are you our mother?"

"No." I frowned, puzzled.

"Yes, you are."

"Who told you that?"

"My sister."

"That's the reason you entered my room?"

He nodded.

"Where is your sister?"

"It's locked."

"Locked? Locked where… and by whom?" I found the idea of a locked-up child nothing but cruel.

"The—the Crying Man."

"The crying man?" I shook my head, confused, but he didn't reply. "What is your name?"

"Sixty-six," he said, but this made no sense at all.

"Listen, I need you to come with me, and together we can look for your—" I stepped forward, extending my hand, but he stepped backward. "Wait, don't run!"

He shook his head. "There is no time… They are calling the witch."

A loud clang in the courtyard drew my attention. The guards opened the main gate, allowing an unmanned carriage pulled by four ebony horses to canter inside until it halted at the center. I turned back to the kid, but he had vanished, so I focused my attention on the happenings outside. The door of the south wing's main hall opened, and a line of men wearing long leather raincoats emerged. Twelve figures approached the carriage. I recognized Von Schroeder at the front, and among the rest, Eric and my father. I stepped to the side of the window to avoid any risk of being seen.

The wooden carriage was longer than usual. It had six wheels, two at the front and four at the back. The windows were barricaded by wood planks and secured with chains and padlocks. A gas lamp hung at each of the four corners, burning redder than usual.

Lightning flashed, and the door at the center of the carriage cracked open. Thunder rumbled in the sky as a woman dressed in a long black garment, her features blurred behind a veil like a black bride, came out and walked down the steps, holding Von Schroeder's hand. I could not hear what they chatted about as they headed to the north tower, but the door remained slightly open after they went in. *This is my chance to find out the secrets Anton mentioned hiding behind Wewelsburg's walls, and I will not waste it,* I encouraged myself.

I hurried to my room and dressed as fast as I could. I was unsure whether there was direct access to the north tower from the west wing, but even if it existed, I didn't want to get lost, so I went through the courtyard instead. To my fortune, no soul ambled the corridors, so I swiftly descended the stairs until I reached the foyer, where I tiptoed, fearing a guard might be patrolling. My intuition was right. I ducked until the guard doing his catwalk headed downstairs, into the basement. I opened the front door just enough to squeeze through, making the least noise possible. Outside, the guards at the main gate were killing time, sharing a cigarette. I made my way across the courtyard, crouching, camouflaged by the night shadows, the sound of my footsteps muffled by the rain.

Inside the north tower was a circular hall with a dome built inside, resting on twelve circular columns with arched pathways leading to tall windows. From the dome hung a circular chandelier. At the center of the gray-blue marble floor, an emblem stood out. It was a dark circle, with twelve zigzagged lines coming out to intersect an outer circle. The crooked lines resembled the SS runes. It looked like an irradiating sun. *A black sun.* Each line pointed to a different window except for three. One pointed to the entrance, and the other two to the doors connecting the east and west wings.

The group had left a trail of watery footprints toward the door heading to the east wing, which I followed to a spiral staircase. Their voices echoed from the basement, so I descended and continued through another set of stairs to a fork. The left path continued down to the entrance of the crypt, sealed by an iron grid door. I hid behind the wall at the intersection and knelt to have a better view of what was happening.

"Who is to be called during the invocation?" I heard the guttural voice of the woman asking, but I could not see her among the crowd gathering next to the door.

"The Black Sun!" Von Schroeder replied.

The woman laughed. "There is no need of a séance to summon He Who Walks Among Snakes. The one who hears the unspoken, beholds the secret, touches the inexistent, smells the subconscious, and tastes the mundane and the divine. Everything that has been said or will be said he already knows, because he is the all-knowing."

"I insist," Von Schroeder said adamantly, presenting a golden chalice.

"Very well, indeed." The woman cleared her throat. "Let's begin."

"Set in position!" The twelve men stood forming a circle

around a concentric sublevel, facing inward, where a firepit nested at the center. "Knights, present swords!" someone commanded, and the twelve straightened their arms and inclined them forward with hands open, palm facing down, in the typical Nazi salute.

Knights? I remembered the fable of the Knights of the Round Table told by my father.

The woman removed her veil and mixed powders inside a chalice. The mixture produced an ashen smoke that quickly saturated the vault with a burnt-flesh smell. She hummed a song as she held the chalice aloft.

"Thee I invoke, the hidden one, whom no man hath seen at any time," she said. "Thou that didst create the darkness and night. Thou that didst give the fruit to taste. Thou that hast brought knowledge to the ignorant. Thou didst convince humanity to love one another and to hate one another." At every sentence she declaimed, the twelve waved their arms as if they were indeed swords, drawing pentagrams in the air.

"I invoke Thee, the Terrible and invisible, who dwellest in the Void Place of the Spirit." The woman continued reciting as she walked around the crypt, chalice in one hand and spreading a white powder with the other, forming a big circle around the twelve. When the woman passed next to the gate, I observed her more closely. She was probably well into her forties, but her hair was entirely white, including her brows and eyelashes, as if she were an albino, though her skin tone was brown. *Could she be the witch the kid referred to?*

"Hidden One: Hear Me!" she screamed. "This is the Lord of the Shadows. This is the Lord of the Forgotten. This is He Whom the Winds Fear. This is the One Who Walks Among Snakes. The One Who Dances on Swords." The woman descended into the sublevel and sprinkled the powder, forming a triangle circumscribed in the depression, with the firepit at the center. Then she stepped into the triangle, close to the fire, and let her chiffon veil fall over her face again.

"Set up the Round Table!" one of the twelve ordered, and they all extended their arms to the right, resting each over the shoulder of the man standing beside them, connecting all members across the room. The shadows cast by the fire on the walls resembled a round table.

"Rise, immortal fire!" the woman commanded, raising her arms up. "Hear me: I am He, the Hidden One! The Serpent Swallowing the Worlds is My name! Come forth and follow Me!" She exhaled, lowering her arms.

Silence fell. Some of the twelve exchanged concerned looks, sweating and visibly tired after the constant arm waving. But then the fire in the pit grew bigger, as if it wanted to engulf the woman. The fire turned blue, shining like a star, forcing everyone to shield their eyes, including me. When the blue fire eased, the features of the woman, somewhat visible through the opaque veil, blurred into a continuous shape-shifting, oscillating between male and female, with sharp features.

"Who are you?" one of the twelve asked.

"You search among the stars, but you won't find Me," a dual voice said, both male and female. "When you look at Me, you gaze at yourselves. I'm the dark snake devouring the universe. Everyone who comes unto Me will experience a new beginning."

"Black Sun." Von Schroeder stepped closer to the woman. "The thirteen welcome you." He performed the Nazi salute.

"Twelve, Obergruppenführer," the voice corrected. "One is missing."

"My apologies. *Reichsführer* Heinrich Himmler is in Berlin with the Fü—"

"Nothing is shrouded from me," she interrupted.

"I wish to inform you," Von Schroeder continued, "we have advanced in the recovering of the sacred artifacts; the Book of Metatron and the Mirror of Azazel are now in our possession. But most important, the children you identified are now in our control, here in Wewelsburg… all except one, still missing."

Children in the castle? Could that be the kid I saw earlier?

"Unfortunately, the war on the eastern front has made continuation of the search inaccessible for us."

"Worry not, everything unfolds accord to the plan." The dual face displayed a bizarre smile from ear to ear.

"Our enemies have recovered Paris and get closer to Germany by the day," an obergruppenführer interjected.

"This war is just a small piece in the greater scheme of things. A lost battle might make you win the greater war… with time and proper help, of course," the voice said seductively.

"But the Führer—"

"Silence!" the voice said, upset, as the body of the woman contorted, arms twisting as if they were broken, head shaking and back bending forward. "Have not I saved your Führer from death twice already?"

"Yes—yes," the terrified obergruppenführer conceded, eyes cast down.

"I'll hold my promise: no enemy will take his life."

"Black Sun, please," Von Schroeder intervened to calm the tensions. "We will abide."

"Yeeeeeeeeeeeeessss." The woman stepped closer to Von Schroeder and, using the index finger of her contorted left hand, smeared down his face the blood coming from the tiny holes above his brow. "I know you will… You know better than anyone what drowning in the pit of sand feels like… eh, boy?" The booming voice laughed, heading back to the fire. "The children! Bring me the children, and I promise you the Übermensch will rise!"

"Long live the Overman!" the twelve shouted in unison.

Why are those children so important? I wondered. *Could this be the secret Anton referred to in his letter?*

The firepit invigorated once more, and the flames returned to their usual color. The faces displaying in the woman's veil dissolved and her limbs and back untwisted, returning to normality. She drew breath agitatedly, as if she had been on the brink of drowning. She removed the veil, revealing her exhausted face. "The séance is over."

At hearing those words, I made my way back, to avoid being discovered. Outside, the rain had receded but obscurity prevailed. The chill shadows granted me safe passage. But instead of going straight to my dormitory, I made a detour to the room where I had found the boy. There was no sign of him, but I peeked through the window, observing the procession of the twelve abandoning the north tower with the woman. She climbed the steps of her carriage and turned back for a farewell. Then her profound eyes glanced up directly at me.

I stepped away from the window and rushed to my dorm, heart pounding, an icy fear climbing my back. I ran the door's bolt and got between my sheets without removing my clothes. I drew the quilt over my head, leaving only a small crack to drag in fresh air.

My trembling hands refused to rekindle my candle. It was pointless to avert darkness anymore.

I had plunged into it.

CHAPTER 6

"ON A DAY NOT FAR AWAY, I hope, it will be you who wears the bridal gown," my mother said, brushing my hair, helping tame my curls. "You will marry a man worthy of you, and you'll have beautiful children."

My lips remained pursed, not to avoid her recurrent marital conversation, but with a fear-induced silence from the nightmarish happenings of last night, still haunting my mind.

"I know what you're thinking," she said, eyeing me in the mirror. "But a woman's life is unfulfilled without children. I could not picture myself not having you or…" She trailed off before pronouncing Anton's name. After a pause, a fleeting smile popped and vanished. "Now you are everything I have."

"Why?" I asked, unemotional.

She put the hairbrush down. "Not having your brother and with my only surviving sister being married to the enemy, the only happiness I can savor now… is through you. Everything else is sour. Time consumes the fascination for life, rendering it purposeless. When you reach my age, you'll understand that watching your children grow is the sole bite of hope that fuels your desire to live another day. We can't have a future without children."

"Amid this endless war, do the children have a future?" I asked.

"Do I have a future?"

"Emma." My mother held my shoulders and turned me to her. "We will survive this war, as we outlived the last."

"But at what cost?"

"At any price," my father said, walking inside the room. "The Reich must thrive."

After seeing him forming part of the ritual, the so-called séance, I wasn't sure who my father was anymore. I doubted the intentions hiding behind his stern countenance, hardened by war. The memory of my father not wearing his uniform seemed otherworldly now. Fed by that paternal strangeness, I could not refrain myself from asking, "Is that what you told Anton?"

My mother slapped me. "Don't you talk to your father like that!"

My cheek throbbed and my breathing turned noisy.

"This nation's greatness was erected upon the suffering of all those before us," my father said. "One day, you'll understand what sacrifice really means… as your brother did—as we all do! Everyone has a duty to fulfill. And we pay the price gladly, because when you look at the world, you'll realize there is no future outside National Socialism. Neither for you nor your children. Understood?"

"I-I'll finish dressing myself in my room." I picked up my dress and rushed outside.

My father's arm extended to detain me, but his fingers curled into a fist and retracted as my mother called his name. The door contained the screams of the dispute, muffled, their words perforating like sharp knives through the wood. I hurried to my dorm, tightening my dress against my chest.

"Peach!" Ania yelled when I passed in front of her room, but I ignored her, afraid that my tears would shed before I could reach my own room.

"Peach!" Ania knocked on the locked door. "Is everything okay?"

"Y-yes, yes, I just need some time alone," I said, the words burning my throat.

"Okay," she replied doubtfully. "But please let me know if you need something. I'll come by later, when you're ready." Ania's footsteps faded away.

My hand wrapped around my locket necklace containing Anton's photo as I rested my forehead on the door, wondering if the terrible things my brother regretted having done, mentioned in his letter, were orders of my father. Maybe there was some truth concealed in my father's words. Maybe I had to be strong and be willing to sacrifice myself, if not for my father or the Reich. I owed it to Gerda—I could not fail her wedding. But I also owed it to my brother. I still had to unravel the mysteries hidden behind Wewelsburg's walls… and what better moment than during the wedding? When everybody would be busy drinking and celebrating. Off guard.

I finished dressing myself with that goal clear in my mind. I pulled on my blue, knee-length dress, buttoned it up to the V-shaped collar, and fastened a leather belt around my waist. Next, I donned my ivory, wrist-length leather gloves but chose not to wear the matching hat. I dabbed perfume around my neck, *Soir de Paris*, a Christmas present from my father, wondering how Anton had spent his last evening in Paris.

"Please, Anton, grant me the strength to uncover all the truth."

The wedding ceremony took place in the foyer next to the main hall of the south wing. It was a small room compared to the hall, but it had a huge hearth of stone decorated with Germanic symbols—the most prominent being the Black Sun. Surrounding the fireplace, candles burning on tall floor stands transmitted a liturgical feeling. The walls were paneled with oak wood up to half-height, with "SS" rune banners hanging above. A cylindrical staircase in the right corner ascended to the second floor. The foyer had direct access to the main hall on the right, restrooms and offices on the left, as well as access to the courtyard.

"Are we late?" Ania asked upon our arrival in the crammed foyer. I stood on tiptoes, looking over the shoulders of the attendees, who were all standing since the few benches were lining the walls.

In the front row, next to the fireplace, stood my parents, Von Schroeder, and Eric, speaking with the obergruppenführer who would conduct the ceremony. He was the one who'd dared to question the Hidden One about losing the war last night, but today he was nothing but smiles, as if the séance hadn't happened at all. Besides the four, no other obergruppenführer was in sight.

In the second row stood Gerda's and Bruno's parents, and behind them, an SS detachment. I spotted Otto and my father's driver, Hermann, among the uniformed personnel, but there was no sign of Reinhard, or Ghislain either.

The doors leading to the courtyard swung open. The SS detachment turned and heiled, synchronized, tilting their arms higher than the usual Nazi salute, creating a tunnel through which the groom and the bride paraded in toward the hearth.

Bruno was wearing his SS uniform, cap, and black leather gloves, flaunting a red armband with the swastika encircled in white around his left arm. Gerda walked hooked on Bruno's arm, carrying a bouquet composed of white and yellow roses, tulips, and lilies. Her bridal garment was a plain gown with tight, wrist-length sleeves and a discrete, V-shaped cleavage surrounded with pearled embroidery. The simplicity of her dress contrasted with the ornate headdress: a round bridal crown with two lines of daffodils entwined in her hair at the back of her head, and an exquisite veil embroidered with flower motifs spread across her shoulders, cascading to the floor.

"Gerda looks beautiful!" Ania whispered when the couple arrived at the hearth and the ceremony started.

"Beautiful, but sad," I replied. Ania gave me a strange look, as if I were not properly sharing Gerda's happiness. But the more I observed her, the more I convinced myself Gerda had failed the eighth commandment for the German woman: marry only for love.

"Maybe it's just because these are sad times," a voice whispered.

I turned to my right, surprised to find Ghislain standing by my side.

"If her wedding is not the happiest day in a woman's life, then when?" I asked softly, to avoid disturbing the ceremony.

"Childbirth?" Ghislain's brow arched. "Oh, I forgot you abhor motherhood," he said, recalling our discussion in the car.

"I don't abhor motherhood. I just detest the inability to choose." I eyed Gerda.

"Maybe that's truly her choice. Maybe because of the circumstances she faced. The call of duty. Her convictions."

I was unconvinced such things should account for marrying an unloved man.

"Would you marry without love?" he asked.

"Never," I replied without thinking twice.

"But if the man you love doesn't love you equally in return?"

"Then I'll die alone, I guess," I said flippantly.

"Does solitude scare you?"

"Less than unwanted company."

"Then I should mince my words to prevent falling from your grace." He bowed, almost apologetic.

"Why should you be concerned about losing my regard? Does solitude scare you?"

"What makes you believe you're the only woman in my life?"

"You live in a castle full of men."

Ghislain chuckled. "Perhaps we are monks practicing celibacy."

"Then you would be right, and these are sad times indeed."

"Why so?" Ghislain turned, puzzled.

"If all men turned celibate, there would be nobody to love women, and we would all die alone."

"I thought death was better than unwanted company."

"It depends…" I smirked.

Ghislain stared at me with his profound steel eyes. "Oh, look, Bruno will declaim his *epithalamium*."

"What's that?"

"Epithalamium. It's a poem written by the groom."

"How—how beautiful you are, my darling," Bruno declaimed, voice shaking nervously.

"Dark are the times like the clouded skies;
Your smile is the waning moon guiding all life.

Rise! Rise! Rise like waves at twilight.
Your bright eyes whisper to me like stars,
A lost sailor navigating through waves of sand,
Paddling without knowing he is aiming at the skies.

Rise! Rise! I scream at the waves of sand,
Because your heart is hidden beyond the stars.
And as the sun chases the moon through the skies,
I chased your heart during the endless night.

And before sunlight turns me back to sand,
I want to hold your hand against my throbbing heart,
Knowing, my darling, that your love makes me believe
That I'm not made of grains of sand, but the dust of stars.

Rise! Rise! Your eyes shining like beams of light.
And with my fingers entwined with yours, at least,
for a moment, allow me to dream about eternal life."

Bruno concluded, and all the attendees clapped vigorously. Gerda blushed, not knowing how to respond.

"Did you like the epithalamium?" Ghislain asked.

"Yes. It was very romantic."

"And what do you think now?"

"About what?"

"Do you think she will learn to love him?"

The bridal couple were hugging and kissing. I sensed Gerda was still emotionally restrained, but after Bruno's display of devotion toward her… "Within time," I said, wanting to believe.

"You sure?"

"During these unfortunate times, having someone by your side who reminds you that you mean everything to him sometimes is the only way to make it through the day," I said, paraphrasing Gerda's words from the day before. Our gazes entwined for a moment, but I could not hold up my end. "Now, if you'll excuse us, the banquet awaits." I pulled Ania away and we joined the attendees, heading toward the hall to continue the celebration.

"Why did you turn him down?" Ania nagged me. "His eyes saw nothing but you."

"Maybe… We'll find out later."

In the hall, servers carrying trays with wineglasses swung around among the attendees, following the beat of the music playing on the wind-up gramophone.

"Let's find a place to sit," Ania said, driving me. "Look, your parents are sitting over there."

"No!"

"Why don't you want to sit with them?"

I could not confess to my best friend I had more important things to do, so I lied. "No, I mean, please go ahead. I need to use the restroom first." I headed back the way we'd come, since the bathrooms were across the foyer, but somebody halted my escape.

"Leaving so early?" Ghislain extended his hand. "Without dancing with me?"

I hesitated. Part of me wanted to grab Ghislain's hand and

dance in the heart of the hall until my feet hurt and I forgot about all the wicked things happening here. But I needed to sacrifice…

"I-I really need to go."

"But if I let you go now, you promise to dance with me?"

"Yes… later," I finally conceded.

"Until later," Ghislain said with a crooked smile.

I left behind the music and gibberish of the hall for the quiet of the empty foyer. I promenaded to the hearth, drawn by the hypnotic flames. My finger traced the Black Sun engraved on the stone, wondering where I should start investigating. The castle was enormous. *The crypt, perhaps?* I was making up my mind about visiting the place where the séance had taken place when the hair-raising sensation of being observed possessed me. I turned and found the boy from last night spying on me through the half-closed entrance door.

"Hey!" I said, but he withdrew swiftly. "Wait!" But when I went out to the courtyard, he had vanished.

The creaking of the wooden door leading to the spiral staircase at the intersection of the south and west wings revealed the path followed by the elusive boy. A hunch told me I would have to descend, since secrets are better kept in the dark.

The atmosphere of the basement was denser, humid. Its thick stone walls insulated all the sounds coming from the surface. An almost inaudible whistle, like the one produced by air currents filtering inside a cave, transmitted a mystical aura reinforced by the archaic decor. At each step, it was as if I traveled a century into the past. No guards chatting, nor maids mopping. There was no one. I assumed they were enjoying the banquet or on military duties.

Scuttling footsteps echoed across the passageway, which I followed. My sense of orientation warned I was approaching the dungeon, according to Von Schroeder. I wondered if it was the one from his story about witches and warlocks.

Finally, I reached a steep set of stairs leading to a sublevel, where the dungeon was located. Von Schroeder's words were true. My trembling feet descended the stone steps, my sweaty hand holding tightly to the metal banister. The torture room was in an arched vault. Up the right wall hung a wooden loge, resembling the pulpit in churches. I imagined the Holy Inquisitor passing judgment from the heights to the accused, shackled and chained to a concrete block on the floor before being hanged with the rope dangling from the pulley anchored to the ceiling. Shivers ran down my spine.

Next to the right wall stood a wooden table displaying a collection of torture utensils: knives, blades, saws, and tweezers. The wood and leather covering the handgrips were scrapped and worn out. The metal looked aged. I wanted to believe its purpose was only historic and decorative, like the suits of armor standing in the halls.

A passage sealed with an iron grid door led to a gloomy stone chamber with shackles and chains bolted against the walls, and at the back, I found two cells. I discerned the figures of a bunch of children among the shadows, gathered against the grid, their eyes glinting in the scarce light filtering inside.

"Oh my God." Horrified, I counted six kids in one cage and one alone inside the other. *Are these the children the Black Sun is so interested in?* "Why are you…" I shook the grid door, trying to open it without success. "Who locked you in there? Is there a key?" But the children remained indifferent to my questions. "Damn!" I cursed under my breath. I had to get them out; I would take them to the hall for all the wedding attendees to see. The perpetrators would not dare to attempt anything against the children once they had gone public, I schemed, even if that would mean also unmasking my father.

The isolated child poked a tiny arm through the bars and pointed at me. "You should go… The Crying Man is coming." The children in the other cell flinched, fading into the blackness inside their cell.

CHAPTER 7

"I NEED TO TAKE YOU OUT." This was my sole chance to release the children. If they caught me, my father could prohibit me from returning to the dungeon. I had to find a way. I browsed through the torture tools on the table, looking in vain for the keys. "Where are they?" I whispered to myself. Footfalls on the stone outside pounded like a ticking clock, getting louder as my time depleted, until the lumbering halted at the door. I abandoned my search and crouched in an angular nook formed by the staircase converging with the wall to avoid being spotted from above.

The visitor descended leisurely, gloved fingers caressing the handrail.

I held my breath and peeked over the steps to uncover the visitor's identity. The man in uniform glanced over the disordered table, presenting a sharp-featured face. It was Reinhard.

"So, we have a nosy visitor." Reinhard sniffed. "Violet… rose… apricot…" He craned his head with eyes closed, chasing through the wind the essences composing my perfume. "Vanilla… jasmine, and peach—delicious." He regained composure. "This piggery has never smelled so good."

I remained silent, naively hoping he would go away.

"Enough of the hide-and-seek, Fräulein Niemeyer. You can

come out."

I gulped. Trying to remain hidden was futile now, so I showed myself.

"Did you stray from the way back to the main hall to come to this place? I hope you've found your visit to the castle's dungeon entertaining," Reinhard said imposingly.

"I would say rather enlightening." I grimaced to repel his intimidation.

"Sure. After the spooky stories told during dinner, you could not miss the chance of visiting Wewelsburg's top attraction and see for yourself if witches and warlocks were still bound to these chains."

"Shockingly, I found something even more terrifying—captive children."

Reinhard smirked. "You don't understand—"

"I do," I interrupted. "No excuse could justify such horror."

He observed me patiently.

"So, please, release them at once," I ordered, attempting to leverage the ranking superiority of my father, hoping he would abide.

Reinhard clicked his tongue several times, shaking his head. "As I was saying," he continued with a euphonious voice, ignoring what I'd said, "I believe you don't understand the situation you're in."

"No, *you* don't understand. Now, if you'll excuse me, I must return to the banquet and speak with my father about this," I said, upset, not really knowing what my father would think about my intercession in this matter, but at that moment, it seemed like the sole viable option to escape from my predicament.

But when I was about to climb the stairway, Reinhard's hand clasped the handrail, blocking my path with his arm.

"Fräulein Niemeyer, are you leaving so abruptly, in the middle of our conversation? How rude! Not the manners of a lady," he said, feigning distress.

"Let me go, or I'll tell my father. I swear."

"Tell him what, exactly?" Reinhard came closer, forcing me to step back. "You think your father doesn't know? That he is ignorant of the existence of these children, locked in a cage so unfairly?"

The confirmation that my father was aware not only of the children's existence but their condition as prisoners was difficult to digest, so I regurgitated the truth. "Everything! I know the children are the price demanded by the Hidden One, the Black Sun, or whatever you call it. I know about the recovered artifacts and all the plans of your superior and his henchman. So, you'd better let me go," I bluffed, trying to intimidate him. After all, Reinhard had not been present during the invocation.

Reinhard laughed maniacally, covering his face, and once he regained calm, he combed back his forelock using his fingers.

"You know, Fräulein Niemeyer… the most effective way to kill a cockroach is not stomping around the room until you crush it. Instead, you sit comfortably and raise your tiptoes slightly, resting on your heels. It requires patience but, eventually, the cockroach will crawl right under your foot." He wiggled his fingers. "And that's not by chance, but nature." Reinhard pressed his temple with the bud of his index finger. "Cockroaches love dark, warm, and tight spaces. Although the sense of safety is transmitted, it's just an illusion played by their primitive brains, incapable of conceptualizing malice incarnated in the shape of a trap."

Reinhard got closer to me. "You don't understand the situation you're in," he repeated with a smooth voice. "Otherwise, last night, your limbic brain would have been disquieted about having a clear passage into the vault, considering this castle is literally swarming with soldiers. And today, you would have been wary about walking here alone." Reinhard sighed, satisfied. "But you have just willingly crawled under my boot… and I will not hesitate in crushing you!" He stomped between my feet, making me jump back.

I wanted to react, but my muscles tensed. My rigid limbs could only back away until my lower back pressed against the table. My trembling hand reached for the torture utensils behind me, searching for a knife. I tried to differentiate the instruments, glancing from the corner of my eye.

"Yeeeeesssssssssssssssssss," Reinhard said, aware of my intentions. "Take that knife and thrust it inside me. I know you want to. You need to. Kill me and become a traitor, just like your brother."

I pointed the knife at his chest with shaking hands. The tip of the blade rested on the Iron Cross hanging from his neck. "Don't you dare speak about my brother, or—"

"Or you'll cut my throat?" Reinhard stepped closer, pushing the knife back, bending my elbows. "Have you ever killed a man?" He reached for my arm.

"Don't touch me!"

"No." He smirked. "You have never even been close to a man."

"Don't push me," I warned.

"Do you know how difficult it is to wash the blood off your hands?" Reinhard ran the bud of his gloved finger down the edge of the knife, and once he reached the hilt, he continued over my hand, passing over my own glove to the skin of my forearm. I flinched with revulsion, and Reinhard seized the opportunity to snatch the knife from me.

"No!" I yelled, but before I could do anything, he clasped my arm. "Let me go!"

Reinhard raised the knife to my eye level and waved it to dissuade me, but I fought to break from his grip anyway. "Let me go!"

"Shhhhhhhhhh." Reinhard pulled me against his chest. "I will not cut you. Don't panic. I would not stain my uniform with treacherous blood." He tossed the knife over the table, and I knew that moment was my only chance to free myself and escape. Gathering all my strength, I kneed his privates. Reinhard bent over in pain, and I pulled my arm to break loose, but he rammed me. I fell backward, unable to interpose my hands. My head bounced on the stone floor.

"*Scheisse!*" Reinhard wobbled, both hands shielding his groin, trying to catch his breath. "How dare you! *Kakerlake!*" *Cockroach*, he called me.

My hands combed through my curly hair, trying to contain the piercing twinge on my nape that disallowed a quick response to get back on my feet. "Help! Please help!" I cried, in hopes somebody would hear me and come to my aid.

Reinhard burst into laughter. "Do you really believe someone will hear you outside this dungeon?" He continued laughing as he approached me. "Not even the bawls of the tortured witches abandoned these walls." He pinned my right wrist against the ground using a shackle bolted to the concrete block.

I punched Reinhard's flank with my free hand to prevent him from securing the shackle, but quickly realized I was causing him no harm. With a racing heartbeat, I searched for something I could use. My hand secured a foot-long metal rod with shackles on each end, welded to the ground through a chain, presumably to chain the wrists of the accuser who would stand for trial. I struck with all my strength; the bar produced a hollow sound when it hit his skull. Reinhard sprawled over me, unconscious.

My agitated breathing calmed a little, but it was too soon to celebrate. First I had to set myself free. I dumped the rod and tried to unbolt the shackle fastening my right arm, but it was outside the reach of my fingers. I had to shake Reinhard's body off me, but he was at least two hundred pounds, and with his arms spread over me, it was impossible for me to roll him aside. So, I pushed him down off me, using my legs until he cleared my torso. With my regained upper-body mobility, I reached for the bolt. Then I heard somebody sobbing. *The kids!* But in the cells, all the children observed me attentively, without crying. With a crippling fear, I slowly turned back to my aggressor.

Reinhard lifted his head from my belly; bland features had replaced his stern look, and he was weeping. "Why do—do you hit me so hard? It hurt," he said in a broken, childish voice. "You were supposed to take care of me."

Scheisse! I located the metal rod from the corner of my eye, but it was out of my reach without making my intentions obvious.

"Don't you love me? Don't you love me?" Reinhard dug his head into my belly. His bizarre behavior made me remember the children's warning about the Crying Man. As this vulnerable boy, he seemed like an entirely different person from the overconfident gruppenführer. It was crazy to think both personalities coexisted.

I inhaled deeply. "Y-yes, I do"—I gulped—"love you." I extended my hand and caressed his hair. "Let me comfort you," I feigned, to reassure him and buy time to creep closer to the rod.

"Then why—why are you so mean…" Reinhard said in a breathy voice that escalated to a booming male timbre. "Why have you chained me?" He clasped my arm and lashed it against the stone.

"Noooooooooooooooo!" I cried as he pulled my wrist closer to the shackle. "Let me go! Please!" I begged, appealing to his last bit of humanity, but he was out of himself.

"But not anymore! You'll hit me no more," Reinhard said, delirious, speaking to somebody else. "Nevermore." With my left arm secured, Reinhard sat over my thighs, restricting the movement of my legs, and extended his arms aloft. "Tonight is the full moon, and the Übermensch shall live!" he said grandiloquently as he ran his hands over my thighs, pulling my dress up.

"What are you doing? No! Please stop!"

Reinhard leaned over me, covering my mouth with his leathered hand, and turned my head aside, exposing my ear. "Shhhhhhhhhhhh, I know this seems terrible to you… but I'm being kind," he whispered.

The children shied away, fading into the blackness of their cells.

I closed my eyelids, squeezing the suffering out of my being through tears during the silent agony that my muffled screams could not voice.

CHAPTER 8

I KNELT, HANDS BEHIND THE STARTING LINE and feet gripped tightly to the ground. The hurdles spread across the track like a series of windows, getting smaller in the distance. The chants of the public packing the Olympiastadion in Berlin resounded. All eyes were on me, including that of my family and friends, who cheered from the side of the track.

I cannot let them down. I need to win gold. Defeat was something I could not swallow. I would be incapable of looking them in the eye, knowing I was not good enough.

But that was not my way of thinking. I had been raised that way, indoctrinated. *"You either strive to be the best or don't even try. The podium has no place for attempts,"* my father had lectured us as children. He was strict, even severe, especially with my brother. *"I demand from you the best because I know you have the potential,"* he constantly exhorted us with his "rigorous" kindness, ratified by the silence of our stern mother.

At home, victories were celebrated, but only when we achieved the highest recognition. *"You don't win second place, you lose first,"* my father used to say, and sadly for me, coming into this world after my brother automatically put me in second place. Anton was bigger, wiser, stronger, and smarter than I was. How could I compete against my brother for the affection of my parents?

A shot boomed, signaling the start of the race, and I sprinted as fast as I could. When I approached the first hurdle, the crowd's uproar shushed, but my mind flooded with voices.

"What honorable man will marry you?" my mother said. *"Women don't respect themselves anymore."*

As I continued the race, each hurdle felt taller, and my shoes were made of stone.

"Marriage is the sole path to happiness. But a gentleman will never fall for a libertine," her voice echoed.

"I'm certain your daughter will marry a decent man," Ghislain's voice emerged, *"and maybe one day, the Führer will award the Cross of Honor of the German Mother to her."*

"That would bring such a joy to this family," my mother concluded.

The words adhered to me like a weight on my shoulders, heavier and heavier at each step, and on my next jump, my knee knocked down a hurdle.

"As women… we need to keep our bodies pure. Mind and spirit," Gerda recited the commandments for German women as hurdles fell one after the other.

"You think your father doesn't know?" Reinhard's voice echoed inside my head.

"At any price," my father's strident voice interjected. *"The Reich must thrive."*

I tripped over the penultimate hurdle and fell on my back, facing the clouded sky. My competitors passed by me as I fought unwavering gravity to get back on my feet, but my body was made of lead. My skin brushing against the cinder track made me feel dirty. I turned in search of vital support from my family, but instead I found him.

Reinhard towered beside me like a giant, looking at me askance with unblinking eyes. *"If you say a word of what happened, do you think your father will care? Nobody is going to believe you. Remember, you started all this. It was you who came to me. So, stop pretending. You are nothing. Worth nothing. You are just a cockroach I can crush with my boot. If you dare to say a word… I'll kill you and destroy everything you ever loved."*

My tears sprouted, and somehow the pressure in my chest faded. I felt lightweight, like a dandelion seed blown by the wind to the sky. From above, the houses of the village looked tiny, as if made of gingerbread, with candy trees and a railroad of chocolate.

But three knocks anchored me back to reality. "Peach, are you all right?" Ania hammered the door. "Peach, open up, please!"

I was not flying. I was overlooking the Alme Valley and Wewelsburg Village from my dorm, standing on the ledge of my window, my toes poking out above the precipice of the moat, a fall of at least sixty feet. The icy breeze burned my swollen eyes. I went breathless, not knowing if it was vertigo or the illusion of freedom. An unrelenting desire to detach from everything.

"Please, Ania, let me alone," I replied with a raspy voice, after endless hours of crying.

Ania insisted, but I didn't concede. I had refused to see my parents, and I would not open for my best friend either. I couldn't look them in the eye after what happened, because I couldn't see myself in the mirror either. Everywhere I turned, Reinhard's lewd face was the sole thing I saw. My mind looped his words like a scratched vinyl, the horrid sensations printed on my skin, the discomfort, the revulsion, the impotence… the shame, forever tarnishing my image to a point I could not recognize myself anymore.

It seemed impossible for me to continue my life, suffering… like this.

"I thought death was better than unwanted company," Ghislain had joked at the wedding.

But he was right. If life had been so unpleasant to me, maybe death would be kinder. I could relinquish my life willingly as long as it would stop the voices in my head and I felt nothing at all. The wound was deep, impossible to heal. I could never return to who I was.

Reinhard was also right. I was nothing. Worthless. I was just a cockroach anybody could stomp.

The best thing to do was to end it all…

I inhaled, and I was about to step into the abyss when someone called from behind me.

"Don't do it," a childish voice said.

I whirled, startled, hugging the timber frame, ready to jump. My visitors were the naughty boy from the other night holding hands with another child.

"How—how did you make it in here?" I questioned my sanity upon confirming the desk was still barring the door. "You're prisoners in the dungeon!"

"We came to help," the boy said, stepping forward.

"Don't get closer. I don't need your help." Tears ran down my cheeks. "I don't want anyone's help." During my tribulation, nobody came to my aid. Maybe I was judging the children unfairly; there had been little they could do, locked in their cells.

"I know how you feel," the other said with a distinctly feminine voice. Upon closer inspection, despite close-cropped hair and an emaciated face, I could see the shape and features were also feminine.

"Are you his sister?" I asked, remembering her as the child who'd warned me about the Crying Man. She was probably six or seven years old. The oversize shirt and pants covering her hands and feet made her look even younger.

She nodded. "I know how you feel." She pulled the shirt up, unveiling marks and bruises across her scrawny torso. This explained the reason for her isolation in the other cell.

"Oh my—" I sat on the window ledge, legs drawn up, the heels of my palms over my temples, trying to digest the revelation. My wrists were reddened and sore, with a skin-peeled mark left by the shackles during my helpless attempts to get free. My insides quivered, imagining this tiny girl going through the same torment, over and over. "Ba-bastard—" I choked on the word, unable to manage the revulsion. My stomach boiled with hatred toward Reinhard, but also toward myself. I was selfishly trying to put an end to my misery, abandoning the children to their fate. *But what can I do? Go to my father, after what I witnessed? Would he listen to me if I tell him what Reinhard did to us?*

I doubted it. My father already knew about the children, and he would not contradict an order of the Hidden One, requesting them for who knew what evil purpose.

My mother? In her eyes, I would be the sole culprit of what had happened to me.

Ghislain, perhaps? I wouldn't have the courage to tell him what happened. Even if I did, and he believed me, I was unsure he would have the guts to confront his superior for me either.

Ania and Gerda? It didn't matter how much they loved me; in this situation, they were as powerless as I was.

Even if I wanted to, I could involve none of them. Reinhard was crazy and capable of fulfilling his threat. *We need help from somebody else,* I resolved. I descended from the window and knelt in front of them. "Where are your parents?" I asked, believing I could escape and search for them. But they shook their heads. "Don't you have someone looking after you?" They exchanged disheartened looks.

"They abducted us…" the boy said, and as he spoke beyond monosyllabic responses, I noted an accent in their German. They were foreigners.

"Only our sister escaped," the girl said.

"But where is she now? She must have informed your parents about what happened… I mean."

Both shrugged without releasing their hands. "It was years ago," the boy said gloomily.

"You've been imprisoned in that dungeon for years?"

"No," the girl said. "We have been to many places."

"Mostly hospitals and laboratories," the boy added.

My goodness. "But where do your parents live?"

"Near Arkhangelsk."

The name didn't sound familiar. "Where is that?"

"Soviet Union."

I stared at them, flabbergasted. We were at war with the Red Army. "Who taught you to speak German?"

"Doctors."

Why are these kids so important they would go to the lengths of teaching them German? Could it be political? Independently of the reason, they needed somebody who could help them return to their parents.

"We have no one," the girl said, as if she were reading my thoughts engraved on my forehead. "Only you."

"Why me?" I sighed. "I mean… I can't even help myself."

"Because only you can see us." The girl released her brother's hand and vanished as if she were a ghost.

I fell backward and dragged myself away.

"Don't be afraid," the boy said. "It's okay, see?" He grabbed something outside of this plane and his sister reappeared—he held her hand again.

"H-how?" I could not articulate the words.

"I don't know, I just can." The boy smiled.

I crawled to them and extended my hand. My fingers reached the boy's tummy and passed through, causing ripples, waving his image, transmitting to me the subtle sensation, almost imperceptible, of my hand moving through water.

The boy stepped back, grinning. "It tickles."

It was some sort of projection, like the movies I had watched in Berlin, but it was three-dimensional and astonishingly real. This explained how they had made it inside the room, and how I had seen him earlier, even as his physical body inhabited the cell. *Could this be the reason they are so interested in them? This… power?* "You mentioned I'm the only person who can see you like this."

He nodded.

"Can you… teleport or something?" I was thinking of the matter transmitter used by Miss Zumeena to teleport Thomas Plummer in the science fiction novel *To Venus in Five Seconds.*

"No, I walked here."

"You wander around, passing through all doors in the castle?"

He nodded again.

"Do you know where the keys to open your cells are located?"

"Yes."

"Then why haven't you set yourself free?"

"I can't," he said, disappointed. "I can only move tiny things. If I try to move a bigger one, my head hurts."

I sighed, pulling my head back, hanging over my shoulders.

"Will you take us out?" the boy asked.

"Out? Where?"

"Anywhere is better than here."

She was right. But even if this boy could guide me to the keys and I freed them and we escaped this castle, we would not pass beyond the guardhouse before the soldiers shot us dead. *Unless…*

I stood and glanced through the window. "A railroad…" I whispered, observing Wewelsburg Village. "If I could take you out of that cage and into the moat, we could descend the hillside of the castle…" My eyes followed a path populated by dense trees to camouflage our escape. "We would have to pass a road sporadically patrolled by soldiers and cross the creek using the bridge heading toward the village… and finally reach the train station, and from there… even Berlin." I was not a railway expert, but at least it would take us away from this place. *Or not… and we all could end up back in the dungeon or dead…* I feared more the former than the latter. After all, I had been about to jump from the window. But the possibility of saving these children before resuming my road to demise…

"Can you guide me safely to the keys and in and out of the dungeon?" I asked the boy. "We need to pass unnoticed to the moat."

He nodded. "A door in the basement of the east wing leads out to the moat."

"Then… I'll see you here after midnight."

"Don't worry, we will leave this castle," the girl said reassuringly, before releasing her brother's hand and vanishing.

The boy walked away, looking back before fading as he traversed the wall.

"I hope…" I said, before collapsing on my bed, wishing all this were just a bad dream.

CHAPTER 9

WHEN THE CLOCK STRUCK 1:00 A.M., the boy reappeared in my room. By that time, I had prepared myself. I'd put on my BDM uniform and collected my scarce money and valuables that could help me on the journey. I prepared my replacement, pillows dressed in my nightgown, which I tucked under the blankets to simulate that I was profoundly asleep. I had tried to pen a farewell note for my parents, but tears flowed instead of ink, so I gave up.

"Are you ready?" the boy asked.

I held the orbed locket necklace hanging from my neck, Anton's memento, and nodded. "Is anybody in the hallway?"

The boy poked his head out through the door and said no. We exited my dorm to a deserted hallway, but this was not necessarily a good omen for me. I had no certainty I was not heading into a trap again.

"I'll go ahead," he said, observing my hesitation.

I followed him through the corridors of Wewelsburg, until suddenly the boy waved his hands in sign of alarm. I flattened myself against the nearest door, hoping the door opening would be wide enough to hide me from the cadets who descended the stairs. It was. We resumed our prowling until we arrived at a hallway with all doors flashing medieval names: King Arthur, King Henry, Henry the Lion, Teutonic Order, Westphalia, and so on. The boy finally halted before a door labeled "Grail."

"Here?"

He nodded.

I turned the handle to no avail. "It's locked. Now what?"

The boy crossed through the door. Seconds later, I heard a *click*—he had undone the lock. I pushed the door gently to avoid any creaking sound and closed it with the same delicacy once inside, making sure nobody had followed me. The room was a study furnished with a desk, chair, bookshelves, and a bench, all carved in wood following the same rune pattern decoration. The photographs hanging on the walls pictured Von Schroeder, along with Himmler and the Führer.

"Von Schroeder's office," I said. "Where are the keys?"

"In the desk."

I sat on the tall chair that felt like a throne, crowned with the Black Sun emblem. I pulled open drawers stuffed with papers.

"The one in the middle," the boy instructed.

"It's locked. Can you open it?"

He turned, puzzled. "I can't see the mechanism."

"Let me try. I watched my brother open my dad's drawer twice." I grabbed a letter opener. It was like a tiny sword, with an eagle and swastika decorating the end of the pommel, and I inserted it in the lock. Then I picked a paper clip up from the desk, unfolded it, and bent the tip into a hook. I inserted the hooked clip on the top of the letter opener and stirred it inside, twisting the letter opener until the lock gave way. "Yes!"

A bunch of things jumbled as I pulled open the drawer, among them a metal hoop with a bunch of keys. But what caught my attention were a couple of books that seemed hundreds of years old. I turned the cover of the first. Written with old calligraphy on the first page was the word *Ravisseur*.

Noises in the hallway froze me. I scanned the room for hide-outs, but it was too late. Footfalls approached. Two men chatted with indistinct voices. I pressed my finger against my lips. I didn't want to find out if I was the only person capable of hearing the boy. We waited until the men had gone.

"We need to hurry," the boy whispered.

I knew that, but there was a reason for the contents of this drawer to be under lock. I picked up a leather briefcase resting on the bench, released the buckles of the flap, and dumped in the whole contents of the drawer. "Let's go." I slung the briefcase strap over my shoulder and across my chest, pushing it around my back to avoid restraining my mobility in case I had to run.

"It's safe now," the boy said, peeking outside. "We need to free my siblings."

My palms started sweating and my breathing hastened at the idea of returning to the dungeon. Reinhard's face still showed every time I closed my eyes, his smell stuck inside my nose…

Enough! I shook my nightmarish thoughts away. I clutched the letter opener close to my chest. I would not commit the same mistake twice. "First, we go to the pantry."

"Why?"

"We need supplies. I won't rescue you from the claws of death just to starve you after. There is a long road before us," I said doubtfully, trying to convince myself this was not an excuse concocted by my mind to delay facing my fears. "But I'll need your help to fool the guards at the gate."

In the courtyard, two sentries guarded the gate, as expected. I would have to cross the yard to the east wing undetected, but this time there was no rain or witch carriage to use as camouflage. "Can you create a distraction on the other side of the gate?" I needed to call their attention, and what better way than to lure them outside the gate?

"I-I… I'll try." The boy walked to the gate, passing unnoticed by the sentries chatting, carefree. He stood at the other end of the bridge and started quivering, hands clenched and frowning, as if he were straining to lift a heavy object. His image flickered like movies do when experiencing issues with the projector. The boy's eyeballs turned white and glowed in the dark, calling the attention of a sentinel.

"What the…"

"Open the gate!" His companion straightened his rifle, aiming at the boy.

Before the sentinel could comply, the boy fled into the woods.

Now's my chance. I scuttled to the entrance of the east wing and descended a few steps, since the door was on a lower level than the yard.

The kitchen was submerged in darkness. Only faint moonbeams permeated the windows, outlining my path to the pantry. I swung open the cupboards and forced my eyes to adapt to the poor light and find the less perishable food. I picked a couple of truckles of cheese, bread loaves, and a jar of jam. I picked a canteen full of fresh water and bagged all items inside my leather briefcase, concerned about the weight, but I calculated there was room for a last item, a tin box of mints—considering I didn't pack my toothbrush.

A spark flashed in the dark, catching me by surprise. The scarce light revealed a hand holding a burning match. A face was revealed when approached by the flame, but the light tempered as the tip of a cigarette sucked the fire in, glowing like embers. Smoke cascaded upward from the man's mouth, bifurcating in his prominent nose and tarnishing the spectacles framing his bushy brows. It was Otto. His eyes rested on me, and I tensed.

Otto jolted the match out, vanishing back into darkness, but his footfalls resounded as his shadow, outlined by the moonlight, marched toward me. I rummaged with a shaky hand inside the leather bag for the letter opener, buried underneath the groceries, but before I could seize it, Otto's physique towered over me, eclipsing the light from the window.

I held my breath, motionless.

Otto lit another match. The warm yellow flame illuminated his expressionless face. Otto stared at me and clicked his tongue with the rhythm of a clock ticking. But despite understanding the analogy that my time was running out, I was petrified. "Leave now," he finally ordered.

Without second thoughts, I circumvented him and abandoned the pantry, clutching the letter opener inside the briefcase. I glanced back as I fled, to ensure he wasn't following me. But Otto observed the wood stick shrinking as the flame devoured it, hypnotized, like it was a spectacle worth beholding.

Back in the courtyard, I halted, unsure how long the boy could act as a decoy for the sentries. I crawled the steps to have a better angle from the gate. The yard seemed deserted and—unusually— quiet, as if it were on purpose and somebody was waiting for... *Emma, stop!* I reined in my paranoid thoughts. *There is no going back,* I convinced myself. I sneaked, glued to the wall, toward the entrance. The gate was closed, but the sentries were out of sight, so I made my way downstairs, venturing underground.

My heart pounded like a metronome as I approached the dungeon. My lungs faltered to inhale the humid air and my legs wobbled as my defilement rekindled inside my mind. "Reinhard…" My mouth turned sour at pronouncing his name. My body tingled as my skin evoked the feeling of his gross hands on me. I had to stop and hunched, hands on my knees, trying to catch my breath, as if I had just run a hurdle race. *I can't do it.* I wanted to escape. To go back to my parents and friends. I wanted to… to go back in time and change what happened… But I could not. Reinhard had imprinted his abuse in my memory, his groping carved on my skin like scars that would haunt me for the rest of my life.

I need to finish it, I reminded myself of my purpose. I closed my eyes and remembered the view from my dorm at the top of the castle. Oddly, recalling my suicidal thoughts helped me feel lighter, relaxed. Having the sensation of imminent freedom at the grasp of my fingers helped me to cope with my terrifying reality.

"Just one step, Emma… One step more… Do it for the kids." I pulled out the letter opener and gripped it, arm extended, as if it were a sword. The tip of the blade quivered like the arrow of a compass, signaling my way down as I submerged myself into absolute terror one step at a time. Even the dim moonlight percolating through the windows refused to descend to the hellish realm of the dungeon, which was lit only by a flickering torch. I made my way through the torture room like a weathervane in a hurricane, swiftly turning toward every corner. It was empty, but the solitude offered no comfort. I could swear the walls were shrinking and the ceiling descending over me. I lurched to the torture instruments and seized the largest knife on the table. *Emma, quick, there is no time to lose,* I encouraged myself and marched straight to the cells, avoiding looking at the chains and shackles lying on the floor that Reinhard had used to restrain me.

"You made it!" the boy said enthusiastically, now in his corporeal form.

"Shhhhhhhh," I shushed him and propped the knife against the wall. "I'll take you out of here." One after the other, I tried the keys until I found the right one. I released the girl first, but when I unlocked the second cell, the children rushed outside and squeezed me all at once, knocking the wind out of me. I was in shock, not from the effusive hug—which was comprehensible—but because I could not believe what I was seeing. Under the torchlight, their skin was abnormally white, as if covered in flour. I stood there, arms aloft, just like the children. Pale as a ghost.

CHAPTER 10

"BUT I SAW YOU…" I mumbled, remembering the previous contact I'd had with the projection of the siblings. Their skin had been pigmented. I struggled to remember my prior visit to the dungeon. *Could the darkness have disguised their skin tone?* I could not tell for sure. Part of me was forcing my mind to block those memories.

"We were not always like this." The girl rolled up her long sleeve, revealing a *68* tattooed on the back of her hand.

I stepped back, freeing myself from their embrace, and read the numbers inked on their hands with dismay: 13, 27, 44, 49, 66, and 88. My mind flashed back to my first conversation with the boy: *"Sixty-six,"* he'd replied when I asked for his name. But my astonishment was far from put to rest. I lifted their chins, and the torchlight revealed features of diverse ethnicity masked under the chalky skin. "My God… are you Hindu?"

"I was born in Madras," number 13 said, referring to the city of Chennai.

"How old are you?"

He shrugged, knitting his bushy brows. He was probably eight.

"How long have you been here?" I asked number 27, but he pulled his head away, casting his eyes down and glancing at me intermittently. "Where are you from?" He had Caucasian features.

"Don't you want to talk with me?" But he remained silent, clasping himself. He was probably six years old, seven tops.

"He can't," answered the girl, numbered 68. "He's mute. He is—was—Jewish," she corrected herself, and all the kids agreed. Apparently, she was the leader of the pack.

"But how do you know? I mean… since he can't…" I had trouble explaining myself.

"Your people call him that way."

My people, of course. I was wearing my BDM uniform, a Nazi uniform, which explained his discomfort. I knelt before him. "Don't worry."

A boy approached my side and snatched my cap, leaving my frizzy hair bouncing free.

"Don't bother her, Forty-Four," rebuked 66, the boy with the projection abilities, but 44 ignored him and donned the oversize cap, which fell over his nose.

"It's okay," I replied and helped him to adjust the cap, revealing his slanted eyes.

He laughed goofily, with an enormous tongue protruding between his teeth. Considering his short nose and tiny ears and teeth, I realized 44 suffered from Down syndrome, hence his more childish behavior.

"You can keep it. It looks nicer on you."

Forty-Four jumped around as if he had received a Christmas present. It was useless to guess his age, considering Down syndrome kids had growth impairment as well.

"Thank you for freeing us," said 49 in broken German. He bowed.

"Are you Japanese?" I recognized Asian features.

"*Hai,*" affirmed the well-mannered boy of six, maybe seven years old.

And finally number 88, who seemed the oldest of the group, probably because of his more robust frame and African features, though he had a malformed left arm.

"And you?" I asked.

"Marrakesh." I had heard of this city in Morocco.

"You should be cold." I rubbed his arms. "The sun is not kind here."

"We—we have to go—now!" 68 exclaimed, with head trembling, limbs stiffened, and eyes partially closed, as if she were suffering a seizure. Her brother, number 66, held her from behind to prevent her from falling.

"Oh my!" I rushed to assist her.

"She's fine, don't worry," 66 said confidently.

"A—a path will be revealed... Hell's flames will protect us..." 68 mumbled, her eyes shifting as if she were reading. Her body contracted abruptly and then deflated. And with wide, unblinking eyes, she stared at me. "It will hurt on the outside, but will break on the inside." Her tiny hand stroked my cheek and dropped to my chest.

What?

"There is no time to waste!" 66 pulled my hand. "We have to run!"

Bewildered, I trusted the children.

Sixty-Six conducted us through the basement. We held hands in a line to avoid leaving anyone behind. The passageways seemed endless, elongated by my anxiety, the fear that our echoing foot-steps would expose our escape. But the last door cracked open, and the castle's moat welcomed us with a cool breeze. I could not avoid remembering my stroll with Gerda and Ania upon my arrival. It seemed so alien now. From strolling one day to running for my life the next. The exit opened feet away from the bridge, but fortunate-ly for us, there was no visible sentry above.

The moon peeked through the clouds, providing enough light to guide our way, but too much to camouflage ourselves in the shadows. "Watch your step," I whispered. The soil was muddy after the recent downpour.

The clattering of jackboots stomping on the stone escalated to a continuous drumming as what seemed like an entire *staffel* of soldiers from the guardhouse marched inside the castle. I urged the children to hide beneath the arched passageway, preoccupied. The hands of my wristwatch were not even close to 3:00 a.m. It was too early for taking a platoon on military exercises. *Were we discovered?*

"We need to go the other way," 66 said, pointing north. It made sense. Surveillance of the castle's southern access was higher com-pared to the northern, just by its proximity to the guardhouse. But we would have to circle the castle counterclockwise, around the north tower and then downhill, heading west.

"Okay, stay low and silent," I instructed, leading the way.

We scuttled in a single line. Shouts echoed in the distance, presumably coming from within the walls. *Have they uncovered the jail-break?* The remaining distance to the grove surrounding the north tower was the same as a hurdle race. *I could make it in ten*, I pondered, but I was not by myself anymore. "C'mon!" I hurried the children, constantly looking behind to confirm seven tiny figures followed my steps. Once sheltered under the foliage of the trees, we halted to catch our breaths. "Is everyone okay?"

"Yes, Mom!" all replied in unison.

Mom? It felt weird. I was about to complain, but their hopeful eyes staring at me restrained me from doing it. "You can call me Peach… and… we need to keep going."

We resumed our prowling, keeping the north tower as visual reference. By the time we were on the western side, the ruckus inside the castle had become rowdy. We continued steadily until the sirens blared. "Run! Run! Run!" I exclaimed, pulling 66 after me by the hand. We rushed down the slope, circumventing the trees.

"Wait! Wait!" the children at the end of the line cried.

I halted, but my feet slid on the mud until I anchored my free hand to the ground. Forty-Four had fallen along the way. *I should have foreseen this.* I reprimanded myself for not considering his condition before planning the escape.

"Are you okay?" I asked, helping him to stand, but he didn't reply. "There is no time to waste!" I pulled his hand, but 44 resisted, pulling uphill. I glanced back and found the reason for his behavior: the hat I gave him had fallen off. "Leave it! Don't you hear the sirens?" I shook his arm to bring him to his senses, but he refused. With no other option, I released his hand and waited for him to retrieve the cap. Forty-Four returned to me elated, as if he had found a treasure worthy of putting at risk his newly regained freedom.

I guided the children through the last stretch of woods until we arrived at the road. "Now, listen to me." I knelt, and the kids surrounded me. "I need you to run as fast as you can. We need to reach that stone bridge and cross the river. It's our only chance. Understood?"

"Yes, Peach."

"Wait here." I hid behind the last tree trunk at the edge of the woods and watched the road to spot any patrol. But as far as my eyesight allowed, none could be seen. I beckoned the children to follow me. We crossed the two-lane road and followed a slim line of trees on the shoulder, heading toward the bridge.

"Fire!" one of the children shouted.

In the distance, a tall column of reddish smoke rose from the castle courtyard.

Bewildered, I slowed my pace. "Otto." His name escaped my lips, as I remembered him playing with matches. "The pantry is burning!"

Fighting the fire was the reason for the soldiers to march inside the castle. *Could Otto be helping me to escape?* The words mentioned by 68 during her seizure echoed in my mind: *"Hell's flames will protect us."* But not everything was good news. At the top of the sinuous road, the headlights of a car flared.

"They found us!" We rushed to cross the bridge. Behind us, the car veered violently, tires screeching on the asphalt, making its way through patches of vegetation as a shortcut to intercept us. "Faster!" I encouraged the kids, but they were already exhaling noisily.

The car sped over the bridge, headlights becoming brighter as it approached. I considered jumping off the bridge, but it was a ten-foot fall, and the creek looked shallow and rocky. Even if we made it safely to the bottom, the creek offered no escape route either. The car passed by our side and the driver pressed the brakes and steered, drifting until it stopped facing us, blocking our way.

Scheisse! I shielded my eyes from the blinding lights. The children clustered behind me in dread.

The car door swung open, and the driver descended, shining a flashlight on us, making it harder to discern his identity. I descried the silhouettes of two more occupants inside the vehicle. *Could that be Reinhard and Von Schroeder?* I thought, fearing the worst.

"Hands up and step away from the children!" the man ordered with a harsh voice.

The children latched on to me, their tiny hands circling my waist.

"Please! Don't abandon us, Mom!" they repeated, frightened.

"I will not repeat it!" The man pointed his gun at us and cocked the hammer.

"Wait!" I held my arms aloft. "We are unarmed! Please!"

The man approached without lowering his weapon, slowly revealing his identity with each step.

"Hermann?" I said, recognizing my father's driver.

Hermann clutched my neckerchief and jerked me off-balance. The button on the collar of my blouse ripped apart. He pulled me away from the children and presented me toward the vehicle.

Not blinded by the lights anymore, I recognized the man riding in the passenger seat.

My father.

He stared at me through the windshield, cold-livered. I was about to rejoice for him being the person who found me when he lowered his head with disappointment before stepping out of the car.

My father pulled something from his coat and extended his arm. A loud *bang* and a flash startled me as Hermann's head exploded, splattering blood over my face. Hermann's hand released my neckerchief and his lifeless body collapsed at my feet. The children cried at the sight of the dead body. My father walked to me with a Luger pistol clutched in his hand, the barrel still smoking.

"Y-you ki-kille—" I struggled to articulate my horror.

My father slapped my face. "What were you thinking?" he yelled rabidly. "Do you know what you have done? Eh?"

I shielded my burning cheek, fingers slipping in Hermann's blood, but I most wanted to protect my ears from his hurtful words.

"Father, I-I-I am sorry, b-but please—" I wanted to explain to him everything that had happened.

"Shut up! Shut up!" My father raised his hand to me, and his trembling fingers curled into a fist as he fought to control his wrath. His body arched as if he were in pain, and he fell to his knees. "Why, Emma?" he sobbed, pressing the Luger against his forehead.

"Father, please!" I tried to help him stand amid my cries. "You need to stand up! Only you can help me! Please!"

"Help?" he said sardonically. "Everything is lost." He rose and stared at me with vacant eyes. "Now I've lost you… just like I lost your brother."

"No, I'm still here." *I'm still alive!* I wanted to shout.

"You shouldn't." My father wiped his tears, coming back to his former self, the methodical and resourceful man he had always been. "You can't stay. You need to leave at once!" He towed me, ushering me into the driver's seat. "Remember the driving lessons your brother gave you?"

"But, Father, if we go back with you—"

"No, Emma. I can't protect you from this."

"But why?"

My father glanced to the children, who observed us attentively—except 44, who was playing with the flashlight he had collected from Hermann. "It's beyond your comprehension," he said dryly.

The Black Sun, I thought.

My father squeezed me against his chest. "My Peach," he whispered. "Now get in, and take—them—with you." He opened the back door and beckoned to the children.

I could swear there was somebody sitting in the back, I thought. The siblings, 66 and 68, sat in front with me.

"I'll see you back at Grandpa's," I said, starting the engine.

"No. Drive west, through Geseke and then Hamm."

"West? Where to?"

"As far as you can from the Reich."

"But—but how am I going to find you?" I asked, disconcerted.

"I'll try to solve things here and send somebody after you."

"What are you planning to do?"

"I'm going to buy you some time." My father half smiled and pointed his Luger to his left arm. "Now go!" he ordered before pulling the trigger.

I closed my eyes as I jammed the transmission into reverse and floored the gas.

The image of my father falling to his knees with his arm covered in blood faded into darkness as the light cones of the headlights retreated from the scene.

CHAPTER 11

EVERYTHING WAS DARK BEYOND THE HALO of light, and to make it worse, my eyes had no wipers like a car's windshield does. My tears distorted the road as if I had suffered astigmatism. I felt like the car was driving itself, unsure whether it was even heading to Geseke. Maybe it was inertia exerting its pull after the sequence of events from the last two days, without knowing how I could stop it.

"Feel it," Anton had instructed during my first driving lesson. *"Be aware of what the car wants to tell you."* My hands sensed the faint vibration of the chugging engine, transferred to me across the mechanisms. *"Recognize every vibration, every pattern, and learn to identify its rhythm. The car will let you know the right time to switch gears. When to press the pedals hard or soft. It will warn you about how much strength to apply on the wheel when you take a turn at high speed, to remain in the road. Just listen to it."*

"How does the car know?" I'd asked, intrigued.

"It senses the conflict of forces," Anton explained. *"One pushing out and the other pulling in."*

"And which one wins?"

"That will depend on you." Anton glanced at the road ahead of us, meditative. *"Inertia can carry you in an undesired direction, but can also*

prevent you from leaving an unwanted place…"

"Look at the sky!" 66 broke my trance. "Planes!"

I leaned over the dashboard. A swarm of tiny cross-shaped shadows furrowed the night sky. "Bombers!" I replied with agitation. "Get on the floor!" The children huddled. I turned the headlights off, unsure whether the planes were hostile, but kept speeding, knowing all the Wewelsburg soldiers would be in our pursuit.

The wheel stiffened, pulling me to the right as the car sensed the slope of a side road heading toward the woods. *The perfect cover.* I veered into the woods without releasing the gas, and the undergrowth scratched the floor of the car. Once insulated by the foliage, I turned the headlights back on. Tree trunks and shrubs glittered, cropped out from obscurity. A small, dark silhouette appeared ahead in the road. As we approached, the figure turned, revealing a face.

"A child!" I screamed in terror of running over the kid. I swerved then stomped on the brake, smashing the car against the fat trunk of a tree instead. The sudden stop compressed my chest against the wheel, and my forehead collided with the windshield, rendering me unconscious.

When I woke, I was sitting on a leather elbow chair inside what seemed to be a train. The Pullman was lined in warm mahogany finishes, lit with petrol lamps hung on brass brackets. My head throbbed painfully and buzzed as if stuffed with insects and about to explode.

"What happened?" I asked the woman sitting by my side, but she gave no response, despite opening and closing her mouth as if she were speaking. "Are you okay?" I inquired, concerned about her well-being—judging by her gray mane and mapped face, she was probably in her seventies. "Ma'am?"

She turned to me with cloudy eyes as if blind and gaped her mouth. Her dentures fell from her gums.

I flinched away from my seat, but my horror escalated at finding all the passengers in the same condition. Eyes clouded, mouths gaping, and limbs wiggling like fish taken out of the water.

Where am I?

The train was not moving. The window framed the darkest of nights, punctured by twinkling stars. But I saw no sign of land on the horizon. The light from the window reflected off a surface below. *Is it water?* It was like an extremely quiet lake, but boundless like an ocean.

My head buzzed painfully, shortening my breathing as if something were obstructing my lungs. *I need air.* I slid the window open, but instead of air, a stream of water flowed in, quickly flooding the Pullman. I waded to the door, hoping to escape, but I was drowning despite being only knee-deep in water. When my oxygen level dropped, I fainted. My face hit the wall of water.

When I woke up again, I sat bolt upright, panting, fighting a tightness in my chest and soaked in sweat. My hands reached my head to control my splitting headache and found my forehead smeared with a viscous substance, an herbal concoction reeking of alcohol. My mind flashed through my last memories before fainting… A car crash… My head hitting the windshield.

Where am I? My mind cleared with no recollection of how I'd arrived at this place. I was sitting on a bunk bed inside a tiny room. Fortunately, not in Wewelsburg Castle; the walls were of timber instead of stone. I was still wearing my BDM uniform, though. It seemed like a cabin inside a train… "A train…" I whispered, remembering my nightmare. "…with petrol lamps hung on brass brackets…" I watched the quivering flame of the petrol lamp lighting the room.

An overwhelming feeling of needing to abandon this place overtook me.

I got to my feet and pushed the folding door aside, revealing a room lit with candlelight, the windows planked with wood. Shelves contained dusty leather books, jars, pyramids, candles, animal skulls, and statues of deities. At the center stood a workbench with a mortar where the concoction smeared on my forehead had been ground. My head bumped against bunches of garlic bulbs. A multitude of plants hung from the ceiling like an upside-down garden.

A murmur coming from the outside called my attention. "The children!" I reminded myself in anguish and followed their voices through the exit.

In the forest's penumbra, I found the children sitting by the campfire in the company of a woman in black. A shiver crept over my skin; she was the witch who had practiced the séance in the crypt at Wewelsburg Castle, who had embodied the Black Sun itself.

CHAPTER 12

I STOOD ON THE STAIRS of the wooden carriage, unnerved.

"Peach!" the children rejoiced and hurried to meet me. "You're all right!"

I welcomed them with open arms. The hollow-eyed woman studied every movement I made.

"We were worried for you," 66 said childishly. "You couldn't wake."

"But I'm fine now… I suppose thanks to you," I said, addressing the woman.

"Thanks to me?" The woman chuckled, poking the fire with a long, gnarled stick, which she held with elegance, as if stirring a cup of tea. But her stylish demeanor didn't end there. She was sitting with a straight back, shoulders slightly pushed backward, legs crossed, and her hand resting delicately over her lap, as if she were perching on a lavish armchair instead of an old trunk. "You should thank Nailah." She cocked her head and looked at me askance.

I became aware of somebody standing by my side. A small child, probably five years old—the kid I nearly ran over with the car. She was wearing a two-piece black robe, like that of a nun, but the veil was a single piece of fabric without a coif, pulled tightly around her face, and her exposed scalp was shaved, transmitting the odd sensation of a mask.

Nailah offered an earthenware bowl with soup. "For you." Her voice carried an accent I couldn't identify.

"Soup is deli-li-li-li-li-licious!" 44 said effusively, licking his lips with his long tongue.

Remembering the woman's actions at the séance, I eyed the bowl with disquiet.

"You can eat it," the woman said indifferently, absorbed with her task at the bonfire. "Why would I tend your wounds just to poison you later?"

It was a fair point. If her intention was to hand me over to the SS, she could have left me in that car until the troops found me.

"Thank you." I accepted the bowl, and Nailah's lips arced in an unemotional grin that, along with her unblinking eyes, transmitted the eerie impression of a doll.

"Come and finish your meal by the fire," the woman instructed, and the children returned to their seats.

I found a spot on a pyramid of logs. The bonfire welcomed me with a warm embrace, repelling the cold of the night.

Sixty-Eight joined me, sitting by my side. "It's tasty." She flashed an uneven denture with missing teeth, making me remember myself at her age.

I caressed her head. The bowl contained a mix of vegetables: cauliflower, broccoli, slices of carrots, and corn kernels boiled with the meat, which was presumably pork—or at least I wanted to believe that, since the species granted a strong flavor. It was far from being the best stew I'd ever had, but it made me wonder what type of food the children had received while locked in that dungeon.

"Who—who are you?" I finally dared to ask.

"I'm like you," the woman answered from across the bonfire, her black pupils shining like marbles. "A defector."

"But I've seen you with—"

"I know what you saw, girl," she interrupted. "I know where you have been. And like you, I'm running away from my people. But your people are not my people. I'm not German, but for the Nazis, somebody with my skills is deemed necessary."

"Your skills?" I questioned, recapitulating the séance. "What are you?"

The woman leaned forward, propping her elbow on her thigh and resting her jaw in her cupped hand. "I can be many things…

Renenet the wise, the mystic"—her eyes narrowed—"or the witch... Who will I be to you?"

I didn't know what to reply.

"Our paths crossing was no accident, girl; there is no such thing as a coincidence."

"If you saw me the other night, why didn't you reveal it?" I remembered her piercing eyes staring at me from the castle court-yard.

"Because I am like you, or rather, you will become like me, a nomad. Soon you'll learn that under the rain of blood flogging this land, nomads need safe passage. I've rendered my services to your Führer, but I'm no Nazi. I've no stakes in this conflict. I'm just a spectator witnessing the end of times."

"Will this war never end?"

"Your war might end." Renenet stood. "Come, children, it's time for you to dream." She collected the earthenware. "Nailah, show them where they can rest, and after that, continue your stud-ies."

Studies? In the dead of night?

"Yes, Mother." Nailah acted as a grown-up, instructing the chil-dren to form a line and follow her inside the carriage.

"Good night, Peach!" The children waved to me as they left.

"Your daughter looks a lot like you," I said, intending it as a compliment.

"My daughter is me... something you'll understand once you become a mother." Renenet glanced at the children marching. "Or maybe sooner... You've gained quite a large family before the rooster crows at dawn."

"I couldn't..." I sighed. "I couldn't turn a blind eye to their suffering... I had no choice."

"That's what you think?"

"What do you mean?"

Renenet sat by my side, and I flinched unconsciously at her im-posing presence. She stared at me with her face divided: one side lit by the flames, the other with her skulled features emphasized by darkness.

"Look at you, so young and fair, like a princess out of a fairy tale." Renenet's fingers caressed my cheek, and I rested my bowl of soup on the logs, uneasy about how to respond. "Any man would fall for you. You could marry, have a home... children, perhaps.

Why are you so willing to spoil your life for the sake of those children, not born from your own flesh and blood, whose fate has been already decided?"

Spoil my life? Reinhard had already ruined it. I had little else to lose. "What do you mean by decided?"

"Nothing you do could change their fortune."

"It's because of the Black S—"

Renenet's finger pursed my lips. "Don't you ever dare to call the Hidden One." Her eyes sought the area with distress, as if the Black Sun would indeed hide behind a tree or a rock.

"Why can't their fates be altered?"

"They have been cursed."

"Cursed by whom?"

She remained silent.

"Can't somebody of your talents"—I tried to make it sound as polite as possible—"lift the curse?"

"You still don't get it, girl." Renenet held my chin. "I washed blood from your face that didn't belong to you." Hermann's blood. "How much more blood needs to be shed for you to realize these children are going to die no matter what you do?"

"We're all going to die," I replied, frustrated, waving her hand away. "And if I have to face death, at least I would prefer to do it outside that horrid dungeon!"

"Precisely," Renenet said overconfidently. "It doesn't matter if you're inside a dungeon or in the middle of a battlefield. You will witness the Harbinger of Death traverse the fields, circumvent all walls, climb endless stairs, and trespass any door to be rightfully on time for the last appointment. Even unwelcome, he is never uninvited, since everyone has been forewarned." She stood, towering over me. "You'll see it with your own eyes, girl; of that, I'm sure. 'Cause you are like me—a gifted."

"What?" I did not know what she was talking about.

"And as thou headest toward the sunset," Renenet professed, and the bonfire rekindled, "worry not if the Harbinger of Death walks ahead of thee; even if thou follow Death's tracks, it is not yet thy time. Worry not if the Harbinger of Death walks behind thee; even if Death follows thy footsteps, thou art still a step away. But if thou seest Death neither ahead nor behind, be prepared, for the Harbinger of Death is many-faced and might be already by thy side."

My whole skin goose-bumped at hearing her words. Considering who she was, I couldn't disregard her warning. "What can I do? Please help me!"

Renenet pointed out an overgrown road. "Leave and never look back. You might still salvage what is left of you."

Despite being plunged into shadows, the path had nothing out of the ordinary. However, I could not get rid of the crawling sensation in my spine that said somebody over there was watching us. "But what will happen to the children? Would you take them with you?" She already had a daughter and seemed uninterested in harming the children.

Renenet shook her head. "They would wake inside the crashed car with no recollection of what happened. And from there, they would face destiny the best they could."

I refused the idea.

"Don't fall prey to guilt. Many parents forsake their offspring for survival. You are in the middle of a war."

"That's a crime."

"Wars blur the lines that define crimes. When it's over, nobody will judge you for what you did for the sake of survival."

"I will." Tears pooled in my eyes. "And that's enough."

"Even if continuing means sacrificing everything?" Her eyes narrowed.

My jaw clenched.

"So heavy are the sins you seek to atone?"

My mouth turned sour, trying to translate into words my suicidal thoughts. I cleared my throat. "Would you sacrifice everything for Nailah?"

"She did sacrifice everything for me," a girl's voice said behind me. It was Nailah, playing with a deck of cards on a mantel.

"I'm sorry. I didn't notice…" I thought Nailah had stayed inside the carriage… carriage? The mobile home made me reflect on the fact that Renenet had indeed sacrificed everything for her daughter. The reasons for their persecution were unknown to me, but abandoning their house, their country, to live as nomads, was indicative of sacrifice.

"No apology needed." Renenet sat on the old trunk.

"Maybe you're right, and the children's fate is written. But maybe mine is too, alongside their names."

Renenet turned to me, puzzled. "Do you even know their

names, girl?"

"Don't call me 'girl.' My name is Emma." I was irked more with myself than with her. I barely knew a thing about them.

"I already knew that," Renenet said, confident of her clairvoyance. "But if you die out there, Emma, know that nobody brings flowers to a nameless grave. You'll become just another dead girl."

No matter how I hated to recognize it, I could not refute her argument. I probably could die—no, I certainly would die.

I quoted, "'Be true to yourself, because I'll only recognize you if you don't forget who you really are.' Those were my brother's last words. He always reminded me I had to be kind." A nostalgic grin popped onto my face. "Maybe If I die doing something kind for the children, my brother will recognize me in the hereafter."

Renenet half smiled and elevated her eyes to a patch of sky outlined by the treetops, the Milky Way splitting the firmament like a road made of stars. Some believed our fate was written in the stars. Maybe all I had to do was to allow the sky to guide my path, even if it signaled away from my past. I elevated my prayers for the hastened recovery of my father, hoping his gunshot wound had been tended. For the heavens to grant my mother the fortitude needed to make peace with the idea of a traitorous daughter. For the well-being of Ania and Gerda. And for Ghislain, wherever he was. I could not embark on my journey with the heavy burden of the past. I would have to learn to renounce my past life, my parents, my friends, my country, maybe even my language, just as Renenet had.

"Renenet? How is it that you, a foreigner, speak German as fluidly as a native?" Unlike her daughter Nailah.

"I've channeled so many souls through myself as a spiritual medium, I basically possess the gift of speaking in tongues. However, I've also intonated so many voices I've forgotten my own."

Listening to her speak about mediumship, my mind revolved around one thing. "Could it be possible for me to speak with my dead brother through you?" Even if she accepted, I was unsure whether I could afford her price.

"Perhaps," Renenet said with faraway eyes. "Perhaps you already did." She stood and paced toward the carriage, followed closely by Nailah, a shadow. "Come inside. Sunrise is about to break, and you need to rest."

"I'm not tired," I said, feeling that my rest when I'd fallen unconscious accounted for a full night of sleep.

"You'd better not." Renenet turned to me. "Tomorrow, you race against Death."

CHAPTER 13

RENENET SHOOK ME AWAKE with a hand covering my mouth. "Shhhhhhhh, Schutzstaffel is here." The roaring engines of the SS vehicles disturbed the early morning quietness of the woods. "Be silent and don't move."

I nodded, trying not to panic.

"Come down here," Renenet instructed the children resting on the upper deck of the bunk bed. The seven children and I squeezed each other, cramming into the low deck. Renenet unfolded a dark veil and hung it from the upper deck, draping it in front of us. "We will play a game called hide-and-seek." She addressed 44, who was at the edge of the bed. "Can you hide?"

Forty-Four nodded.

"Good."

There was a pounding on the carriage door.

"Everything will be fine," I whispered, forcing myself to believe it.

Renenet attended the door, leaving the bedroom sliding door ajar.

"*Guten morgen*, Frau Bahiti," a male voice greeted when the door cracked open.

"Gentlemen," Renenet replied dryly. "What brings you to my

humble abode? I hope not a tarot reading. My child still dwells in slumber."

Nailah? I wondered where she could be, since we occupied the bed.

Their boots made the wooden floor creak as they stepped in. "We were patrolling the surroundings and wanted to pay you a visit. Routine, you know? I hope you don't mind."

"Of course, no."

"Oh my God! Are these for real?" the man asked effusively, but there was no response from Renenet. "Hey, Pete, look at this—the skull of a baboon." The man chuckled, but Pete grunted.

"What are you looking for, exactly?" Renenet asked.

"Obergruppenführer Von Schroeder has lost something. And you might know their whereabouts."

"I don't," Renenet replied solemnly.

"That's an unreliable statement coming from a… witch. Maybe you should throw the bones or conjure the dead to divine their location."

Renenet didn't falter under his mocking provocation.

"Those are too many dirty bowls for feeding two mouths, Frau Bahiti. Hmmm?" His tone was tainted with irony as he indicated the earthenware we'd used for dinner.

"It would surprise you how much four ravenous horses can eat."

"Peckish enough to use silverware?" the soldier asked wryly. "Pete!"

Footfalls headed in our direction, and the point of a rifle poked in, pushing the door open. Pete entered the room, rifle first. He was wearing a double-buttoned long coat, tightened around his waist by a bag belt. His helmet and collar flaunted the SS runes. I held my breath and squeezed my eyes, believing we were about to be discovered. I wondered about the location of my briefcase; the letter opener would be handy in this situation.

Pete's probing eyes scanned the room but overlooked us. As if the bed had been completely empty.

It's the veil! I remembered the veil Renenet wore during the séance. The fabric had turned opaque when it displayed the Black Sun's face. That explained why we could see through but not the other way around.

"My horses are my family," Renenet said crossly, "and I will spoon-feed them if I deem it necessary."

Pete knelt and picked up a flashlight from the floor. It was Hermann's; 44 had brought it with him. Forty-Four's chubby arms extended to prevent it, but I clasped his mouth with my hand before he could say a thing. The other children helped me to keep him at bay. I feared our movements would make the bed creak.

"It's obvious you haven't found what you came looking for, so I advise you to continue your search elsewhere."

"Your kind is unwelcome here," the soldier said with a steely voice. "You'd better leave. Favors are quickly forgotten."

"Watch your words, young man. My kind feeds the tongues of tattlers to the horses."

"Circles of salt and bunches of garlic will not shield you from bullets, witch."

"You clever man," Renenet said sardonically. "Garlic and salt don't repel bullets, but they do stop witches from entering houses and stealing younglings. Tell me, *soldat*, did you sprinkle salt on your doorstep before leaving your family to join the war?" The soldier didn't utter a word. "Poor little Ada, so lonely, looking through the window at night without knowing somebody is looking back at her from the darkness."

"Don't you dare to harm my child, witch!" The soldier pulled the bolt of his rifle, loading a bullet into the chamber.

"Shoot!" Renenet confronted him bravely. "I can walk Death's Road both ways, but I'm sure your daughter can't."

Pete dropped the flashlight and rushed to the workshop amid the ruckus. "Put the gun down. Jesus! Karl, they are not here. Let's go." The pair of booted footfalls faded until the engines roared and the cars left, allowing the silence to settle once more.

"Wait here," I instructed the children before emerging from the bedroom. In the workshop, Renenet was sitting at the table with Nailah, as if this whole time she had never abandoned her mother's side.

"Now you understand why I can't take the children with me?" Renenet said dispiritedly, and I nodded. "I'll help you to cross the checkpoint, but I'll have to drop you on the outskirts of Lippstadt."

"Thank you," I said, both happy and disappointed at the same time. Lippstadt was just halfway to Hamm. Once there, I would still need to figure out how to complete the other half without the car.

"One more thing." Renenet rummaged in her cabinet and

pulled out a black pouch. "You'll need this."

"Is it for a spell?" I asked doubtfully, examining the beige powder inside.

"The most powerful spell women possess—makeup," Renenet said, and I frowned. "How long do you think you'll survive out there with seven children looking like walking skeletons?"

I spent our journey to Lippstadt brushing makeup on the children's exposed skin. Unfortunately, even after disguising their ivory skin tone, they would never pass as normal. Their close-cropped hair, to avoid catching lice, along with their malnourished thinness and the old rags they were wearing, would make them stand out in a crowd. We had to avoid human contact as much as possible.

At the Geseke military checkpoint, Renenet presented Von Schroeder's safe passage letter, and her magical veil helped us fool the soldiers once more. This fact made me consider that even if I had not crashed the car, I would not have crossed the checkpoint by myself. Perhaps Renenet was right; there was no such thing as coincidence, and our paths were meant to cross.

The carriage halted. "We've arrived," Renenet said casually, submerged in her work at the bench. I could not help wondering how four unmanned horses could find their way to Lippstadt, but after what I'd seen, I thought it was better not to ask.

"Let's go." I gestured, and the seven children marched out under the wary look of Renenet. "Before leaving, please thank Frau Bahiti for her hospitality," I said awkwardly, channeling my mother.

"*Danke, Frau Bahiti!*" all the children but 27 said in unison. Twenty-Seven brought his open hand to his mouth and waved it away as if blowing a kiss. I assumed that was the equivalent of "thank you" in sign language.

"What are you planning?" Renenet asked.

"We'll try to take a train to Hamm… or Dortmund…" I sighed. I'd never been to Hamm before, contrary to Dortmund, which I'd visited some years prior. But I wanted to believe there was a reason behind the instructions my father gave me. "As long as we remain as far from Wewelsburg as possible, we'll be fine." I attempted to conjure a smile. "Thank you again."

"Offering a bowl of soup and a place next to the bonfire is the least we nomads can do."

I climbed down the stairs of the carriage and looked back at Renenet. "I hope one day I can return the favor."

Renenet smiled mildly. "If our paths are fated to intertwine again, so it will be…"

"Wait!" Nailah emerged from behind her mother and hopped down the steps. "This is for you." She presented a card with her tiny hand.

I squatted and received the card. "Thank you… but what does it mean?"

"It's the eight of swords." The card depicted two sets of four stylized swords facing each other, blades intertwined as if woven. The roman numeral eight appeared on both ends. "You're being tested," she said with a drawling voice that seemed comical, considering she was a child. "An outcast who has become a hostage of your own thoughts. You are blindfolded by your own scrutiny, walking aimlessly in a field sown with swords. Your compass to elude obstacles is only your self-inflicted wounds. But once you undertake the road of the helpless, not even the spilled blood will guide your steps back home."

"Oh, well…" I said, hearing my grim destiny. "I'll take it. Thank you." I pocketed the card.

"No matter how exhausted you are," Nailah added, "don't falter. Death will offer no vindication."

"I will not," I said enthusiastically, clinging to hope.

Nailah scuttled back to her mother, and the horses cantered, pulling the black carriage away and leaving us by the side of the road under the bright sun.

What would Anton do in this situation? I inhaled deeply, a memory from when I was five or six years old coming to my mind. Anton and I had gone to the fields at Grandpa's farm to fly our newly built kites. A gale blew, snatching the kite from my tiny hands, which were incapable of securing the string. I had burst into tears, and not even Anton's offer for me to take his kite could appease me. I wanted to fly a kite alongside my brother, not in turns, and not by myself, since we had drawn our faces on them. *We will go on an excursion!* Anton declared back then and rushed to the kitchen. He packed delicacies cooked by Frau Weber, and holding my hand, he led me into the woods. After a long walk, we settled below a tree to eat our delights, but not even the sweeties could outshine the somberness of losing my kite. *"I'll show you a magic trick,"* Anton said, draping his arms with the tablecloth we used for our picnic. *"Close your eyes, and don't open them until I tell you,"* he instructed, and after a minute, when I opened them, he unveiled my kite in his hands. Truth was, Anton had climbed the tree to retrieve it, but for me, at such a young age, it was nothing but an act of real magic.

"Today is a lovely day for an excursion!" I declared, arms akimbo, under the skeptical looks of the children. "What? Have you never been on an excursion before?"

They shook their heads.

"But you do know what an excursion is, right?"

They exchanged looks.

Feeling remorseful, I explained to them as we traversed the vegetation. An excursion was the most heartwarming way I could devise to take them off the road, far from the people who wanted to harm them.

My people.

The sunbeams warming my skin, the fresh air filling my lungs, and the country breeze waving my hair were truly reenergizing. Nature relieved the feelings of persecution, especially for the children, who had been locked up for a long time.

"Where are we going?" 66 asked, holding his sister's hand.

"The City of Lippstadt. We should be close now…" I said, unsure, wondering if it had been a bad idea to roam away from the main road. No houses were visible yet.

"Are we lost?" 68 inquired.

"No! We are just… finding our way," I said confidently.

"How?"

"There are many ways, like using a compass, which unfortunately I don't have right now, but… we can use the sun." I pointed to the sky, but the sun was at its zenith. "Once it starts tilting west, of course."

"And when the sun has gone down?"

"We'll arrive before twilight, don't worry." I snickered, but the children stared at me dubiously. "But even if night falls, we can still use the stars." I tried to regain their confidence with my BDM explorer skills.

"Can you read the stars, Peach?" the children asked, amazed.

"It's not that difficult. You just need to find the constellation Ursa Major, the Great Bear"—*Or was it Ursa Minor?*— "and it will point directly to Polaris, the North Star." I tried to sound confident. "Yes... as easy as that!"

"I found a star!" 44 shouted out loud. "North Star! North Star!" He danced.

"A star?"

The children quickly gathered around 44's discovery, so I had to pass through them. It was certainly not a star, but finding it in that place was equally rare.

"It's a flower called edelweiss." I caressed the pointy white petals that resembled a stylized star. In the center, yellow pods bulged like a tiny sunflower. Edelweiss usually grew at high altitude, hence they were often considered an alpine flower.

"Can it guide our way?" 44 asked, thrilled at his finding.

"Do you know sunflowers? They have the skill of chasing the sun, so certainly they can guide our way," I elaborated.

"But that's not a sunflower, Peach," 88 interjected.

"No, but the edelweiss is a... cousin, yes, a cousin of the sunflower," I lied, not knowing that edelweiss indeed belonged to the sunflower family. "But you know what the coolest thing about the edelweiss is?"

They shook their heads.

"They have a song!" It was a military march I'd learned from my brother, called *Es war ein Edelweiss*, "It Was an Edelweiss."

"Sing it for us!" the children said, eyes alight with excitement.

"I-I..." I hesitated. Truth was, I could not remember the lyrics precisely. But to avoid deflating their enthusiasm, I sung it for the children, with a more melodic rhythm and improvising my own verses to fill the gaps.

> *I found it abandoned*
> *on a cliff at highest peak,*
> *a fallen star from the sky,*
> *I picked the prettiest flower...*

I picked up the edelweiss and placed the stem in 44's chubby hands.

> *…and gave it to the loveliest*
> *child dearest to my heart,*
>
> *Edelweiss! You are my star!*
> *My shining edelweiss!*
> *Guide us back to the sky!*
> *Holla-hidi hollala,*
> *Hollahi diho.*

The children sang the chorus along with me while 44 ran around with the flower aloft, making airplane sounds. We followed the path where we'd found the flower, hoping it would lead us to Polaris. Not long after, we arrived at a farm.

Rolls of hay were scattered across the fields, leaves bleached like an old man's beard, as if abandoned. Months had passed since the wheat fields had been harvested and rolls baled—farming knowledge taught by good Herr Huber during my stay at Grandpa's farm. Arriving at this farm carried the sensation of returning home. I daydreamed about walking into the kitchen to discover what Frau Weber was preparing for lunch, hoping a tasty soup and a hot bath could cleanse my mind of my tribulations. But instead of the house, I ventured to the barn first.

The barn was a two-story, timber-framed building with a gabled roof. The gate had a rusty latch. I pulled on the padlock to find it was broken, only superimposed to deter unwanted visitors. We sneaked inside, and the interior told a similar story: dried bales of hay in heaps, disarrayed farming tools, no horses nor carriage in sight.

"It seems abandoned." I deliberated. "Stay here."

"Where are you going?" 66 inquired.

"To the house. I need to confirm it's truly abandoned." I didn't want to take any risks.

I walked toward the front door, rehearsing my excuse in case somebody opened it. "Do you want to buy a truckle of cheese to support the Bund Deutscher Mädel?" My uniform provided veracity to my story, and knocking on strangers' doors for collecting funds was a regular BDM chore. No acting was necessary.

I called three times, but there was no answer.

I peeked through the dusty windows. The interior seemed disordered enough; maybe not to consider it abandoned, but certainly not recently inhabited. *Maybe they moved somewhere else because of the war.* We had abandoned our family house in Berlin. I twisted the knob, but it was locked. My moral compass restrained me from breaking a window to get in. I hated the idea of somebody storming our abandoned house. Besides, borrowing the barn as a hideout was everything we needed for now. I didn't expect we would spend much time in this city, anyway.

"It's empty," I informed them after my reconnaissance mission. "You need to wait for me here. I'll go downtown to locate the train station." *And figure out the least crowded route to it.* "I'll buy the train tickets to Hamm, and—if I can spare some *reichsmarks*—I'll buy extra food too." I pulled the food from my briefcase, realizing that for eight mouths, the provisions I'd collected from Wewelsburg's pantry would only be enough for one meal, two at the most.

"Are you going to come back?" 44 asked, on the brink of tears.

"Of course I will." I crouched. "Do you think I would abandon you?" But they remained silent, making me believe someone had abandoned them in the past. "I'm not leaving you, okay? I'll buy the tickets and we'll go together to Hamm."

"But what if somebody comes when you're not here?" asked 13.

"You hide"—I pointed to a nook formed behind two tall stacks of bales—"and don't come out until my return. Is that clear?"

"Yes." The children lumped together around me, hugging me by surprise.

My timid arms uncurled to embrace them too. "I'll be back soon. I promise."

CHAPTER 14

WAR HAD NOT YET TAKEN A TOLL on Lippstadt. The terra-cotta tiled roofs showed no sign of bombings. Pedestrians ambled the sidewalks and cyclists rolled down the cobblestoned street, dodging the sporadic cars that passed by. It was like traveling back in time, before the war. A military presence patrolled the streets, but no SS forces, which appeased my mind. At least they were not actively looking for me. I could blend in with the crowd. Girls wearing BDM uniforms were common.

"Excuse me, ma'am," I interrupted a woman daydreaming about wearing the dress displayed in a shop window. "Do you know where the train station is?"

"Oh! Yes, yes, you're on the right track. Just follow this street down."

"Thanks, and could you please point me in the direction of the market as well?"

"After crossing the railroad tracks, head north, and before you get to the Lippe River, you'll find it beside St. Mary's Church. You can't miss it—the bell tower looks like Frankenstein's castle." She frowned, displeased.

Upon arriving at the train station, I confirmed that at least the architecture of the station was less gloomy than the mental image

I'd made of the aforementioned church. It was a staggered building, taller at the center, with a timber-framed structure and tiled roofs. But despite the welcoming facade, a heavy military presence made me wish I were walking into Frankenstein's lair instead. Several military personnel carrier trucks were parked on the right side of the building. At least a hundred soldiers could be inside. Unfortunately for me, the only way to verify it was going in.

I did so, under no suspicion of the soldiers guarding the entrance. Once in the main hall, I headed directly to a map hanging on the wall. My eyes followed the rails from Lippstadt, making a stop at Soest before continuing to Hamm. "That's the one!" I said to myself, joining the ticket office line but feeling a little concerned, since the departure board was not listing any outgoing train to Hamm.

When I reached the front of the queue, I asked, "Excuse me, at what time is the next departure to Hamm?"

"No trains to Hamm for now," the gray-haired man said.

My heart sank. "Do you know when the service will be reestablished?"

The man shrugged as he counted five-reichsmark coins, piling them in stacks. "Only Soest for now."

I stepped aside, weighing my options. Riding to Soest sounded like a reasonable idea for putting land between us and Wewelsburg. But even after buying the tickets, how would the children pass unnoticed onto the platform? *Could we access it from the back?*

A bell clanged as a train arrived. A group of soldiers marched to the platform, and I blended with the contingent, walking slightly behind to avoid raising suspicion. The train had only freight wagons. The soldiers opened the latches and slid the doors aside. They placed wooden planks with steps to be used as a ramp. Hundreds of women emerged from the gloomy interiors, disheveled, wearing scarves to tame their uncombed hair and some to disguise their scrawny faces. They descended with effort, carrying mostly personal items and tiny bags.

"Where are you heading?" a young boy wearing a uniform asked me, most probably a fresh recruit from the *Hitlerjugend*, Hitler Youth.

"Hamm," I said, distracted, my gaze glued to the women.

The soldier boy mentioned something about Hamm, but my consternation about what I was witnessing rendered his words inaudible. A group of three officers coordinated the efforts to line up the women for registry.

"…I could not avoid noticing you," the soldier boy said, adjusting his spectacles. "You are beautiful."

"Oh…" I raised my eyebrows. "Thank you—I suppose," I said, almost to myself.

But he smiled, pleased with his flirting skills. "What is your name?"

"Um… Mildred," I answered, using my favorite doll's name.

"I'm Johannes."

Now we were acquaintances. "Why are they bringing these women?" I dared to ask.

"Oh, they are coming from Auschwitz," he said, unaffected.

"Are they…"

"Jews," he said, completing my sentence. "Yes, Hungarian Jews."

A few wore armbands or the Yellow Star badge sewn on their clothes, the six-point star containing the word *Jude* inside, with mock-Hebraic typography. After their registry, the soldiers steered the women to the carrier trucks at the side of the station to avoid the main hall.

"Where are they taking them?"

"To work in the factory."

After the last woman descended, a young man hopped out from the wagon before the troops slid the doors closed. He was dressed all in black, and he looked familiar, but at that moment I could not remember from where. The man in black walked nonchalantly, and the officers didn't pay attention to him. The officers' uniforms flaunted SS runes. *SS troops! They're in Lippstadt searching for me!* The conjectures built with the speed of my racing heart.

"What is your business in Hamm?" Johannes asked.

"What?"

"I mean, why do you need to travel?" he clarified.

"Oh!" I cleared my throat, cold pearls of sweat condensing on my forehead. "M-my aunt—to visit—my aunt…" I amended, trying to sound as calm as possible. But my betraying tongue tripped again the moment I peered at a board hanging on the wall behind Johannes, where a Wanted poster displayed a photo of me, offering a two-thousand-reichsmarks reward. "She—she is sick."

"Are you okay? You suddenly turned pale." Johannes held on to my shoulder, genuinely concerned about my well-being.

"I am." I waved his arm off me, but I frowned, puzzled by a carmine line descending from under his cap across the back of his neck. "Are you?" It resembled blood.

"Stop her!" the SS officers shouted.

"I need to go," I said as the train chugged, preparing for departure.

"Are you sure you're all right?" Johannes asked, but it was too late for a reply. An officer pointed his gun at me. I pushed Johannes aside and bolted away.

I dodged the travelers in my way until the end of the platform. I imagined the height difference as if it were a hurdle on the track, and I jumped with greater enthusiasm. This time, my life depended on it. The loose gravel cushioned my landing, and I resumed my escape, parallel to the rails. I glanced back, measuring my advantage against my pursuers. The soldiers' gear was slowing them down.

The train gained momentum, speeding just behind me. I couldn't put the children at risk by returning to the farm while I was being pursued, and I remembered the woman's instructions about the market and the river being across from the railroad tracks, which sounded like the best plan to elude them.

"Halt the train! Halt the train!" the soldiers yelled to the engineer, but it was too late.

I leaped across the rails, landing safely on the other side just before the locomotive passed by, blocking the path of my pursuers. The engineer pulled the brakes, but the seconds it took the heavy train to come to a halt granted me enough time to secure my escape. I zigzagged through alleys without stopping until I found the peculiar bell tower of St. Mary's Church. The building had bulging domes like those of a sultan's castle, with one smaller, pointy tower erected on top holding a cross. The church certainly transmitted a baleful feeling. A perfect hideout for Doctor Frankenstein to conduct his experiments.

I pondered on my next move while I caught my breath. The market would be the perfect place to blend with the crowd, and I had provisions to buy. But SS forces didn't stand around with their arms crossed; they might raid the surrounding areas, and a bag full of groceries would make it harder for me to outrun the soldiers. Besides, the way back to the farm was long, and the children were expecting me. I opted for going back, following the Lippe River as an escape route.

Fortunately, greenery surrounded the riverbank. I lay down under a copse of shrubbery for a few minutes, allowing the blood to flow back into my throbbing legs. I remained vigilant, making sure nobody followed me. Once rested, I skulked through the overgrowth, heading west until I reached the outskirts of town. Then I headed south, in search of the farm.

The sun was setting by the time I reached the fields. My throat was dry. My swollen soles hurt. The shoes of my BDM uniform were far from optimal for enduring a high-speed sprint through the city, plus the extra hours of trekking in the wild.

The barn was within eyesight, but even dead tired, a part of me refused to walk the last stretch. *What will I tell the children about my fiasco? How will I explain to them we're going nowhere?* Now I was a wanted fugitive, and it was just a matter of time before the SS forces stormed the barn and enslaved the children inside that horrid cell again. And I… I gulped… most probably would end up hanged for treason. *"Become a traitor, just like your brother."* Reinhard's words tormented me, and I caressed my neck anxiously, as if an itchy rope were fastened to my collar.

Traitor.

I never liked the sound of the word. It was even less palatable written on a board over the chest of your dead body swinging from the gallows. *Could I go back to Papa and ask for forgiveness?* Doubt pierced what I'd thought was my iron will. *Could I just disappear, as Renenet advised?* My faint shadow cast over the barn's gate lasted until the last sunbeams bled and vanished.

"I-I want to go home…" I rustled as my voice broke into sobbing. I squatted over the dirt, cuddling my legs against my chest. My tears dropped to my grubby knees. I wiped the dirt with my jacket sleeve, remembering how my mother had cleaned my knees after my wanderings as a kid. *"Tomboy's knees,"* she used to say. The memory made me smile.

"At least I had the joy of having a mother," I said to myself, remembering those less fortunate than me… and that thought gave me the strength to remove the broken padlock and unlatch the gate. "I'm home!" I trumpeted, and the children crawled from behind the hay bales.

"Peach! You're back!" The children rushed to embrace me, their faces flushing with happiness. "We were worried about you!" Their electrifying hug recharged the batteries of my exhausted body.

"When are we leaving?" 88 asked.

I paused. "Not today," I said grimly. "There…" I crafted my white lie. "There was an issue with the trains to Hamm, but the friendly man at the ticket office asked me to return tomorrow."

"We will spend the night here?" 13 asked, concerned.

I caressed his face. "I'm afraid so." But 13's worried face twisted into a gleeful grin.

"Come, Peach, come!" The children towed me around the fort they had built with hay bales.

"This is your bed." Forty-Four pointed to a series of makeshift beds made of hay covered with pieces of fabric they had found in the barn.

"Thank you," I said, on the brink of tears, as the children jumped happily over the hay beds.

"Have you been crying?" 68 asked me, squeezing my hand.

"No—no. Too much sunlight, I think," I lied flagrantly, but I could not fool her. She had a gift for knowing the things that would happen, as she'd showed me during our escape from the castle.

"It's fine to cry," she said with a voice mature beyond her years. "Sometimes I cry at night. The heart needs to breathe."

CHAPTER 15

THAT NIGHT, WE GATHERED AROUND an oil lantern we found hanging from one of the wood beams. The flame, even tiny, worked as our fireplace. After my failure to gain more provisions, we had to adjust our meal to only what I had collected from the pantry at Wewelsburg. For our main dish, I used the letter opener to slice the bread loaves and placed cheese slices on top. For dessert, I smeared strawberry jam on the bread. I distributed the slices among the children, and we passed them around, along with the water canteen. I bit the tasteless dessert, yearning for Frau Weber's natural strawberry marmalade, but witnessing the exhilaration on the children's faces at the chemically colored jam made me feel spoiled. Or rather, I felt sorry at hearing of their mistreatment, increasing my guilt. After all, the culprits of their misfortune were my people.

"We'll play a game," I said enthusiastically. "I wished we could have had time before to get to know each other, but you know… circumstances have been… far from ideal." I giggled nervously. "So, I'm going to introduce myself and say something about me. Then it will be the turn of the person on my right, and so on."

Sixty-Eight looked at me, troubled, being the next in line.

"As a reward, I'll give you one mint." I flaunted the tin box of mints, which the kids beheld as gold. "Understood?"

They nodded timidly.

"My name is Emma Niemeyer, but everyone calls me Peach. My brother gave me this nickname, mocking my round pink cheeks when I was little. His name was Anton... He... he passed away recently... killed in combat. I enjoy running and I practice hurdle racing." I smiled. "I love feeling the cold air hitting my face, the sensation of blurring everything I leave behind me and focusing only on the goal ahead of me. I dream about participating in the Olympics and winning a medal... if the war ever ends."

I opened the tin lid and hurled a mint into my mouth.

"Your turn." I nudged 68.

"I-I'm Sixty-Eight—"

"Not the number. Your real name," I pointed out.

She turned to her brother, who nodded slightly.

"I'm Valeska Volkova," she started timidly. "Jov is my twin."

I could not avoid arching my brow, since they were not so identical as I would expect of twins.

"We were born in a frosty town to the north of St. Petersburg, by the White Sea. We have a sister called Lara. I like to go to school and play hide-and-seek in the forest."

"You always cheat on me. You know where I'm hiding." Her brother, 66—Jov—complained, and everybody laughed.

"Because you're bad at hiding," Valeska clarified. "That's why the Crying Man found you." She went silent and the faces of both turned grim.

"Your sister was with you that day, but she remained hidden and escaped?" I reconstructed the story based on what they had said back in Wewelsburg.

"Yes."

I handed them their mints while I caressed Valeska's back reassuringly. "You're free now. And soon you'll be back home to play with your sister." I tried to avoid delving into painful memories. Speaking about the Crying Man was equally painful to me.

"No, we're not." Valeska's vacant eyes reflected the quivering flame.

I pulled her chin to face me. "Valeska, I need you to have trust. This is the only way we can survive, okay?"

She nodded.

"Good. Now it's the turn of the handsome boy with the hat."

Forty-Four was still feasting on the bread with one hand and holding the edelweiss flower I'd given him with the other.

"What do your parents call you?"

"*Du.*" He licked the marmalade smudged around his mouth.

"Du? Like *Drud?*" This was a German name meaning "strong."

"Nooo, like *'Hallo, du! Bringen wasser!*' She shouted this when she needed water for the cows or wanted me to feed them."

"She?"

"My mother. She is beautiful." Forty-Four smiled.

"But surely your parents gave you a real name besides 'you'?"

He shook his head.

"Were you attending the cattle?" I asked, concerned.

Forty-Four nodded and bit his slice of bread. "I lived in the barn."

My God! I was unsure of being able to continue my inquiry. "But you spent nights at the house, right?"

"They allowed me in only on Sundays. Mom always washed me before going to church."

I could not conceive of the treatment this nameless child had received in his own house—not much different from the cell in Wewelsburg. "But how—how did you end up with… them?" I asked, fearful at hearing the answer.

"On a Sunday after church, my mom told me I had to be a good boy and go with the uniformed men."

"And she walked away… without remorse?" I asked, incredulous.

"Noooooo!" 44 screamed vexedly. "Mom promised me. She will come back for me. I trust her… like you said."

"I… understand…" I could not avoid the mournful tone of my words. "You're waiting for her to come." I handed 44 the tin with mints, a gesture he celebrated as if he had won the lottery.

After 44, next in line was number 27, but he was mute.

For God's sake, Emma, what are you doing? What will you ask him about? His Jewish name? I squeezed my head with the heels of my hands. *Emma, you're an idiot.* I realized my mistake, forewarned by Renenet. *What am I supposed to call them? Dopey, Sneezy, Bashful, Doc, Happy, Grumpy, and Sleepy?* I imagined myself christening 44 as "Happy," but it felt even more heartless than the Nazis who had numbered them. *What did you expect, Emma? You are a Nazi.* "I'm sorry, kids, I-I-I just can't…" I stood and turned away to avoid them seeing my tears.

A pair of tiny arms circled my waist, and one boy leaned his head against my back. "It's okay, Peach," Jov said reassuringly. "You can call me Sixty-Six."

Another pair of hands joined Jov's. "I'm Manu, but you can call me Thirteen."

One by one, all stood and joined the embrace.

"Hoshi is my name, but Forty-Nine is fine too."

"Mine is Jayvyn, but you can call me just Jay, or Eighty-Eight."

I dabbed my tears and turned around, shaken by the gesture.

"His name is Lemuel," Valeska said, caressing 27's head. "But he says you can call him Twenty-Seven. He doesn't mind. We're used to being addressed that way."

"No, it's not okay," I said with trembling chin, angry with myself for feeling so powerless.

"Maybe not, but you're the one person who has done the most for us," Jov said.

"Forgive me for not being able to do more."

The children smiled.

"Now, let's get to bed. It's late, and tomorrow we have a long trip to Hamm."

The children lay down, showing their personalities in the way they slept. The twins embraced each other. Forty-Four—my heart ached knowing I had no other name to call him—sprawled with my cap over his chest and the flower by his side. Hoshi held his body straight, hands entwined over his chest, like Tutankhamun's mummy. Lemuel lay in fetal position, sucking his thumb. It made me anxious that I'd not yet earned his trust; though I would not blame him. The sight of the women at the station today illustrated that Jews had a lot of reasons to fear us. And finally, Manu rested his head on Jay's shoulder, always the quieter two of the group. I assumed they felt the loneliest, being older than the others.

I turned the knob of the oil lantern to pull the wick of the burner down, dimming the flame, scared of sleeping in the dark now more than ever. Yet slumber eluded me. The anxiety of not knowing how to travel to Hamm chased away my dreams. Reading had always calmed my nerves, so I reached for the contents of my leather briefcase that I'd collected from Von Schroeder's drawer.

I browsed through a leatherbound book so old it seemed unearthed, but all its pages were blank, making me wonder if taking it had been worth the trouble. Then I examined some folders containing medical reports with diagrams of the tests to which they'd subjected the children. Most of it was medical jargon I could not understand, but my hand flew to my mouth at the pictures of their fragile bodies, naked, showing the progression of their skin-bleaching procedure. My nails bit into my palms, wrinkling the bloodcurdling documents as my breathing turned noisy. *You were right, Anton.* My hand descended to my neck in search of my necklace containing the photos of my family, but I grew alarmed when I could not find it. I searched inside my bra and blouse to no avail. My mind replayed all the situations in which I could have lost it.

"Hermann!" I panicked, hoping I'd not awakened the children with my outburst. Hermann had held me by the collar and pulled me forcefully, probably breaking the chain. I imagined my necklace resting inside Hermann's dead hand, and I shuddered.

But I could do nothing about it now. I had lost the locket. *Forever.*

I shut my eyelids, forcing myself to descend into the deep, reinvigorating sleep I so desperately needed.

Instead I descended the staircase into the dungeon at Wewelsburg. I headed to the cells, following the echoes of crying to free the children from incarceration, fearful that Reinhard would arrive. Fortunately, this time I had the key with me, but when I unlocked the door, the children were not there. The crying came from a baby wrapped in a blanket lying on the cold stone floor of the cell. I picked up the baby, but as I unwrapped the blanket, searching for the face, I found nothing in the bloodstained rag. Drops of blood on the ground trailed into the torture room, and as I felt a liquid dripping down my thighs, I realized with horror the blood belonged to me. But that was not the worst. My belly had bulged. I removed my jacket and unbuttoned my blouse in despair to uncover my bloated belly—I was in late pregnancy. Tiny hands and feet bumped my belly from inside as the baby turned around, and then a shape crossed my skin of what seemed like the scaled tail of a crocodile…

I yelled in terror and— I woke up, thankful it had been only a nightmare. My skin crawled at the stroke of the night breeze percolating through the gapped wooden walls of the old barn. I peeked at my wristwatch, unsure how long I'd been asleep. *Half past one*, it declared. I tucked myself up to my neck with my jacket, and once comfy, I glanced at the children.

There, I saw him.

A man dressed in black knelt alongside 44, his right hand hovering like a spider over 44's sleeping face.

CHAPTER 16

THE MAN OBSERVED 44 with a solemn expression. Forty-Four's eyelids were slightly open, showing his eyes bouncing from one side to another, as if he were having a disquieting dream. Without removing my eyes from the man, I slid my hand inside my briefcase and extracted the letter opener. With subtle movements, I stood without calling his attention and stepped closer to him.

"Who are you?" I pointed the blade at the back of his neck.

The man turned his head slowly. His features were those of a young man, probably my brother's age.

"You can see me…" he said with a euphonious voice.

"What do you mean by that? Of course I can see you."

He tried to rise to his feet.

"Don't move." I glanced at the gate; a plank still rested across the metal brackets. "How did you get in?"

He looked up, and my gaze followed to the window in the gabled roof. But during the fraction of a second that took me, he moved behind me at a speed so high that his image blurred.

I whirled, my letter opener leading the search, and found him comfortably sitting on top of a tall heap of bales, legs crossed, with fingers entwined around his kneecap, as if he had been there all this time. At least thirty feet stood between the two places, and no human could have covered such distance in less than a second. The man stared at me with gleamy olive-green eyes, which appeared to produce light on their own, since my silhouette was blocking the oil lantern, keeping the stranger in shadow's dominion.

"I remember you…" My mind regurgitated memories of the man now that I was finally face-to-face with him. "I saw you atop a mountain of rubble after the bombing in Kassel, holding a girl by the shoulder." Baffled, I lowered my knife. "And I saw you descend from that train along with the Hungarian Jews at the train station…"

"Then you can indeed see me. You should feel proud of that." He crooked his head. "Or perhaps… scared; always depends."

"Why do you keep saying that?"

"I'm simply stating what should be obvious by now. Not everybody can see me. Most people can't."

I'm able to see Jov's projection. Was that proof of what he said?

"It's called second sight," he continued. "You were gifted with this ability…"

Renenet had called me a gifted, like her.

"Or cursed. It will depend on you."

"Second sight…" I repeated. "But what does it do? What does it allow me to see?"

"It allows you to glance into other realms outside the dominion of men. Realms in different planes of existence that coexist, all intertwined within a delicate balance. You will witness all the stories told through the ages by your kind."

My kind? Does he mean other gifted? Stories about… "You mean like monsters and demons and ghosts?"

"Everything you have refused to believe exists," the man said with a sepulchral tone.

"But I've never seen a ghost in my life." I was rather disappointed at never having experienced the supernatural.

"Are you sure?" He raised a brow. "Or is it that dead people are so embedded in this reality that you can't tell them apart?"

I gulped.

"Look at your feet," he ordered. "Do you see him?"

"What?" I could see nothing but fodder scattered over the ground.

"A scrawny man is crawling toward you. He lived here centuries ago and contracted the plague. Can you see his buboes bulging the size of apples and his skin reddened, with his innards bleeding underneath?"

"I can't see him." But as I examined the fodder closely, I identified stems moving slightly, which I could attribute to a wind current in other circumstances.

"He is begging for water, pulling your skirt."

A sensation crawled up my leg, but I could neither confirm nor deny whether his words were playing tricks on my mind.

"Maybe it's just a matter of time," he finally said. "You are young yet to uncover your abilities. What is now sporadic, soon you will need to bear during your everyday life."

"Why me?" My heart sank, as if I'd been diagnosed with a terminal illness.

"Why not?"

I shook my head and raised my knife, along with my concerns about this stranger. "Who are you?"

"I have a thousand names."

"I need only one."

He paused for a few seconds. "You can call me Sidney, then."

"What are you doing here, Sidney? What is your interest in the child? I saw you watching him in his sleep."

"You already know why I'm here. You said it yourself; you saw me doing my job. That little girl standing over the mound of rubble had died during the night, crushed by the roof that collapsed. The last two women who descended from that train perished days before in Auschwitz, but refusing their own demise, both boarded that train along with their friends, believing they still belonged to this realm."

"Are you… Death?"

"No. I'm the Harbinger of Death."

The words gargled inside my throat. "You—you will not take him." I stepped forward.

"That was never my intention," he said reassuringly. "I just came for him… to take him for a stroll."

"A walk… to where?" The barn had remained closed.

"There is no such thing as a sudden death. All condemned to death are forewarned. When a judge passes sentence after reading the verdict, the accused doesn't know when it will be carried out. That's the purpose of the first visit. I come one night during their sleep and take the accused for a stroll to the very place where they will sigh their last breath. Standing before their corpse, I notify them the sentence will be carried out… eventually.

"The accused awakens with a new opportunity to change the outcome I've presented. Unfortunately, people forget their dreams and, incredulously, believe they pose no influence over the waking world. Then, in time, they walk the ill-fated footsteps to the last reunion."

His chilling words made me recall Renenet's warning at the bonfire. *"It doesn't matter if you're inside a dungeon or in the middle of a battlefield. You will witness the Harbinger of Death traverse the fields, circumvent all walls, climb endless stairs, and trespass any door to be rightfully on time for the last appointment. Even unwelcome, he is never uninvited, since everyone has been forewarned."*

"Why?" I fisted my hands. "Why do you want to take the life of an innocent?" I confronted Sidney, feeling powerless.

"Why not?" Sidney repeated.

"Because that is… evil!" Tears sprang into my eyes, remembering 44's sad story. "After… everything he has suffered."

Sidney stared at me, unemotional, as if my words had no meaning to him.

"Is there anything I can say to change your mind?"

"It's not up to me to pass judgment." Sidney descended from the bales of hay. "I'm only the courier." He walked away.

"Wait!" I chased him across the barn, but he blended with the shadows and vanished.

I carried the oil lantern over his path but found no footprints. Not a single trace of Sidney's presence, as if he had walked through the wall. Fleeting like the wind.

CHAPTER 17

WHEN I OPENED MY EYES the next morning, I sat upright and glanced at the children, who were still sleeping. All but 44, who was missing. The plank was off the brackets and the gate was ajar.

"*Scheisse!*" I put on my shoes and jacket and went after him.

The breeze blew cold. The sun was still hiding behind the hills, with faint orange beams peeking timidly across the horizon. But birds had already awakened, chirping as they revolved around the sky. I scanned the fields until I found 44 chatting with a woman sitting on a hay bale. Forty-Four was jumping happily around the woman, so I assumed I had nothing to worry about.

"Peach!" 44 shouted when he noticed me, and ran to me.

"I'm glad to see you're safe."

"I'm with Maria. She said we can stay at home with her instead of the barn."

"I see…"

Maria glanced at me from head to toe and smiled mildly.

"Why don't you go and wake up your siblings? It's almost breakfast, okay?"

Forty-Four assented. "See you, Maria." He blew us a kiss before bolting to the barn. "*I-del-wiz! I-del-wiz!*"

Maria waved at 44, holding the edelweiss flower, which I presumed he had given to her. She looked fortyish, but her face was all mapped out, and with her hair unkempt, she was probably younger. She was wearing a white blouse, pants, and knee-high boots plastered with dirt and manure, making me believe she was the person tending the farm.

"So, this is your farm…" I said. "I'm sorry for—"

"Don't," Maria interrupted. "The boy already told me." She beckoned, tapping on the dried hay. "Sit."

My mind wandered, trying to imagine what 44 could have told her, but it didn't really matter. Maria beheld the sunrise in silence for an entire minute, making me feel awkward sitting by her side.

"As you get older, fewer and fewer things bring you joy. For me, daybreak is one of those pleasures. Awaking still confused, before the everyday burden of being alive falls upon me, it's the only moment in which I can truly stop and just… feel." She cast her gaze down to the edelweiss flower.

"Do you like it?"

She grinned nostalgically. "It has been a while since the last time I saw one."

"We found it near here."

"My son used to bring me flowers from his camping trips. He loves hiking."

"Is he in the Hitler Youth?" I asked without thinking.

"Quite the contrary. He hates Nazis." Maria chuckled. "Inherited it from his mother, I guess. He evaded the Hitler Youth and military conscription. My son, along with many boys, formed a group to protest Hitler's totalitarian regime… *Edelweiss Pirates* they called themselves." Maria caressed the now-withering petals of the flower as if it were the face of her son. "Later, they were declared enemies of the Reich."

"I'm sorry," I said, speechless, alarmed such things were happening. "I hope he is all right."

"He is being held prisoner in a concentration camp in Cologne, doing forced labor with the Jews. I haven't seen him in years…"

The image of the Hungarian Jews descending from the train became vivid in my mind. "I'm really, really sorry… I know what you must think of me…" I said, remembering the way she had observed my uniform.

"You are just a good girl wearing stupid clothes, unaware of what they symbolize."

My lips remained pursed, digesting her words.

She waved a finger at me in negation. "No Nazi would cross the country to save the lives of those children."

"Well… I-I don't know, I'm…"

Maria raised her hand. "No need to explain. You can stay in the barn for as long as you want… or move inside the house, if you don't mind sharing it with me, three chickens, two pigs, and the ghosts that haunt me."

I could not avoid giggling.

"These are hard times. I had to sell the cattle. No seeds left to sow the fields. Not much to offer, besides a glass of milk and a pair of eggs."

"Thank you, Maria. You're very kind. But we're not planning on staying—"

"The child told me. Hamm, right?"

"We will board the train to Hamm today."

"A train?" She turned, puzzled. "Didn't you hear the radio, girl?"

I shook my head.

"Hamm was bombed. The British hit the railway hard this time. So, no trains to Hamm for at least a few days."

"It can't be…" I cursed under my breath. At this pace, the SS would apprehend us before we could leave Lippstadt.

"Shake away the long face. I'll take you to Hamm myself."

"Would you do that for us?" A silver lining shone amid my hopelessness.

"Yes! But I hope you don't mind that my carriage doesn't have padded seats. The only things I transport are pigs and bales of hay."

"Hay is comfortable enough." I smiled, but my enthusiasm faded as quickly as it arrived, remembering the situation we were in. "But… on second thought, I don't want to expose you to being caught helping us across military checkpoints." I sighed. "The SS is after us… so… I can't accept your offer, Maria. We'll find another way to Hamm."

"I appreciate your concern, girl, but I have nothing else to lose."

"But your son—"

"Perhaps it would be for the best. Captured by the Nazis, sent to Cologne to do forced labor… but being able to see my son."

I remained silent, perplexed by her words.

"One day you'll understand… Nothing is more terrifying than

the thought of dying alone."

Her words made me comprehend that the unattended farm and barn were not a product of her laziness, but a reflection of the lack of purpose in her life. My mind wandered, imagining how this farm had looked when Maria had her family. Golden wheat heads bending down, pulled by the wind; her son and husband feeding fodder to the cattle; Maria preparing hot soup in the kitchen for their supper. Maria sat every morning on a bale of hay to find a purpose to keep living, deprived of what she loved the most.

"Besides," Maria added, "I would like to contribute my share toward reuniting that lovely youngling with his mother."

I grinned gloomily, knowing 44 would never reunite with his mother; back at home, nobody expected his return.

"Come," Maria said, stretching her back, "let's have breakfast. We have a long journey ahead of us."

We traveled on a horse-drawn, four-wheeled carriage designed to transport cargo inside its wooden frame. Maria had the brilliant idea of stacking bales around the perimeter so the children could travel safely hidden in the middle. I joined Maria in the driver's seat, but we agreed that at the first sign of danger, I would jump back with the children.

"Don't worry." Maria steered the reins of the horses away from the main road, following a narrow trail outlined by dense shrubbery. "I've traveled these roads since I can remember. I know how to avoid the Nazis. Just a few days ago, I went to Dortmund, passing next to Hamm, so I know where the fuckers hide."

"I hope." I glanced back now and then, concerned the SS could follow our tracks.

"What are your plans once you're in Hamm?"

"Mmmm… take a train, I guess."

"To where?"

"Far west… the Netherlands, I suppose."

Maria guffawed. "Have you ever been at the front line?"

"No," I replied, feeling ashamed. "Have you?"

"No, but my husband fought in the Great War," she said, turning serious. "Decades later, while lying on his deathbed, he still woke up in the night with nightmares about the horrors he had endured in the trenches… So, believe me, girl, when I tell you that's some shit you don't want to carry with you through the rest of your life. But I assume you will not listen to me, anyway."

"I really appreciate your advice… It's just that…" I struggled to assemble the words. "Considering the horrors we're running away from, the retellings of death on the battlefield don't seem so alien… even sound liberating, in a way." My suicidal thoughts surfaced under Maria's concerned gaze. "I'll check on the children," I said, to avoid further questioning.

"Peach!" the children welcomed me to the hay fort.

"Oh my goodness!" I gasped. The drops of sweat produced by traveling under the sun had washed their makeup away, exposing the children's unpigmented skin. "Your skin needs to be retouched." I pulled out the makeup bag from my briefcase and improvised a brush with my scarf. "Who wants to be first?"

"*I-del-wiz!* Me! Me! I want first!" Forty-Four raised his chubby hands. "I want to be ready!" he said, overexcited.

"Ready for what?" I dabbed his face with the powder.

"See my mother."

My hand froze, and a tingling sensation migrated from the back of my neck to my scalp. "What—what did you dream last night? Remember?" I asked, terrified of hearing his answer.

"My mother came to visit me while you were asleep."

"What did she say?"

"That she misses me, but we will be together soon." Forty-Four smiled widely.

"Forty-Four, please. I need you to focus." I pulled him closer. "Did your mother take you someplace?" I remembered Sidney's words about taking the accused for a stroll to the place where they would sigh their last breath.

"She held my hand, and we walked and walked and walked…"

"Walked where?" Feeling irksome, I squeezed his arms. "Please remember!"

"I don't know! I couldn't see well, there was fog around us… but…" Forty-Four's eyes circled around his eye sockets to connect with his memories. "A pond! There was a pond… with beautiful white swans swimming around… I counted seven!"

"Cool! That's where your mother lives? I want to visit there!" all the children responded with excitement, but Valeska, who stared at me, remained inexpressive.

Now what? Should we avoid ponds? I rubbed my face.

The sun was setting by the time we arrived at the city of Hamm. Traveling off the road to bypass military checkpoints had slowed our pace. Devastation welcomed us. Hamm had been recently bombed, and like Kassel, was hit hard. My mouth gaped at the ragged skyline of the city. Near half of the buildings lay in ruins.

"Are you still thinking about trying to travel by train?" Maria asked, concerned.

"I… suppose."

Maria halted the horses. "This is the closest I can leave you. Follow this road. You'll find the main railway station ahead."

I hopped down from the carriage and walked to the back. I removed a bale of hay, opening a way into the fort. "We've arrived, kids." I offered my hands to help them down.

"Thank you, Maria. I really don't know how we would have come this far without your help. I don't know how to repay your kindness."

"It's nothing, girl."

My cheeks heated. "Sorry, I never told you my name," I said, embarrassed by my rudeness.

"Save it," Maria said. "My father used to say, 'We are all strangers walking in a foreign world.'" She smiled. "Maybe one day, I'll be the stranger breaking into your barn."

I smiled. "That would be nice."

"Until then." Maria whipped the horses with the reins and cantered away. "Farewell!"

"Goodbye, Maria!" The children waved.

"Come, kids," I said, holding their hands. "We need to find a new home."

CHAPTER 18

ONCE IN HAMM, I used the same strategy I'd followed in Lippstadt: find a hideout for the children, then explore the city to devise a way out. However, contrary to Lippstadt, Hamm was too urbanized to find a comfortable barn on the outskirts of town at a walkable distance. Our best bet amid the havoc was to find an abandoned house livable enough to shelter us for a day. The children hid behind the foliage of a bushy thicket while I ambled the neighborhood until I found the perfect place.

The hollow facade of a building stood on foot as if it were the lid of my dollhouse, with some windows still holding the wood frames, burned and with smashed panes. A complete story of its bombing could be reconstructed by studying the shuffled floors and walls, like a collapsed house of cards. At the back of ground zero, a set of rooms looked almost intact, saved from obliteration by a couple of columns that had prevented a skewed wall from falling over. I twisted the knob, but even unlocked, the door was jammed against the frame. With effort, I kicked the door open.

The last sunbeams of the day guided my way in. Judging by its contents, the room was a laundry, making me wonder if the building used to be a hotel. I found a couple of service carts packed with linens, perfect for improvising beds. In the center of the wall stood a boiler as tall as a phone booth and at least twice as wide. It had four wrought iron doors arrayed two by two. I removed the latch and opened one at the bottom, revealing the furnace. I examined the coal inside; it was still usable. I searched for ways to ignite it, until I came across a box of matches, which I used to light a flame to a rag.

"This will keep us warm through the night," I said to myself, rejoicing at the sight of the burning coal. *There should be more coal somewhere around here.* I glanced at the adjacent room, but having no windows, it was pitch-black. I ruled in favor of bringing the children to our new home.

By the time I returned with the kids, the coal had produced a bright and warm flame. They marveled at our fireplace.

"Where is the chimney?" Jay asked.

"Look at that pipe." I pointed to a wide metal tube running up to the ceiling.

"Can we see it from outside?" Manu wondered.

"Not today," I answered. "It's late now and we need to prepare for bed. Here, help me stuff these." I handed them pillowcases, a final touch for our makeshift beds.

Before going to bed, I prepared our supper. I sliced the last loaf of bread and truckle of cheese and smeared the remaining marmalade. The amount was so tiny I had to divide the food among them. Half the children got cheese, the other half marmalade.

"What are you going to eat, Peach?" Jov asked with concerned eyes, realizing I had not saved a portion for myself.

"Uh? I'm fine, don't worry," I assured him, but they didn't seem convinced, so I relied on my acting skills. "When I was looking for this place, I came across a kind old lady who shared a frankfurter with me… It was so yummmmmmy"—I circled my belly with my hand—"that when I noticed, *boom!* I'd eaten it all. I'm sorry I could not save a piece for you."

"You can have dessert, then," said 44, handing me the box of mints.

A smile snapped on my face. "Oh! Thank you!" I swallowed a handful of mints and went to bed before the rumbles of my ravenous stomach could deter my sleep. Fortunately for me, the quivering flames of the furnace were hypnotic, banishing my sleeplessness. I fell into a deep, emotionless sleep.

     M. Ch. Landa

My eyes peeled open in the middle of the night, and I found him squatting by my side. Sidney's shimmering eyes were resting on me, as if he had been watching over my sleep the entire night.

"I wondered if you would wake up," he said in a soothing voice.

Why? I reflected, still transitioning from my dreamy state back to vigil. *Forty-Four!* my brain cells shouted in unison, like a series of light bulbs plugged into the current. *This is his second visit; he has come back to take 44 with him!* I reached for the knife in my briefcase.

"Don't worry," he said, as if he could read my thoughts. "I'm not here to take him with me."

"Then why are you here?" I sat upright.

Sidney remained silent, his green eyes dyed amber in the light of the flame, like iridescent stones.

"Or… are you here to notify me about my oncoming death?"

"The idea of dying is so scary to you?" His evasion of my question made me suspicious about his true intentions.

Could he be here to notify another of my children? I panicked at the idea. "Not anymore." *How could it be?* I had been one step away from jumping through my window in Wewelsburg Castle. "What happens…" My rambling mind concatenated the words. "…if I try to kill myself without receiving your visit first?" I pictured my way down from the heights. "Do I die?" *Or just break all my bones and agonize for weeks?*

"Death's doors won't open without an invitation. If they do, it's because you received the invitation, even if you don't remember. Just like a child who receives a pistol as a present that will kill him in old age."

"That's unfair. People have the right to know—to choose…" I said, my mind scheming. "What if I want to die instead of him?"

"Would you be willing to sacrifice yourself in his place?" His eyes narrowed.

"Can you guarantee they'll be safe?"

Sidney meditated for a moment. "There is a way. It's called Lazarus's medallion," he explained. "It's made of the purest gold, and you, as the substitute soul, need to carry it along the Pilgrimage of Death to Mt. Touriel."

I'd never heard of that mountain before, but trekking was one of my favorite activities. "And that's it?"

"And sacrifice yourself by jumping into the magmatic river inside."

Oh! It's a volcano! The thought of burning alive in lava made the idea of jumping from a window more appealing. "But how is it by doing that the life of the other person is forgiven?"

"Pagans believed the most precious possession, far beyond gold, jewels, and riches of this world, is the kind heart of a person who will sacrifice for another. The moment a substitute soul jumps into the fires of Touriel, the magma melts the gold of the medallion, and like a burning metal claw, it sinks inside the chest and solidifies again, encasing the heart in gold. That's the offering pagans make to the gods. If the substitute is indeed kindhearted and the sacrifice is accepted, the heart will remain enclosed in gold, pure, lasting for an eternity as a memorial of those who did the right thing. However, if the substitute heart was consumed by egoism and the sacrifice is rejected, the gold will melt along with the heart, eradicating from existence the wrongdoings… Or at least, that's the story shared by Lazarus after he rose from the dead."

I hearkened to the story, wondering about its veracity and whether I could save the children's lives, even if that meant sacrificing mine. "How do I get this medallion?"

"Getting a Lazarus's medallion is not the troublesome part." Sidney browsed inside his jacket pocket. "It is completing the Pilgrimage of Death." He pulled aloft a golden chain, and a disk of glinting gold dangled, with a pentagram engraved upon it and five small orbs embedded at each vertex—blue, red, green, yellow, and black on the top. "All you have to do is engrave your name on the back and say aloud, 'I, Emma, take thy sins as mine, and before thee as my witness, I willingly renounce my life so thou canst continue thine,' and you add the name of the person you want to sacrifice for."

"How do you know my name?"

"To deliver a letter, a courier needs to know the name of the recipient."

Though cryptic, I could not argue with his logic. Besides, I was really concerned about something else. "What if I don't know his name? If he is nameless, never christened before. How do I make the exchange work?"

"But he has a name," Sidney clarified, searching in his pocket once more. A tiny leather book spread open on his palm, and the pages turned by themselves like a raffle roulette until his index finger dropped like an arrow pointing to the winner of the prize. "His name has been called," he confirmed, and slapped the book shut.

"Hey! That's unfair! I couldn't read it!"

"No need for that. You know the name. You gave it to him."

Happy? I wondered, remembering my faulty attempt to name them all after the seven dwarves.

"But don't worry." Sidney got to his feet, eyeing the kids sleeping soundly. "If you truly want to sacrifice yourself by aiding their cause, you can choose another kid."

"What do you mean?"

"All have been called," he said impassively.

A lump formed in my throat, remembering Renenet's words, the children's curse and that their demise was unavoidable. "Can I… can I walk the Pilgrimage of Death as a substitute of the seven?"

"A life for a life; that's how things work," Sidney explained. "Lazarus walked out from the sepulcher after the fourth day, fully conscious of the sacrifice perpetrated by the substitute to absolve his life. Lazarus's heart was so overwhelmed by debt to his savior that he continued in his savior's footsteps as if they were his own. From that day, the name of Lazarus was no more." Sidney pocketed the medallion. "Genuine sacrifice lies in abnegation and the responsibilities that come with it." Sidney stared at me. "Could you, as their mother, pick one for saving and endure the guilt of abandoning the others?"

My mind regurgitated crazy thoughts, trying to digest the moral dilemma. "But I'm not their mother," I finally said.

"You are now." Sidney looked in my eyes. "But be aware, it doesn't matter how pure your soul might be. No single soul could outweigh seven."

Pure? I thought, considering my stained soul couldn't outweigh even the most sinful. The Crying Man had robbed me of my purity. After my nightmare from last night, the fear that a being could grow inside me gnawed me from within. I had failed to preserve the commandments for the German woman.

Sidney paced toward the adjacent room.

"Wait!" I said, and he halted at the doorjamb. "Was that the true reason you came here? To notify the rest of my children about their imminent death?"

"No." Sidney glanced back. "I enjoyed talking to you last night.

I don't have the chance to speak with people very often… Most can't see me for who I really am. And fear prevents the few who can from uttering a word." The way he referred to his existence sounded quite lonely, making me feel sorry for him. "Farewell." He stepped into the insoluble darkness prevailing inside the room, as if he were king of the world of shadows.

CHAPTER 19

THE NEXT MORNING, I WOKE with the odd sensation something was different. As though I had gone to bed in one place and awakened in another. Maybe it was unfair to ask for a sense of familiarity while staying in an abandoned place. But I could swear something floating in the air permeated inside me, producing a hollowness not attributed to my involuntary fasting.

"I'll leave earlier today, kids," I told them, rummaging in the service carts, searching for clothes I could wear. "We need food and a way out of this city."

"Will it take long?" Jov asked, worried.

"I'll be back as soon as I can." I superimposed an oversize sweater against my figure. "This can work." I wore it instead of my BDM jacket, just rolling up the sleeves. "And now, the final touch." I wrapped an old scarf around my head to cover not only my frizzy hair, but my features as well. I could not take any risks, knowing there could be posters hanging around showcasing my likeness. I was a wanted fugitive.

"During my absence, please look inside these carts for clothes you can use. We might have to sleep in the open, and nights are getting colder. We won't always be so lucky to have a boiler to warm us. Do you understand?"

"Yes, Peach."

Valeska approached me. "Peach, when you're in danger, don't fear—jump!"

I could not make sense of her words, unable to imagine how jumping could be useful against a Nazi squad. "Thanks for the advice. I'll keep it in mind." I squeezed her cheek. "Take care of everybody, okay? You're in charge now."

She nodded.

Outside our hideout, the debris of what once was an imposing building echoed like the cave behind a waterfall. Precipitation dripped all over the place. It was just a drizzle. I was not concerned about getting wet, but if by the time I wanted to take the children out the rain had not receded, their makeup would not last more than a few blocks. Not enough to make it to the train station.

This time, I switched the priority of my activities, roaming the streets of Hamm until I came across a grocery store. I chose a couple of loaves of bread, a liter of milk, a truckle of cheese, a few frankfurters—I had a promise to keep to the children—and a jar of blackberry jam.

"*Guten Morgen*," I greeted the shopkeeper, head down, placing everything on the counter.

"Guten Morgen," she replied. "That will be forty reichspfennigs for each loaf, twenty-three reichspfennigs for the liter of milk…" She continued jotting the tally.

I reached into my briefcase, but to my surprise, it was empty. The contents had been removed except my money. Waking up so absentmindedly, I hadn't paid attention to the weight shift of the briefcase. *So, the children played a joke on me. One day they are innocent angels and the next they turn into rascals.*

"That will be five reichsmarks and fifty reichspfennigs."

I paid, thinking on how the two-thousand-reichsmarks reward offered for my head could be useful now to cover expenses. *Maybe I should turn myself in.*

The bright side of having an empty briefcase was that I had more room to carry the groceries. However, not having my letter opener with me made me feel unsafe, unprotected. I considered returning to the hideout to leave the groceries, but the train station was within sight, and I had to figure out whether there was train service.

The countless rails of the marshaling yard looked like the roots of a tree, the branches sending trains all over Europe. Unfortunately, bombs had hit the railways and the station, damaging it at least partially. Some hundreds of workers labored under the rain, doing the repairs. A few trains were still on rails, but I could not judge from the distance whether they were operational, forcing me to go into the station to investigate. But this time, instead of walking through the front door, I followed the railways, hoping I could blend in with the workers to avoid the soldiers guarding the station.

I passed unnoticed until I reached the platform. "Mildred! Mildred!" somebody called behind me. It was Johannes, the soldier boy I had met in Lippstadt's station.

Scheisse. I froze in my tracks. *What do I do now?* I wondered, unable to deduce Johannes's intentions. *Could he turn me in?* He seemed oblivious to my identity, but I could take no risk.

"I'm sorry. I need to go back," I said, making my way back as quickly as possible.

"Wait!" Johannes said. "What happened with your aunt?"

I halted my escape at the sight of Sidney striding on the rails, heading my way. But it was not only him. Amid the workers, I recognized people in bloody, ragged clothes, heavily mutilated. Rain fell on them but didn't dampen their clothes nor wash their blood; drops passed through them. The puddles of water remained undisturbed under their footsteps. I glanced back to find the platform crowded with undead among the living, still waiting to catch a train, as they had before dying in the bombings. It was like peeping into hell, but as if it had overlapped with this world, just as Sidney described.

"Second… sight." My lips trembled, pronouncing the words.

But these people were more than a ghostly vision. Their unblinking eyes stared directly at me, aware of my existence. Their bloody mouths gaped, and asynchronous voices flooded my head with pleas to ease their torment. I shut my eyes and covered my ears with my hands to impede it from driving me mad, but to no avail. The cacophony of voices brought me down.

"Leave! Please! Leave me alone!" I begged, rocking on my knees.

Suddenly, the voices went silent, leaving only my shaken breathing resounding in the stillness. I cracked my eyes open, still fearful as I rose until my nape hit a metal tip.

"Don't move," a soldier pointing a machine gun against my head warned. Another soldier tugged off my scarf, exposing my identity. "You're coming with us."

This time, I found myself surrounded not by living dead but by a bunch of Nazi soldiers. Resisting detention was pointless, being unarmed and outnumbered. So I gulped and stood with my hands up. A soldier snatched my briefcase.

"Hey!" I complained.

The soldier behind shoved me forward. "Move!"

"I hope your aunt gets well soon!" an ingenuous Johannes shouted, standing on tiptoes to crane above my escort, which meant he would not get a single reichsmark out of the reward. *What a waste.*

The SS soldiers led me through the station amid the murmurs of everybody, a teenage girl escorted as if I were Jack the Ripper. Outside, they forced me inside the back of a car to sit between two soldiers, dissuading any thoughts of escape.

"Peach!" somebody called.

Among the crowd outside the station, I identified Jov, his face stricken with desperation as he watched them take me away. But as much as I wanted to tell him not to worry about me, I didn't do it. That day I learned that as a bearer of the second sight, I could not trust my eyes anymore. I could not tell for sure if what I was seeing from Jov was his projection or his actual self and by warning him, I would put him in danger.

As the car departed, I hoped my eyes could convey my message to him. *Don't worry about me; stay safe, always.*

The ride was brief. The car drove parallel to the Lippe River for about five minutes before parking outside a hotel. The building was half-destroyed, as if it had been cut on a diagonal axis and had collapsed in onto itself, but the remaining half stood and even seemed inhabited. I wondered what kind of person would lodge in a place like this. Unless you were like me, of course, a runaway hiding from the Nazis.

Two soldiers escorted me to the third floor. At the end of the corridor, where the collapsed ceiling had blocked the passage, my escort knocked on room number 313 and patiently waited.

The door opened, and my heart shrank at the sight of him.

It was Reinhard, the Crying Man.

CHAPTER 20

THE SOLDIERS ESCORTING ME clicked their heels and straightened their right arms. "Sieg Heil."

Reinhard didn't reply, only eyed me with disdain. He was unkempt, as though he had ignored his grooming for days: disheveled hair, grown beard, the once-neat white shirt of his uniform stained and sleeves rolled up to his elbows, with a pair of suspenders doing their best to keep the shirt inside his pants. Reinhard finally spoke something, but I could not hear his words. My heartbeats were trashing my eardrums and my mind refused to process the simplest instruction: breathing. Only my skill to balance on my bones kept me standing.

"Get in!" The soldiers shoved me inside.

Reinhard pulled a wooden chair from the four-chair dining table. "Sit," he instructed, and the soldiers forced me down to the chair.

Considering the condition of the building, the interior seemed mostly intact, besides some cracks on the walls. The furniture of the room comprised two velvet armchairs facing a tiny wooden table, with an outstanding rectangular silhouette of dust on the wall, most probably outlining where the TV set was once located. Flies circled around a tower of dirty dishes protruding over the kitchen sink. Three large flowerpots decorated the corners of the room, but the plants had withered long ago. The sole vestiges of greenery were the fern-patterned curtains, which remained shut. A flickering incandescent bulb kept the room alight most of the time. The door leading to the bedroom was closed and had diagonal scratches forming an X.

"She was carrying this." The soldier handed my briefcase to Reinhard and approached his ear to whisper something inaudible. Instead of being interested in the contents, Reinhard beheld and fingered the insignia on the brooch.

"*Reichsadler,*" he said, touching the Imperial Eagle standing over the swastika. "Do you know what it means?"

My lips remained pursed; I was still emotionally comatose.

"It's Roman. It was the insignia of the imperial power, '*Translatio imperii.*'" Reinhard turned to me. "It's Latin. It means 'transfer of rule' and describes the tradition of how the imperium has been transferred from emperor to emperor and to kings through the centuries… until it arrived to us."

But despite addressing me, I didn't return eye contact. My gaze fixed on the vacant space of the TV as I battled to control my shallow breathing and unclench my fingernails from the backs of my thighs.

"You can leave now," Reinhard instructed his men, resting my briefcase on the table. "Please inform Ghislain and Otto that we've found her." The soldiers clicked their heels and heiled before departing.

Ghislain is here and searching for me?

Reinhard walked to the cupboard in the kitchen barefoot, his boots nowhere in sight. The voices in my head debated whether this was my opportunity to escape. The door was unlocked and Reinhard distracted. I was uncertain whether the soldiers had gone back to the vehicle or were guarding the door. But Reinhard was carrying his pistol sheathed in his belt. Judging by my distance to the entrance, he would have enough time to shoot me before I could open it. My opportunity vanished as Reinhard returned carrying a bottle of *Courvoisier* cognac and two glasses.

"Here," he said, pouring a glass for me.

Reinhard sat on the chair opposite me, laid-back, raising his glass. Needle scars on the inside of his left elbow called my attention. My reaction must have been noticeable, since he unfolded his sleeve to cover the tracks. Reinhard extracted a cigarette pack from his breast pocket and offered me one, but my apathy disdained his gesture. So he pulled one out with his lips and lit it. "You might not believe me"—Reinhard blew a cloud of smoke—"but I'm glad to see you again." He flaunted a malicious smile. "I was hoping to meet you again, but you left Wewelsburg so abruptly, taking everybody by surprise. Nobody was more astonished than your mother." He pondered, swirling his glass of Courvoisier. "Poor Frieda Niemeyer." He sipped.

I gulped at hearing her name.

"She was torn apart. Who wouldn't be? Two tragedies in her family," Reinhard said with an alcohol-coarse voice. "First, losing that quisling, whom she fondly called son," he said, referring to my brother Anton. "And now, her beloved daughter following in his treacherous footsteps." His words drilled inside my head, spawning images of my mother in tears. I felt pathetic for disappointing her with my actions.

Reinhard emptied his glass and refilled it. "So much suffering, and for what?" The cigarette hung from the rim of his lips. "Everything for what?" He tipped his chair back over the hind legs.

But I didn't answer.

"Everything for what? Damn it!" Reinhard spat out the cigarette. He stomped on the floor with the forelegs of his chair and slammed the table with the palm of his hand. "Answer me!" he huffed, with a wild hair tuft falling across his eyes, arteries popping out on his temple and neck.

I shut my eyes, squeezing out my tears.

Reinhard combed his hair back using his hand as he took a deep breath, and a fake smile returned to his face.

"Everything for taking the children with you," he said calmly, opening my briefcase. "For taking them to the uncertain. Wandering without a purpose or destination. Enduring cold and hunger." Reinhard picked out a frankfurter and devoured it. "But since you don't want them to suffer, and you want to put a smile back on Mommy's face, you are going to tell me where the heck they are." He finished by licking his fingers as he dropped the bag on the floor.

My wrath surged, and thoughts about having my letter opener with me and pushing it into his throat crystallized inside my mind.

Despite my fatigue and yearning to go back to my family and

my old life, there was no turning back—especially for the children. Living on the run, even malnourished and suffering in poverty, was a brighter future for them than the grim imprisonment and torture inside that dungeon. I would make sure it stood that way, even if I had to pay with my life.

"I know not having the children seems terrible to you…" I said, paraphrasing the words he'd used before raping me. "But I'm being kind." I extended my middle finger.

Reinhard burst into laughter and walked toward me. He leaned until his nose touched my ear and whispered, "I know why you are here, *Kakerlake.*" Cockroach, he called me again. "Better swallow the cognac. It will make things easier for you. Trust me." His alcohol breath made me nauseated.

Reinhard went to the bedroom and swung the door open. Blinding light flooded the room. The bedroom was gone, collapsed along with a portion of the building, leaving a window instead, framing the cloudy city skyline.

"My apologies." Reinhard unbuttoned his trousers. "But the hotel is amid renovations, and the bathroom is still missing." The arc formed by his urine splashed and dripped down the three-story concrete slide formed by the collapsed wall tipped against the door frame. "I hope you are good at keeping your balance while peeing," he said, shaking his penis.

I could feel nothing but revulsion, remembering what he'd done to me.

Reinhard returned to the dining table, leaving the door to the precipice open. At least it refreshed the polluted air and helped me cope with my claustrophobia.

Reinhard unsheathed his pistol and placed it in the center of the table. "Now you and I will have a more intimate conversation."

CHAPTER 21

REINHARD POURED HIMSELF ANOTHER GLASS of cognac. "Wolfrick," he said, referring to Von Schroeder, "ordered me to besiege the entire Reich to find you." He squinted, waving his finger at me. "But I know you too well. All I had to do was sit comfortably and wait for you to crawl under my boot... and so you did, proving once more that cockroaches love tight, dark, and warm places." He waved his arms grandiosely.

I scowled at him. "You sit here like a coward while a boy does your dirty work."

Reinhard's brow arched.

"Don't feign ignorance."

"Why would I? I got you. Nothing else matters."

"You used Johannes, the Hitlerjugend, to guard Lippstadt's and Hamm's railway stations."

Reinhard pondered for a moment. "Why would I deploy a Hitlerjugend from Lippstadt to Hamm when I can order my loyal soldats to form a line from here to the Rhine and they will adhere to my commands?" He chuckled. "Have you forgotten your apprehension? *SS-Schütze*, who captured you, told me you called everybody's attention with your screams, begging to be left alone, despite being by yourself."

Could that be the truth? But I saw Johannes as clear as… Then I remembered the blood dripping from his nape. *A wound, a deadly head wound. Johannes is dead as well.* That explained why the soldiers had disregarded him. I only saw him because of my second sight.

"You are fucked up here, you know?" Reinhard pointed to his temple. "Fräulein Niemeyer, you need help. Professional help." His hand reached for mine across the table. "The Reich can provide the help you need. We have doctors and the facilities to—"

"To turn me into a monster, like you did with those poor children?" I slapped away his hand.

Reinhard's semblance grew serious. In a split second, he grabbed his pistol and, pointing in my direction, pulled the trigger. The bullet passed next to my right ear and hit the wall behind me, deafening me terribly. Reinhard leaned over the table, and he pulled me toward him. "Don't you dare ever touch me again," he spoke rabidly through his grinding, clenched teeth. "Do-you-understand?" He poked the searing muzzle of the gun into my neck.

I growled, containing my screams.

"Alcohol eases the suffering…" Reinhard pressed my head against the table and, uncovering my neck, poured my glass of cognac over the burn. "You would have made things easier if you had swallowed it!"

My fingernails bit the timber as the burning sensation radiated across my head and back.

"Now, up!" Reinhard released me.

I cannot show frailty to this monster. I straightened in my chair, still dizzy, with my ear buzzing.

"This is your last chance." Reinhard rested his pistol on its side in the center of the table. The barrel was longer than on my father's Luger, and a red number nine was engraved in the wooden grip panels. "Where are the children?"

"I won't tell you… but if you kill me, you'll never find them." I set my jaw.

"You want to challenge your odds, girl?" Reinhard said calmly. "Let's play a game, then." A Machiavellian smile popped up on his face. "Have you ever played Ten to Midnight?"

"Was that a game you played with your father?" I said sarcastically, unable to imagine the sadistic games Reinhard liked to play.

"My mother, actually." It was harder for me to believe Reinhard had a mother. "Right now, my soldats are afoot, tearing down every goddamn door of this shithole, and it's just a matter of time to find your precious punks. So, your clock is ticking… the Clock of Death is ticking." He rotated the pistol on the table, simulating the staggered movement of a clock hand from one to twelve. "And when the clock hand reaches midnight… you die."

For a moment, I wondered if he would have the guts to kill me, considering he still had to explain my death to my father—who was his superior. "What will your superiors think if you return to Wewelsburg empty-handed?" I tried to regain control of my breathing. "You need me alive." My only card to play was to convince him that hurting me would bring him trouble with my father.

Reinhard smirked and cocked his head. "You don't believe me, right? Just glance back and find out what happened to the last person sitting on that chair."

I dared to turn back with a racing heart, and just like with the missing TV set, a dozen of bullet holes outlined the silhouette of the person sitting in my place, sprayed with dried blood. Overwhelmed at being in front of Reinhard, I'd not paid attention to the firing wall when the soldiers towed me in.

"Ten bullets." Reinhard tapped the clip with one finger. "And ten minutes surrounding midnight that would be fatal to you." With two fingers, he illustrated the cone formed between 11:00 p.m. and 1:00 a.m. of his imaginary clock relative to the position of the gun on the table and my distance from it. "Now, let's find out if your time to meet the grim reaper has arrived."

Reinhard's words made me remember Sidney's midnight visits. But after my visions at the train station and the incident with Johannes, I questioned not only Sidney's existence but my sanity. Maybe Reinhard was right, there was something wrong with my head, and all the twisted things I'd seen so far belonged only to the realm of my imagination.

"No roulette is more entertaining than Ten to Midnight. Trust me, Russian is too quick to be fun," Reinhard said sympathetically. "Let's roll!" With a twist of his wrist, Reinhard put the gun in motion, the barrel circling until it finally stopped, pointing at thirty past nine. Reinhard pulled the trigger. I shut my eyes and shuddered as the bullet passed by, hitting the wall. "Where are the children?" He put the pistol back in motion, but I didn't utter a word. This time the barrel pointed at six—his direction—but before it had totally stopped, he spun it again. "I can do this all day long."

As the pistol revolved on the table like a child's top, I pondered the idea of seizing the gun before he could. Unfortunately, even if I did it, I was sitting too close to him. There was no way I could move away from his reach in time to aim at him.

"You are overly confident of your luck, to keep your trap shut." Reinhard pushed the trigger, and the expelled bullet smashed the flowerpot to my left, electrifying my nerves.

"No."

"What?" Reinhard gave the pistol a rest and walked around the table. He stood behind me and I shivered at his proximity. He squeezed my shoulders while whispering in my ear, "'No' is all you know how to say?"

My insides battled to contain the seaquake of negative emotions.

"I thought we understood each other. That was the impression you gave me the day you seduced me. I must confess, you know how to turn a man on."

My blood boiled at listening to him speak as if raping me had been my fault.

"Now you return to me, acting unkind," he continued. "And your attitude… hurts my feelings. But you need to understand that for what I want to do to you… I don't need you alive."

My stomach churned at the thought of his disgusting plans.

"Tick-tock, tick-tock… Any minute, my men will find your hideout. You are just making things harder… I need you docile." Reinhard collected my unresponsive hand and dropped it, plummeting it onto the table. "Like this."

I focused my eyes on the pistol lying inches away from my hand.

"What? You want the gun?" Reinhard asked, figuring my intentions. "Go on… take it…" His hand manipulated mine to grab the pistol. He folded my fingers around the handle and pushed my index finger inside the trigger guard, then forced my shivering hand to point at my right temple. Reinhard positioned his head on the other side, his scruffy beard scraping my cheek. "Shoot! That is what you want, right? To put an end to my life… This is your chance. This is a Mouser 'Red 9' C96." Which explained the red number nine on the grip. "Its long barrel and the high-velocity cartridge provide an unmatched level of penetration. One nine-millimeter bullet can penetrate your skull and mine. In a second, we'll be lying on the floor, dead next to each other, holding hands like star-crossed lovers. Just like *Romeo and Juliet.*" Using the barrel of the Red 9, he pushed my trembling chin to face him. "Don't you want to be my Juliet?"

I wanted Reinhard dead, but I lacked the courage to pull the trigger. Even if I had wanted to, I couldn't tweak a muscle. I was paralyzed, witnessing in terror his eyes turning aqueous and tears rolling down.

The Crying Man had emerged again.

"A tragedy…" Reinhard said with a broken voice. "What a beautiful tragedy we could have become!" He snatched the Red 9 from my hand and hit me with its butt.

"Pathetic!" Reinhard poured Courvoisier until it spilled over the table. "Let's resume the game!"

I collapsed over the table, a pounding ache spreading through my jaw. Part of me acknowledged this could be my end. *Next round, Reinhard will pull the trigger and I'll share the destiny of the previous person sitting on this chair.* Slain, my body disposed of, thrown into the rubble through that door. *I should have pulled that trigger,* I scolded myself. *I should have paid the price with my own life.* Perhaps if Reinhard were dead, my children would have a greater chance of surviving. Even if I was not with them, a Good Samaritan would eventually cross their paths.

"Get up!" Reinhard ordered.

I peeled my eyes, disoriented, and noticed the head of a child emerging through the closed entrance. Jov's projection peeped through the door like a sunbeam flashing through the clouded sky. "I found you!" he said, relieved.

His presence was what I needed to harbor hope again.

CHAPTER 22

I RAN THE BACK OF MY HAND over my mouth, smearing it with blood. My lower lip was bleeding.

"Are you all right?" Jov asked.

I assumed Jov had followed us from the railway station to this place, meaning two things. First, soldiers hadn't found them yet, otherwise Jov would not be projecting himself here. Second, Reinhard could not see or hear Jov, since he was not "gifted" with the second sight as I was. Knowing the children were safe for now granted me temporary relief. However, I could not risk saying a word to Jov, which could put Reinhard on alert. I had to play along until we could devise a way to get out of this place together. This seemed impossible, because even having Jov's invisibility on my side, he could hardly interact with the real world, as he'd proved to me back in Wewelsburg. In practical terms, Jov was just a ghost.

I nodded, answering Jov's question.

"I'll help you get out of here," he said.

"Just a few drops… There is still plenty of blood to be shed." Reinhard placed the Red 9 pistol at the center of the table. "Time to roll again!" He put the roulette back into motion.

Jov observed with consternation as the spinning pistol stopped slightly behind 11:00 p.m. My eyes drew an imaginary line from the barrel that passed a couple of inches away from my right arm. I closed my eyes and jumped at the loud *bang*. I could sense the gust of wind generated by the bullet.

"*Ufffff*, we are getting so close," Reinhard said.

Jov's eyes peeled with dread at the sick show, and he covered his ears with his hands. Now he was aware of my situation: my luck was running out. Jov searched around for something he could use against Reinhard while Death's roulette spun over and over. Reinhard shot round after round, the empty, ejected shells bouncing over the floor with hollow *ping* sounds.

"Not talkative yet?" Reinhard set the roulette in motion again. This time, the barrel finally pointed at midnight. "Ha! It is time now!"

My mind turned blank in disbelief at the pistol aiming directly at my chest.

"*Auf Wiedersehen*, Fräulein Niemeyer."

Oh my God. I gulped.

"Nooooooooo!" Jov shouted, trying to stop Reinhard, but it was too late.

Reinhard squeezed the trigger, but the pistol expelled no bullet. He pressed it twice, but the mechanism of the Red 9 just clicked, the firing pin jolting back and forth on an empty chamber every time. No bullets were left inside the magazine. "It seems cockroaches have more than one life… But rein in your enthusiasm. I fired only eight times. The other two bullets are lodged in a sack of meat and bone down the defile." He motioned with his head toward the door.

I sighed, light-headed, my blood descending to my feet. For a brief instant, my sight clouded with multicolored dots. I was about to faint.

"I'll come back," Jov said, hurrying toward the door.

"Go back to them," I whispered, hoping Jov would escape with his siblings. There was nothing else he could do here.

"What did you say?" Reinhard asked as he loaded a ten-round stripper clip through the chamber of the Red 9. "You're a crazy bitch indeed."

Reinhard poured himself another glass of Courvoisier with terrible aim, spilling more on the table than inside the glass. He was drunk, and possessing a gun made him even more dangerous. Considering his aim with filling the glass, next time he fired his Red 9, the bullet might hit me even if the roulette pointed at 8:00.

"Wa-wa-it—wait," Reinhard held his hands aloft. He stood with effort and sheathed the Red 9 inside his trousers. He wobbled to the door, recently remodeled as a balcony, and unzipped his pants. Leaning over the frame, he pissed again. His aim was worse than with the cognac, splashing the floor upon which he was standing— barefoot.

I could not avoid grimacing with revulsion. *Emma, you need to focus*, I scolded myself. *I will push him over*, I resolved after analyzing the situation. I would have to stand from my chair in silence and ram his back. Reinhard would not have enough time to take his gun out and turn around to shoot me. I just had to be careful to avoid grappling with him, otherwise I would end up at the bottom with him. I would have to push him while he was facing away from me. *You can do it*, I encouraged myself, trusting my speed at the track would help me accomplish the feat.

I funneled my weight onto my arms, resting one hand on the chair and the other on the table to slide myself out. I watched Reinhard from the corner of my eye, playing with his urine like a little boy, wiggling his penis around. I swung my left leg out, about to push myself up, when the main door cracked open. *Guards?* I panicked, wishing Jov was still here to warn me, and returned to my initial posture.

Reinhard glanced over his shoulder, but nobody walked in. Soldiers guarding the entrance peeked inside, as disconcerted as I was. With the same gentleness as the door had opened, it closed by itself again, as if carried by the wind, subverting my plan. Reinhard headed back to the table, zipping up his trousers. *Scheisse.*

"What were we doing?" he asked casually. "Oh, yes!" He pulled out his Red 9. "Let's roll."

It's over now.

Jov's projection trespassed into the room. "I need you to be ready, Peach," he instructed. "At my signal, secure the door. We can't allow the guards to get inside."

I arched my brow, dubious. Jov's plan solved only one part of the equation—the smaller one. Reinhard was by far our biggest threat.

"Trust me," Jov reaffirmed.

With no better option at hand, I would try anything.

Reinhard disposed himself to set the roulette back in motion, and Jov studied the movements, holding his left hand aloft. Using his right hand, Jov influenced the result, and the barrel ended pointing at three.

"Ohhhh." Reinhard frowned, displeased. "Next will be the good one."

Jov stopped the spinning pistol at six—pointing Reinhard's direction. "Now!" Jov lowered his left hand. But despite hearing my cue, I remained paralyzed by Reinhard's gaze.

Suddenly, a battle cry erupted. "*I-del-wiz!*" I recognized 44's voice. An invisible force knocked Reinhard down from his chair, and I watched, bemused, not quite grasping what was happening.

"The door!" Jov reminded me.

I rushed toward the entrance. The knob started twisting as I shouldered the door. The guards pushed inward, but I ran the bolt. "Open up!" They slammed the door.

Reinhard, lying on his back, kicked an invisible someone away, and a flowerpot smashed at the other end of the room. As earthenware pieces crumbled over the floor, reality unfolded, revealing 44 draped under a sheet of emptiness. *Renenet's invisibility veil!* I thought, realizing 44 had stolen the veil from Mrs. Bahiti before we separated. Or maybe Renenet had given it to him? That was irrelevant now. What mattered was that, using the invisibility veil, 44 had outwitted the soldiers, and he had walked in when the door opened… to save me.

"You damned chimpanzee! I'm gonna kill you!" Reinhard got back to his feet and went after 44, flexing his muscles with a maniacal face.

"Noooooo!" I yelled, fearful I could not arrive in time to protect 44.

But when Reinhard crossed the firing line of the Red 9 resting on the table, Jov, with great effort, squeezed the trigger, and a loud *bang* filled the room.

The expelled bullet hit Reinhard's left thigh, and he staggered, leaning against the wall. "I-I'll kill you all!" he babbled through grinding teeth, suppressing the pain. Reinhard's eyes sought his gun, but without the firm grasp of the shooter, the recoil effect of the shot had pushed the pistol across the table and onto the floor. He crawled after his Red 9, but before he could grab it, I smashed the bottle of cognac over his head. Reinhard collapsed, blood flowing from his shaved nape.

I tried to catch my breath to calm my trembling hand, holding the neck of the broken bottle. *Is he dead?* I wondered, imagining myself cutting Reinhard's throat with the sharp, zigzagging rim of glass. But as my breath quietened, I dumped the bottle aside. *My children,* I reminded myself. Keeping them safe was the only thing that mattered to me now.

But my peace was short-lived.

A guard broke the window, and pushing his arm through the bars, he pulled the curtain aside, taking sight of me. "Get in!" he instructed his partner, who shot at the lock to open the door. They were seconds away from breaking through.

I rushed to 44's aid. "Are you all right?"

"Peach!" He hugged me effusively.

"Not now! We need to escape!" I tied a knot with the invisibility veil around his neck as if it were a cloak, and I hurried him. But we met Jov's serious eyes looking through the frame of the collapsed bathroom, sharing the bad news that jumping was our only way out.

CHAPTER 23

OUTSIDE, IT WAS STILL DRIZZLING. I glanced over the precipice, measuring the inclination of the wall tilted against the structure, forming a three-story concrete slide, which, to our good luck, the plaster and paint were still on, relieving us from most of the friction. It was a forty-five-degree incline or more, but enough to cushion our landing over the rubble using our legs. However, a profuse crack at the center concerned me. Our weight could split the wall in two, but hearing the kicks slamming against the door forced me to disregard safety measures. I picked up my leather briefcase and strapped it across my chest. "Are you ready?" I asked the kids, but 44 clutched me, burying his face in fear. "Just imagine it's a slide at the playground… but bigger." Remembering 44's story, I wondered if he had ever been on a playground before. "It will be fun," I reassured him, not only for him but for me also. My legs were shaking. "Don't worry, just jump…" I said, echoing Valeska's words unintentionally.

"Peach, when you're in danger, don't fear—jump!" she had said to me. *I hope you're right, Valeska.*

We sat at the edge, wrinkling our noses with disgust at the puddle of Reinhard's urine. "Ready?" I embraced 44, hoping Jov's ghostlike condition would keep him safe from any harm. "Now!"

I pushed myself over the edge and screamed as we sped down, everything blurring past our sides. My legs flexed in anticipation to propel me into running, but when we reached the bottom, 44's weight pulled me down and we rolled over the debris. I pulled 44 against my chest and used my arms to protect our heads. When we stopped, I opened my eyes, finding metal rods in front of us. A couple of inches more and we'd have died, impaled like the bodies previously disposed of by Reinhard. "Are you okay?"

Forty-Four nodded. "It was fun! Let's do it again!"

"Over there!" soldiers shouted from the hotel room.

"Hide!" Jov shouted.

My legs refused to respond, but the sound of the bullets persuaded my aching body to crawl behind a column.

"We need to make it there." I pointed to a partially crumbled wall twenty steps away, while the bullets carved the borders of the column, discouraging any intention to peek. "Jov, please tell us when they reload."

Jov came out from behind the column, invisible to the soldiers, waiting for the precise moment to give us the instruction.

"Cover yourself." I rearranged 44's veil, trying to cloak most of his body to camouflage him. Our abrupt descent had torn pieces of the veil off, and 44 examined the holes with sadness. "Cheer up! If we make it through this, I'll ask for a new veil from Renenet. I promise."

But the veil was the least of my concerns. Rain was washing away the makeup from his skin, revealing his characteristic whitish tone, a cruel reminder that for him, persecution might never end.

"Now!" Jov signaled, and I pulled 44's hand. Unfortunately, 44 was not a runner as I was, and the firing resumed. We completed the last stretch under a rain of bullets.

"They hit you!" 44 said, alarmed, when we reached the wall. I hesitated to look, fearful of finding my clothes stained in blood from a bullet wound disguised by the rush of adrenaline. I held my breath and dared to glance down. A bullet had hit me, and liquid streamed out through the bullet hole. *Milk*, I discovered with relief. The bullet had hit the milk bottle inside my briefcase.

"I'm fine." I dumped the bottle. "We need to continue." I towed 44 through the passages formed by the destroyed walls, searching for an exit to the concrete maze. "This way!" I said with excitement, sighting a door at the end of the corridor. But as we rushed toward it, the floor we were standing on collapsed, falling one story down and taking us with it.

"Owwww," I moaned, caressing my limbs.

The cloud of dust dissipated, revealing a room before us. I stepped in, realizing it was a boiler room similar to the one we'd been staying in, but properly furnished to work as a household. It smelled like cooked food rather than mustiness. At a tiny table, a man in his forties, his wife, and their daughter, probably ten, stared at me gape-mouthed, spoons in hand. The decoration called my attention: two *menorah*, seven- and nine-branch candelabras, and a hexagram, the six-pointed star, hanging from the wall. They were Jews hiding from the Nazis.

"Please, help us!" I begged with a hoarse voice after inhaling a mouthful of dust.

The man put his finger over his mouth, signaling me to hush. He stood from his chair and, holding my arm, led me back into the corridor, where 44 waited for me. Once I was outside, he closed the heavy metal door and secured it.

"Hey! Let us in! Don't be cruel." I hammered the door. "Please! Nazis are chasing us…" It occurred to me that under my oversize sweater, I was still wearing my BDM uniform. *I am a Nazi. Why would Jews open the door to a Nazi like me?* I sighed.

"Peach, I can hear their footsteps. They're coming," Jov said.

Climbing back to the surface was impossible. We had to continue down the corridor. Unfortunately for us, after the turn the ceiling had slumped, blocking the path.

"*Scheisse!*" I stomped to release my frustration, but my heel thudded with a metallic reverberation. I was standing on a lid to a sewer hole. "Stand back!" I squatted, secured the handle with both hands, and heaved it open. The interior was pitch-black, and judging by the pungent smell of backwater lodging in my nose, I figured it led to the sewer system, but since we didn't have anywhere else to go, this seemed like our only chance. "Get in." I guided the children inside and closed the lid after us. We descended using the wrought iron ladder bolted to the stone wall. At the bottom, my feet splashed in a six-inch pool of stagnant water. "Where are you?" I said, forcing my eyes to adapt to the darkness.

"*I-del-wiz!*" 44 said, hugging me.

"Hold me and don't let me go. Jov? Where are you?"

"I'm here." His voice came from the darkness.

"Are you able to see?" I asked, concerned, unable to sense him.
"I can… hear."
"What do you mean by hearing?"
"For me, everything is like echoes."
"Okay, follow my sound." I extended my arms, reaching stone on both sides. It was a corridor, around seven feet wide, with a ceiling way above my head. Two choices. *Left or right?* I chose right.

I fumbled our way through the dark tunnel, following the distant sound of running water, until we arrived at an intersection. My feet sensed a ramp down, increasing the depth of the water level. Dim sources of light coming from the ceiling—most probably street gutters, since rainwater was sprinkling down from them—revealed a large, arched sewer tunnel, probably twenty feet wide. "Here, there is a ledge attached to the wall." I helped 44 avoid sliding down the ramp.

A *clang* echoed down the tunnel. Beams of light broke into the darkness. SS soldiers carrying flashlights descended the stairs. "They're coming!" We hurried down the sewer to the next tunnel intersection, but footsteps splashed from that direction as well. "They're surrounding us… This is a trap." We continued down the sewer tunnel, searching for stairs to emerge to the street. But then, suddenly, I halted. *What if this is what Reinhard wants?* I imagined him waiting for us nonchalantly at the surface. *Jov shot him, Emma,* I tried to convince myself, but I could not avoid my claustrophobic feelings of being trapped, dirty and stinking in backwater. *"Kakerlake."* Reinhard had fulfilled his desire to make me feel like a cockroach. But like a cockroach, we would have to outsmart him once more in order to survive.

My light-deprived eyes identified a nook encasing a metal door. Pipes were coming out from the top, maybe electrical… *A control room!* I examined a padlock on the latch. *Nobody would lock something if it were of no value.* It could be the perfect hideout until the search was called off. "Please guard the hallway for any light until I open this door," I instructed the children. I put my briefcase on the floor and rummaged for my letter opener, but I remembered the children had emptied the contents. "Come on!" I searched in the surroundings and found a piece of a flat steel bar, but the edge was too blunt to force it inside the padlock.

"Let me go!" 44 squealed behind me.

An SS soldier dressed all in black had secured 44 from behind.

He was wearing a gas mask and held no flashlight, explaining how he had approached undetected. The soldier would have assumed 44 was alone, since Jov was invisible to him and he had not noticed my presence, concealed inside the nook. He was planning to flee carrying a kicking 44 under his arm, but I leaped onto his back.

"Let him go!" I searched for an opening between his helmet and gas mask to plunge my steel bar into his neck.

The soldier bucked, twisted, and reared like a bull in a rodeo, trying to throw me off, but I hooked my arm tightly around his neck. He released 44 and cast himself backward into the water. The canal was not deep enough to cushion the dive, and my head and back hit the rocky bottom. We wrestled underwater, surfacing just to grab a breath of air before submerging again. I used all my strength to maintain the choke, because it was like fighting a crocodile. My survival depended on it.

"Peach!" 44 and Jov screamed in terror, standing on the ledge.

The soldier's hands pulled my head, but I did not falter. He smashed me against the wall of the canal. The pain weakened my limbs until I lost the choke hold. The soldier pushed himself away, creating distance between us. We emerged waist-deep in the backwater of the canal, facing each other. I pointed my flat steel bar at the fully armed soldier, knowing this could be my last stand.

"Stop!" the soldier said with a voice muffled by the gas mask, putting his hands in the air. "Please stop, Peach."

"What?" I said, confused at being called by my nickname.

The soldier unfastened the straps from behind his head and removed the mask, revealing his identity under the dim lights.

"It's me, Ghislain."

CHAPTER 24

"GHI-GHISLAIN?" I ASKED DOUBTFULLY, trying to recognize his features amid the scarce light of the sewer, still in disbelief we were meeting again under these circumstances.

"The one and only," Ghislain said, exerting pressure with his hand on his bleeding trapezius. Apparently, my attack had found its way to the base of his neck, hopefully not hitting an artery.

I sighed in relief. "Ghislain!" Tears ran down my cheeks. I wanted to wade to him and fling my arms about him, but seeing him in full gear, displaying the SS runes on his helmet, reminded me we were now on opposite sides. He was a Nazi, and I was a traitor.

"Why are you here?" I wielded my flat steel bar in his direction.

"Calm down, I'm here to help you." He extended his hand to reach me, but I stepped back. "Come with me. Please, you must trust me." He beckoned.

Despite any feeling Ghislain might harbor for me, Reinhard was his superior, and the chain of command he had sworn to uphold would force him to abide by Reinhard's orders. I could not trust Ghislain anymore. *"All I had to do was to sit comfortably and wait for you to crawl under my boot,"* Reinhard's lunatic voice played inside my head. I would be the cockroach crawling into the warm embrace of Ghislain, where I could feel secure. But not anymore. *I will not fall into his trap again.*

"No!" I shook my head. "I won't. Please stand back."

"Peach, don't." Ghislain's face lit up with a golden shine, and his beautiful steel eyes stared at me. Unfortunately, it was not only his face lit up, but the entire sewer. "Peach, look out!" he yelled.

I turned around and found the source of the light.

A *flammenwerfer*, wearing a gas mask, walked out from a tunnel intersection next to us, vanquishing the darkness with the flames burning at the tip of his flamethrower. He opened the gas valve connected to a cylindrical tank carried on his back, and the tube regurgitated a shining ball of fire. The air ignited, as if the flames came into existence spontaneously, in a hypnotic spectacle. I could not react in time, but as the whip of fire unleashed in my direction, Ghislain submerged me. The flames burned over the surface, brightening the murky waters.

I surfaced, battling to catch my breath while Ghislain counter-attacked, shooting with his handgun. But the flammenwerfer wore an armored apron, shielding him from the bullets. Ghislain kept pressing the trigger as he towed me to the edge. "Take cover!"

I crawled inside the nook, where 44 was cowering.

"Where is Jov?" I asked 44, but he shook his head, eyes shut. I dared to peek out and saw Jov standing behind the flammenwerfer, trying to mess up the flamethrower with his limited capacity to influence this world.

Ghislain came out of the water and rolled to cover, and after him, a curtain of fire sealed the nook. I flinched away from the irradiating heat, feeling like we were inside an oven. *We're going to die charred*, I thought, having trouble breathing as the fire consumed the oxygen. Ghislain pulled a grenade from his belt, unscrewed the cap at the end of the stick, and pulled the wire, igniting the device.

"No!" I yelled, thinking about Jov, who was standing next to the soldier, invisible to Ghislain.

"Get down!" Ghislain tossed the grenade at ground level and ducked, wrapping his arms around his head.

The flammenwerfer blew up in a tremendous explosion, the grenade's explosive power magnified by the gas of the flamethrower, which shook the entire sewer system.

"Jov! Jov!" I coughed and tried to go after Jov, but Ghislain's arm prevented me from doing so.

The flames receded, and the smoke dissipated, revealing the remains of what once was a human being, now just unrecognizable pieces of bloodless, carbonized flesh adhered to the armor. All the blood had evaporated. Just like all signs of Jov.

Ghislain pulled me around to face him. "We need to go now. Do you understand?" He jolted me to bring me back to my senses. "Do you understand?"

"Yes! Yes!" I pulled myself free from his arms.

"Follow me." Ghislain marched away.

I reached for my briefcase and 44's hand; he was still in shock. "Come on."

We fled through the dark sewers, but as we did, I could not avoid glancing back to the burning remains, hoping Jov had returned to his corporeal body in time.

CHAPTER 25

THE WATER LEVELS ROSE ABOVE THE CANAL as the torrential flow increased. Street gutters discharged jets that looked like waterfalls. It would be dangerous to remain belowground any longer. Ghislain guided us through the flooded tunnels until we arrived at a dead end. He climbed the ladder of a sewer hole and cracked the lid open. He studied the surroundings to confirm the area was clear. "It's safe. You can come out," he said, pushing himself up.

We emerged in the interior of a partially destroyed warehouse. The ceiling had an enormous hole where the structure had partially collapsed, and on the floor lay the fuselage of the four-propeller plane that had crashed into it. Metal panels from the wings looked like a cheese grater from the bullets of antiaircraft machine guns. The holes were so wide I could pass my hand through some. Despite the fire that had consumed the plane after the crash, a series of concentric circles with red at the center were still visible in the body paint of the flank. It was a British bomber, just like the ones that had raided Berlin a hundred times during the sleepless nights I spent hidden inside the cellar. The warehouse had been abandoned after the crash.

Ghislain removed his helmet, and now I could see his features with clarity. Despite the dirt on his face, I still found him handsome. When our eyes met, I glanced away, wondering how I looked. I didn't have a mirror with me, but considering the condition of my clothes, my hair should be a mess after being submerged in the stagnant water. I could confirm it reeked horribly. I had never felt so grubby in my entire life.

"Are you ready?" Ghislain asked as we caught our breath. "We flee at once." He removed the slim magazine of a submachine gun he was carrying strapped across his chest, then blew on it and shook it to dislodge the water before plugging it back in. He unfolded the stock and propped the gun against his shoulder.

"Yes," I answered, avoiding eye contact. I adjusted 44's invisibility cloak around his neck, but oddly enough, Ghislain did not question the artifact's existence. *Could he have known?*

"Now, follow me quietly." Ghislain skulked around the plane, with his machine gun leading the way.

The dense, dark clouds peeking through the hole in the ceiling made me feel it was already nighttime, but when I glanced at my wristwatch, it was not yet 5:00 p.m. After everything I'd gone through, my quiet memories of the time at my grandfather's farm were a lifetime ago.

We exited the warehouse through a broken window leading to a narrow alley. We followed Ghislain through the heavy rain to the main street. He crouched behind a pile of rubble and flashed his open hand above his shoulder, so we crouched behind him. "That's our transport," Ghislain whispered, flashing the keys of a car parked in the alley across the street.

"*Kommandeurswagen?*" It was a metallic-gray, two-door, 4x4 version of the Volkswagen Beetle, built for military purposes. Ghislain nodded. But an obstacle blocked our goal: a soldier guarding the corner.

"I'll take care of him. Wait here." Ghislain was about to move out when a personnel carrier truck rolled down the street. The truck halted in front of us and five soldiers jumped out of the cargo compartment.

"Turn up every goddamn stone!" Reinhard shouted, standing on the edge of the truck, clutching the Red 9 in his hand.

My heart pounded.

"Find the cockroach!" Reinhard's eyes shone with steel determination, unconcerned with the dried blood covering his nape and neck, and his trousers dyed crimson, displaying the bullet hole with no bandage applied to the wound. He even seemed vigorous, considering he'd been stumbling-drunk just an hour ago. "Let's go!"

Reinhard tapped on the metal side and the truck moved forward, escorted by two *Kübelwagens*, light military vehicles considered the German equivalent of a Jeep, with the signature spare tire on top of the hood. I had loved those cars since I first laid eyes on them. I'd imagined myself exploring Africa's savanna in one.

"What do we do now?" I whispered, concerned, as the soldiers spread to inspect the buildings nearby. It was just a matter of time before they found us.

"We need a distraction." Ghislain took the remaining grenade from his utility belt and unscrewed the metallic cap without pulling the wire. "At my signal, you run straight to the Volkswagen."

"What are you planning to do?"

"I'll go to reason with them."

"Will it work?"

"I'm a Nazi officer." Ghislain winked and walked straight to the soldier guarding the corner. "Hey!"

The soldier saluted upon identifying the rank in his uniform.

"We need backup! Flamethrower blew up into pieces. I got hit!" Ghislain pressed the wound on the back of his neck, which was still bleeding. He issued orders, pointing at a location down the road, and the soldier complied.

"Oh my God, please don't do it," I whispered, observing how Ghislain had pulled the cord of the grenade behind his back and slid it inside the soldier's backpack when he patted his back. The soldier ran, calling for his companions. Ghislain beckoned us, and we rushed to the car. But in my mind, I did nothing but count the seconds remaining to the explosion in terror: *one, two...*

"Over there!" a man shouted, and a burst of bullets hit the same ground we were running on. Ghislain provided cover fire.

"Four... Five!" I yelled, and then the grenade blew, providing a distraction, but I didn't dare look.

"Get in!" Ghislain had the passenger door open by the time we arrived. Forty-Four hopped into the back, and I sat in the passenger seat. Even before I could properly close the door, Ghislain turned the ignition and floored the gas, revving the engine. The Volkswagen pulled out from the alley into the street as bullets punctured the metal hood and side of the car. "Get down!" Ghislain yelled, twisting the wheel. The car veered violently, then sped up, leaving behind our attackers.

"Why did you do that?" I asked.

"What?" Ghislain fixed his eyes on the road.

"The grenade!"

He glanced at me. "Do you believe they'll think twice before killing us?"

Soldiers deployed at every corner proved Ghislain's point as they opened fire against us. The Volkswagen crossed through lines of bullets, breaking the windshield and windows.

"Forty-Four, get down!" I screamed amid a rain of shattered glass.

Ghislain retaliated with his machine gun, granting us some cover. "Reload it!" He handed me the gun. "Magazines are on my back." He leaned over the wheel, creating a space between his back and the seat.

I glanced at the machine gun in my hands, perplexed; I had never held one before in my life.

"Now!"

I extended my left arm across Ghislain's back to reach the magazines stored at the left flank of his utility belt. I hunched to extend my reach, but as my fingers secured the magazine, Ghislain stomped on the brakes and the inertia propelled me into the dashboard. I craned my head above the dashboard to find out the reason for the sudden stop: a huge personnel truck towering over our tiny Volkswagen. *Scheisse, Reinhard has found us.*

"Hang on!" Ghislain switched gears swiftly and sped up, maneuvering the car to circumvent the truck. "Load the gun!" Ghislain reminded me as he drifted the Volkswagen in a zigzag down the street, to hinder the aim of the shooters.

"I don't know how!"

"First, press the button by the side to release the magazine."

I followed the instructions to replace the empty magazine.

"Now, pull back the cocking handle."

I did it, loading a bullet into the chamber, and turned to Ghislain with excitement.

"What are you waiting for?"

"What?" I asked, puzzled.

"Shoot! Shoot at the wheels of the truck!"

Oh my God! I do not know if I can—

"Noooooooooow!"

I took a deep breath and turned back. *You can do this, Emma.*

"Forty-Four, stay low." I jumped into the back seat. I secured the machine gun with both hands and propped the stock against my shoulder as Ghislain had done. Using the sight, I aimed at the truck's front tire through the rear twin windows of the Volkswagen, and I squeezed the trigger. I could hear nothing but the rattling mechanism, spitting the bullets amid continuous puffs of fire coming from the barrel. The stock compressed my shoulder joint every time the handle jolted. My collarbone ached terribly and my muscles pinched. Bullets in the magazine drained until the machine gun's cocking mechanism stopped, but the truck's armored tire exploded. The driver hit the brake and the truck spun on the road.

"Yes!" I crowed at leaving Reinhard's truck behind.

"No time to celebrate!" Ghislain rebuked, looking through the rearview mirror. The two Kübelwagens from the escort had joined pursuit of us, but unlike the heavy truck, they were faster and quickly paired with us. "Shoot them!"

"I'm out of ammo!"

A Kübelwagen slammed the Volkswagen's driver-side flank, pushing us off the road, but Ghislain controlled the car despite the wet pavement and veered the wheel back toward them, pushing them away. He drove the car across the bridge over the channel running parallel to the Lippe River.

"Get down!" Ghislain said.

I descried through the frame of the rear window the second Kübelwagen aligning behind us. A soldier stood and pulled his rifle over the windshield. I ducked before he opened fire. The bullets punctured the back of the Volkswagen, ricocheting inside the engine in the rear. Forty-Four and I screamed in terror in the back seat, eyes shut and covering our ears from the deafening clatter, until the engine blew and the fire ceased.

"Shit!" Ghislain exclaimed as he lost control of the car.

I raised my head to find the Kübelwagen at our flank, preparing to charge us, but this time it pushed our Volkswagen against the bridge railing, which didn't hold. During those brief seconds of the fall into the Lippe River, 44 and I levitated amid a shower of shattered glass and shrapnel. The Volkswagen plunged into the chilly waters. With all windows broken and the chassis full of bullet holes, the car flooded instantly. I had time only to hold my breath before immersion.

The current, augmented by the downpour, dragged us downriver. Ghislain struggled with the door until finally he kicked it open. He clasped my arm and pulled me out, and I hugged 44 against me. Ghislain towed us back to the surface, and I could breathe again. "Swim to the banks!" Ghislain ordered, helping me to remain afloat while holding on to 44's weight. I waded the last yards to the riverside, carrying 44 in my arms. I knelt on the sand, exhausted and coughing water out of my lungs.

"Are—are you all right?" Ghislain asked breathlessly.

We could not be all right until we were safe. The current had carried us who knew how far, but at least we found ourselves surrounded by vegetation. It seemed far enough from an imminent Nazi threat. The rainfall receded into a drizzle. *We survived after all.* I glanced down at 44, who still rested unconscious in my arms. "No, no, no!" I put him down, fearful he had breathed in water. "Forty-Four, wake up!" I bowed over to determine whether he was still breathing.

Forty-Four's eyelids opened, and his sleepy eyes stared at me, smiling. "Mama…"

Two red stains appeared on his cloak, and as they spread, the invisibility trick vanished, turning what I had thought was Renenet's special veil into a piece of ragged linen 44 had picked up from the laundry where we were hiding. My mind traveled back in time to when the SS soldiers knocked at Renenet's door, looking for us. *"We will play a game called hide-and-seek. Can you hide?"* she had asked 44 back then, and we'd turned invisible.

It never was Renenet. She knew 44's special ability. It had been 44 all this time… protecting us.

"My God…" I uncovered 44's torso with trembling hands, revealing two bullet wounds, one in his chest and the other in his belly.

"Hold the pressure!" Ghislain placed my hands on 44's wounds as he browsed his utility belt for first aid items to contain the hemorrhage.

"Mama!" 44 repeated with faltering voice.

"Yes, yes… Mama is here," I sobbed, witnessing how 44's blood pumped out through my fingers. "Don't worry, Son, you'll get well soon."

Forty-Four extended his arm, as if his chubby fingers wanted to trap the sun that had peeked timidly through the clouded horizon.

"Mama, you have come for me."

I glanced back to find what he was looking at so eagerly and caught sight of Sidney standing on the other shore of the river.

"No, no, no, look at me!" I said, terrified, knowing the reason for Sidney's presence.

Sidney walked on the water's surface without disturbing it, and he halted in the middle of the river. "Edelweiss, Edelweiss," he called. "Son, I've come for you."

"Edelweiss…" I whispered. "I had named him… Edelweiss." I pushed Ghislain aside and squeezed 44 against my chest, guilt corroding my entrails. I could have saved him from dying if I had only known his name… but he had saved me from Reinhard. "No, no! You will not take him from me! You hear me?" I screamed at the top of my lungs toward the river under the perplexed eyes of Ghislain. "Please! Don't listen to him! You will stay here… with me."

I kissed Edelweiss's forehead, but when I lifted my eyes, I saw him running on the water, heading toward Sidney. I waded into the river after his spirit, still carrying his body with me, but when the two souls met, I halted. Edelweiss hugged Sidney with an ear-to-ear grin, full of excitement… finally happy. Sidney smiled at him tenderly, showing an emotion that, for the first time, trespassed his impassive facade, and both walked away, hand in hand, until they vanished.

With my heart falling apart, my arms uncurled, releasing Edelweiss's lifeless body into the waters of the Lippe. "Edelweiss… find your way to Polaris." I swiped my hand across my face to remove my tears, but I only smeared it with his blood instead.

Ghislain held me while a piece of my heart sank into the murky depths of the river. "Swans," he said, breaking the long silence. Seven white swans had lifted off from the waters and hovered over the river. I stared at them with tearful eyes as they circled, until the last ray of sunlight extinguished.

CHAPTER 26

WE JOURNEYED BACK TO THE CHILDREN under a tunic of shadows. The night surveillance was tighter in Hamm, especially in the areas surrounding the Lippe River and the railway station, forcing us to detour around the periphery. Finally, we "acquired" a transport—or rather, Ghislain stole it—a *Lieferwagen* parked on the street.

"And how exactly do you plan to flee Hamm? We need a van," he'd responded when I confronted him, questioning the morality of the action.

I could not avoid feeling saddened that somebody was losing the means to support his family, even if it meant life or death for us. Ghislain drove through the quiet streets at the lowest speed possible and with headlights off to avoid calling the attention of the patrols.

It was well past midnight when we arrived at our hideout. When I opened the door, I crumpled to the floor at the sight of the children cowering in one corner of the room, hugging each other as they had when I'd found them locked inside the cell in the dungeon.

The children hesitated to approach me, staring with concerned eyes at the Nazi officer standing behind me.

"Don't worry," I reassured them. "Ghislain is a friend. He

helped me."

Jov approached timidly. I was gladdened to see him unharmed by the explosion his spectral being had undergone, but my excitement evaporated when I noticed traces of blood coming out of his ears.

"My goodness! Jov!" I held him close to me. "Are you okay?"

Jov's eyes turned aqueous. "I-I can't hear you," he said with trembling lips. Somehow the flames had not burned him, but the sound wave produced by the explosion had affected his ears. "I only hear a buzz."

"I'm—I'm… sorry… I-I've failed you…" My tears streamed uncontrollably. "I could not protect you… I could not save Edelweiss. If I just…" *If only I had not been caught*, I reprimanded myself with a phrase that would accompany me for the rest of my life, along with the image of Edelweiss's dead body dangling from my arms.

The children cuddled me until my breathing had eased and my tears dried on my face.

"It was the only way." Valeska caressed the dried blood smeared across my face knowingly. "He knew what would happen… yet he didn't hesitate for a second to go after you."

"But—but why? I didn't deserve his sacrifice…" I stammered. Just days ago, I was about to jump to my death from a window for failing to uphold the commandment for German women about keeping my body pure. I had betrayed my parents' trust and disappointed my best friends. My entire life was ruined, and I had lived my last few days expectant of the moment I could put an end to my misery. "Why would somebody sacrifice himself to save me? I am worth nothing…"

Ghislain's hands rested on my shoulders. "Don't say that… Am I not here?" He squatted by my side.

"Why? Why are you here?" I said incredulously, trying to grasp the reason behind his decision to sacrifice his military career and put his life on the line to save a traitor like me.

"Because you still owe me a dance, remember?"

His answer drew a small nostalgic smile to my face. I had promised him a dance at Gerda's wedding.

"Besides, they still need you," he said, glancing toward the children. "I have lost people dear to my heart. It consumes you from within. But despite the tragedy, keep going. Mourn your beloved by living. Those who truly loved you depart this world fulfilled in knowing you outlived them."

"How do you know?" I asked naively.

"Because I would," Ghislain said solemnly. "Now, go rest. I need all of you strong for tomorrow's journey. We leave before dawn."

"But we're hungry, Peach," said Jay.

"Oh my!" I pulled the groceries out of my bullet-holed brief-case. I'd wasted the milk during the chase, and the bread and frank-furters had been submerged in the waters of the Lippe. The black-berry jam, still in a sealed jar, was perfectly edible, and the cheese salvaged by peeling the exterior. "This survived. I'm sorry."

"Blackberry!" Their eyes grew in amazement, as if it were a delicacy.

"Please share it equitably," I instructed.

Ghislain sat on the floor, his back propped against the wall. He unbuttoned his jacket and shirt to examine the wound on his neck—the wound I had inflicted.

"Please, let me help you," I said, remorseful. I searched for a clean piece of linen I could use as a bandage and tore two strips from it. I filled an old bowl with hot water from the boiler.

"I'm fine, it's just a scratch," he said, minimizing it.

"Are you suggesting I am incapable of hurting you?" I submerged a piece of cloth in the water, then wrung it out.

Ghislain winced as I dabbed the wound carefully. "On the contrary, you nearly killed me."

"I didn't know it was you…" The person I was trying to choke to death. "I can't even conceive of what would have happened if I had… and found out later." Carrying the blame of one dead person for a lifetime was more than my conscience could bear. Considering carrying another was unthinkable. "Besides, I don't know what I would have done without you." I crisscrossed the strip of cloth around his neck and armpit three times and tied it with a knot.

"I thought solitude didn't scare you," Ghislain said, quoting our discussion from the wedding ceremony.

"Sometimes… when I fear losing people dear to my heart."

Ghislain smirked. "Don't move." He snatched the linen from my hand and, after dipping it into the water, gently cleansed my bloodstained face. "The dirt makes your skin paler," he whispered. "Now you can flaunt your pink cheeks to honor your nickname,

Peach." He stared at me with his sterling-gray eyes. "You have beautiful eyes."

My heart raced, and my breathing faltered. "I-I-I need to feed more coal." I got to my feet. "We don't want to freeze during the night," I babbled.

I dumped the remaining coal we had found inside the furnace. The black coal rested over the powdered bed of the ashen remains of the burned ones. As I poked them, I could not help but wonder how long it would take before we all burned and turned into ashes as well.

CHAPTER 27

A PAIR OF FIREFLIES REVOLVED close to the furnace with their green-blinking tails, lured by the flickering flames. I wondered how long before the allure turned deadly for them. I'd pretended to fall asleep to appease Ghislain, but the truth was I could not sleep, nor did I want to. Every time I shut my eyes, the same image was engraved on the interior of my eyelids—Edelweiss's motionless body dangling from my arms. I observed his image, expectant, waiting for his eyelids to open and look back at me, for his mouth to conjure his name and his extremities to reanimate, for him to run and jump around like he always did… but his image remained frozen in time. Vivid like a photograph but hollow and static as wax, submerged in an endless sleep from which nobody ever awakes. A dream we unequivocally call…

"Death." The word slipped through my lips.

As if I had pronounced an invocation, the pair of fireflies flew toward the adjacent room. The bugs plunged into darkness, flaring their location only now and then. As their air dance pulled them together, the next time they shone, they did not dim again; they remained static, as though pinned on a blackboard. As the twin green lights approached the door, they were lightning bugs no more, but a pair of alluring green eyes.

"You've been expecting me, I see," Sidney said with a velvet voice as he emerged from the shadows.

I sat and glanced around. The children were sound asleep, and Ghislain sprawled with his back resting against the entrance door, head hanging from his shoulders. I tiptoed to the doorjamb, careful not to step on anybody. I stood facing Sidney with fists and jaw clenched. I wanted to hit him, to scream at him. I wanted him to explain to me why—

"I don't know why," Sidney said calmly, as if he had listened to my thoughts. "You can still unleash your anger on me if that is helpful, but I can't answer questions to which not even I have an answer. I'm just the messenger, remember?" He pulled out the small leather book from his jacket pocket and turned the pages swiftly. "Only names are whispered to me. Nothing more."

"Whispered by whom?"

"Don't know."

I frowned with incredulity.

"Do you put a face to every voice you hear in your head?" he asked.

"I'm not crazy, wandering through the city deciding who deserves to die and who doesn't."

"I don't pass judgment on people."

"Then who does?" I asked, feeling irksome.

"They judge themselves."

"Cut the crap, these children were cursed," I echoed Renenet's words. "Thing is, they're too young to have cursed themselves... and they... just want to have a normal life... My God!" I pressed my forehead with the heel of my hand to contain the headache caused by my frustration. "Why are these kids so important, for Christ's sake?" I murmured, to avoid waking Ghislain and the kids.

"Do you want answers? Why don't you see them for yourself?" Sidney stepped back, returning to the realm of shadows. "Follow me."

I inhaled deeply before following the greenish twin stars into the darkness, arms extended before me, fearing I would collide with furniture at any second. But after thirty, forty, and even fifty steps inward, it never occurred. I glanced back to the doorjamb framing the boiler room, distant and aloft, like when you peek into the interior of an apartment through a window on the third floor of a building. However, I had walked without sensing the minor declination of the terrain. Looking down, I could see myself as clear as standing under the midday sun, but there was no source of light. If that was not odd enough, upon waving my fingers I realized my body didn't cast any shadow. This place was like a boundless void, so strange that standing over what I could tell was solid ground was my sole anchor to sanity.

A spark flared in the blackness and quickly combusted into a bonfire, but it was no ordinary bonfire; the flames were blue. The bonfire was twenty feet away from me, but even if I walked in its direction, the distance remained constant, as if at every step the soil between expanded in equal degree.

Sidney appeared by my side.

"Before the dawn of civilization, the Watchers descended from heaven…" he said, and the sky rumbled. Dark clouds were punctured by God rays, and humanoid figures descended through the blinding beams of light, arms wide open, as if crucified. "…in a time in which man and ape were barely distinguishable." A tribe of primitive humans pointed to the heavens, witnessing in awe the phenomenon that defied their understanding. "The Watchers taught men how to read the stars, how to speak and write, how to sow the fields, track time, and foretell seasons, how to produce fire and wage war, and when they were ready, they taught them about the occult."

As if I were strolling through a museum, I found myself surrounded by imagery of men and women learning the arts, as recounted by Sidney, in the style of Renaissance paintings. However, the faces of the Watchers were blurry, with indistinct features, as if they had shaken their faces faster than a camera shutter could capture them. Despite the nakedness of the celestial beings, I could not attribute any gender to their slender bodies. All had long hair—I would say waist-long—but it never fell over their shoulders; it appeared suspended in the air as if pulled up by an unseen wind.

"Within time," Sidney continued, "the Watchers' devotion to humanity fermented into love. And human wombs conceived offspring of beings that enraged the Will, who sent his angels to punish the Fallen." The visions presented a pregnant woman tied by her extremities to a wooden frame, as if it were a medieval torture device. But she was not being martyred; she was giving birth to a shapeless being under a rain of blood spewing from her vagina. Standing by the woman's side, a hunchbacked midwife assisted her.

"The Fallen were judged and condemned to perpetual imprisonment in everlasting sarcophagi." The landscape became a rocky gorge carved with huge human figures on both sides, facing each other. Each figure was holding different things, depicting each art taught to men. "The Valley of the *Grigori,* or the Valley of 'those who are awake,' who watch from day to night over humanity in silence, atoning for their sins, as their cursed offspring begotten with women, the Children of the Damned, prowl the earth… through millennia, until your epoch." Sidney turned to me. "Over generations, the seed has been diluted, yet the genes of the Grigori still run through the veins of humankind, recessive with most, but now and then, the gifts of the Grigori materialize in ill-fated children."

"Are my children descendants of the Grigori?" I asked in disbelief.

"Your children are bearers of the original sin—the deeds committed by the Fallen."

That explained the inhuman abilities I'd witnessed with my… own eyes… *scheisse.* "It's… it's my ailment…" I could not articulate the words. "Is the second sight that I suffer a curse from the Grigori as well?"

"It's hard to say." Sidney pondered. "The second sight can be a subtle remnant from the original seed, but it's not the only way to get it. People who traverse the threshold of death and return to their plane of existence will develop the second sight within time as well. *Once seen, it cannot be unseen.* Like how the primitive humans learned to see the Watchers, people peeking into the other side will never see the world as they once did."

The celestial conspiracy sounded so crazy that my mind struggled to digest the implications of what Sidney said. But there were still a lot of pieces that didn't fit into the puzzle. "Even if my children suffer this condition, what does this have to do with the Nazis? Why do they want to have them so desperately?"

"What do they gain?" Sidney asked rhetorically, and my mind traveled back in time to the dinner upon my arrival to Wewelsburg Castle.

"Übermensch," I said, remembering Von Schroeder's words.

"Could you imagine it?" Von Schroeder had said. *"A being with superior strength and reflexes, with outstanding psychic abilities, capable of bending the trajectory of a bullet in battle or manipulating the vital signs of his enemy and forcing him to surrender. Just imagine the possibilities of having the ca-*

pacity to control the elements or simply to possess a foe's mind to exert control over their body. There would be no more wars. Such could be the power of the Overman."

"To create the Overman." My mind flashed upon the medical documents I had extracted from Von Schroeder's desk. "They need my children… whatever is in their blood… this seed, the genes from the Grigori, to create the Overman," I answered myself. "But… but they need them alive."

"Correct." Sidney confirmed my chain of thought.

"But you come every night to tell me they're going to die." I frowned, confused. "Why?"

Sidney waved his arms, and the darkness surrounding the bonfire withdrew, unveiling where we had been all this time. I saw myself sitting on a pyramid of logs by Renenet's side. It was a memory, frozen in time, from the night I had spent with her. Renenet's carriage and horses were there as well, but no sign of Nailah and the children; I assumed they had already gone to sleep by that time. Everything was exactly the same, except the color of the fire. It was electric blue.

Sidney motioned his index finger as if conducting an orchestra, and the static image played like a vinyl record on the gramophone. *"We're all going to die,"* the version of me said, and repeated as if someone forced the stylus to play the same part again. *"We're all going to die."* Then Sidney halted the replay.

"The only difference is when," he explained.

"But you know when! And how! And… probably why."

"You have access to that information as well. But I wonder…" Sidney turned to me. "If you're so desperate to know, why haven't you asked her yet?"

"What do you mean?"

"Valeska," Sidney clarified. "The girl you so vehemently protect, she knows it. The gift—or curse—she inherited from the Grigori grants her the capacity to see the events of what you call the future."

Sidney was right; I knew it. I'd known since our escape from Wewelsburg. Valeska had even informed Edelweiss that in order to save me, he had to sacrifice himself…

"Are you afraid of what she might say?"

I shook my head as tears flooded my eyes. "I've never done it because…" I sobbed. "Because that would be like confessing I don't know what I'm doing or where I'm taking them. And—and as a mother, I cannot do that. A mother should always offer reassurance and direction… and—"

"Would you sacrifice everything for Nailah?" my voice in the recording interrupted me.

"She did sacrifice everything for me," played Nailah's voice, but she was nowhere in sight. I remembered she had been behind me, sitting on a mantel, playing with a deck of cards.

The recording paused.

"Even if you're willing, you can't sacrifice for those children or the children's children forever. The imprisonment of the Grigori will last until the heart of the last of their cursed descendants has ceased to beat." Sidney squinted. "Many had, have, and will have an interest in those children, either from this existence or from beyond."

The playing resumed. *"It's because of the Black S—"* my voice said.

"Don't you ever dare to call the Hidden One," Renenet interrupted, and the vision paused again.

The Black Sun, I thought, unable to comprehend what it really was, having as sole clue Renenet's aberrant impersonation. "There—" I was about to ask Sidney what I could do, when my recorded voice interrupted me again.

"What can I do?" I had asked.

Renenet's recording pointed in our direction, Sidney's and mine. We were standing on the overgrown road. The version of me in the vision stared directly at me now. I relived anew the crawling sensation up my spine I'd experienced that day. *"Leave and never look back,"* was Renenet's advice.

I confronted Sidney. "Why should I escape and run in fear?" I forgot to be intimidated by something or someone that was not even physical.

"Perhaps because what you search for has already found you," Sidney said in a sepulchral tone.

I turned to him, baffled, but he motioned his head toward the bonfire.

What I'd thought was a two-dimensional vision was in fact three-dimensional. I ambled around, trying to notice something out of place. My curiosity lured me to the version of myself. I didn't know if it was out of vanity, in the same way you observe yourself in a mirror, but standing there, I noticed something strange inside my unfinished bowl of soup resting on the logs. My faint reflection on the surface of the soup suddenly waved, as if a pebble had fallen inside. I tried to pick up the earthenware bowl, and to my surprise, I succeeded. I stirred the soup with the spoon and pulled out the contents: cauliflower, broccoli, carrots, and corn kernels, but as I continued stirring, the spoon became entangled in hair. First I thought it was corn silk, but as I pulled the spoon out, I realized it was human hair!

The bowl and spoon fell from my trembling hands, but despite hitting the ground, the bowl didn't break. The soup surged abundantly, spilling as if it were an entire pot. Tufts of black hair unfolded and spread upward like an upside-down jellyfish. A head found its way out from the bowl as if it were a portal. It resembled the elongated head of a horse, but when I tried to identify the features, my vision blurred, as if my eyes could not focus on it. Yet amid the fuzziness, eyes and mouth were recognizable, round, and hollow, like holes pinched in fabric.

I stepped backward, searching for Sidney, but he was nowhere to be seen.

A slender being finally came out, towering at least five times my height, and limbs sprouted out with a slimness almost insectoid. The being squatted on its long hind legs, bringing its head to my level, with its long hair suspended in the air, waving as if it were underwater. The being's arms were shorter, ending in eight-fingered hands with lengthy phalanxes, resembling the legs of spiders that crawled the ground after their prey… in this case, me.

From its mouth, a sound erupted that I could not identify as words. The spider-hands shot off after me, and I, as recommended by Renenet, followed the overgrown road back to where I'd come from, guided by the distant image of the boiler room framed in darkness. I glanced back as I ran for my life, heart throbbing in my ears. The creature was upon me, and at every stride of its slender legs, sharp-clawed feet stomped ahead of me, left, right, left, right.

The exit to this nightmarish world was within my grasp, but before I could reach the door, the spiderlike hands clasped around me and pushed me back. The wicked being groped me, and I squealed in despair, hoping Ghislain or the kids would wake up and attend my cry for help.

But they were sound asleep, unaware of the terrors that watched their sleep from the shadows, while a feeling of darkness weighed on my chest and hollowness gnawed my insides.

CHAPTER 28

I AWOKE SCREAMING.

Ghislain was jolting me. "You okay?" He wiped my sweating forehead. "Christ, you scared us to death."

The children stared at me with concerned eyes.

"I'm sorry I worried you," I said, holding my head. "I'm fine... I just... I had a nightmare..." My eyes moved as though magnetized to the dark doorjamb, wondering if it had really been a nightmare. But I could remember everything that happened vividly: the void, Sidney's recounting of the story of the Grigori, the visions, and, unfortunately, the frightening beast that hunted me. At the thought of it, my breath shortened, and I sensed something stuck inside my throat. I coughed violently, feeling my entrails squeezing to dispose something lodged deep in my stomach.

"Peach, are you all right?" Ghislain inquired.

I vomited a mixture of saliva and bile, but the object obstructing my pipe was still stuck in my throat.

"Peach! Peach!" the children cried in despair.

I shoved my fingers inside my mouth and pulled out the object. I gasped a mouthful of fresh air once my windpipe was clear but witnessed in horror the object lying on the floor.

It was a tuft of black human hair.

"My God," Ghislain said with preoccupied eyes. "You might have swallowed it without noticing in the river or sewers."

Or with the vegetable soup… I wondered with disgust, remembering my experience.

Ghislain caressed my back. "Please take your time, but we must get ready for departure. It's time now."

I got to my feet. I could not endure another hour, another minute, next to that room. "The sooner we leave this place, the better." I put on my BDM jacket, which I had left there the day before, and packed my belongings inside my briefcase.

The streets were deserted and the sky was dull, without the faintest snippet of light peeking out from the horizon. They were the same streets and the same sky I had seen just hours prior, upon our return to the hideout, but somehow, they felt different. As if days had elapsed. As if that void I visited had been not only a pit of horrors but a time machine as well.

We fled Hamm in the same way we arrived, hoping we had left all evils behind.

I must admit, the Lieferwagen Ghislain stole was a considerable upgrade to our means of transport. The children could travel more comfortably inside the cargo bay. It was secure, since it didn't have windows at the back, so no nosy eyes could spot the children from outside. It even had the perfect cover story: the sides of the van advertised *Lauterbacher Biere*, Lauterbacher Beer, since it was a delivery vehicle, and we even found a few cases of beer when we opened it, making it the perfect escape vessel.

"We'll head west," I said as I jumped into the passenger seat.

Ghislain observed me from the corner of his eye while hotwiring the engine. "Where in the west?"

"As far as we can. The Netherlands. I don't care."

"The Gestapo still has dominion over the Netherlands."

"France, then."

As we drove away from Hamm, we also left the carpet of clouds behind, which appeared pinned to the city's skyline. The country roads gleamed with sunlight. The view of trees and bushes on the shoulder of the road, combined with the wind massaging my face and blowing my dirty hair, was truly a blessing. Almost therapeutic.

Ghislain drove the van quietly, hardly uttering a word. The children in the back produced all the hubbub.

"I know I've already asked this," I said, breaking the silence. "But I really need to know. Why are you here? Why are you helping us?"

Ghislain glanced over me briefly, then his eyes returned to the road. "Your father asked me to."

I sighed hopefully. My father had fulfilled his promise of sending somebody to help me after all. "But why you? I mean, you're not his subordinate."

Ghislain shrugged. "I guess he deduced I would be in the vanguard of your search, led by Gruppenführer Schmidt."

Reinhard. I shuddered.

"After all, Schmidt is the confidence man of Obergruppenführer Von Schroeder. It was simple logic to assume I would be close enough to the action and have the possibility to solve things without suspicion."

"Solve things?" I echoed, remembering that last time my father tried to "solve things," pieces of Hermann's brain had splattered over my face.

"My mission was to find you, then I would address the situation to extract you without causing commotion and hide you in a safehouse until all this had ended."

"I don't believe that would have appeased Reinhard. He is too obsessive to let me go."

Ghislain turned to me, acknowledging with his silence that I was right about my assessment.

"This won't end until one of us is dead."

"Not necessarily. Reinhard's clock is ticking—everyone's clock is ticking. The war is approaching its end, and it doesn't seem we're on the winning side. You'll see it yourself once we're in the Netherlands. The front line is moving closer to the fatherland by the day. Your father accounted for this too. Keeping you hidden until the war ends is his priority."

"How long will that take?"

"It's difficult to tell." He shrugged. "Months… a year, maybe."

A year on the run? I considered. A few days had passed, and I'd been nearly killed a couple of times already. "I don't think I can endure that much—that we can endure that much," I corrected myself. "Now you're in this with us. You've become a traitor, just like me." I could tell by his expression Ghislain hated being associated with that word. "I'm sorry about it. The last thing I wanted was to drag people into my mess."

"That's the soldier's life: follow someone's orders and confront the consequences on their behalf."

"So, you followed my father's orders, then?"

"No, it was not an order. I owed him."

"What debt to my father would justify betraying your country?" I said, trying to make him elaborate more, but Ghislain didn't take the bait.

A moment later, he finally broke the silence. "I'm not."

"Yes, you are."

"I'm sorting things through," Ghislain said, more to himself.

Then I realized we were heading directly to a checkpoint at the outskirts of Bergkamen. "Where are you taking us through?" I asked, disconcerted, assuming he would know how to evade them.

"Don't even dare to move a muscle," Ghislain said as he decreased the speed. "Everybody back there, please be quiet."

I stuck my hand inside my briefcase and secured my letter opener, expectant of how things would unfold. At the boom gate stood two sentries chatting and smoking, with their rifles hanging from their shoulders. Ghislain stopped the car, and the sentries disposed of their cigarettes and approached us, one to each side.

"Sieg Heil!" greeted Ghislain.

"Sieg Heil," replied the sentry. "Papers, please."

Ghislain pulled out his documents, creased and stained after their immersion in the stagnant water.

The sentry squinted, battling to read it. "Brigadeführer Fleischer?" His eyes studied Ghislain's face and the papers, back and forth, having issues with matching his features to the watered-down picture.

"Affirmative."

Meanwhile, the second sentry approached my door holding his rifle, finger on the trigger and eyes fixed on me.

My chest tightened, and I clutched my knife. I followed the sentry's movements with unblinking eyes as he passed by, inspecting the Lieferwagen. His reflection in the mirror showed how he knelt and leaned over the ground to inspect the underside of the van. *Damn!* It was just a matter of seconds before he opened the back door and found the children inside. I thought about jumping out of the vehicle and attacking the sentry while he was on the ground, but my eyes darted to the stall by the side of the road, where a third soldier observed us. There was no way I could deal a blow without the aid of Ghislain, who was… chatting nonchalantly.

"…yes, I know Carl Meyer very well, from the Eighth SS Cavalry Division, right? Last time I heard, they were stationed in Hungary. But I've heard nothing from him since the Romanian front collapsed."

"Aye," the sentry agreed. "So, where are you heading, Brigadeführer Fleischer?"

"Dortmund," Ghislain said. "We carry precious cargo."

"*Weizenbier?*" the soldier asked, nodding to the beer label on the van.

"Let me show it to you." Ghislain jumped out of the van.

I shut my eyes. *What is he doing?* I pulled out my letter opener and held it close to my chest, expecting the worst.

"So, Corporal Fiegel…" Ghislain already knew the sentry's name. "You and the guys spend the whole day here, out in the rain and sun, far from your families, doing this important job to keep the Reich safe, and what do we do for you in return? Hmm?" he asked rhetorically. "We have abandoned you… So, as we were approaching, I said to myself, 'We need to share a couple cases of beer with these guys. It's the least we can do.'"

The back door of the Lieferwagen was pulled open.

Followed by silence.

An appalling silence.

I hopped out of the van, letter opener in hand, ready to confront the sentries, but then, laughter burst.

"*Danke! Danke!*" the sentries said, overlooking the children. They passed by my side carrying a case of beer each. I hid the letter opener behind my back.

Ghislain swung shut the back door of the Lieferwagen and returned to the wheel. "Get in," he said, peeking through the window. "I'm not betraying the fatherland. I just know what the fatherland needs," he said quietly, with a sense of accomplishment.

The cheerful sentries pulled up the boom gate, granting us passage.

"Please hurry," I murmured, hoping Ghislain would floor the gas and leave the checkpoint as soon as we could. But Ghislain turned to me with puzzled eyes.

"Oh, wait… I forgot." He descended from the vehicle and headed toward the sentry and asked for a cigarette, which was happily provided.

"Was that really necessary?" I asked him, upset, when he returned.

"What?" Ghislain drew a mouthful of smoke as he started the van. "Relax. I have it under control."

I rolled my eyes.

"What were you thinking to accomplish with that knife?" he asked, glancing at my hand still clutching the letter opener.

"You mean like yesterday in the sewers, when I nearly killed you?" I responded archly.

"Feel proud. This time you were about to get us all killed, not just me." Ghislain smirked.

But this time his smile triggered the opposite effect in me from the usual glee. Furious, I snatched the cigarette from his mouth and hurled it onto the fast-moving road.

"Don't smoke in front of the children."

All six children were behind us, listening to our quarrel.

Ghislain chuckled. "Are you really mad at me?"

"No," I responded dryly, glancing toward the passing greenery out the window.

We went silent for most of the rest of the journey.

Ghislain followed a route across Lünen, Recklinghausen, Gladbeck, and Dinslaken. At every checkpoint, Ghislain knew a shortcut to bypass it or was an acquaintance of the sentry or a sentry's relative, or he devised an inventive way to convince the sentries to grant us passage, just as he had done at Bergkamen Checkpoint, which raised my suspicions about him. Crossing the country seemed so easy and perfect with him at the wheel.

Could Ghislain be deceiving us and still working under Reinhard's orders? He had risked his life for me back in Hamm, there was no doubt about it, but there was something elusive about this easiness in traveling. *Maybe it's just his connections, built during all his years in the SS.* But his attitude was also confusing. *"I'm not betraying the fatherland,"* he'd said, and, *"I'm sorting things through."*

Am I becoming paranoid? I wondered, observing Ghislain speaking seriously on the phone at one of our stops for gasoline in Dinslaken.

"It's decided," Ghislain notified me upon his return. "We'll take a rest in a safehouse in Kleve before crossing to the Netherlands through Nijmegen. Intelligence expects that the enemy attack will engage far south, through Düsseldorf and Duisburg. It's the safest option for us."

"Says who?" I asked, questioning the label of "enemy." Perhaps the best thing that could occur was for us to be "rescued" by the so-called enemy, as the proverb stated: *The enemy of my enemy is my friend.*

"My informant." Ghislain turned to me. "Why?"

No names. I'd hated military hermeticism since my infancy. I'd had to deal with it from my father and Anton as well.

I crossed my arms. "I'm not sure how trustworthy your sources are."

"Unfortunately, they're the only sources I have. So, unless you have a better idea, that's where I'm heading."

I had no better plan.

We continued heading north, parallel to the Rhine River until Wesel, where we crossed to the west bank of the river and continued farther north to the city of Kleve. As we approached the city, the landscape changed. Military forces were everywhere, but despite my growing concerns, Ghislain tried to appease me.

"The forces stationed here are *Luftwaffe*, Second Parachute Corps, if I'm correct. Believe me, they have greater concerns to worry about than a bunch of deserters."

"Why are you so sure?"

"We're weeks away—days, even—from this place being ravaged by war."

I listened to Ghislain's words while observing civilians ambling along Kleve's streets, mixing with the uniformed men, trying to have a normal life.

"We're approaching the front line, and here, soldiers desert all the time."

"But what about the children?" I wasn't concerned about my future as a traitor—I already knew there was only one.

"Hermann Göring's Luftwaffe doesn't have an interest in the

children, simply because they are ignorant of their existence. These children are a secret jealously kept by Himmler and his SS staff."

I turned to Ghislain, skeptical about that. It felt as if the entire Reich were after us.

"Secrets. Everything is about secrets. Envy and conspiracy proliferate the most among the highest ranks in the Reich. Treachery is not a sin if you win the favor of the Führer."

Ghislain returned my look as I battled to digest the workings of a world that at my young age I failed to comprehend.

"Our sole threat is the SS," he continued. "The closest detachment to this place is the Second SS Panzer Corps, stationed in Brummen, Netherlands, some thirty kilometers north from here… We'll be all right. Don't worry."

Despite his encouraging words, I struggled to believe we would blend among the crowd and nobody would care about us. But, anyway, did we have any other option? Unfortunately, every time I asked the question, the answer never changed.

Ghislain drove past Kleve into the river marshes surrounding the village of Niel, in Kranenburg, just a couple of miles away from the Dutch border.

Humid grasslands composed the landscape, which seemed regularly flooded by the rising river. Thickets of willows and elms surrounded the pastureland, the sole remnant of what was once a dense forest. Settlers had cut down the trees to parcel the land, erect farms, and build an intricate system of water channels sprouting from the Rhine River.

Barley fields shone gold under the sunlight as the Lieferwagen crossed the dirt roads. Staring at the landscape calmed my nerves, feeding the illusion I was returning to the safety of my grandfather's farm. Far from the violence and madness prevailing in the world. Away from the evil and the wicked who enjoyed inflicting pain on others.

"Birds!" the children shouted at the sight of a flock of birds circling above us.

"What are they? Godwits?" Ghislain leaned over the wheel, glancing upward.

"*Sie sind Krähen,*" Valeska said, unexcited.

I poked my head out through the window and turned to the sky. Dozens of ebony-feathered birds glided along with us. Catching sight of me, the birds produced shrill caws.

"You were right, Valeska." I returned to my seat. "They're crows."

"Why are they following us?" Ghislain asked. "Crows are not endemic to this region."

"They escort us," Valeska explained.

"Escort us to where?" I asked.

The crows glided toward a country house at the end of the lane, where they perched atop a brick chimney jutting above the tiled roof.

"Is that gloomy house our safehouse?" I inquired of Ghislain dubiously.

"It seems so."

"Have you ever been here before?"

"No. But being dark and abandoned is a good thing."

"How is that?"

"You said it yourself. We're traitors, and under this regime, in order to stay alive, traitors should hide even from sunlight."

I couldn't stop thinking about the Jewish family I'd found living in the dark basement below the ruins of the building.

Are we fated to live like that? I shivered, fearful of what I was slowly becoming.

A cockroach.

CHAPTER 29

A STRONG CURRENT CAUSED BY yesterday's torrential rain flowed through the water channel, spinning a big paddle wheel attached to a mill at the side of the cowshed where Ghislain had hid the Lieferwagen.

"No windmill?" I asked.

"What do you mean?" Ghislain frowned, puzzled.

"Are not windmills a signature of the Dutch lowland landscape?"

"Yes… but what is your point?"

"Well, this house looks… out of place." I pointed at the double-hung windows and the fancy portico of the three-story house that didn't really match the architecture of other houses and farms we had passed on our way here.

"Nobody can pluck a house from a place and sow it somewhere else." Ghislain sighed. "Unfortunately, there's no other option at hand. Unless you want to sleep in the van or the fields, better get used to the idea."

Ghislain climbed the steps to the portico, where a rocking chair moved gently in the wind. "Let's see if I got it right."

I assumed he was referring to the instructions he'd received during his phone call. Ghislain counted the timber planks and stomped on one next to a rocking chair, which creaked as he pressed it with his boot. He knelt and, using the pads of his fingers, pulled out the plank.

"Be careful," I said as he stuck his arm in the hole.

Ghislain retrieved a set of dirty keys, and after repositioning the plank, he unlocked the front door. "Shall we go in?"

"What do you think?" I asked the children. "Do you think it's safe?"

"Yes! Let's go in!" Jay, Hoshi, and Manu responded enthusiastically.

I eyed Valeska. "Should we go inside?"

She finally assented, but clutched her brother's arm as we walked across the threshold.

Contrary to my judgment from the outside, the interior was cozy. The furniture was made of leather and cedar. Wood panels covered the lower half of the walls and straw-yellow wallpaper ran up the top half to the coffered ceiling. I expected to find Nazi paraphernalia garnishing the entire place, but the predominant decoration comprised crucifixes and small holy relief sculptures. Too many even for a devout Christian.

"Was the last tenant a priest?" I asked.

"No idea," Ghislain said, inspecting the chimney.

"Or maybe a writer." I caught sight of a Simplex typewriter in front of a leather armchair in the living room. Despite being loaded with a red ribbon, the page inserted was blank, just like the pile of sheets beside it. As if someone had planned to write a novel but had left suddenly before starting it. Judging by the thickness of the dust covering the furniture, I guessed the house had been uninhabited for around a year.

The lush staircase had handrails carved out of cedar, and an extravagant chandelier hung from the ceiling, with details in cut glass and plated with gold instead of gilt brass.

On the second floor, the door facing the stairs revealed an enormous bathroom lined with black-and-white marble tiles, a double sink, and a white bathtub. My eyes grew with excitement as I imagined taking a much-needed bath, with hot water, after so many days on the run.

I swung every door open, unveiling four bedrooms, and at the end of the corridor, the last door led to the master bedroom. My reflection welcomed me on an ornamented oval mirror hanging above a dressing table. I wrinkled my nose at my disheveled clothes and frizzy hair. On the table I found a brush raveled with auburn hair. "A woman's hair," I deduced. A golden crucifix on the nightstand called my attention. The eyes were hollow, as if somebody had used a nail to puncture two holes where the eyes should be. I grabbed a Bible lying next to the crucifix and sat on the four-poster bed, which was covered with a padded wool quilt, making it very comfy. When I browsed the Bible, I noticed all pages of the first five books—from Genesis to Deuteronomy—were crossed from corner to corner with red ink strokes. I preferred to leave the book the way I found it and walked to a mahogany wardrobe. I pulled the double doors open. It was full of clothes. I shuffled the clothes and realized with excitement it held both mens- and womenswear. I took out a light reddish-brown chemise dress and superimposed it over my figure in front of the mirror. It hung from my shoulders to my knees, the waist aligned with mine. It had flower-patterned embroidery around the V-shaped collar. The dress was old, like the ones worn by my mother during her youth in the 1920s. It reminded me of a photo of my parents during their honeymoon in Paris. My mother was wearing a dress like this, hugging my father; both seemed thrilled, and in the background stood the Champs-Élysées.

My lips arced with joy, wondering if a matching cloche hat was inside the wardrobe. I could finally be rid of my BDM uniform, which, putting the filthiness aside, I didn't feel comfortable wearing anymore.

Heading back to the wardrobe, I glanced through the curtains of the window; the sun was sinking, fuzzy like a lighthouse on a distant shore, surrounded by an ocean of clouds flooding the grasslands, dispelling the trees' and shrubs' cut-out shapes under a golden veil of haze.

"Peach! Peach!" The voices of my children broke my trance. "Peach, hurry!" they were calling from downstairs. I rushed across the corridor and down the stairs, following their voices to the kitchen as if their lives depended on me.

"What's happening?" I asked upon my arrival.

"Look!" The kids presented what they'd found in the cupboards: packages of pasta, lentils and peas, cans with tomato sauce, sardines, grape and pineapple juice, and even V-8 vegetable juice, among plenty of other things. "Look at all the food here!" They bounced around, as gleeful as if they had found a treasure. Given the deplorable conditions they had endured in the past, they certainly had.

"There is even wine!" Ghislain said, holding the bottle aloft as if it were a trophy.

I rejoiced, knowing that, at least for as long as we stayed in this house, my children would not suffer hunger.

CHAPTER 30

THAT EVENING, WE HAD A FEAST. Ghislain cooked spaghetti Bolognese with the ingredients available, substituting the beef with canned pork, but considering the recent standard of meals we'd been having—if we ate food at all—this tasted like paradise. I cooked a simple soup with a mixture of lentils and peas, imitating Frau Weber's cuisine as I'd observed from moseying through the kitchen. For beverage, we had wine, with grape juice as the equivalent for the children, of course.

"Do you like it?" I asked the children at the large dining table.

"It's tasty!" declared Jay, his mouth smeared with red sauce.

"I want more!" Hoshi said, waving his spoon.

"Of course! You can eat all you want." I reached for the pot and poured a ladleful of soup. "I'm glad you like it. We prepared it with much dedication especially for you." I glanced at Ghislain, sitting opposite me at the head of the table. He smiled mildly.

"Forty-Four would have loved it!" Manu said.

I froze.

"He loved lentils," he added quietly amid the sepulchral silence.

The children cast their eyes to their plates when they met mine, feeding my guilt. But I had nowhere to look. I was literally surrounded by incriminating stares. Hundreds of tiny portraits of a multitude of people upholstered the dining room walls. The portraits were so close together that the straw-yellow wallpaper in the back was almost invisible. It looked like a record of mugshots, making me wonder if police officer was the proper occupation of the last tenant of this house, or photographer, perhaps? Maybe they were not criminals… maybe I was the criminal, and they were my jury. Hundreds of incriminating pairs of eyes staring at me all at once, declaring in unison, *"Edelweiss's death was your fault."*

"I know… it's my fault." I put the pot aside, rather brusquely, shaking the entire table. "Everything is my fault!"

Manu started crying, and I gasped out loud.

Ghislain tried to calm me. "Peach, he didn't mean to say that."

I shut my eyes and shook my head to clear my thoughts. "I know… I'm sorry." I extended my arms. "Please, come here."

Manu stood from his chair and ran around the table to find his way to my arms.

"I'm sorry," I whispered as I caressed his head.

"I'm sorry, Peach…" Manu babbled.

"No. I'm the one to blame."

"Come, kids." Ghislain rose from the table. "Bring your plates. Let's wash the dishes together."

"Go with your siblings." I tapped Manu's back.

The tiny troop marched to the kitchen, leaving me in the company of the unfamiliar faces decorating the walls. All photos displayed serious faces, not even the slightest smile. But among all, one picture drew my attention, drawing me closer for further examination. The photo was of a mature man, probably in his forties or fifties, with a pointy mustache and a scruffy beard, nothing extraordinary about him. The uncommon part was the face of a woman showing behind him, over his left shoulder. The image of the woman was faint, seeming almost phantasmagorical, blending with the sepia tonality of the background. I examined other photos, trying to identify a similar pattern that might prove the effect was just a byproduct of the background, but there were none. All were clean.

"Maybe I'm the only one able to see her," I said, discouraged, as a sufferer of the second-sight disease. *Maybe all these people are already dead.* I abandoned the dining room before my unhinged thoughts could creep out from the drawers I'd locked them in.

I had to cleanse my mind, and what better way to do it than with a hot bath? The so-desired hot bath we all desperately needed. Ghislain shoveled coal and ignited the boiler in the kitchen, and the pipes conducted the hot water to the tub on the second floor. I bathed the children by turns. First Manu, Lemuel, and Hoshi, and once they were clean, I dressed them in clothes I'd found in the wardrobes of the different rooms. I found no children's sizes, but I did my best to roll up the cuffs of the trousers to avoid them tripping. "Tomorrow, I'll stitch them, I promise," I said, helping them jump into bed.

"Peach!" Jay's voice came through the bathroom door. He was taking a bath with Jov. "The water is getting cold!"

"I'll ask Ghislain to shovel more coal!"

I headed downstairs, but I couldn't find Ghislain inside the house. When I walked to the portico, I found him sitting on the rocking chair, writing in a small book. "Ghislain?" I asked, interrupting his concentration.

Surprised, he closed the book and tried to conceal it, clumsily. "Yes?" he said, trying to sound as normal as possible.

"What is that?"

"What?"

"The book you're holding."

"Oh! This…" Ghislain brought it forward, eyeing it as if it were the first time he had seen it. "It's—it's just a notebook I found in the cupboard… used to jot down recipes, lists of ingredients, and things of the sort."

The lie was obvious. Ghislain rarely hesitated in his words. *What could be written inside that notebook that would make him behave like this?* I wondered, realizing after events I'd confronted, I'd grown skeptical of all men, starting with my father. But this time, I played along.

"I didn't know you were into writing."

"Neither did I," Ghislain said, his eyes fixed on the pitch-darkness. "But something about the peace of this place triggered the desire to jot down my thoughts."

Ghislain was right; an unnatural peace surrounded this place. I could hear no sound: no military trucks passing nor airplanes flying over, no crows cawing or insects chirping; water had stalled in the channel, and not even the wind dared to howl. It appeared as if we were insulated from the world, and there was nothing beyond the curtain of darkness around us. Not even the stars or the moon dared to shine, and only our outlines cast by the lights over the scrub confirmed something existed beyond the wooden steps of the house. The calmness brought about by not having to worry about anything in the world was spellbinding. The more I thought about it, the more alluring it became.

"I've been thinking we should stay here for a couple of days." Ghislain picked up his glass of wine from the floor and sipped. "After everything you and the children have gone through, some days of sedentary life in the countryside will suit you well. Don't you think?"

I pondered his proposal, leaning over the banister. Ghislain joined me, a glass of wine in hand.

"I don't know," I said, sighing. I could not fathom the idea that all of a sudden we found ourselves freed from persecution just by hiding in the middle of nowhere. The tentacles of the SS extended across the globe, and nothing would dissuade Reinhard from seeking vengeance. But the truth was, this was the best we had been since we escaped from Wewelsburg. My children could enjoy tasty meals, hot baths, clean clothes, and sleeping on comfy mattresses.

"I thought you enjoyed the country life," Ghislain said.

"What made you think that?" I asked, remembering how I missed my days in Berlin.

"You radiated happiness the day you romped into my life. Remember?"

Romped? I blushed, remembering Ghislain had observed me sprinting from the barn into my grandfather's house, jumping over my imaginary hurdles.

"I remember." I stared into his sterling-gray eyes, as I had that day, brightened by the sun, now darkened by the night sky. That moment seemed so distant, like night and day, as if all those fond memories belonged to a previous life.

"Your cheeks were pinker than usual, making your eyes look like lapis lazuli under the sunlight, beaming with determination. You balanced gracefully at each jump as if you were about to rise through the skies. I thought I would die that day, incapable of finding a different reason why I was being visited by the most beautiful of Valkyries."

Ghislain's comment sparked a smile on my face. "You asked, 'From whom are you running away?' but Valkyries run from no one. They are fearless warriors. Me, on the contrary… I run all the time."

"But you never answered my question."

"That's because my mother interrupted us, but honestly, even if she hadn't, I didn't really know what to say…" I sighed; my hands clung to the banister. "But looking back… I think… all my life I have been trying to run away from my fate. Away from my mother's desires of me becoming the perfect mother. From my constant struggle of succeeding in the footsteps of my brother to gain my father's admiration. From having to prove to anybody that I'm the perfect daughter, the perfect sister… the perfect woman." *The perfect mother…* I didn't have the guts to dare say it.

Ghislain gently pulled my chin to face him. "Maybe you're not running away, but running toward your destiny."

"What would my destiny be, then?"

"What waits for you at the finish line?" Ghislain whispered with a silken voice as he approached me, the tips of our noses rubbing.

"I don't know what—"

"It was me waiting for you at the finish line…" Ghislain sealed my lips with his.

I closed my eyes as a stream of sensations invaded my whole being, satiating every cell in my body with an intoxicating substance that made me forget who I was and where I was.

It felt like the elation of climbing to the podium for the first time. The fullness of my mother's praise. The comfort of my father's hug. The excitement of playing children's games with Anton. All of that together, but none at the same time. It was different. Or maybe I was different. At my tender age, it felt like love.

It didn't matter how beautiful and pure the feeling was; fate mocked me once again. At the moment Ghislain clasped my waist and pulled me toward him, my mind played the awful memories I thought I had overcome but which were in fact lurking below the surface, hidden in plain sight. Ghislain's soft touch reminded me of Reinhard restraining me against my will. My ghosts transformed Ghislain's gentle lips into Reinhard's lewd tongue crawling over my skin. Ghislain's embrace turned claustrophobic as my mind evoked the painful sensations of Reinhard forcing himself on me.

I could not bear it anymore. I pushed Ghislain away, unwinding myself from his arms.

"What happened?" Ghislain inquired.

I waved a dismissive hand and walked away from him.

"Emma, what's wrong?" He held my arm.

"Please... don't." Tears ran down my cheeks. I thought about explaining everything to him, but my mouth could not dig out the words I'd buried under six feet of silence, that I'd hoped would remain that way for the rest of my days. "Just... don't... please."

I frowned at him coldly, and as Ghislain released my arm, so did the oppression congesting my chest.

"Forgive me, please," he said, despite not having anything to apologize about. Being with him was what my heart craved the most, but it was equally painful at the same time.

"Ghislain... I-I..."

He turned to me with his eyes sparkling in hope... but I cowed.

"...I still need to bathe Valeska. Could you please feed the boiler?"

Ghislain assented solemnly, lips pursed.

I walked inside the house, convinced that my inevitable fate was to die alone.

CHAPTER 31

"IS THE WATER HOT ENOUGH?" I asked Valeska, sitting on the edge of the bathtub while I massaged her foamy head with the pads of my fingers.

"Yes. You should not try too hard, I'm bald anyway." Their hair had been close-cropped to avoid lice.

"But it's already growing!" I said overenthusiastically. "Soon you'll have long, beautiful hair!"

But Valeska remained downhearted.

"What? Don't you like long hair?"

"I had waist-long hair before our kidnapping."

A lump formed in my throat. "You remember your life before the incident." I had nearly forgotten most of my memories from when I was younger than her.

She nodded. "I remember everything… Mommy and Daddy and my sister… our house, the cattle, the forest…" she recounted as she played, reshaping the foam with her tiny hands.

I sat beside the tub, resting my folded arms over the edge. "Do you remember the first time you realized you were special?"

Valeska turned to me, puzzled. "You mean cursed?"

I didn't know what to say.

"It's okay; you don't need to say anything. I know what it is. But no… I don't know when it started. For me, it's been like this since I can remember. I grew up believing it was normal that all days repeated more than once, and that everybody experienced it that way. I enjoyed celebrating my birthdays multiple times though… so many birthdays that I should be an old woman by now." Valeska giggled, but her joke carried an immeasurable truth. She indeed had the wisdom of an elder.

"But then…" I hesitated and rested my head on my arms. "You knew evil men would come after you and your siblings, yet you went to play hide-and-seek with them on that day?"

She nodded. "I'd seen my life from birth to death so many times that I'd forgotten."

"But why didn't you say anything to your parents? I mean, they could have done something!" I frowned with frustration.

"Do your parents listen to you?"

Remembering my experiences, I could not argue.

"But anyway, there was nothing I could have done to avoid it."

"But what about forging our future? About free will? Can we change nothing?"

Valeska turned to me briefly, then returned to her play. "If a tree drops a leaf on the river, it doesn't matter the direction the wind is blowing. It will fall down the waterfall anyway."

Valeska's words reminded me of our fall into the Lippe River inside the Volkswagen. The unavoidable current of destiny carried us, rendering our efforts to keep Edelweiss alive meaningless. "But what if you swim against the current?"

"Then you suffer. Regardless of your actions, the current will carry you to the place where you ought to be."

"But then what is the purpose of all this?" I stared at her, baffled, unable to accept the way the world works.

"To experience it."

"To experience it despite what you've suffered?" I knew better than anyone the terrors to which Reinhard had subjected Valeska, and I could not share her optimism about envisioning a painful future.

She smirked. "And to be here with you."

I frowned.

"I've been familiar with your face since I was very little. I've seen it so many times. All my life I've waited to meet you."

My heart cracked from the inside.

"When we lost our parents, Jov was saddened, but I encouraged him by saying that soon we would have a new mother who would care for us as nobody had done before. So my brothers survived locked in that cell, clinging to the hope that one day, a girl with a heart of gold would take us with her and we would have nothing else to fear."

Her words made me remember my first encounter with Jov. *"Are you our mother?"* he had said back then. I could not wrap my mind around somebody I didn't know being so happy and eager to know me, despite all my flaws and mistakes. "But—but you still have everything to fear…" My voice broke. "I don't know what I'm doing, nor what to do to save you! I'm lost… and I feel like I'm just dragging you with me into perdition…"

"We're not asking you to give us something you don't have." Valeska caressed my head. "Because everything you have, you have already given it to us."

"But…" I sobbed.

"You gave Edelweiss the kindness and devotion he'd never had. Despite the suffering he went through in his life, he left this world happy, knowing he was loved at least once."

"I didn't do enough." The image of his lifeless body dangling from my arms still hurt like a raw wound.

"Nobody but you made him feel loved, special."

I remembered Edelweiss's radiant face when I played with him. For the first time in a long time, I felt a pinch of warmth inside my chest, realizing I had helped him to fill the void of love left by his biological mother.

It made me smile.

"Don't worry about the future." Valeska squeezed my hands. "You'll live long enough to have children of your own and suffer the aches of old bones." She said this with nostalgic eyes. "What a loving mother you will be… I'm already jealous of them."

I chuckled. "We'll get old together, I promise."

"I'm already old!" Valeska said, showing me her wrinkly fingers. "See? Time to get out!"

"Oh! I see!" I wrapped her in a towel and helped her rub her hair. "I hope when I get older, I can be as wise as you."

She smiled.

"Do you want me to help you dress?"

"I can do it by myself. Now it's your turn to take a bath," she said, heading to the door.

Children of my own… I undressed myself, thinking about what had happened earlier with Ghislain. *How could I?* I entertained the idea of one day getting married, but how could I possibly if every time I was kissed and made love to it rekindled the pain inflicted by Reinhard? Eternally haunted by the phantom pain of the wounds.

I plunged in and lay on the bottom of the tub, hoping the water and soap could rinse away not only the dirt on my body but also from my soul. It was invigorating, scrubbing my body and washing my hair after so many days. Once I finished, I leaned back against the tub, with no intention of getting out until the skin of my fingers and toes had wrinkled like Valeska's did.

Children of my own… I considered this again, but after what I had gone through, I could not see myself becoming a mother. *Adopt the children, perhaps?* If we survived, of course… Maybe we could find a house like this one… farm the land… Maybe Ghislain could help me… Building a home. A home with Ghislain. And maybe… within time…

Emma, you can't! I scolded myself. *I won't have a place to call home ever again. I'll never know what loving passionately feels like, get married, or have children… ever! And if that does happen… it's only because one is already growing inside me…* I panicked, remembering that another day had gone by without having my period. I recalled the nightmare I had. Walking into Wewelsburg dungeon, my pregnant belly, and the poking hands, feet, and demon tail of… a monstrosity, just like the father. *Reinhard… Damn you… A thousand times damn you.* I cursed his name until exhaustion. How could I carry and give birth to a product of rape? How could I even look my parents in the eye to share the news if I ever saw them again?

No. I was not strong enough to stand before my parents. I would have to lie to them and to everyone else… but to do it convincingly, first I had to lie to myself and to the unfortunate being in my womb… but I lacked the strength. I was weak. I was nothing like Valeska. I could not see the blue sky behind the dark clouds, no matter how hard I tried.

I sighed, wishing I could have Valeska's resilience.

I submerged my head, thinking maybe it was best to keep running from my destiny… *But how do I run away from something I carry with me?*

The window… I thought of the window leading to the precipice at Wewelsburg. *Just one step to end it all.* Or I only had to wait here, immersed in water until my lungs ran out of oxygen... But when I was close to fainting, a force erupted inside me to hold on to life. I resurfaced, gasping and agitated, but as I regained my calm, I reached for my towel and came out from the tub.

As I dried myself, I noticed carmine speckles tainting the towel whiteness, and rubbing the sticky substance between my fingers, I realized it was blood. *My blood.*

And that night, amid my sobbing, I welcomed my period.

CHAPTER 32

THE NEXT MORNING, I WOKE EARLY. I was not drowsy; on the contrary, I felt reenergized. I wondered if it was merely the effects of a bath or sleeping on a decent bed after so many days on the road. *Maybe it's all of that combined*, I concluded. I stared at the nightstand and frowned. The golden crucifix was missing. I searched under the bed, fearing I had pushed it off during my sleep, but I could not find it.

I gave up the search, and after a quick toilet to take care of the mess of my period, I opened the wardrobe, excited by the riches within. I dressed myself with the light reddish-brown chemise I'd found yesterday. It was quite a challenge to fit inside the cloche hat, given the frizzy nature of my hair, but once I tamed it, I loved the hat. I walked down the hallway pompously, waiting to be seen in my new outfit, but to my surprise, everyone seemed still asleep. The house was quiet as a tomb. Heart squeezing, fearing that something bad had happened, I peeked inside the rooms and confirmed the children were sleeping. Finally, when I arrived at Ghislain's room, the door was ajar. The bed was made, and his SS uniform rested on top, perfectly folded. I ran my fingers over the fabric, remembering my father. He had the same devotion to his uniforms, to the point of refusing somebody else polishing his boots. It occurred to me that Ghislain could have abandoned us. I rushed down the stairs and circled the house, but my search for him turned futile. Outside, it was cold. The fields were still velvet with the morning mist, the sun not yet showing. The rocking chair was vacant and I found no trace of Ghislain.

Did he really leave? I sighed and sat on the chair. I rocked, the planks creaking beneath me, pondering whether my attitude last night had driven him away. "Alone again," I said, believing we were back on our own.

A silhouette appeared on the road. It was a man pulling a wheelbarrow. I walked down the steps of the portico to have a better look, and as the man approached, the mist revealed Ghislain, dressed as a civilian.

"What are you doing?" Puzzled, I observed the contents of the wheelbarrow: flowers, dirt, and a shovel.

"Reinstating the garden." He drove the wheelbarrow to the side of the house, where an abandoned garden was hidden by the undergrowth.

"Where did you get the flowers?"

"I saw them growing on the shoulder of the road on our way here." He unloaded the wheelbarrow.

"But why are you fixing the garden? We're not planning to stay long."

He began weeding with a hoe. "You said it yourself. This is a gloomy house, and nothing brings more life to a place than a garden." Ghislain grunted, battling to pull out a deeply rooted weed. "Even if we leave today, the next tenants will have a nicer view. Don't you think?" He ran his forearm across his forehead, drying the droplets of sweat that had condensed. "Besides, you like flowers too, right?"

"Why do you say that?"

"Maybe judging by the flowered print on your dress?" Ghislain looked at me from the corner of his eye as he dug the holes. "You look beautiful."

"Thank you." My heart bloomed at the fact he had noticed.

"The other day on the banks of the Lippe, you called the boy Edelweiss."

"Edelweiss..." I whispered. "We came across an edelweiss while we wandered the outskirts of Lippstadt, pretty rare. I gave it to him, and it made him so happy... It looked like he'd never been so happy… Maybe he'd never received a present before…" I turned gloomy.

Ghislain turned to me. "Do you know what giving an edelweiss to a loved one means?"

I shook my head.

"It's a promise of dedication."

This made me felt guiltier about failing my promise of dedication to Edelweiss. "I think he would have loved this house…" I glanced around, my eyes turning watery. "He liked to run and romp and…" My throat tightened as I imagined him playing in the fields.

"Peach." Ghislain held my hand. His was grubby with wet dirt, but I loved the smell. "You did everything you could. And I know that if his life had been in your hands… you would have traded yours instead."

I gulped.

Maybe I had the opportunity, I thought, remembering Sidney's words about Lazarus's medallion. All I had to do was pick him, take Edelweiss's place in the Pilgrimage of Death, and now he would be alive… but back then I could not tell who among my children was next to die, since all were cursed. I wished the next to die was me. My soul was not worthy enough that my sacrifice could account for all the souls of my children. But at least my death would free me from the suffering of losing another.

Sidney… I had not seen him since our last night in Hamm. *Did he visit me last night?* I could not remember. After taking the bath, I'd gone straight to bed and fallen asleep as soon as I closed my eyes.

"I wish I could find edelweiss flowers in the marshes to cheer you up. Unfortunately, sedges cover the fields," Ghislain said. "I could only find these."

"What are they?" I examined the plants, which had long stems attached to root balls.

"These are buttercups." Ghislain pointed to the vibrant yellow petals forming the flower's corolla. "And these are cuckoo carnations." They were a beautiful pink flower with elongated petals that forked into slimmer ones.

"They're beautiful… How do you know so much about flowers?"

"I helped tending gardens."

"I would never have imagined you as a gardener, seeing you in your uniform. You're always so serious."

"I didn't come into this world wearing a uniform."

"I imagined your father served in the militia and acted as role model." A similar situation had occurred between my father and Anton.

"My father was…" Ghislain's expression turned serious. "He fought during the Great War. But despite his dutiful service to the fatherland, for the rest of his life he harbored feelings of resentment and abandonment. I never judged him, nobody dared to. He was an amputee, so nobody could argue he hadn't sacrificed enough. Even when he complained about how unjust the government was to the veterans, he rarely spoke about what he witnessed on the battlefield, and never on how he had lost his leg. Comparing pictures of him before deployment and after the war, even only a few years apart, the change was so drastic he appeared to be two entirely different people.

"'War changed him,' his close friends and relatives used to say, but as I grew older, I understood that war had regurgitated him. In my father's eyes, he should be dead. He often insinuated that my mother would have received more money for the corpse of her husband than receiving him maimed, unable to work the land. For him, he was not only crippled but half-dead. Death failed to take him entirely, and my mother received a living dead man instead, with one foot already inside the coffin. Then, my father made sure the other would join it soon, drinking his way straight to the grave. But unlike the bullets that ripped apart his leg in battle, alcohol is a sluggish assassin. I imagine he figured that out as well, so one night he killed himself."

My heart went out to him. "I'm sorry to hear it."

"My father's passing didn't affect me. His death was forewarned. However, after his suicide, my life was never the same. My mother sold the farm and all our possessions, and holding my shoulders, she said to me, 'You're a man now, and it's time for us to part ways and attempt to rebuild our lives.' She handed me half the money and boarded a train without looking back."

A lump formed in my throat. "How old were you?"

"Ten."

I winced. "I can't imagine how difficult that was. What happened?"

"I wandered here and there until the money ran out. Then I had to learn to survive on the streets, how to protect myself and work for food. Until the day a man offered me a roof over my head and food on my plate. I wasn't the only boy he adopted; most of us were orphans from the Great War. His house is where I learned about gardening, among many other things. But it was no easy feat; he was a prominent military man from the Nazi party, and he instilled in us all the German values under extreme rigor… And years later, here I am." Ghislain finished transplanting the buttercups and carnations to their new home.

"He must be a kindhearted man," I said, thinking about the good deeds he'd done, adopting all those children.

"You tell me," Ghislain said, half smiling. "The man who took me off the streets was none other than Obergruppenführer Wolfrick Von Schroeder."

I could not conceive it. *Von Schroeder being kind?* I refused to accept it. Even if Von Schroeder had not hurt me directly, he was Reinhard's superior, and my children had suffered all those horrors under his watch. For me, Von Schroeder was evil incarnate, despite the kindness shown toward Ghislain.

"I didn't come into this world wearing a uniform," Ghislain repeated. "But despite parting ways from the soldier's path, life has ways of putting you back on track." His words echoed the river analogy Valeska had told me last night. "Now I'm a soldier fulfilling my duty," he said with irony.

Deserting would be the right word. "Thank you for fulfilling your duty to my father and saving me," I said, realizing I had never thanked him for saving me in Hamm.

"I didn't save you to fulfill my duty—"

"Peach!" Jay interrupted us, shouting from the house entrance. "Peach, please come quickly. Twenty-Seven has disappeared!"

I ran inside the house, followed by Ghislain. When we arrived in the room, the children were surrounding Lemuel's empty bed.

"What happened? Where's Lemuel?" I asked, remembering I had seen everybody resting on their bed before going downstairs.

"I don't know," said Hoshi, who'd been sharing a bed with him.

"Oh my God." I exhaled, ambling around the corridor, trying to think where he might be. *Valeska!* I resolved and walked toward her. "Valeska, please, you need to tell me where your brother is. I know you can, so please focus."

She extended her arm with her finger pointing toward the… window?

"Did he go outside?" I asked dubiously, since I hadn't noticed him leaving the house—at least not through the front door.

"No, inside," she clarified.

"Inside?" I pondered, and amid the silence, I heard a series of thuds.

"Maybe—"

"Shhhhhh," I hushed Ghislain and pressed my ear against the wood panels covering the walls, amplifying the noises. "Lemuel!" I yelled, hammering the wall. "He's inside the wall." I turned to Ghislain. "Please, help me get him out."

Ghislain fumbled with the wood panels, looking for an opening, until finally he pulled a door open. "It's a hideout," he said, crawling in. A few seconds later, Ghislain came out holding Lemuel, looking scared, in his arms.

"Thank God!" I hugged Lemuel. "Why did you go in?" I forgot for a second he was mute.

Lemuel recounted a story with his hands that I could not interpret, but Valeska translated.

"He says the door opened, and a voice coming from the interior invited him in."

"A voice? Did you see someone?"

Lemuel shook his head.

"It was too dark," Valeska translated.

Ghislain crawled out of the wall, dusty and with his hair covered in cobwebs. "It looks like the passageway connects all the rooms, maybe the entire house. These are common in safehouses."

"Did you find someone inside?"

Ghislain jerked his head. "No, but I found this." It was the golden crucifix with hollowed eyes that was missing from my nightstand.

CHAPTER 33

"WE LEAVE AT ONCE," I said to Ghislain.

The golden crucifix had appeared inside the passageway without a coherent explanation for how it had arrived there. The incident bolstered my aversion toward the house. The sensation of being watched, previously limited to the dining room, had proliferated to the entire house.

After I relaxed, Ghislain convinced me to stay at least one more night. "The kids can't leave like that." He gestured to their oversize clothes, which still required mending. "Besides, we still need to recover and gather our strength. Once we cross that border, we don't know when we'll have food in our mouths or a comfortable bed to sleep in again."

He was right.

I spent the rest of the day on the portico, sitting on the rocking chair with needle and thread in hand, stitching the clothes to fit my children. Sewing was good for keeping my mind busy, reining in my paranoid thoughts and distracting me from the discomfort of this time of the month. However, I could not prevent my eyes rising from time to time to scan the horizon, fearing that at any moment, Reinhard would show up on the road. But every time my fears were about to materialize, it was only Ghislain pushing the wheelbarrow. When he finished transplanting the flowers, the garden looked beautiful. Unfortunately, it was too late for me to enjoy it; I was impatient to abandon the house. Ghislain, on the contrary, looked like one of those flowers he had transplanted, eager to put down roots. He cared for repairing the house as if he were the owner. After hearing his story, I understood that was what he yearned for. It helped him to satiate his need for belonging.

With Ghislain working on the repairs so diligently and me sewing the clothes, surrounded by a bunch of rascals who could not stop romping around, I wondered if this was what being married and having a family would be like. I was too young to be a housewife. I pricked my fingers innumerable times with the needle, so by the time I finished, the pads of my fingers were red and swollen. Out of devotion to my children, I could not utter a single word of complaint. It was more important that their sleeves were long enough to hide the numbers tattooed on their hands and their trousers short enough to prevent them from tripping as they ran.

Because if I was sure of one thing, it was that my children had to run. They had come to this life to be persecuted for who they were. Condemned to pay with blood for a conflict caused by their ancestors, whom, despite being their descendants, they did not know or care to. It made me wonder how many generations this hate would last. It seemed like enough to outlast the diluted genes of the accursed ones. Maybe until the person punished for belonging to their kind shared more with the accuser than the accused.

After a long day of preparation for our departure, that night we had a special dinner, planning to eat and drink as much as we could. We would carry canned provisions with us, since we were leaving the van behind. "We'll cross the border on foot," Ghislain explained. "If we want to pass unnoticed, we need to blend in with the people. Tomorrow, we'll head southwest through the farm corridor between Nijmegen and Groesbeek to avoid German forces. Then, we'll continue toward Grave to cross the Meuse River. Hopefully by then, somebody will be kind enough to lend us a car." Ghislain winked at using the word *lend* as a euphemism for *steal*. From his days living on the streets, he was no stranger to stealing. Surviving, as he used to call it. In his defense, perhaps he was right; we were just trying to survive. I just hoped Renenet was right when she said, *"Nobody will judge you for what you did for the sake of survival."*

"Then we'll drive south through Uden and Eindhoven, circumventing the Eighty-Fourth Corps, which should be positioned somewhere around 's-Hertogenbosch." Ghislain traced our route over a map using his index finger. "If we make it into Belgium, we'll be safe... at least from the SS... Then we'll need to worry about the war. Yankee invaders won't welcome Nazis with open arms... even if we're deserters," he concluded with a gloomy expression.

After the cruelty I had witnessed so far, after being hurt and hunted by my own kind, the invaders didn't sound like horned devils to me. I was looking forward to crossing enemy lines and leaving the battlefield behind. To run away from all the conflicts of the world to a peaceful land. But we were swimming against the current. I was fearful of what Valeska had prophesied becoming truth; that despite our efforts, we would still end up at the bottom of the waterfall...

When I finished my dinner, I walked to the porch, carrying a glass of wine with me. I needed to breathe fresh air, and staying inside the house had become stressful. Maybe it was only my trauma creating persecutory delusions. The sudden halt in experiencing my visions of dead people and Sidney's visits after we left Hamm made me reconsider that maybe the disease I was suffering was not second sight but psychosis.

"That would explain it all," I said to myself, sipping my wine and resting the glass on the banister. That would explain the hallucinations and the delusions... *But how would you explain what the children did, and Renenet?* I could not, and as time passed, I questioned the veracity of those events myself. Unfortunately, I knew if I could ever tell my story, nobody would believe me. "But I have proof!" I had the documents recounting the horrors done to my children. "That should help." I stared into the pitch-darkness, and seconds later, I wondered when I had begun talking to myself. Maybe I was indeed going crazy.

A loud song coming from the living room broke the silence. I saw the children through the window gathering around Ghislain, who was making a gramophone work properly. It was a rhythmic jazz song led by a trumpet and the coarse voice of a man singing in English. I understood the lyrics, given the fact I had a good proficiency in the language because my aunt, my mother's younger sister, had married an Englishman and moved to England. Before the war, we visited them during the summer. I'd enjoyed playing with my two cousins.

"*Oh, when the saints!*" the man sang.

"*When the saints,*" echoed a chorus of women after him.

"*Go marching in,*" the man sang, and the women repeated. "*Oh, when the saints go marching in.*" The chorus echoed each line. "*Yes, I want to be in that number when the saints go marching in.*"

The song continued playing while Ghislain danced goofily with the children. I rejoiced at seeing them playful and joyful, even Jov, who after the injury to his ears, caused by the shock wave of the explosion, had been withdrawn. He was adjusting to his impaired sense of hearing, I guessed. I smiled, thinking that my happiness didn't depend only on myself anymore.

Ghislain held Valeska's hands and turned her around in the center of a circle formed by the children. Gently, he taught her the basics of swing dance. Valeska had never laughed like that. I tried to picture her as a grown woman, a beautiful girl enjoying her youth, wishing I could see that image turn into a reality. I made a toast for Valeska and the children.

Ghislain came outside, displaying an ear-to-ear smile. "Come, it's your turn to dance." He extended his hand.

"Oh! No! Please, dance with the children," I said, embarrassed; I could not tell if my cheeks were hot from his proposal or from the glasses of wine I had drunk.

"You owe it to me." Ghislain cocked his head. "Remember?"

"C'mon, Peach!" the children encouraged me.

"All right, but—"

Before I could finish, Ghislain pulled me inside the house.

I was rigid at first, but after a couple of pushes and pulls and a few turns, my rusty body recovered its mobility. Slowly, happiness erupted from my interior, and I could not stop smiling. We did a barrel roll then switched partners. I continued dancing with Jov, then Jay, and I realized we were all holding hands and turning around, laughing and shouting.

The songs played one after the other, and while exhausting, dancing relaxed me; it even helped relieve my menstrual cramps. Not only was it good for me; as the time passed, one by one, my children collapsed into the armchairs, and then their fatigued eyelids shut. Ghislain and I continued spinning on the dance floor, and as the rhythm of the music slowed our moves, we drew closer. He held me against him, this time triggering no unwanted memories.

"When was the last time you danced?" he asked softly.

"I can't remember. During my last visit to Berlin, I believe. Life on the farm was never this exciting."

He shrugged. "We are on a farm, in case you haven't noticed yet."

I poked his chest. "Of course I know, you silly."

"Any place can be heaven in the proper company," Ghislain whispered, caressing my cheek.

"Or hell…" I voiced the unfiltered words of my subconscious, and the stream of unwanted memories flooded my mind once again. I squeezed my eyes painfully, trying to get rid of Reinhard's image. "I-I'm sorry." I stepped away.

"What did I say?" Ghislain tugged my hand, genuinely disconcerted.

"Nothing." Everything was my fault. "I need a breath of fresh air." I headed back to the portico, grabbed my glass of wine from the banister, and swallowed the remaining liquid to drown my memories.

"I know you hate this place," Ghislain said behind me. "Please forgive me for persuading you to stay one more day."

"It's not that… It's—it's just…" I stuttered, unable to complete a sentence. I gulped, as if by doing so, I could push the words inside me back to the confinement of my heart. I averted my eyes, incapable of staring at Ghislain, or I would break into tears. Darkness was less demanding. Less painful.

"I understand." Ghislain sighed before retreating.

His footsteps faded inside the house, emphasizing my solitude.

"Maybe you should get used to solitude," I whispered to myself, firmly believing I would be alone for the rest of my life.

How fragile life is, I reflected, holding the glass loosely between my fingers, waiting for the moment it would slip from my grasp and fall to the ground and shatter into a thousand shards. Once broken, not even the most skillful artisan could glue it back together. An unsolvable jigsaw puzzle—that is what I had become. Nothing, no one, would stitch my torn pieces back together.

The wooden planks creaked behind me, and I whirled in surprise. It was Ghislain.

"It's for you." He handed me a folded paper flower. An edelweiss. "No edelweiss grow in the marshes… so paper is the only thing I had at hand. But I promise you that one day, I'll climb the tallest mountain and bring to you the prettiest flower I can find."

Before I could utter a word, he walked away.

A promise of dedication. I remembered Ghislain's explanation behind the meaning of giving an edelweiss to a loved one. I held the flower dearly against my heart. "A loved one…" I sighed.

CHAPTER 34

THE NEXT DAY WE PUT OUR PLAN IN MOTION. We had breakfast, and despite wanting to carry the entire contents of the pantry with us, we packed only enough provisions to avoid hunger through the day. "We need to travel light, in case we need to run," Ghislain advised. "Besides, we don't want to draw too much attention." I took his advice to heart and reconsidered my outfit, favoring overalls with a blouse and a jacket on top.

"We need to cover our tracks," Ghislain instructed us, making sure we were not leaving any proof of our stay. He disposed of the van. I burned my children's discarded rags. We made sure to leave no other belonging behind. Ghislain locked the front door and returned the keys beneath the planks, where he had found them. "We're ready," he said optimistically.

We left the same way we arrived, escorted by a murder of crows. Their cawing granted a baleful aura to our pilgrimage. When our procession passed next to farms, people went inside their houses and hid behind the curtains, as if we were a walking premonition of what was about to happen. But oddly, the quietness propagated with every step, as if the unnatural peace granted by the house had journeyed with us, surrounding us like an invisible bubble. The only disturbance was the sound of our shoes brushing the blades of grass, and as we advanced, it turned melodious. Yards turned into miles just like minutes turned into hours.

"Welcome to the Netherlands!" Ghislain informed like a tour guide after we crossed a pond. "If I'm correct, that should be Wyler." He pointed to a village on the far right of the horizon. He pulled out binoculars to look.

"Where did you get those?" I asked.

"I found them in the house." He blew the dust out of them and handed them to me. "But they're not much use now. Once we're on top of the hill, we'll see the world," he said jokingly.

When we climbed the wooded hillside and reached the clearing at the summit, we did see the world, or at least the less pleasant face of the world.

The face of war.

A swarm of planes crowded the sky like shining metal birds, creating an almost hypnotic view.

"Bombers?" I asked, believing the planes were heading toward Kleve or Emmerich and would pass us.

"At that height and in plain daylight?" Ghislain shook his head.

Bombers resorted to the night, to cloak themselves with shadow against the antiaircraft fire. He looked askance at me without uttering a word. His gloomy expression conveyed his hunch that these aircraft carried something more dangerous than incendiary bombs. "Invasion."

Those metal gliders transported an army of soldiers.

Antiaircraft guns located across the landscape, camouflaged in scrubland and farms, chugged continuously, drawing in the skies trails of smoke puffs that looked like candy floss. The puffs looked almost harmless, until the first airplane got hit, setting it ablaze in a matter of seconds. The turrets of the planes counterattacked, shooting bright beams of light among the bullets, and hundreds upon hundreds of soldiers jumped from the planes, spreading their parachutes like dandelion seeds carried by the autumn wind.

"Finally, war has reached us…" I said, flabbergasted, looking at it through the lens of the binoculars. The bubble of peace surrounding us had snapped. "Is this how the invasion of Germany begins?"

Ghislain observed with worried eyes the German soldiers emerging from trenches behind the tree line to fight the invaders. He winced, unable to hide his frustration. His hands jerked with the patriotic desires of holding a rifle and jumping inside those trench-es to combat the enemy for the sake of the fatherland.

But we were just spectators on this battlefield. Planes swooped in flames while motionless paratroopers glided aimless, killed be-fore they could set foot on foreign soil, and the soldiers on the ground were shot down, falling into the deep trenches they had dug themselves without knowing it would become their own graves. For the first time face-to-face with war, I repented with my whole heart my desire to witness the front line. The impersonal sensation of the horrors was overwhelming. There was no time to mourn a tragedy when the deaths escalated to the hundreds. Even when a thousand soldiers stormed onto the battlefield, they died as if they had fought the war alone… or at least, that was what I thought, until I peeled my eyes and saw him…

A man dressed in raven black making his way through the bat-tlefield.

The Harbinger of Death.

Sidney, who had previously visited each of those soldiers during their slumber and had unveiled their incoming and inescapable deaths, was now ready to reap their souls. He welcomed with arms wide open the souls carried by the inexorable current of the river of life to the waterfall of destiny. But it was not a single man this time; that many souls required an army. Hundreds of copies of Sidney popped into existence as far as I could see, holding every fallen soldier with a welcoming embrace, putting an end to the pain, the anguish, and the agony with his gentle touch before vanishing.

Among the hundreds of troopers, it was only me attesting the terrifyingly beautiful omnipresence of Death.

Peach! Peach! I read Ghislain's lips as he jolted me, bringing me back to my senses, reconnecting my ears to the commotion of gun-shots, explosions, and wailing. "We need to go back to the house!" He pulled my hand as an airplane in flames glided over us, the fu-selage grazing the treetops, leaving a dense trail of smoke behind. "We need to get out of here, now!"

Ghislain led the retreat, carrying Valeska in his arms. I held hands with my children, and we fled from the battlefield.

"What are we going to do now?" I asked him, with wheezing voice, during a momentary break under the canopy of the woods. Our gasping had become louder than the roaring of the guns be-hind us.

"We hide and wait," he said, running his hand through his hair with apparent frustration.

"But for how long?"

He shrugged. "They need to cross the Rhine to have access to Berlin. They have evidently chosen Nijmegen as the entry point, contrary to the south border, as intelligence said…" He lost himself in his thoughts. "But capturing Arnhem will not be a simple task. Its being surrounded by rivers constrains the armored forces of the invaders to the use of the bridges, working like a funnel." He shook his head. "Besides, Arnhem is heavily defended, so unless they deploy heavy artillery, the siege could last for days… or weeks, if they even break through at all. The Second SS Panzer Corps will provide aid, without a doubt. Invaders could be stationed here for the entire winter."

The SS would swarm to this place to repel the attack at any minute, without doubt. That was terrible news for us.

I gulped. "We need to find a way through."

"But not today. We can't risk being caught in the crossfire. We need to wait for the vanguard to move north of Groesbeek. That'll open a passage behind enemy lines." Ghislain acknowledged this with difficulty, as he accepted the fact that this was the beginning of the end for the Reich. The enemy was at our doorstep.

When war knocks at your door, stay close to Father and everything will be fine, my brother Anton had written in his last letter. Unfortunately for me, my father was hundreds of miles away. Our sole chance for survival rested on Ghislain's judgment now.

"Help!" said a faraway voice.

"Valeska?" I turned around, counting my children. "Where is Valeska?" But they shook their heads. "Oh no! We need to find her. Quick! Let's split up."

"Please help!" Valeska yelled, and I followed the sound of her voice through the foliage. "Come!"

I hurried, fearing a soldier had captured her, but when I arrived, she was alone. I knelt and pulled her against me. "Thank God you're all right." I caressed her face. "But please, don't do this ever again, do you understand?"

But Valeska extended her hand, pointing to the sky. Above us, an unconscious man in military uniform was hanging from his parachute, trapped by the branches.

"Oh my…" I backed off. "Is he dead?"

Blood ran down his left ear; he probably had hurt his head during the landing, causing a contusion. Faint grunts coming from the soldier answered my question.

"Don't get any closer," Ghislain warned me upon his arrival.

"He's unconscious," I said.

He circled the paratrooper as if he were dealing with a wild beast. Without removing his eyes from the hanging man, Ghislain squatted and collected a rifle tangled in a bush, which presumably belonged to the soldier. Versed in using all kinds of armament, Ghislain held the rifle as if it were his own and cocked the handle.

"What are you doing?" I asked as he aimed at the soldier's chest. "Don't!"

His finger rested on the trigger.

"Don't!" I interfered in time, pushing the barrel away. The bullet passed close to the unconscious soldier, puncturing a hole in his parachute. "What the hell are you thinking?"

"Why do you think he's here, huh?" Ghislain yelled, the arteries protruding on his temple. "Do you think he'd have mercy on us? We're at war!"

My stomach tightened at every word he pronounced.

"No! You're at war, not me!" I rebuked, my whole body quivering. "Nobody ever asked me if I wanted this damn war! Don't you see not only the enlisted suffer?"

Ghislain stared at me in silence, digesting my sour words.

"If you're so desperate to kill, the battlefield is that way. I won't stop you. You have a gun in your hands; what are you waiting for?" I pushed him. "*Wir Folgen Dir!*" I quoted the words on the poster on my bedroom wall at Wewelsburg Castle. "Follow your Führer into battle if that's what your heart really craves. But I won't allow you to kill an unconscious and unarmed man who's done nothing but jump from a plane in flames to his certain death."

Ghislain rested the stock of the rifle on the dirt and took a deep breath. "Okay."

I waited a moment to be sure he had stood down. "Now, I'll get on the branch and cut him down, and we're going to take him with us back to the house and tend his wounds, if necessary."

"What?" Ghislain frowned. "Are you planning to bring the enemy into the house?"

"Your enemy, not mine. You see the colors of his uniform. I see only a human being who desperately needs our help, and I'm going to do what I would expect from somebody if I were in the same situation." I pulled out the letter opener and handed my briefcase to Valeska. "You're welcome to help… or leave. My children and I can carry him home." I walked to the tree.

It was an old elm with a dense crown; I could almost guess its age by the thickness and cracks of the bark, wide enough to fit my fingers inside, perfect for climbing. It was tall but shaped like an inverted chicken foot; the hardest part was reaching the junction of the branches. I started climbing with effort, battling with my feet to find the support needed.

"Let me help you." Ghislain offered his hands and propped me up.

Once on the junction, I climbed to the branch that passed above the man; I straddled it and started severing the parachute lines one by one. "This is the last one, are you ready?" I took a deep breath, hoping he could survive the fall, and squeezed my eyes closed while cutting the remaining line until I heard a slam. I descended from the tree.

The children squatted around the soldier. He was just a boy, barely older than me. My hand covered in blood, I held his head, confirming my theory about his contusion.

"Hey! Hey!" I tapped his cheek, but he didn't respond.

"We can't waste a minute longer. Help me pull him to his feet," Ghislain instructed.

I hooked my hands under the soldier's armpits and pulled up his torso. Ghislain squatted in front of the soldier, and holding his right hand, he pulled the boy across his shoulders and stood, balancing the weight evenly. "Grab the rifle," he said.

I slung it behind my shoulder. "Let's head back home."

We marched back, carrying in our arms the first invader into the fatherland.

CHAPTER 35

UPON RETURNING TO THE HOUSE, we installed our guest in a bedroom. Ghislain sat by the bed with the rifle resting across his legs, expectant, his eyes fixed on the soldier like a wolf stalking a deer. He waited patiently for his prey to commit an error that would justify taking his life, but to his misfortune, the soldier refused to wake. He was a prisoner of delirium, perspiring with fever.

"Jim… Jim," he called repeatedly as I applied the cold compresses to his forehead. But despite my efforts, his fever did not recede.

Hours later, he finally woke up.

"How do you feel?" I asked in English as he regained consciousness.

"Who—who are you?" The boy cowered against the headboard at waking up in front of an unknown man pointing his own rifle at him. But his countenance swapped from fear to suffering when a discharge of pain shook his entire body. "Ahhhhhh!" He contorted, trying to reach his foot.

"Please, don't move! You must rest," I said, battling with my brain to conjugate English sentences properly. My language skills were rusty. "You hurt yourself during the fall. We found you hanging from a tree, unconscious, with your parachute twined around the branches. I freed you, but you hurt your ankle at landing." I uncovered the swollen ankle I had diagnosed when I removed his boot. "But don't worry, it's just a sprain, nothing serious. With a series of hot compresses, you will be like new in a couple of days."

The soldier stared at me with unblinking eyes.

"Sorry to overwhelm you, it's just… I used to run, so I know a thing or two about sprains." I giggled. "I'm Emma, by the way, but everybody calls me Peach."

But the boy remained silent, his gaze diverting to the barrel of the gun pointing at him.

"Oh, I understand. His name is Ghislain." I tried to ease the awkward introduction. "Please put the gun down," I hissed at Ghislain in German, then switched back to English. "Don't worry—"

"You are just a bullet away from the hereafter. You already survived a plane crash. You better don't put your luck to test twice," Ghislain said in English.

"Please, don't listen to him. We're friends," I said, disregarding Ghislain's imprudence. "Who are you?"

"I'm Bill, Bill Hurlbart of the 508th Infantry Regiment, 82nd Airborne Division… Where—where am I?"

"On the wrong side of the world," Ghislain said sardonically.

"Ghislain, please!" I took a deep breath and regained my composure. "You're on the German side of the border, in the river marshes near Kleve."

"Kleve?" Bill asked, more to himself, lost in his thoughts. "My unit!" He looked shocked as his fuzzy mind cleared. "I need to find them!" He tried to stand.

"Not so fast, Humphrey Bogart!" Ghislain got on his feet, holding the rifle menacingly.

"Wait!" I interposed myself between the two. "You can hardly limp to the door, yet you want to crawl all the way to Nijmegen?"

Bill's lips pursed with impotence. The artillery blasts were audible in the distance. He knew his countrymen were the ones being shelled.

Ghislain signaled his ear. "Yes. That's the call for you to crawl… but back to America!"

"Ghislain, please! You're not helping here," I grumbled in German. "So, the best thing will be for you to leave."

"But he's—"

"I can take care of myself. That wound on your neck is testament to that."

Ghislain grimaced, but handed me a key. "Lock the door when you leave." He strode to the door, rifle in hand, and when he swung it open, the children, who had been eavesdropping, collapsed to the floor. "Up!" Ghislain marshaled the children back to their rooms.

"Is he a… soldier?" Bill asked.

Was Nazi *the word he was looking for?* I pondered for a few seconds. "He was…" I resolved. "In other circumstances, maybe you and he would have faced each other on the battlefield… but not today." I smiled at the thought that despite all the horrible things that had happened, at least I had prevented these two soldiers from killing each other. "Forgive him. He's moody and apprehensive sometimes… but he's a fine man."

"He's jealous—rightfully. You're beautiful."

Jealous? "Oh!" My cheeks burned. "I'll leave you to rest and visit you later… I-I…" I showed him the door key.

"I can hardly limp to the door," Bill said, echoing my words.

I smiled and left the room.

Downstairs, Ghislain rummaged through Bill's belongings. "Did you lock him up?" He emptied the contents of Bill's backpack over the table and browsed through the items: canned rations of stew, hash and pork and beans, bars of chocolate and wafer, compass, and a Bible, among other personal items.

"Bill is a soldier, not a monster."

He turned to me, startled. "You call him 'Bill' now?"

"Ghislain, please," I said, trying to avoid an argument.

"We don't know his intentions…" Ghislain went silent, examining a deteriorated teddy bear with the stuffing coming out through what looked like a bullet hole in its chest.

I wondered what type of man would carry a teddy bear into war. "You were saying, about his intentions?" I said sarcastically, and snatched the bear from his hand. My finger caressed the sheepskin burned on the edge while I scanned Bill's backpack until I found a matching orifice, assuming a bullet had caused it.

"Like I said, we don't know his intentions." Ghislain removed the lid of a metal container the size of a shoebox, unveiling controllers.

I turned to him, puzzled.

"It's a radio receiver," he explained, pulling out an antenna and plugging in a black handset. "He could inform his superiors of his position, and before we know it, an army could be on us."

"Don't exaggerate. He doesn't even know where he is."

"If you hadn't told him."

"Ghislain, not even I know where we are," I said, upset. "Now, if you'll excuse me, I need to go cook dinner." I took the teddy bear with me.

I knocked three times before opening.

"Come in!" Bill shouted from the interior.

"I imagined you would be hungry, so I brought you some food." I placed the tray over his lap. "Sardines. I hope you like it. We have little to offer."

"Thank you. It smells delicious."

"Really?" I asked, dubious of my culinary skills.

"Try eating my rations for a week and everything will taste like paradise."

"The canned stew sounded tasty…" I went mute, realizing I had confessed to poking around in his belongings. "I'm sorry…"

"Don't worry. I would have done the same."

"Here." I pulled the teddy bear from my apron pocket. "I sewed it."

Bill's fingers caressed the red stitches.

"Unfortunately, red thread was the sole available… I used the other colors on the children's clothes."

"Thank you," he said, clamping his lips.

"At least your girlfriend will be happy that you keep it in good shape," I said, assuming it was a departure present.

"I have no girlfriend… It's my brother's."

"Jim?"

He turned, bemused.

"You called the name in your delirium."

"No, Jim was… He was my best friend since I could remember. We were neighbors. We studied together. Conscripted together… And three months ago, we jumped together… in Normandy…" Bill's eyes turned vacant.

"It was like yesterday?" I asked, referring to the mayhem I had witnessed.

"Much worse. Most never made it to the ground alive. Jim among them... 'I'll see you down there' he said, before pushing me out of the C-47 in flames... but the bullets... just passed through us." His index finger simulated the trajectory of the bullet hitting the teddy bear in the chest. "It was a present from my older brother, Max. This bear was his most prized possession when we were children; he never shared it with me. But the night before my embarking, he gave it to me, frustrated he couldn't enlist... He's paralyzed... polio... and needs to be hooked to a ventilator to survive. 'Take the bear,' he said to me. 'That way I'll feel like I'm there to take care of you, as you've done with me all these years...'" Bill's voice turned coarse, and his eyes reddened.

"And he certainly did," I said, remembering the bullet passing through the teddy bear inside his backpack, missing Bill by mere inches. "Your brother took care of you."

Bill nodded, tears streaming down his cheeks.

"I'll allow you to rest." I collected the tray and headed to the door.

"Peach?"

"Yes?"

"Thank you for saving me."

CHAPTER 36

THE NEXT MORNING, I FOUND BILL DOWNSTAIRS. He stood propped on a cane that presumably he had found in the wardrobe in his room. He observed attentively the fields framed by the window of the front door.

"You should rest in bed," I advised, breaking his concentration.

"I'm much better now," he said, looking at me from the corner of his eye.

"You heal fast."

"I owe my recovery to your hot compresses."

"I could have helped you descend the stairs."

"I woke before daybreak, and the bedroom has become… claustrophobic." Bill's sight seemed lost in the foggy marshes, but I realized it was not his eyes but his ears that were astray. The echoes of the rattling guns and thudding of bombs exploding far off had disturbed the countryside quietness usually experienced at dawn. I could not judge him; even I battled to keep away the memories of the horrors unfolding at the front line.

"It seems no hour is too early to wage war," I said, breaking the silence.

"For soldiers in combat, war has no intermission. It hasn't stopped since I jumped from that plane and won't end until I return home… afoot or in a casket."

Ghislain passed in front of the house pushing his wheelbarrow, committed to tending his garden before the first ray of light shone on the horizon.

"Why are you really here? This isn't your house or your belongings," Bill said, acknowledging he had inspected the house.

"We…" I wasn't sure how to phrase it. "…are nomads." I resolved myself to the bittersweet taste of fulfilling Renenet's prophecy. "Yesterday, we crossed the border to escape, but we got caught by the battle. We were heading back here when we found you."

"Are you deserting?"

"He doesn't like to use that word." I observed Ghislain dutifully working the land. "But I really don't care."

"It's because of the children?"

I stared at him briefly and glanced away.

"I couldn't help noticing their… peculiarity."

"It's like you said. I'm fighting a war without intermission, which hasn't stopped since I set foot in the dungeon where the children were captive and won't end until they're in a place where nobody can harm them anymore. But, unlike you, that safe place can't be my home, because the war I fight is against my own people."

"Why are the Nazis so interested in these children? Why are they so special?"

"Because my children… might be the key they need to tip the scales of the war."

"I—"

Ghislain walked through the door, hoe in hand. He stood before Bill, towering over him by at least five inches, but Bill didn't cower.

Ghislain eyed Bill from head to toe. "I'm glad you recovered…"

"Thank—"

"Death is not condescending to the wounded," Ghislain added, and continued his journey to the kitchen.

"Don't listen to him," I said.

"No, he's right. Rights and codes are meaningless in no-man's-land. To fight the powerful, the weak have no other option than gathering to become stronger." Bill turned to me. "Peach… I can help you."

After an intensive day convincing Ghislain, the three of us sat at the table after dinner to hear Bill's proposal.

"If you allow me, I can use my radio to contact HQ. I'll explain the situation and request an escort. I'm sure my government can offer you a way out. They'll be very interested in the intelligence you could provide," Bill said, referring to Ghislain's military knowledge.

Ghislain pondered for a moment, lips pursed, but finally shook his head. "I won't defect... never."

"Ghislain, please!"

"Peach, how are you even considering this?" He spoke in German, hoping Bill couldn't follow our discussion.

"He genuinely wants to help us. And honestly, how many options do we have?"

Ghislain took a deep breath. "Okay." He leaned back and switched the conversation back to English. "How long will it take for this escort of yours to arrive at this location?"

"I don't know... a day, hopefully less." Bill shrugged, unconvinced.

"I knew it!" Ghislain chuckled, making me wonder if he was just testing Bill's proposal. "Your leaders will not divert personnel from the siege; Arnhem and Nijmegen are too crucial for your military strategy to jeopardize it by helping strangers stranded in the marshes." Ghislain pointed at Bill's map, and the clattering of the artillery getting noisier as time passed backed his argument—the battle had turned fiercer by the hour. "Your field officers are too busy trying to make it through the day. Even if the escort arrives, our bodies will be dead cold by then. They monitor all communication channels day and night. Schutzstaffel will arrive first. So, no way you'll use that thing."

Ghislain was right. Reinhard would expect us to commit the slightest mistake and reveal our position.

"Then I'll do it myself," Bill said thoughtfully. "My condition has improved enough that I can make my way back to the battlefield and search for my lieutenant. If I can take a child with me, I'm sure I can convince him to send some men."

"No, no," I said adamantly.

"I'll take care of him."

"I-I can't entrust any of my children to you." I could not bear the idea of something happening to them because of my poor judgment.

"You said it yourself, there's no way I can get aid if I can't provide proof… It doesn't matter how much I'm willing to help you, unfortunately; I don't set the priorities," Bill concluded, disheartened.

I sighed.

"Peach, we can still resume our plan," Ghislain said in German. "We don't need him."

I closed my eyes, resting my head on my hands, elbows pinned on the table. I meditated on the idea of walking back into the battlefield, but the cacophony of explosions turned into a bellicose tune in my head, a musical background for the image of Sidney's baleful march through the falling soldiers. "I'm not exposing my children to that again…" *Or rather, to him.* I gasped in defeat, glancing at the portrait tiles dressing the walls, the single proof that all these people in the pictures had ever existed… *Proof… a proof of existence.* "I have the solution!" I exclaimed eagerly.

"What do you mean?"

Without saying a word, I rushed upstairs. I found my children sitting on the steps, eavesdropping on our conversation. But I didn't care about the gloomy scenario they had heard, because I had found the solution to our tribulations.

"Peach! Where are you going?" my children called with surprise as I sidestepped them on the way to my room. From the wardrobe, I extracted my briefcase and returned to the dining room.

Bill's eyes widened when he caught sight of the Reichsadler, the shining brooch of the Imperial Eagle standing over the swastika. "Here!" I showed them the medical records that detailed the procedures done to the children. Even though the records were written in German, the photographs were so graphic that Bill averted his eyes, battling to digest the horrors. Ghislain was in shock, but likely more for the fact of me having classified documents in my possession. "Here is everything! Take it all with you." I pushed the briefcase to Bill. "This should be proof enough that we speak the truth, right?"

Bill stared at me with severe eyes.

The next morning, limping on a bandaged ankle, Bill undertook the crucial quest to find his lieutenant on the front line, carrying with him all the contents of my briefcase except the letter opener and the weathered tarot card given to me by Nailah, which I had almost forgotten about. Ghislain had returned all of Bill's equipment but his radio. A measure I backed, not distrustful of Bill's intentions, but because of its weight. Taking it with him would add stress on his swollen ankle and hinder his movement, and the success of this operation relied mainly on speed.

I could not appease my mind after hours passed without a signal from Bill. I walked in circles, eight-of-swords card in hand, wondering what might have delayed him, remembering Nailah's baleful reading. *"Your compass to elude obstacles is only your self-inflicted wounds."* Could his injury have worsened with the long hike? Or had he been captured by German forces? Maybe he arrived safely to his unit but found his lieutenant slain, or simply refusing to help us… and Bill would continue fighting his own war, disregarding us.

"Relax," Ghislain comforted me. "If he hasn't returned by nightfall, tomorrow we resume our plan no matter what. But right now, you gain nothing by worrying."

He was right. I collapsed in the rocking chair on the portico and inhaled the chilly breeze to quench my anxiety. Little by little, I fell asleep, watching the calming image of the fields. But the cawing of the crows disturbed my soothing dream, fluttering over a person walking up the road, heading toward the house.

"Bill?" My eyes battled to adjust to the sunlight. I squinted, and my sight sharpened.

But the visitor was not Bill.

It was Sidney.

CHAPTER 37

A MURDER OF CROWS REVOLVED ECSTATICALLY, as if about to migrate to a distant, warm land. *"Some crows don't migrate, they linger over the winter,"* I remembered Herr Huber explaining to me as we observed the dark-feathered birds fluttering over the crops at my grandparents' farm. *"But winter's famine turns them voracious, to the point of feeding on newborn lambs,"* he'd added. Imagining the crows pecking a baby lamb to death gave me the creeps.

On the first day of that winter, Herr Huber shot some crows with his rifle and hung the dead birds upside down around the house. *"I'm driving the crows away,"* he explained to me, but I was unable to understand the reason behind it, considering we didn't have any newborn lambs. *"It's not for the lambs, it's for us. Crows are the harbingers of death,"* he'd clarified.

From that day on, I'd thought of crows as a bad omen.

Now, watching Sidney heading our way amid a whirl of crows, I confirmed the words of Herr Huber.

Death was here, just like Renenet had prophesied. *"You will witness the Harbinger of Death traverse the fields, circumvent all walls, climb endless stairs, and trespass any door to be rightfully on time for the last appointment. Even unwelcome, he is never uninvited, since everyone has been forewarned."*

I jumped up from the rocking chair. "Ghislain?" He was nowhere to be found as I looked around. I prowled inside the house, clutching the letter opener, and ran the bolt on the door. I called Ghislain again, but there was no response. The house was submerged in silence, except for the back door in the kitchen, pounding repeatedly against the frame, creaking as the wind blew like a wheezing lament. The living room was empty, but as I marched fearfully into the dining room, with each step I revealed a somber figure sitting at the head of the table. "Von Schroe—" I whispered, breathless, and the eight-of-swords card fell from my hand.

"Obergruppenführer Von Schroeder to you, Fräulein Niemeyer," he said, removing his cap. "And yes, I'm here. I have always been intrigued about visiting this house, fascinated with the stories." He glanced at the pictures hanging around. "I told myself, 'What better occasion?' but I should confess that your unceremonious reception disappoints me. After we welcomed you with arms wide open at Wewelsburg."

His words fueled my rage at the haunting memories, as if he had poured gasoline into my bloodstream.

"Welcomed you like one of us, like family. Yet you dared to steal my property..." Von Schroeder shook his head, clicking his tongue. "Ungrateful."

"They're not your property!" I fled toward the stairs in search of my children. When I crossed the hallway, I found Reinhard in the kitchen, leaning forward, using the blade of the hoe to remove the sludge from his boots. Reinhard elevated his sight, his maniac eyes unveiling from behind his tufts of hair, and he winked at me.

Heart pounding, I climbed the stairs as fast as I could, but Reinhard dashed after me nimbly, as if his leg had fully recovered from the bullet wound. In my hurry, I tripped and fell prone just steps before arriving at the top floor.

"Don't make this harder, Cockroach!"

Reinhard seized my right ankle, but I kicked him off and clambered inside the first bedroom in the hallway. It was Jov's room, but there was no sign of my children. I latched the door.

"Open up!" Reinhard demanded, hacking at the door.

I flinched at the edge of the hoe protruding through the wood, my whole body startling with every thud. It was a matter of seconds before Reinhard tore the door down, so I headed to the bathroom that connected the bedrooms, something he didn't know.

But before I made it to the door of the adjacent room, a hand hooked my neck—Von Schroeder's. He threw me against the double sink, but I threw up my arms before smashing into the mirror, which shattered into hundreds of shards, slitting my hands. I clung to the basin to avoid falling.

"You treacherous scum," he spat at me.

Von Schroeder's words reignited my fury. My fingers fastened around the handle of the letter opener, and when Von Schroeder pulled my shoulder to face him, I unleashed a reverse blow, aiming at his face. He blocked my blow, but the tip of the blade plunged into his cheek.

"Bitch!" Von Schroeder backhanded me, knocking me down. "Damn you!" He strode to the bathtub, leaving a trail of blood droplets staining the checkered tile floor, and washed his wound under the faucet. "Do you know what you just did?" I remembered his ailment, hemophilia, or the "disease of the kings" as he referred to it, meaning his body would have a hard time healing that wound.

I struggled to stand as Reinhard approached my flank and kicked my belly, flipping me over. I wriggled in pain, unable to breathe but with a compulsive sensation of vomiting at the same time.

Reinhard's boot squeezed my windpipe, pinning me down as he leaned forward. "I'm going to squash you like the cockroach you are!" he whispered, peeling his lips away from his teeth.

"Bring her," Von Schroeder ordered, holding a white handkerchief against his cheek.

"Yes, sir." Reinhard rolled his arm around my waist and lifted me up with ease. He carried me downstairs almost unconscious. Back in the dining room, Reinhard dumped me on a chair. "Sit! Hands on the table!"

I straightened with effort and noticed an SS soldier guarding every corner of the room and Ghislain sitting across from me. He stared at me with bleary, unblinking eyes, but his nostrils were flaring. I could not decipher his countenance. Was he being considered a traitor like me, or a confessed criminal, cooperating with Von Schroeder? Maybe he had collaborated with them all this time and now was delivering me? I could not blame him; Von Schroeder was like a father to him.

Von Schroeder tossed the bloody letter opener onto the table. "It's over, Fräulein Niemeyer." He removed the handkerchief. The cut on his cheek was an inch wide and still bleeding. "This time, I hope your intelligence outweighs your bravado and we can sustain a more civilized conversation. Don't force me to use coercive measures again."

Reinhard stood by his side, hoe in hand. Black-clad, he looked like a Doberman, baring his teeth, waiting for the instruction of his master to murder his victim.

"Now, Fräulein Niemeyer, would you be so kind as to share with me the children's whereabouts?"

I gulped. I didn't know; their bedrooms were empty, but I could not tell. *Could Ghislain have taken them someplace safe?* His face gave no clue. But even if I knew, I would never tell him. "Don't know…" I finally answered.

Von Schroeder snapped his fingers. "Search every corner of this house, even if you have to tear it to pieces."

"At will, Obergruppenführer," a soldier replied, clicking his heels, and then signaled toward the entrance. The wooden planks creaked with the stomping boots of the squad pacing inside the house. The ceiling squeaked with the furniture being pushed, followed by a series of thuds as the objects contained fell on the floor. Soldiers hammered the flooring to inspect the basement. Windows crashed, home appliances were broken into pieces. Soldiers were indeed destroying the house.

Von Schroeder leaned back, listening to the cacophony of destruction as if it were an anthem of Frideric Handel. He pulled out the gold watch from his pocket and placed it on the table. This time I was close enough to recognize the emblem engraved on the lid. It was the circle with the twelve zigzagged lines shooting out that I had seen on the floor of the north tower in Wewelsburg Castle. It was the Black Sun.

"Your time is depleting." Von Schroeder smirked, tapping the table with his index finger with the rhythm of a hastening clock.

"No, your time is depleting," I countered. "Don't you hear the hammering of the cannons? The thumping of bombs or the wind gusts caused by bullets?" I said, quoting his words back in Wewelsburg Castle. "Your enemies are at the gates, and a squad of Americans are heading here as we speak."

Von Schroeder's smile vanished, but his seriousness lasted only a few seconds before he burst into laughter. He enjoyed it, despite his cheek wound bleeding profusely. "Bring me the pouch!" he ordered, and a soldier fulfilled his wishes. "When I was younger than you, a stranger gave me an unexpected gift. Little did I know, it would change not only my life, but my destiny and the lives of those around me... forever. You were fated to be sitting here by my side, Fräulein Niemeyer. So, I brought you three presents to help you clear out your future. The first..." He pulled out a teddy bear, stitched with red thread—Bill's. "You're right, we came across the Americans on our way here... A one-man squad... He was carrying this." Von Schroeder ran his leather-gloved hand over his cheek and smeared the blood on the teddy bear, cleaning his fingers meticulously. "Not tough enough to be a soldier, I would say."

All the soldiers laughed at his joke. I exchanged looks with Ghislain and sagged on my chair, my heart plunging, fearing the worst.

"But don't worry, he isn't dead... yet," Von Schroeder amended. "He is being taken care of, waiting for you with Little Gustav."

I failed to grasp who Little Gustav was; I assumed he was a torturer, though Reinhard was too much of an expert in the matter of inflicting pain to need somebody else.

"Your confession can make a difference in your American friend's destiny... So, what will it be? Painless or torturous?"

I inhaled deeply, trying to unravel the lump in my throat. *But what can I say?* I could not betray my children, and even if I wanted to, I didn't know where they were hiding. Valeska knew this was coming, so I hoped she had taken her brothers to safety. It didn't matter what my answer was. I knew deep inside I would end up dead. "I don't know..." I mumbled, barely audible, as I battled to contain my tears.

"What?" Von Schroeder asked.

Reinhard swung the hoe, and the blade sank into the wooden table right in front of me. "Answer the question, goddammit!"

"I don't know!" I cried.

"Then you leave me no other option..." Von Schroeder rummaged through the contents of the pouch and extracted a rope. "This is the second present for you." He tossed it to Ghislain. "Tie a noose, Son."

CHAPTER 38

GHISLAIN OBSERVED THE ROPE IN SILENCE.

"We've come a long way to this point. Now it's time to put an end to what we started." Von Schroeder paced behind Ghislain. "You did a good job keeping us informed at every moment." He rested a reassuring hand on Ghislain's shoulder. "You should feel proud of your service to the fatherland."

"'A good job keeping us informed'…" I repeated in disbelief, my heart shrinking as Ghislain would not meet my eyes.

"Didn't you know?" Reinhard said sarcastically. "I must admit, you truly fooled her," he said, addressing Ghislain.

My suspicions had been correct. Ghislain had only saved me as part of a larger scheme. He had deceived me to lure us to this house, God knew for what reasons. "Why?" I questioned bitterly, remembering his words, his promise, refusing to believe everything was a lie. "Why did you do it?"

But Ghislain remained silent, winding up the rope.

"Because it was an order," Von Schroeder responded on his behalf, and he was right. Why would Ghislain betray the orders of his superior and foster father? For the children's sake? For me?… No, I had been a fool.

"Done." Ghislain handed the hangman's noose to Von Schroeder.

"Splendid! Let's put it to use." Von Schroeder pranced outside.

"Move!" Reinhard forced me to follow.

"You did a splendid job," I bitterly congratulated Ghislain, who walked ahead of me.

He peered at me over one shoulder but didn't utter a word.

"Be quiet." Reinhard's gloved hand gripped the back of my neck and drove me like a puppet.

Outside, Von Schroeder circled the property like a real estate buyer, examining it in detail. During our wander, I noticed their military vehicles parked behind a copse of trees behind the house, explaining why I hadn't noticed their arrival. Guessing the number of soldiers dismantling the house, and counting the ones guarding the grounds, they were probably more than forty men. This didn't surprise me. Von Schroeder would not risk coming near the front line outnumbered.

"That will do." Von Schroeder pointed to a wooden beam protruding from the mezzanine. The dining room was visible through the windows. "Perfect height." He measured with his extended thumb and a closed eye, like a painter drafting his masterpiece. "Fix the ring and anchor the spike."

Two soldiers used a ladder to reach the wooden beam and nailed in a metal ring. They passed the end of the rope through, which would be tied around the spike hammered to the ground.

"The sun is sinking," Von Schroeder said, pointing to the horizon. "I hate spending the night outdoors. I'll be returning before night falls, and you can come with us. Tonight, you can sleep in a cozy bed along with your family that waits for you at Wewelsburg… or you can follow in the footsteps of your treacherous brother and rot in a cold ditch along with your American friend."

"Don't you dare speak of my brother, you son of—" I charged him, but Reinhard restrained me.

"Only sharp words are what you have in that filthy mouth of yours? Be aware that the tongue is a two-edged sword, and every time you swing it, you might end up cutting yourself."

Von Schroeder threatened with the noose, and I could sense the hairy and gritty rope fastening around my jaw, pulling my skull until my vertebrae snapped. My throat tightened at the thought, shallowing my breath. My distressed eyes diverted, uselessly searching for an escape, until I caught sight of Sidney traversing the fields in our direction. Invisible to all but me, cursed with the second sight.

Maybe this is it… this is the way I will die. Hanged. What does it matter now?

"I-I-I…" I stammered, but remembering my brother Anton, the suffering of my children, and my own tribulations as well, I gathered the strength I required. "I think… you should go fuck yourselves."

"The kitten has fangs," Reinhard joked.

Von Schroeder sniffed. "Bring her."

Reinhard pushed me closer to the improvised gallows, but before the grotesque spectacle could start, the sound of motors approaching interrupted us. A car escorted by two gray BMW motorcycles with sidecars, driven by SS troops, pulled into the driveway. A figure climbed out of the back of the car.

My father.

My muscles relaxed, and I inhaled as if I had emerged from water near drowning. "Fa-father," I said, feeling giddy.

"Why such relief? You thought I was about to hang you?" Von Schroeder half smiled. "We don't hang women. We're not monsters."

Even if I wanted to believe him, I could see nothing but a devil in uniform.

"Let's get inside the house," Von Schroeder ordered.

"Emma!" my father said once we were inside, and I rushed to him.

"Father! I-I'm…" But I could not elaborate in words, only tears.

"I'm glad you're safe." My father caressed my head. "Everything will be fine. Don't worry."

"What brings you to the western front, Hans?" Von Schroeder stood behind his chair, his folded arms resting on the top rail.

"You know well what."

"If it's not obvious enough, I'm in the middle of rescuing our children and punishing the kidnapper," Von Schroeder said.

Rescuing our children? Kidnapper? I could not believe his words, after all the atrocities perpetrated.

"And everything is under control."

"It doesn't seem like that, by the look of your face," my father said, indicating the sight of blood dripping down Von Schroeder's jaw over the insignias on his chest. Despite more than an hour elapsing since I'd inflicted the wound, no clots had formed.

"Blood needs to be shed to achieve greatness. The line that divides us from our enemies has been drawn with blood. I swore to be unmerciful to whoever crosses that line. Do not force me to uphold my oath, Hans. Turn around and go back out the same way you arrived."

"I won't leave without my daughter."

"We have unfinished business with her. I give the orders here. You have no jurisdiction on this matter."

"You're wrong." My father pulled a paper from his coat and presented it. "I come from Berlin. I have here your instructions to cease your current operation and return."

Von Schroeder snatched the paper and read it.

"The Führer is aware of your shady agenda. I've informed him myself. We can still return and work things through. But don't force me to expose all your crimes—"

"My crimes?" Von Schroeder put his hand to his chest solemnly. "Are you judging me of crimes when I have done nothing but aggrandize the fatherland? You accuse me, when I have endured the unthinkable to bring us within an arm's length of glory, shedding my blood at every step to attain the supreme?" Von Schroeder ran his hand over his cheek and presented the bloodied leather gauntlet to my father. "Have I killed? Yes, many times, and I would kill each one of them again if needed. I would kill all those undermen standing between us and our dream of raising humanity to the heights of the gods. I would bring the gods to their knees so they can look me in the eye if I must…" Von Schroeder took a deep breath and relaxed. "Because I'm only fulfilling my duty. The obligation entrusted to me. Is that a crime? You should tell me." He poked my father's chest with his finger. "You did the same in that laboratory of yours… How many unborn were aborted and how many sick have you sacrificed for the sake of racial hygiene?" Von Schroeder frowned, pointing at me. "Have you told her? Have you told your daughter about *Lebensborn?* About your plans for mating her with Brigadeführer Fleischer"—Von Schroeder pointed to Ghislain—"in order to breed the perfect Aryan race?"

"Enough!" My father slammed the table.

"Father?" I asked, unable to digest what I'd heard. *Was I only an experiment to him? Was I only a womb to bear as many pure-race children as possible?* But my mind didn't stop there... *Was even my rape in the dungeon planned as well?*

"Emma, it's not like that..." my father said, hands trembling, visibly agitated.

"It is like that, Hans! Accept it! We both have our hands stained." Von Schroeder forced a bloody handshake with my father. "We're both criminals... The only difference is... I'm not a traitor." Von Schroeder pulled my father closer, and in a swift move, he unsheathed his pistol using his left hand and shot my father in the flank.

CHAPTER 39

MY FATHER. AS A CHILD, I ADMIRED HIM like a giant, firm like an oak tree. The man who could face any challenge and fight any battle and would persevere until emerging victorious. The man who had helped me to stand every time I fell. Now, his trembling legs stepped back, and his knees gave as his baffled face rejected his downfall with an extended arm and flexing fingers, as if clinging to the pedestal I'd erected for him. But like all colossi in history, my father collapsed.

I pounced to his aid, but soldiers restrained me. I sobbed uncontrollably, arms curling, imagining I could ease his pain with a phantom hug. My father's men attempted to take up arms, but the gun barrels of Von Schroeder's henchmen were already pointing at their heads. Surrounded and outnumbered, the discouraged troopers had no other option but to surrender their weapons.

"Take them out," Von Schroeder instructed. "You know what to do," he said with a baleful tone.

The muzzles of the machine guns conducted the unarmed soldiers outside the house as if they were wearing the colors of the enemy. Not a minute later, a series of gunshots resounded.

"It's a tragedy to watch countrymen falling under enemy fire," Von Schroeder declared, acting aggrieved, implying his intention to attribute their deaths to the American invaders as part of his scheme, making clear he would tell the same story to exculpate our murders as well.

"Ba-bastard." My father coughed the foul word amid the puffs of blood erupting from his punctured lung. He drew his gun and pointed with a quivering hand, but Von Schroeder kicked his arm away, and the bullet smashed a portrait on the wall.

"You'll never call me that again!" Von Schroeder stomped my father's wound with his boot heel.

I struggled to set myself free as my father wriggled in pain, but I could not unclasp the soldiers' hands from my arms. "Leave him alone, you bastard," I said to divert his attention from my father.

Von Schroeder turned to me, blowing like a bull about to charge. The arteries in his forehead bulged, and blood leaked from the twin holes above his eyebrows, passing across his lacrimal caruncles as if they were bloody tears. "You never asked what your third present was," Von Schroeder said, battling to regain his characteristic equanimity.

I had totally forgotten about it. Bill's teddy bear had been the first, and the rope had been the second. I could not imagine what kind of monstrosity could be next.

"Bring the last present," he ordered Reinhard, who smiled wickedly, as if he had been waiting for this moment the entire time, and when he returned pushing the "present," I understood the reason for his morbid glee.

"Mo-mother?" I cried, having believed she was safe hundreds of miles away.

"Emma! Thank the gods!" she said with relief, but when she laid eyes on my father, she crumpled to the floor, just like her encouragement. "Hans! Hans!" she wailed, and pulled my father's head into her lap, resting a caring hand on his wound.

"Frieda…" My father met her hand.

"Monster! What have you done!" my mother confronted Von Schroeder, who was still clutching the murdering gun.

"I fulfilled my promise. I've reunited your family." Von Schroeder searched in his pocket for something. "A family of traitors." My orbed locket necklace containing Anton's photo dangled from his fingers. Von Schroeder's henchmen had retrieved it from Hermann's dead body, meaning he knew my father had aided me in my escape. "Frieda, you take me for a fool if you believe I'm not aware you knew your treacherous son provided the intelligence to the Czechoslovak government used for Heydrich's assassination in Prague. And helping the French Resistance in the liberation of France—"

"What do you want from my son?" My mother scowled at him. "He's already dead."

"Not even death can purge the stain of treachery," Von Schroeder said coldly. "Even in the afterlife, your son will be branded a backstabber."

At Von Schroeder's mention of death, Sidney passed by the windows, his eyes fixed on me as he prowled outside. My heart pounded as he drew closer to my agonizing father. *If Sidney touches my father... I need to avoid that at all costs...* Unfortunately, I was trapped in the silent agony of an imminent danger invisible to everyone else, even Ghislain at my side.

"Unfortunately, perfidiousness is contagious and transmitted through vermin like the plague," Von Schroeder continued lecturing us. "A trusted son conspired with foes to kill a fellow countryman and convinced his selfless mother to connive in his crimes, becoming a partner in crime with her silence. Then the seed of disloyalty was sown in a bright daughter, who kidnapped the future of the Reich, assisted in and cloaked from her crimes by her own father, one of the top and finest obergruppenführers and a close friend." Von Schroeder dumped my locket on the floor and aimed at my parents. "The only way to stop subversion from spreading is to exterminate all the vermin."

"No!" I interjected. "I did it. It was me who shot Hermann. It was me who set Wewelsburg on fire. Blame me! Not them. My parents were not involved... Please, forgive them!"

"Could a girl be the sole mastermind behind this plot?" Von Schroeder paced toward me. "Or was there somebody else? Hmmm?" Von Schroeder tapped Ghislain's shoulder. "A dutiful soldier assigned with the mission to find the kidnapped children. A son entrusted by his father with such a paramount task, despite the rumors about his collusion with the traitors." Von Schroeder flung his arm around Ghislain's shoulders and guided him in front of my parents. "But can a father's love blind a man to the point of negating the evidence proving his son is a double agent? Of refuting the idea his son schemed to flee the country with the girl and the children, contradicting the wishes of his father?"

Despite the sudden revelations, Ghislain remained silent, jaw clenched and crestfallen.

"I believe a father's heart is never mistaken." Von Schroeder's gentle hand turned Ghislain's face to meet his eyes. "But you need to prove the rumors wrong, Son. You need to prove your loyalty, your nationalism." Von Schroeder put his gun into Ghislain's hand. "Shoot the traitors and prove them wrong! Show them your commitment to the cause, to the fatherland!"

Ghislain aimed loosely at my father, following the orders of his own father and superior, but my mother interposed her body in the line of fire. Ghislain hyperventilated and frowned, evidencing his internal struggle between the soldier and the man.

I begged, appealing to his humanity, "Ghislain, don't listen to him! I've seen the good in you! Please, don't do it! I know you're not like them!"

"Nonsense. I accepted you into the pack. You are like us now." Von Schroeder squeezed Ghislain's nape. "You're a wolf, and this is your prey. Bare those fangs and pull the trigger. Show me I did the right thing, saving you from the streets and welcoming you into my house like my son."

Ghislain gnashed his teeth as he clutched the gun. After what seemed like a never-ending moment, his breathing finally eased and he lowered the gun. "I'm sorry... but I'm certain now I would have served my country better if I had died in the streets." He handed the gun back to Von Schroeder. "Taking my own life, as my real father did, would have been more patriotic than following your commands."

Von Schroeder's eyes turned stern as the man he'd once regarded as his son became a stranger. "A father's heart is never mistaken. Your father was a coward and took his own life to avoid witnessing his son inheriting his destiny." He shook his head slightly. "But no... you will not. Suicide is an honorable death... You'll share *their* destiny... You'll have a traitor's death. Seize him!"

Two soldiers, once brothers-in-arms with Ghislain, forced him to his knees.

"It's not that I'm evil, boy." Von Schroeder addressed Ghislain as if he were still the ten-year-old boy he had met in the streets. "I just hurt people in the name of great things. Something a commoner like you will never understand..." Von Schroeder aimed his gun at my mother and squeezed the trigger twice, wounding both thighs.

"Nooooooooooooooo!" I yelled, as if the two bullets had punctured my heart.

My mother collapsed, but as she endured the pain, her eyes searched for my father's. The shaky fingers of her hand tottered across the floor until they found my father's hand and both intertwined.

"You b-bastard!"

"Shut up!" Von Schroeder shouted, deranged, veins twitching in his face and drops of blood pumping from all his raw wounds. "You took something from me, and now I'm going to rob you of what you care about the most." He waved a bloody, inculpatory finger at me. "Now, pull those rats out of their hideout!"

Moments later, his henchmen walked in carrying cans and poured gasoline on the walls of the entire house.

We'll burn alive... I realized, and as I continued falling into my bottomless pit of despair, something snapped inside me.

"It was you! You forced me to do it!" The dam withholding my feelings, my secrets, and my suffering crumbled. "I did it because you left me no choice. Reinhard couldn't continue torturing and raping my children, as he did to me." I confessed my personal horror before everybody. In front of my moribund parents, who had never envisioned such a bleak future for their daughter. In front of Ghislain, the man who had saved me and for a moment made me believe the illusion that love was still possible for me. And in front of all those soldiers, men who had turned a blind eye on the abuse. But I made my voice heard, especially for the man who had hurt me. "I did it because I'm no longer afraid of you!" I turned my rabid eyes on Reinhard. "You'd better kill me, because even if you shackle me, this time I'll bite, and I'll tear you apart and spit, and to my last breath, I'll curse your name... I swear... I swear you'll pay for what you've done."

My father stared at Reinhard with protruding eyes, choking on his bloody anger.

Ghislain attempted to rise, but his custodians twisted his arms, forcing him down. "Reinhard, you son of a bitch!" he mumbled through clenched teeth.

But despite the consternation provoked, Reinhard's face drew into a Machiavellian smile, as if everything I had said had been a compliment. "Only great pain is the ultimate liberator of the spirit," he said proudly, like an artist admiring his work; meanwhile flames grew behind him, as if we had descended to hell.

Fire spread wildly across the papered and wood-paneled walls. The temperature increased, and the glass covering the hundreds of portraits cracked and exploded. The photos holed and charred until their ashes floated away like gray snow. The structure creaked as it succumbed to the heat, and soldiers exchanged worried looks as they waited for their superior to issue the order to abandon the building. However, Von Schroeder's hell-bent countenance reaffirmed he was not planning to leave the house empty-handed. He held his Black Sun pocket watch close to his chest, as if counting the seconds for a prophecy to be fulfilled. But despite Von Schroeder's quiescence, none of his subordinates dared to move an inch. They turned into sweating statues, as they feared the man more than burning alive.

"Sir," a panicked soldier finally spoke. "So-somebody is typing on the typewriter," he stammered with unblinking eyes, staring toward the living room.

"And?" Von Schroeder replied calmly, without removing his attention from the watch.

"Nobody is sitting in front of it..." the frightened soldier explained. "It's typing itself... a g-g-ghost!"

Sidney, I deduced, considering he was invisible to all but those with second sight. *Finally, Death has stepped inside the house...*

Von Schroeder chuckled. "What would you expect from *La Casa del Diablo*? This house is a passageway to the other side, used by the devil to drag the unwary to hell. Hence its name. The Devil's House."

The eyes of the human statues circled around, trapped in their sockets, as they realized the place we were in. Even I could not help wondering if all those portraits belonged to unwary souls dragged to hell. My spine prickled at the thought we had spent days in this house, until it became hell itself.

A soldier rushed downstairs. "Sir, we found the children, hiding in a passageway inside the walls!"

"*Consummatum est!*" Von Schroeder said, pleased, and closed the lid of his watch.

"Peach! Peach!"

The soldiers carried my kicking children outside amid their screams.

"Don't you dare hurt my children!"

"Everybody out!" Von Schroeder finally issued the anxiously awaited instruction and then turned to me, still restrained by his henchmen. "Fräulein Niemeyer, you are right. I never gave you a choice. To compensate for that, I have a fourth present for you. I'll give you the chance to save one of your loved ones. Who will you choose, I wonder? Will you drag one of your doomed parents outside before the burning house collapses, or will you save your treacherous sweetheart from suffocating on the gallows?" He stared at me with bloodshot eyes as a fresh stream of blood tears ran down his face.

I spat on him. "Bastard!" I wriggled to set myself free from my captors, fueled by rage and impotence.

Von Schroeder ran his forearm over his face to wipe the saliva. "I hope you reach old age and repent of what you have done until your dying breath, just like I'll carry this wound of yours for an eternity. Tie him up!" Ghislain's custodians drove him out of the house.

"No!" I wailed, but Reinhard punched my belly and I fell to my knees, stifled, battling to endure the pain and get back on my feet as soon as I could.

Von Schroeder picked up his hat from the tabletop and wore it. The Totenkopf insignia, the skull and crossbones, gleamed, reflecting the flames. "Sieg Heil!" he saluted my dying father, then walked away.

CHAPTER 40

THE WALLS OF THE HOUSE WERE MADE OF FIRE. The air turned dense. Burning. Unbreathable. I could not stop my coughing as I crawled to my parents. But despite the heat, I found my father trembling as if he suffered hypothermia. His clothes were drenched in blood. "Papa! Mama!"

"E-Emma!" My father extended his tottering hand with fixed, unresponsive eyes, like a blind man trying to uncover the world.

"Papa!" I said with choking sobs. "Please hold on, I'll take you out." Amid his suffering, I dragged my father by his armpits a few steps with great effort, but the way back to the entrance seemed unattainable. *I won't make it on my own.* "Mama!" I called, but she was unresponsive. My mother was oblivious, beholding the flames devouring everything while she treasured the locket with Anton's photo against her chest. "Mama! Please!" I shook her out of her trance. "Please, help me! We need to get out!" The ceiling cracked above us. "I need you to drag yourself using your hands... I can't carry both of you! Mama, please!" I refused to choose one over the other. I had to save both.

A series of thuds on the window drew my attention. Ghislain's boots were kicking the window as a hangman pulled him up the gallows. Ghislain grunted and jerked in despair as his fingers tried to make room between his neck and the noose to breathe.

"*Verräter, Verräter!*" The soldiers chanted "traitor" to Ghislain as the executioners tied the rope to the spike.

But despite my desires to run to Ghislain's aid, I could not simply abandon my parents. Certainly, Von Schroeder had forced me to pick whom I would save, condemning the rest to death. "Mama, please!" I begged, wishing we could teleport outside.

"No." She stared at me. "Everything is lost for us now... It's time for us to reunite with your brother."

"E-Emma... go, go!" my father ordered, regurgitating blood.

"No! No! Please!"

My father fumbled for my hand. "P-please... for-forgive me for not doing enough... f... you."

"Emma, listen to your father for once!" my mother said. "I wish I could be the mother you deserved... You, worth gold..." She smiled and caressed my cheek, smearing blood across my face. "Now, before you leave, indulge the last whim of your dying mother and pull me to your father's side." I closed my eyes, squeezing my tears out, rejecting the reality I was living. I refused to accept this was the end for my parents, but the window exploded, bringing me back into my infernal reality. With no other option... I fulfilled my mother's last will.

"Hans... tomorrow we will wake up in Paris," were my mother's last words as she cuddled with my father. The place where they had spent their honeymoon.

I shut my eyes, trying to imprint that last image of them in my memory, together, as I always loved to see them. Then I turned away.

As I abandoned the burning house, I found him still sitting in front of the typewriter, legs crossed, unconcerned at the flames engulfing the living room. Sidney had typed, "13, 27, 44, 49, 66, 68, 88," the numbers of my children, repeatedly across the entire sheet, using the red ribbon.

"I hope you had enough time to say goodbye," Sidney said, unsympathetic.

"Why? Why?" I confronted him, enraged. "Why did you have to do it?"

Sidney stood and walked toward me, eyes alight. I stepped back.

"Because someone has to..." Sidney said with a calm voice as his eyes returned to their usual green hue. "I didn't have a choice either. The Will named me at my birth to endlessly repeat this chore. Just like your children, I am also subject to punishment for the crimes committed by my bearers." Sidney sighed. "I like to think of it as a penance, to convince myself that I have some control of my destiny…"

"But you have the power…" *The power to change things, unlike me.*

Sidney shook his head. "I have only the power to say that today is not your day." He strode toward the dining room to consummate his task: to reap the souls of my parents.

"No!" I tried to go after him, but Sidney snapped his fingers and the kitchen exploded. I flung my arms in front of me, and the shock wave sent me flying through the entrance door. I landed and rolled on the dirt, extinguishing the fire caught by my clothes. My ears rang. I coughed violently, trying to expel the smoke in my lungs.

"Ma-ma… Pa-pa." I staggered to my feet but could only witness the house collapsing onto itself, like a funeral pyre, turning to ashes the last vestiges of my parents' existence. I stood watching the embers climb into the moonless sky, flying into the night like ephemeral fireflies.

From the sea of fire, a figure emerged. It was Sidney, immaculate and unburned, as if he dwelt in a different dimension, where the flames could not reach. A dimension juxtaposed over ours. Sidney helped my parents get up. Despite their bullet wounds, my parents seemed as healthy as if they were alive. They glanced at me one last time, and their preoccupied faces changed to longing smiles. But my uncontrollable weeping prevented me from returning the smile. My parents held hands and walked after Sidney until their figures vanished from this plane of existence.

I could have tried to convince myself that seeing my deceased parents was just a mirage produced by the flames or a delusion concocted by my mind to deal with the trauma of their demise. But at that point, I had accepted that my visions were real. And that the condition I suffered would be my punishment for the rest of my life. Or, like Sidney said… *my penance.*

As I beheld the hypnotic fire devouring my world, somebody stood by my side.

Ghislain had survived.

CHAPTER 41

GHISLAIN WAS STILL WEARING THE NOOSE around his reddened neck like a loose tie. The other end of the rope was burned, meaning it had been the fire that set him free, or rather, destiny that wanted him to live, unlike my parents. Not that I wasn't happy to see him alive, but in those moments, after going through so much in so little time, I felt numb. I could feel nothing else. As if my nerves had been inhibited from signaling my brain, to avoid experiencing more suffering.

"I'm sorry," Ghislain said, but I didn't reply, my eyes fixed on the pyre. "A month ago, I met with your father. The concern about the future of the Reich was growing. On the eastern front, we had lost nearly four hundred thousand soldiers… dead, wounded, missing, sick, or captured. The Red Army outnumbers our forces six to one… Naturally, your parents grew worried about you, about your future. In their eyes, you would be safer married to a man who would take care of and protect you during the hardships our country will endure after losing the war. Like most parents, they wanted the best for you, and they believed that, somehow, that person was me… an orphan, raised to follow orders… And I accepted your parents' proposal without even seeing a picture of you, because amid all the orders I've received to do many awful things… taking care of someone and growing a family seemed like the noblest thing I could do with my broken life."

"It doesn't matter what they wanted… They're dead now," I said balefully.

"My promise of your safekeeping conflicted with the duty to my country… to my adoptive father. I desperately needed to keep you hidden until the end of this war rendered meaningless all these conspiracies and struggles for power, but the only tools at my disposal were those of my master." Ghislain chuckled darkly. "I guess now I know to whom my informant pledged allegiance." He turned to me. "It's my fault, Peach. Your parents are dead because of me."

But despite his words, I could not blame him. Ghislain was simply confronting the consequences of the decisions of his superiors—living the soldier's life, as he described it. Von Schroeder used him to get to me and to my father. We had all been just pieces on his chessboard, knowingly or unknowingly.

"It's not your fault. You didn't pull the trigger. I'm thankful for that." I was guiltier than him. Ultimately, it was my decision to rescue the children, not his.

"Yes, it is. I can't hold a beautiful flower in my hands without withering it." Flames had reached Ghislain's garden; the buttercups and carnations were charred. "I promised your parents I would always take care of you, and standing before them, I want to renew my vow. At dawn, I'll take you to Switzerland. I have some contacts within the Italian clergy who will put you on a ship to South America. You'll be safe there. I promised you I'd climb the tallest mountain to bring you the prettiest flower I could find… Now I know it's not a flower but bringing your children back that matters to you."

I turned to Ghislain. "Do you know where my children are?"

He nodded slightly.

"Then take me to them."

"You don't know what you're saying, you—"

"Don't tell me I don't know what they're capable of while my parents' bodies are still burning." My heart ignited at the thought of it. "I absolve you of the promise you made to my parents for my safekeeping! Just… take me to my children… and I'll rescue them, even if it's the last thing I do." I had nothing else. My entire world had crumbled and turned into ashes before my eyes. The idea of saving my children was the last bit of hope giving purpose to my life.

Ghislain remained silent for a moment, then agreed.

When the first sunbeams flashed across the horizon, the house had burned entirely to the ground. The imposing three-story building had turned into a thick layer of ashes and burnt coals carpeting the house's charred carcass, with a few standing poles still on fire. My footsteps were cushioned, like walking on snow, printing a high relief. When I made it to where the dining room once was, I used a stick to uncover the skeletons of my parents, still cuddling, as I had seen them for the last time. All traces of who they had been were gone… their features, their hair, their clothes. Even the locket treasured by my mother had melted, leaving only a golden trace in the bones of her hand and rib cage.

Like Renenet had prophesied, my parents had become the nameless. Nobody would bring flowers to their graves, and I was certain no flowers would ever grow again in this haunted place.

A tiny rectangular shape called my attention, and when I picked it up, the ashes slipped down, revealing the oddly unburnt eight-of-swords tarot card. "'But once you undertake the road of the helpless, not even the spilled blood will guide your steps back home,'" I pronounced Nailah's fateful last words, and an urge to cry possessed me. My actions had led my parents to their deaths, but after a full night wailing, I had no more tears to shed.

Then, the sky cried for me. Droplets of water fell from the gray clouds above.

"Peach, it's time," Ghislain said. He was wearing a black SS uniform.

"Where did you get that uniform?"

"Your father's escort." The soldiers sacrificed for backing my father.

"Do you feel comfortable wearing it?"

Ghislain lowered his eyes to the skeletons of my parents.

"Where are they keeping my children captive, then?"

"*Kleiner Gustav.*"

"Who is Little Gustav?" I asked, intrigued, remembering Von Schroeder mentioned they had taken Bill to Little Gustav.

"It's a what rather than a who… Little Gustav is a train. A war train."

I didn't know what that meant.

"Come with me."

We went inside the cowshed, where we took shelter from the drizzle while Ghislain explained.

Schwerer Gustav, or Heavy Gustav, was a rail supergun mounted on a train wagon, but it was no ordinary wagon. Heavy Gustav was a 150-foot-long, forty-foot-tall, 1,500-ton super-weapon that required two parallel railway tracks to run on. Heavy Gustav's hundred-foot-long barrel could shoot five-ton explosives or seven-ton concrete armor-piercing rounds at a range of twenty-nine miles. It was first used in the siege of Sevastopol in '41, firing only forty-eight rounds before the city surrendered. But despite Heavy Gustav's power, the logistics required made it impractical. Setting up Heavy Gustav at firing range from Sevastopol had required four thousand men and five weeks, and then another five hundred men to operate it.

During the following years, Nazi engineers focused their efforts to produce lighter, smaller versions of Heavy Gustav, trying to scale its firing power. From those efforts, the Little Gustav prototype came to life. Little Gustav was a rail gun the size of a normal wagon and could be attached to an armored train, simplifying mobilization through the regular railway system. The deployment of the cannon was streamlined with pneumatic stabilizer legs, decreasing the number of operators needed to just a few. Despite being smaller rounds, the projectiles used an experimental, enriched version of *RDX* explosive, which delivered twice the explosive power of TNT.

"Where is this train located?" I asked eagerly, more interested in its whereabouts than the technical specifications.

"Close. A few kilometers south of here." Ghislain unfolded a map on the floor of the cowshed and pointed with his finger. "If the information I overheard from the soldiers is correct, Little Gustav is on the border, west from Kranenburg, providing artillery support to forces fighting in Groesbeek. Considering the number of American soldiers deployed, Groesbeek will fall, inevitably, forcing Little Gustav to retreat east to Kleve. We'll intercept them somewhere along this route."

"And if the information isn't true?"

"Then it would be wiser to reconsider Switzerland."

A hunch was better than nothing. "How will we make it there? You disposed of the van."

"We'll use one of the BMWs." Ghislain waved toward the motorcycles used by my father's escort. "In other circumstances, soldiers would have destroyed the vehicles and taken those guns to prevent them from falling into the enemy's hands. But since they wanted to simulate that your father and his men were surprised by enemy forces, they did not. I guess Von Schroeder never imagined I would survive the hanging or that you would have the impetus of seeking revenge on your own."

"He guessed wrong."

Ghislain smiled mildly. "I've collected all the armament carried by the soldiers and what was hidden in the compartments of your father's car." He pointed to a pile of rifles, ammunition, and grenades. "I hope you know how to use one of these." Ghislain handed me a machine gun.

"Are we going to blow up the train?" I asked at the sight of the grenades.

"Let me explain." Ghislain used the muzzle of a rifle to draw a diagram of the train in the dirt, comprising nine aligned rectangles. "This is the composition of the train: first the locomotive, entirely armored to protect the wheels and the boiler. The weapons at our disposal are incapable of damaging it, so our best chance is to hijack it. The second wagon is the systems car; it carries a secondary boiler to feed pressure to Little Gustav's pneumatic system. It carries a pneumatic crane to load the cannon and the ammunition deposit. The third wagon is the cannon itself, Little Gustav, a 360-degree turret with a telescopic barrel. The cannon's firing controls are in the turret, but the stabilizer legs are deployed from the crane.

"The fourth wagon is a *Befehlswagen,* a command car, where the telecom and planning room are located. This car also contains the detention section, where the children and your American friend could be captive.

"The fifth and seventh wagons are twins. Both have quad fifty-caliber antiaircraft machine guns on top. The sixth and eighth wagons are twins as well; both are personnel carriers with lateral doors for deployment and a central hump with a series of slits for firing, working as mobile pillboxes. In the case that we engage in fire, our best chance is to throw a grenade and pray to God that it finds its way through the slits." Ghislain held up a stick grenade.

"The ninth and last wagon is usually a vehicle carrier for military transport," Ghislain explained, completing his diagram. "Now that you're aware of what we'll deal with, here's the plan. We need to sneak in while the train is stationed, with Little Gustav deployed and actively firing. A patrol of soldiers will cover a hundred-meter perimeter around the train to spot any enemy intrusion. We need to elude the guards and board the second wagon, the systems car, and hide there until the train sets back in motion. From there, we make our way into the personnel car to rescue the children and the American. All wagons are connected through a narrow passageway, which we can use to mount an offensive with the help of your American friend, reducing the SS forces' numeric advantage in combat. This diversion will buy us time to deal with our escape plan.

"Engineers identified a malfunction during the initial testing of Little Gustav. When the pressure on the firing pin surpasses the recommended limits, it jams the cannon in the best of cases, but if it's forced, it can detonate the round inside the chamber, blowing up the entire cannon. Because of time constraints to put Little Gustav in action, they never fixed the problem, only issued warnings to the operating personnel.

"This could be our way of revenge… blowing up their precious weapon and escaping before the detonation occurs by detaching Little Gustav and the rest of the armored train from its connection with the systems car and locomotive." Ghislain's eyes lit with determination as he turned to me. "What do you think?"

Suicidal, I thought, but I didn't really care anymore. "What other option do we have?"

"None. If the train advances inside German territory, our chances get slimmer by the mile. As a soldier, I would rather attempt to hijack Little Gustav than assault Wewelsburg Castle." Ghislain was right. Out here, Nazis were exposed to the enemy. But Wewelsburg was a fortress. With Little Gustav we might face fifty men; in Wewelsburg, it would be at least five hundred.

"Will Von Schroeder be on the train?" The icy desire for vengeance hijacked my heart.

"I can't tell for sure. I recognized his vehicle parked in the bushes. Maybe it's being transported by piggybacking on the train, or he made his way back to Wewelsburg using the road. There is no way for us to know."

"Okay, let's go… The sooner we go, the sooner we can put an end to this." I strapped a bag containing the grenades and the machine gun onto my back.

"One last thing. I need you to wear this." Ghislain handed me an SS uniform collected from my father's escort. "This should be closer to your size."

"I'm not wearing that," I replied without thinking twice.

"This is not about who you are, this is about survival. This is camouflage. Or how do you plan to pass unnoticed while we infiltrate the train?"

It made sense. Everybody would notice my curls a mile away.

"All right, turn around."

Ghislain paced to the door. The pants were larger than I expected, but I hid the excess inside the knee-high boots. I rolled up the sleeves of the jacket into the inside to avoid raising suspicion; SS uniforms should be perfectly tailored. I exploited the fact that my hair was wet to tie it and hide it inside the *Stahlhelm*, the emblematic Nazi steel helmet. I glanced down at myself, pondering what my parents would think if they could see me dressed like this, but when I noticed a bloodstain on the jacket, it reignited my fury.

"I'll miss it," Ghislain said, staring at the remains of the house. "Not the house itself, but the time I spent with you and the children." He looked at me from the corner of his eye, as if he expected me to say something, but I remained silent. "I'll bring the BMW."

CHAPTER 42

THE RAINDROPS TRAILED ACROSS MY GOGGLES as we rode the BMW at full speed through the fields. The bellicose tune of war got louder as we approached the border between Groesbeek and Kranenburg, with the artillery sounds standing out over that of the motorcycle engine. A fierce battle was unfolding. My hands got clammy inside the leather gloves as I held the machine gun attached to the sidecar, as Ghislain had instructed, "always pointing at the horizon." But my horizon seemed nothing but gloomy, with the sun draped under dense, dark clouds. *Maybe I'll leave this existence without looking at the sun ever again.*

"How are we going to find it?" I shouted over the loud engine.

"Don't worry, Little Gustav will guide us to him!"

Ghislain was right again. As we advanced, the rumble of Little Gustav's cannon stood above all the artillery. It was like the roar of a lion, resounding across miles with the purpose of scaring off intruders… but instead of fleeing, we were about to enter its territory.

Ghislain pressed the brakes, and the bike tires slid over the mud. "There!"

In the distance, Little Gustav stood on an armored train, just like Ghislain had described it. The stabilizer legs of the cannon were pinned to the ground, and the telescopic barrel towered over the train like a mast. The operators fired the cannon, and despite the stabilizers, its powerful recoil shook the entire train. A shell the size of half a man ejected from the chamber amid a cloud of smoke. The projectile expelled through the muzzle at high speed, drawing a trail across the clouds. A mushroom-shaped cloud erupted over a distant target in Groesbeek, and seconds later the shock wave caused by the explosion reached us. The show left me breathless. It was a fearful weapon, without doubt.

Ghislain removed his goggles and stared at me. "Are you sure you still want to do this?"

I pulled my goggles down to have a better look at his sterling-gray eyes. All the memories I'd shared with him became vivid inside my head. "I'm sorry," I said, both trying to make peace with the past and asking forgiveness for involving him in this suicidal mission.

"For what?"

But instead of answering him, the tightness in my chest and restlessness of my legs found its release in Ghislain's wet lips, kissing him by surprise.

"I'm sorry too..." Ghislain cupped my face in his hand and kissed me again, effusively, pumping a shot of adrenaline into my bloodstream, endowing me with the clarity and determination I needed. "I wasn't there for you in Wewelsburg when you needed me the most..." His jaw muscle jumped. "But I'm here for you now... always." Ghislain revved the engine. "I promise." He released the brake and twisted the grip, opening the throttle. The motorcycle skidded over the muddy ground before dashing off.

My heart pounded as we approached Little Gustav.

"Planes!" I descried a squadron of fighter planes hovering over Groesbeek.

"Americans," Ghislain clarified, and I recognized the stars and stripes painted across the wings and fuselage.

The antiaircraft machine guns mounted on the armored train expelled a continuous stream of ammunition that glowed as though made of light. A stream of bullets caught the pilots by surprise, taking down two planes, and the survivors veered toward Little Gustav for a counterattack.

"Little Gustav is withdrawing!" Ghislain said as the stabilizer legs and cannon retracted like a scared spider. "They'll try to elude the planes' attack by sneaking away inside German territory."

"But that thwarts our plan!"

"I know! I know!"

When we reached the railway, Ghislain drove parallel to the tracks. The armored train left us behind. A reduced number of wagons attached allowed the powerful locomotive to speed hastily. The American airplanes nosedived, and their bullets drew spark lines along the train before soaring off again.

"We need to abort! It's too dangerous! We'll catch them down the road!" Ghislain yelled as we were catching up with the train.

"No! We need to keep going!" I insisted, fearing that if we lost them now, they would be gone forever.

"But we don't have a plan B!"

"Yes, we do!" I hung the bag containing the grenades across my shoulder and picked up the machine gun Ghislain gave me. I stood on the sidecar, balancing on my feet as we pulled alongside a flatbed wagon hauling vehicles.

"What are you doing?"

"I'm getting my children back!" I jumped for the moving train without considering how slippery my boots would be because of the rain and landed halfway on, the swing of my legs threatening to drag me off the wagon. I trailed my fingers across the surface, searching for something to hook on to, to no avail. Amid my despair, I released the machine gun to clutch the ledge, and the giant metal wheels crushed my weapon.

"Peach! Are you all right?" Ghislain kept the bike running parallel to me.

"Yes! I'm fine!" I climbed on top of the wagon platform. The wagon was transporting the vehicles used by the soldiers during deployment, just as Ghislain had expected. None of them was a Horch, the car used by Von Schroeder, meaning he was not on board.

"Peach! You need to jump back! It's too dangerous!" Ghislain beckoned.

"No way! I must end this! I'm sorry!" I said, meaning every word. I moved ahead, sneaking between the vehicles. "Just five cars to go," I reminded myself how many wagons I had to cross, according to the diagram. The next car was the "mobile pillbox," as described by Ghislain. It was like a giant toaster on wheels, with doors and slits running along both sides. Trying to break into a car crammed with SS soldiers was a terrible idea, leaving me no other option than to go over the roof. A banister ran around the top that I could use to climb up.

I used a block of wood to wedge the car tires as a step to prop myself atop the tunnel, trying to make the least noise possible. I advanced, crouching, to the ledge of the roof. A squared "hump" protruded in the center of the roof, with two slits facing each direction. I descried four soldiers inside, two guarding each flank.

Emma, you can do this. I took a deep breath and uncorked the cap of the grenade without pulling the cord. I placed the stick between my teeth and, holding the pole of the banister, climbed to the roof. From the top, the train seemed endless. I squatted to keep an eye on the soldiers and have time to react in case I was spotted. Seven, eight, nine steps I counted. I was close to the hump when a soldier turned in my direction. I froze, holding my breath. His eyes scanned the horizon, passing over me first without suspicion, but a second later, his face grew alarmed. Despite wearing my SS disguise, I forgot I was biting the grenade! I removed it too late.

"Hey!" The solider stuck the barrel of his rifle through the slit. "Intruder!"

I rolled on the roof to clear his line of fire but shut my eyes instinctively at the detonation, losing the notion of my surroundings. I almost fell over the edge but held to a post of the banister and trapped my foot against another. My body cambered over the precipice like a plank about to break. The ground passing at full speed beneath me stole my breath. *I'll fall,* I thought.

"On the left flank! Quick!"

At least my predicament had put me outside his firing range. A metal latch opened and the metal doors beneath me flung open. Two soldiers poked their heads out, glancing upward with their rifles, and they were about to shoot me when a burst of bullets knocked them down.

Ghislain approached, driving the BMW with one hand and shooting the machine gun mounted on the sidecar with the other. "Peach! Hold on!"

The soldiers retaliated from the interior, their bullets hitting the motorcycle's sidecar. Ghislain pressed the brake to dodge their attacks by falling behind.

"Alarm! Alarm!" the soldiers screamed.

Fearful, I used my mouth to pull the cord of the grenade and flung it inside. The explosion shook the wagon, and a stream of smoke erupted through the door, quickly dissipated by the wind. The armored walls had protected me from any harm, but my ears were buzzing. I climbed back to the roof and ignited a second grenade, which I tossed through the slits to ensure clearing any threat. I jumped over the hump and caught a glimpse of what waited for me in my journey toward the locomotive.

"There! There!" An artilleryman pointed at me, instructing the gunner sitting on the quad-barrel antiaircraft machine gun mounted on the end of the next car. The gunner gyrated the plane-hunting machine gun to align the sight to me.

"*Scheisse!*" My sole option for cover against such a weapon was hiding in the basin formed by the tunnel between the wagons. I sprinted as fast as I could. The sight finally aligned with me, but I slid over the last stretch of the roof before the gunner pulled the trigger. I ducked just in time before the shining bullets flew over my head with a deafening rattle. I cowered, pulling my helmet against my head, believing the bullets would carve their way to me through the armor.

The firing finally ceased, but I was really in a predicament now. There was no way I could elude the machine gun. Throwing a grenade from the other side of the wagon to hit the gunner behind protective plating was like trying to hit a bird perching on a treetop with a stone.

"Peach!" Ghislain yelled from his BMW. "I'll call their attention. Once they come after me, that will expose the machine gun's flank! Use that opening to hurl a grenade!" He sped up the motorcycle and attacked the machine gun.

"Enemy on the road at two o'clock!" the artilleryman informed the gunner, who veered the machine gun and fired. The huge bullets hit the dirt, raising four columns of dust that trailed after an elusive Ghislain, who maneuvered his motorcycle to pass behind the trees bordering the railroad. Trunks exploded, splintering in all directions as the shining bursts of ammunition cut the trees down as though they were made of cardboard.

I peeked to confirm Ghislain's hypothesis, but the artilleryman had expected our plan. He shot his pistol at the first sight of me. The bullet hit my helmet with enough force to throw me back. I fell flat, disoriented. A blurred figure showed up, upside down, superimposed on the cloudy sky. My eyes adjusted, revealing his identity. Sidney stood on the edge of the wagon, as if he were a statue on a pedestal.

"Am—am I dead?" I removed my dented helmet to see if the bullet had made it through.

"Not yet," he said, impassive as usual.

"Then why are you here?" I pulled myself up.

"You summoned me this time."

"Oh…" I pressed my temples with the heels of my hands to put my shattered thoughts back together. "So, it was me this time…" I gulped at the thought that soldiers had died by my choices. But my well of remorse had dried up and refilled with rage after what they did to my parents. I didn't care what could happen to them anymore… nor me. "Then stick around… I might die any second now." I pulled a grenade from the bag and uncorked the cap, preparing to test my aim.

"Why are you so eager to arrive at the end of your journey?" Sidney descended and strolled by my side, unconcerned about the bullets passing through his ghostly image.

"I'm not. But forty soldiers and two machine guns still stand in the way of saving my children, and I'm not giving up." Bullets hitting the roof were a cruel reminder of what waited for me upon exiting my hideout. "Since you're staying, at least you should be my eyes and let me know when I can peek over." The artilleryman would have to reload the magazine any moment now.

"Would you sacrifice anything to reunite with your children?"

I stared at Sidney. "I-I… would pay any price."

"So be it." Sidney looked ahead. "I won't be your eyes, but I will be your guide. I'll show you the boundaries between life and death." His image multiplied endlessly along the train on both sides, left and right, one after the other, forming a passageway, as if I were looking at the endless versions of him created by the illusion of two mirrors facing each other. Sidney crouched and stood, adjusting the position of his hands over time to create a moving tunnel for me. "I'm a timeless being witnessing past, present, and future all together. I know the trajectory of every bullet, so I'm creating this safe passage, which you need to follow rigorously. If you touch me, you could die."

"Are you expecting me to follow your tunnel straight to the machine gun?"

"A weapon designed to attack airplanes, not humans. The space between the barrels creates a gap wide enough to fit a person safely in the middle." Sidney was right. Engineers had designed the weapon to attack targets hundreds of yards away; the barrels aligned in angles to converge in the distance, but at close range were imprecise. "You need to worry only about following my instructions, understood?"

My logic refused considering such a ludicrous plan. But Ghislain would not survive long in the open; also, the passing landscape had changed, now showing the outskirts of a town. *Is that Kleve?* God, we were rushing inside German territory. As Ghislain had explained, our chances were getting slimmer with every passing mile. There was no other way.

"Don't worry, Emma, this is the hurdle race you have prepared for all your life… It's time for you to win the gold."

CHAPTER 43

DOES SIDNEY KNOW ABOUT MY DREAM *of winning gold at the Olympics?* An eerie sensation electrified my body, like déjà vu. His words made me wonder how long he had been watching me. How long had Death had his eyes on me? But that odd familiarity with Death pushed me to trust him and follow his crazy plan. If I failed and died, at least I would have the comfort of knowing I had done everything I could to rescue my children. Because deep down, I knew if not for them, I would have died, jumping from that window in Wewelsburg or tortured by Reinhard in Hamm. I owed my life to them.

"Okay, I'll do it." I knelt, hands on the floor, holding the grenade as if it were a baton I had to hand over in a relay race. *This is your race, Emma! You must win gold!* I convinced myself, trying to regain control of my breathing.

"On your mark!"

I rubbed the print of my boots against the wet metal, to ensure I had the best grip at my start.

"Set! Go!" Sidney signaled.

I stepped over the wagon and sprinted, following the path formed by the multiple images of Sidney aligned like dominoes, without thinking about the bullets flying at me.

"Left, right, duck!" Sidney instructed me ahead of time, miraculously letting me avoid all the bullets.

My ears buzzed as gusts of wind passed by my sides. I pulled the cord of the grenade, knowing I had scarcely four seconds to make it to the end of the wagon. As I approached the infernal machine, Sidney's projected tunnel narrowed, showing me that the way across was not circumventing it, but passing above.

"Jump!"

I stepped on a ledge at the front to gain impetus and jumped over the machine gun—amid the incredulous eyes of the soldiers—passing through the gap between the protective plates. I dumped the grenade in midair and landed on the metal tunnel on the other side, rolling and ducking to reduce the impact. The grenade exploded behind me with a jolt, dispersing shrapnel.

My ears were partially deaf from the blast, but I could hear Sidney's voice clearly in my head, as if he could speak directly to my soul. "Go! Go! Go! You need to continue."

I leaped over the next car, a personnel carrier car. Soldiers inside the pillbox were waiting for me, poking out the muzzles of their rifles through the slits. But I didn't care. I ran as if they were spectators who came to see me competing.

"Left, left, right, duck!"

I followed Sidney's instructions religiously, but in a sidestep, my boot slipped slightly on a shallow puddle of rainwater formed by the cavity of the sunken roof. My shoulder passed through Sidney's projection and twitched with the ardent pain of the graze of a bullet, proving to me that my life truly was in peril.

Standing over the hump, I ignited two more grenades and dumped them inside the slits. I caught sight of Ghislain wriggling his BMW on the road as he engaged in combat. I continued my race, sensing the wagon shaking at each explosion. When I was about to reach the end of the car, Sidney appeared before me, creating a dead end. "Stoooooop!"

I leaned backward to compensate for the inertia and skidded with my boots to a halt before touching Sidney. Before I could catch my breath, the reason for the abrupt stop became clear.

A shower of bullets trailed along the train roof to the antiaircraft machine gun at the end of the next car. An American aircraft overflew just some yards above my head and a gust of wind blew my hair. The American planes had followed the train inland after all. In the sky, a squadron of bombers hovering at high altitude released a series of bombs that landed in the surroundings, erecting geysers of dirt and smoke, shattering trees and nearby constructions. A bomb hit the last wagon and blasted the vehicle transport away. The jolt propagated across the entire train, bringing me to my knees to avoid falling.

After unleashing their destructive cargo, the pilots maneuvered their bombers for retreat.

"*Amis! Amis!*" the alarmed soldiers screamed, German slang for American soldiers. I was no longer their biggest threat. They concentrated their personnel and armament to retaliate against the invaders. The antiaircraft weapon trailed the airplanes' trajectory across the sky, leaving its flank exposed. This time I didn't wait for Sidney to show me the way. I ran halfway through the car and hurled a grenade at the feet of the distracted gunner and the artillerymen feeding endless ammo belts to the insatiable guns. Sidney materialized behind them, but I cast myself prone and crossed my arms around my head before he shared the touch of death. The explosion blew the crew away.

"Just one more wagon!" I encouraged myself as I got back to my feet. My path ahead was now cleared.

The command wagon differed from the previous; the only access from the roof was through a metal hatch. The idea of dropping my last grenade inside to neutralize any threat crossed my mind, but I refrained from doing it. I was unsure where the detention cell was located, and the blast could harm my children or Bill. I'd have to go downstairs and figure it out.

I gripped the two handles and pulled with all my strength, but the hatch didn't give an inch. *Maybe it's latched.* I attempted a second time, but suddenly, the hatch flipped open. I fell on my buttocks. A soldier nearly seven feet tall towered over me as he climbed onto the roof.

"Stowaway!" the giant said, grinding his teeth.

I tried to crawl away from him, but his sturdy arm held me by the collar of my uniform, and my feet wriggled as he lifted me with ease. I punched his arm and kicked his flank, unable to reach his face, but I inflicted no harm to his muscular body.

"Do you know how we deal with stowaways?" He motioned toward the road.

My blood rushed at the idea of falling from this height. *I would die.* But when the mountain of a man rotated his torso to gain momentum to throw me, his motion brought me closer to him, and I managed to elbow his face. He released me.

"Bitch!" the man grunted, blood running from his broken nose. I stepped back.

"Helmut! Are you okay?" somebody called behind him. Five soldiers had climbed to the roof. "Step back. We'll take care of her."

"I'll kill her!" Helmut screamed, enraged.

I would have no chance against five fully armed soldiers. My gaze drifted to the road, searching for Ghislain, hoping he could help me, but he was nowhere to be seen. *Is he all right? I hope so,* I prayed, since I had not seen him since the bombing. With all guns pointing at me, I revealed my last grenade with a trembling hand and started pulling the cord, willing to blow us all up before being captured.

"Don't force us to shoot you!" the leader of the group barked. "I was a friend of your brother's. We—we can work this through. Just put the grenade down," he said nervously. But was it true, or was he just messing with my head to persuade me? "Your father would not have wanted this for you."

But instead of being a call to reason, those words burned like a red-hot iron on my raw wound, reenergizing my wrath.

"Sidney, this is a suitable moment for you to show up," I mumbled, ready to pull the last stretch of the cord, cold beads of sweat rolling down my face.

As if he had heard me, Sidney passed by my side, looking at me askance. He strode toward the soldiers as a shrill sound in the sky grew louder. Behind them, an American airplane swooped from the sky with its guns spitting fire, tracing a path of sparks over the ironclad roof.

"Incoming!" a soldier yelled, and they spun to confront the attacker, but their weapons were no match for the high-caliber artillery of the plane.

Sidney passed among the soldiers, gently touching their shoulders as the rain of bullets pierced their bodies. The glowing trail of death approached me next, and with nowhere to run, I squeezed my eyes and braced for the impact. But the rattling of the machine gun halted, and the airplane whooshed above me, leaving behind a powerful gust of wind that knocked me back. I opened my eyes and ran my hands over my torso with incredulity, feeling only my heart banging against my rib cage. The track of smoky bullet holes running across the roof had stopped just inches from my feet. "I-I'm alive!" I declared with a nervous laugh. "Sidney?" I called, but he had vanished.

Three airplanes followed the American fighter in close pursuit, with the *Balkenkreuz*, the beam cross, printed on their wings and fuselages. "The Luftwaffe," I whispered as the planes performed an intricate dance in the sky, a dogfight.

If Göring's air forces were already here, SS were next. *You must focus, Emma.* I had no time to waste. I inhaled deeply and tiptoed through the butchered bodies, collecting with revulsion a machine gun and a few grenades before descending the ladder. Inside, I found myself in a quiet corridor running the length of the car. The armored wall had slim windows at the top, allowing the sunlight to filter in. I advanced, pushing open the door of each room using the muzzle of the machine gun, my finger hooked around the trigger.

The first room was a meeting room. A collection of maps draped the table, and diagrams filled every inch of the blackboards hanging from the walls. The following room was a comms room crammed with radio and telegraph equipment. A voice broke through the static of the radio. "Ground support is now on its way. I repeat, ground support is coming. Hold your position."

"*Scheisse!*" I had to hurry before reinforcements arrived.

The door to the adjacent room creaked open, revealing the bars of a cell holding my children and Bill captive. My children were hugging each other, huddling in a corner. But before I could rejoice about finally finding them, Bill issued a warning. "Peach, look out!"

As I stepped inside the room, a gloved hand trapped the barrel of my gun, neutralizing my capacity to aim. Two soldiers emerged from behind the wall. Before I could react, the soldier holding my gun pointed his handgun at my head and squeezed the trigger twice.

"Peach!" my children screamed in unison.

There was no way in this world a trained soldier could have missed such close shots. Yet the bullets passed beside my ears with a deafening buzz, grazing my curls and hitting the wall behind me.

The soldier's eyes widened in disbelief. "What the f—"

I seized the opportunity to kick him in the groin. When he curled in pain, I hit his nape with the butt of my machine gun, rendering him unconscious. Bill poked his hands out through the bars and choked the second soldier from behind against the cage until he fainted.

Having neutralized the threat, I finally exhaled.

"Peach! Peach!" My children swarmed the gate, their tiny hands coming out to welcome me. "You came for us!"

"My children!" I knelt to hug them through the bars. "I'll never abandon you. You hear me? Never!"

Bill watched our emotional reunion with a hopeful smile on his battered face. His ragged uniform exhibited wounds in his body as well. They had mistreated him while captive. *Tortured.* "Are you okay?" I asked.

"Now I am."

I returned the smile.

CHAPTER 44

I EXPLAINED GHISLAIN'S PLAN TO BILL as I opened the cell.

"Any surviving soldiers will be here any minute, and reinforcements are on their way to intercept the train." I handed him the machine gun and all the grenades I carried except one, which I fastened to my utility belt. "I need you to guard the end of this wagon and not allow anybody to pass through." We stripped the passed-out soldiers of their weapons and dragged them inside the cell. I picked up the handgun that had failed to kill me. *A lucky charm.* "We need enough time to hijack the locomotive and set up Little Gustav for an explosion."

"You know how to do it?" Bill asked, skeptical.

"I hope Ghislain instructed me well enough." I expected things would align for me, as had happened so far.

"Where is he?"

"We'll meet at Little Gustav." I avoided Bill's eyes, unsure of Ghislain's whereabouts. But there was no turning back. We had to remain confident even if we had to rely on a lie.

"I'll do my best."

"I know you will…" I remembered the story about his brother. "Sorry for dragging you into this."

"I crossed the Atlantic to fight Nazis… and here I am. Fighting to my last breath."

"Thank you, Bill." I patted his arm. "Come, children, follow me."

The metallic doors at the end of the wagon revealed the breathtaking war machine, Little Gustav. But even with the barrel and legs retracted, the moving cannon was anything but little, compared with a tank or a truck.

"Hold tightly and stay behind me." I placed Valeska's hands around my waist so I could hold the gun.

We advanced through a narrow corridor between the first set of stabilizer legs, which resembled the hind legs of a giant grasshopper. The tubes and wires attached to the legs transported me to the pages of Jules Verne's *The Steam House*, as if the steam-powered mechanical elephant described in the novel had come to life. Metal steps led us to the turret with the telescopic barrel. A single panel controlled the pressure pumped into the huge pistons that adjusted the inclination of the barrel and rotation of the platform, allowing it to shoot in any direction. The size of the projectile chamber was so huge that a standing person could fit inside. I harbored no doubt that the engineers who built this artillery monstrosity had visualized themselves conquering the world atop this mechanical spider.

After passing through the second set of stabilizer legs, we arrived at the system car mentioned by Ghislain. The first section had a pneumatic crane with a cabin mounted on a rotating platform, primarily used to load the cannon's massive ammunition. The second section was the ammo deposit, with the five-foot-long shells stockpiled behind steel roll-up doors. It was like looking at bullets magnified by a microscope. The third section was the ancillary boiler and coal supply, which fed pressure to Little Gustav and the crane through a maze of pipes.

"Wait for me here." I instructed the children to hide inside the armored shed storing the ammunition. "No matter what you hear, don't come out. Understood?"

They assented without objection.

A bloody passageway around the boiler connected to the locomotive. I circumvented the bodies of fallen soldiers, who, judging by the size of their wounds and the caliber of the bullet holes around them, had died during the aerial attacks.

The locomotive looked like a torpedo, aerodynamic and

chromed by the armor dressing it so extensively that the wheels were invisible. Only the chimney popped out, protected by a metal plate at each side. I peeked inside the cabin through a slim window on the door. An engineer operated the train while arguing about the reinforcements with a man outside my field of view. The thought of shooting the engineer crossed my mind, but we knew nothing about how to operate a train. I would have to sneak inside and force them to comply at gunpoint. I twisted the handle, but the door didn't budge. Unfortunately, the engineer caught sight of me through a rearview mirror.

"They're here!" The engineer reached for his handgun.

I ducked before the bullets pierced the window and glass chips showered over me. The vibration of the bullets hitting the metal door transferred across to my back. During a break in the fire, I poked my pistol over the windowsill and shot blindly. But after my gunshots, they resumed their attack. Fearful they could make their way to the door and catch me off guard, I reached for the last grenade in my utility belt. Judging by their closeness, I activated the grenade and counted three seconds before hurling it inside.

"Grena—" The engineer's shriek was drowned by the blast, and silence settled afterward.

I peeked inside the cabin and found the engineer shivering on the floor, the right side of his face soaked with blood pouring from the shrapnel buried in his flesh. Missing patches of scalp revealed the white of his skull. His squinting left eye turned to me, and he growled as his shallow and agitated breathing gave pass to a final, wheezing sigh. Sidney walked onto the scene like the actor who remains hidden behind the curtains, waiting for his cue. He knelt beside the moribund to concede the long-awaited peace with a tender caress.

"You're getting better at killing," he said.

The gruesome image of a man dying by my hand, which I had vehemently avoided so far, tore the cloak of wrath I had wrapped myself in. My feelings, numbed by the psychological pain of my trauma, flared, overwhelming me with guilt. *All those grenades. All those men. What have I done? I need to help him...* Blame-infused, I recklessly passed my arm through the broken window, scraping my hand on the sawtoothed edges. I stood on my tiptoes, hyperextending my arm, and with my fingers grazing the handle, I realized I needed the keys resting in the engineer's hand to remove the lock.

"*Scheisse!*" I hammered the metal door, leaving bloody prints at every blow until sorrow brought me to my knees. My death-tainted hands quivered at the thought of the soldier's words, *"Your father would not have wanted this for you."*

"I didn't want this either… but they forced me…" I babbled, rocking on my knees.

Sidney's phantasmagorical presence crossed the door. "All killers tell themselves the same argument."

"But… I'm just trying to… save lives…" I wailed.

"Save lives by taking lives?" Sidney quirked an eyebrow at me. "How is that fair?"

Fairness? I wondered, elevating my eyes to meet Sidney's. "I should be at school running for sport, not to save my life. Passing a baton, not a grenade. What did I do to deserve my misfortune?"

Sidney's lips remained pursed.

I shook my head. "Life is not fair… not even in death."

"Do you think he deserved to die?"

The disfigured face of the engineer flashed across my mind. I didn't know what kind of man he was. What kind of brother, husband, parent, or son he had been in life.

"What makes your cause more just than theirs?"

"Innocence." I gulped. "My children are just innocents caught in a war of bloody-minded men." I thought about the atrocities committed by their persecutors: the killings, the abuse, the torture, the concentration camps. All of them were guilty of monstrosities by act or omission. No, there were no innocents among their ranks. Not even my father and brother. I funneled my feelings of impotence to my fists, clenching until the sensation of pressure surpassed the pain of my blood-dripping wounds.

"How many peccant sinners are you willing to sacrifice for innocents? Fifty? A hundred?"

"Only one… me," I answered with reinforced conviction. "But when you come to collect my soul, you can ask me again how many bastards I dragged to hell with me."

"Why are you so willing to sacrifice yourself for them?"

"Because I know how it feels to be robbed of your innocence. The darkness weighing on your chest, the hollowness gnawing your insides." I got back on my feet. "There is no hope left for me to dream of. The only happiness I could ever savor would be through them." I echoed the words of my mother, finally unshrouding the mystery of motherhood. "It doesn't matter if it costs me everything I have left."

"Peach! Peach!" The dim voices of my children emerged through the ruckus of the locomotive, and without thinking twice, I hurried after them, thinking the worst. But upon my arrival at the ammo deposit, all my concerns eased.

"Ghislain?" I asked incredulously, witnessing a miracle. "Ghislain! Ghislain!" I rushed to him.

"Emma!" Ghislain hugged me so profusely that he put back together all the loose parts inside me.

His abdomen flinched at my embrace. "Are you all right?" I asked. A wine-colored stain had expanded across the flank of his ebony uniform.

"I will be, once all of you are safe…" He glanced over at my children. "…and we've blown this infernal machine." He pushed me aside and strode to the boiler feeding Little Gustav.

"Ghislain!" I went after him, trying to explain our predicament. "The locomotive… The engineer is… dead." I didn't want to admit authorship of his murder. "But the cabin is locked… The locomotive is out of control!"

Ghislain kept shoveling coal to the raging flames.

"We can't stop it… unless… Jov helps me open the door!" He had helped me before.

"We'll deal with that later." Ghislain examined the pressure valves. "We need to set up the cannon to explode and load the remaining shells onto the wagon with Little Gustav… then we'll detach it."

"But maybe we can escape now." My children were safe, and I could not care less about blowing up Little Gustav. I just wanted to get as far away as possible from this train.

"There is no other way, Emma." Ghislain's tousled hair waved in the wind and his steel eyes shone with determination. "We need to cover our escape."

"Cover? But Bill can—" I thought of the remaining soldiers confined to the rear wagons.

"We just passed Weeze, and we're heading south at full speed, where the bulk of Nazi armed forces wait for the enemy. We're running out of time. *Wehrmacht* loom across the horizon."

CHAPTER 45

REINFORCEMENTS WERE APPROACHING, but we were far from being ready.

"Emma, get in the cabin. I need you to operate that crane," Ghislain instructed as he rolled up the steel doors, exposing the person-size shells.

"Me? But I've never operated a crane before!" I worried, remembering it took me weeks to learn how to drive Papa's car even with Anton's instruction.

"You better learn quickly while I prepare the cannon."

"But—"

"Trial and error!"

Without another option, I jumped inside the cabin of the crane. The seat had a control panel on each side, full of buttons. I quickly identified a black knob to switch on the system. The crane shook as the boiler pumped the pressurized steam through the metallic arteries of the mechanized arm. "Good! Now what?" A button labeled DEPLOY blinked with an orange light. "Could it be this?" I dared to press it, and the stabilizer legs of Little Gustav woke from slumber with a loud, metallic roar and spread outside the wagon, extending its anchors. "No, no, no!" I turned it off, but before I could override the instruction, the anchors plunged into the soil for a moment, yanking the entire train.

"Peach, what are you doing?" Ghislain screamed from the cannon, struggling to keep his balance.

"Sorry! I'm trying!"

"Use the levers!"

I held the levers at the end of each armrest. I moved the left lever to the side and found it controlled the turret rotation, and if I moved it back and forth, I controlled the angle of the arm, up or down. Subsequently, the side movement of the right lever controlled the arm extension and the back-and-forth movement the rotation of the gripper. Finally, a smaller lever by the side controlled the clamp of the gripper. "Now I'm ready!"

"Peach! Load it!" Ghislain signaled me. "I'll guide you!"

"I'm on it!" I rotated the crane and carefully approached the first projectile, knowing mishandling them would kill us all. My breathing shortened as I nudged the gripper around the shell, pinned from the point and the back. I clamped the pincers with utmost care, and once secured, I extracted it. I dried my clammy hands on my pants before continuing.

"You're doing great! Now, into the cannon!" Ghislain cheered, guiding me, hands on the shell. "Lower it slowly!" He motioned since I could barely hear him amid the noise. He spun his fist, instructing me I had to rotate it, and then extended his fingers to release it inside the cannon chamber. *Good!* I could read Ghislain's lips as he raised his thumbs.

I sighed, fearful of suffering a shoulder contracture due to the overwhelming tension.

Ghislain approached the cabin. "We need to load the remaining five on Little Gustav's turret!"

I grumbled at the arduous effort but operated the gripper anyway. Ghislain guided me to pile up the projectiles. One, two, three went by, but during the fourth round, an explosion in the communications wagon broke my concentration. Bill emerged from a dark cloud of smoke and rushed to find cover behind Little Gustav's metallic limbs. He had lost his defensive post. "Ghislain, Bill is in trouble! Children, take cover!"

Soldiers showed at the entrance and over the wagon roof, opening fire. I put up my arms to shield me from the bullets that smashed into the windows, tracing crystal webs.

"It's bulletproof, Peach!" Ghislain reassured me amid my

screams. "Keep loading them!" He replaced the machine gun magazine and peeked up to counterattack.

"But they'll blow up the bomb!" I said, alarmed at the bullets ricocheting over the crane's metallic arm.

"Just one more and I'll start the countdown on the timer! It's now or never!"

Ghislain was right; we were so close now. *We should end it.* I continued the strenuous procedure without guidance this time. I forced my eyes and my mind to disregard Sidney, who appeared and vanished time and time again as he welcomed the falling soldiers into his benevolent arms.

Death was drawing closer to us.

Step by step.

I deposited the penultimate shell, and Bill used the crane arm as cover for retreat. He limped to the cabin, bleeding from his calf. "I'm out of ammo!" He grimaced, trying to manage the pain.

"In the back!" I instructed, thinking that even if he could not find ammunition in the armory, there were a bunch of dead, armed soldiers in the boiler passageway. I collected the last projectile. *Finally!* But my enthusiasm was short-lived.

"*Kettenkrads* at two o'clock!" Ghislain alerted.

A convoy of Kettenkrads, a hybrid vehicle, half motorcycle, half tank, approached the right flank. The front of the vehicles was that of a motorcycle, with a front wheel controlled by handlebars, and the rear resembled a tiny tank for cargo. Its treads allowed Kettenkrads to traverse difficult terrain—like the muddy soil surrounding the railroads after a rainstorm. This light, personnel-carrier vehicle was the fastest in the Reich's *panzer* division, making it the perfect choice for sending reinforcements in a situation like this. The strategist Von Schroeder had sent a battalion of men on wheels to reclaim his train.

A soldier riding the cargo compartment of the Kettenkrad at the vanguard stood up. My blood iced as I recognized Reinhard. But a concoction of feelings erupted in my entrails, a fierce battle between trepidation and anger to gain control over my actions. *Of course it had to be him.* In his mercy, Von Schroeder had robbed Reinhard of the ecstasy of ending my life. Now, unleashed, Reinhard would not refuse the joy of inflicting pain on me. And I... I had convinced myself only the sweet taste of vengeance could quench my grief over the assassination of my parents.

Our paths crossing again—like Renenet said—was no accident. But this time I was determined to do everything in my power to ensure this coincidence was the last.

Reinhard motioned, providing tactical instructions to his men, and the convoy split into three. The first group aligned parallel to the train, driving as close as possible to allow the soldiers to jump over, like pirates boarding a vessel. The second group, carrying sharpshooters, remained in the rear, providing covering fire. The third group, led by Reinhard, assaulted Little Gustav.

Ghislain ducked behind the control panel to avoid the bullets coming from multiple directions, unable to retaliate. We had less than a minute before all those soldiers boarding the train made it to Little Gustav. We were massively outnumbered, underequipped, and wounded. Our situation was spiraling downward to a single outcome. *Defeat.*

Reinhard's eyes met my gaze, and he smirked knowingly; once again the cockroach had crawled under his boot.

So this is the waterfall at the end of the river? I remembered Valeska's analogy of fate. But I was too rebellious. This was a fate I refused to accept, even if I had to swim upstream.

My heart pumped burning wrath into my bloodstream. "I-will-not-allow-it!" I clutched the levers controlling the crane and yanked them toward Reinhard, releasing the last shell in midair. The driver of Reinhard's Kettenkrad eluded the projectile, which bounced over the ground, knocking down a few Kettenkrads like pins in a bowling alley before exploding.

Then, inexplicably, time came to a halt. I became a prisoner of a heartbeat that expanded forever. Incapable of reacting, I witnessed the shell cracking open in slow motion, rays of light leaking out. Black feathers fell out of the sky, shed from the raven wings of Sidney, who—unconstrained by time—glided gracefully. The Harbinger of Death fluttered around, gently touching the shoulders of the time-frozen soldiers, their timorous faces alight with the radiance of doom, in a macabre waltz beheld only during seasons of war. In a disquieting, yet liberating, abscission of souls.

Clocks ticked again and a blinding fireball expanded, engulfing the nearest Kettenkrads, and a torrent of smoke erupted violently. A wind tsunami carried a deafening noise, hitting everything around as if crashing against an invisible wall. The mighty shock wave rocked the armored train, almost derailing it. The sudden tug propelled me against the shattered bulletproof glass. As I pulled myself back to my seat, my sight turned blurry and crimson and my fingertips slick and warm as I reached for my aching forehead. Ears buzzing, I strained my eyes to see through the now almost-opaque window, traced with a multitude of fractures, but which miraculously still held together. The explosion had wiped out more than half the Kettenkrads and soldiers, but the remaining were still determined to continue the fight.

"Just one more bomb… to finish the work," I rambled, out of my mind, thinking about collecting another projectile from Little Gustav, when I caught sight of Reinhard. He pointed a *panzerfaust*, a rocket-propelled grenade launcher, directly at me. "*Scheisse!*" I veered the crane's arm to knock him down, but his driver pressed the brakes and I missed. Reinhard fired, but the sudden jerk of the Kettenkrad messed up his aim. The rocket passed the cabin and collided with the metal shed where my children were hiding. The layers of armor burst open like bones in an exposed fracture.

"Nooooooo!" I yelled, drunk with anger. Nostalgic about Death's tragic peace, which I had just witnessed, I threw myself into the turmoil of my sensations, subconsciously begging for Sidney to put an end to my suffering. "I'll show you how to squash a cockroach!"

CHAPTER 46

I LUNGED THE CRANE ARM AFTER REINHARD, the claws of the gripper open like a hungry crocodile. But with my imprecise movements, I plucked the driver instead, his legs kicking in the air. Reinhard jumped over the crane arm, hanging from the pipes feeding the pistons. "You're going nowhere!" With a swift move, I slammed the crane arm against Little Gustav's stabilizer legs. The driver fell to the ground and disappeared, left behind by the speeding train. But Reinhard flew against Little Gustav's hind legs, and I lost sight of him.

"Peach!" Ghislain showed up at the cabin, cradling his left arm.

"Are you okay?" I asked, startled, but before he could answer, anguish tangled around my throat. "My children?"

"Shaken and scared, but alive."

I sighed with relief, as if the air locked inside my lungs had been pressuring my insides.

"I need cover while I detach Gustav." Ghislain descended to the wagon connection, and I interposed the crane arm to shield him from bullets while Bill provided covering fire. Ghislain removed the metal pins and uncoupled Little Gustav, but the pipes feeding the pneumatic pressure maintained the car attachment. He slammed the pipes with the pins, frustrated that he had not accounted for this in his plan. "I'll go to set the timer and bring a mallet to sever the pump lines!"

"Ghislain, wait—"

But before I could warn him, he ventured over to Little Gustav in the midst of gunfire. The stressed pipelines were shaking and with the slightest yank could break at any second. But upon Ghislain's arrival at the turret, Reinhard emerged from under the barrel and charged him.

"Ghislain!" I screamed as the two wrestled on top of Little Gustav.

The gunfire stopped from both sides, each fearful of hitting their own man. I had my hands tied as well, so I descended from the crane, eager to run to Ghislain's aid. But the SS soldiers had the same idea and started approaching the cannon stealthily.

You need to act now! Think, Emma, think! My gaze wandered around for a tool to cut the pipes. *The slightest yank could break the pipes at any second...* The thought echoed in my head, *A yank, a powerful yank...* and I remembered how the deployment of the stabilizer legs had yanked the train when deployed. "Ghislain, hold on to the crane!" I rushed back to the cabin, praying he could free himself from Reinhard in time. "Please, Ghislain, you can do it." I activated the switch, bringing Little Gustav back to life with a deafening roar. "Ghislain, c'mon!" I hurried him as the legs started spreading.

Ghislain landed a hit on Reinhard's jaw, knocking him off, and sprinted toward the crane's arm.

The leg anchors buried into the ground, plowing the soil as they drilled deeper. The yank broke the pipelines, releasing a jet of steam, and finally detached Little Gustav from the locomotive.

"You-will-not-escape!" Reinhard ran and jumped at the last second, hanging from Ghislain.

The sudden halt caused by Little Gustav and the strong inertia twisted metal like paper, compressing the whole train. The rear wagons derailed and ramped, piling on top of the cannon.

As the locomotive left behind the crash site, the loss of steam pressure in the piping system affected the crane. The metal arm deflated, and in its descent, Reinhard's feet dragged across the wooden ties and gravel in between the rails, but he refused to let Ghislain go.

Then the projectiles on board Little Gustav exploded.

There was a flash, and pieces of the armored wagons flew into the sky as a mushroom cloud erupted. The powerful shock wave expanded, rippling the ground as if it were a sea wave. Fortunately, by then we were far enough away to avoid most of the explosion's destructive power. However, the soil undulation transferred through the railways. The locomotive jolted as if it had passed over a bump and started running off its rails.

I turned to the front instinctively, and my children rushed to me. "Peeeeeeeeeeeaaaaach!" They clustered around me, and I hugged them. The locomotive tilted to the right, like a boat about to sink, and when it hit the ground, inertia sent us flying several yards before we landed and rolled to unconsciousness.

I woke up, face flattened against the cold mud, coughing out the dirt lodged inside my mouth. When I tried to pull myself up, an electrifying pain ran down my shoulder, and my arm faltered. *Is it broken or dislocated?* I acknowledged either was a small price to pay, considering I had survived the train derailment.

"Va-Valeska? Jov? Children?" I rolled over. My sight was blurry from the concussion; I was unable to recognize them among the shapes scattered across the field. A source of light drew my attention—the locomotive wreckage on fire. The silhouette of a man heading toward me eclipsed the flames.

"Ghislain?" I asked, straining my eyes as he approached, only to realize that the man was not Ghislain but Reinhard.

CHAPTER 47

REINHARD LUMBERED ACROSS THE TRAIN DEBRIS, dragging Ghislain's slack body like an ox pulling a yoke. "Are you awake, Sleeping Beauty?" He snorted. "You robbed me of the pleasure of waking you with a kiss…"

"You—you… devil!" I grunted.

Reinhard snickered briefly and grimaced as he pressed his flank. Blood had wicked through the textile layers of his uniform. "People call upon that name, carefree, jesting about invoking her… Until one night, she appears before you. Uncalled. Uninvited." Reinhard ripped his jacket and shirt open, exposing his torso. He was bleeding profusely from multiple tiny wounds, as if a shotgun had hit him.

Shrapnel from the explosions, I concluded.

"And once you have seen her face, her true face, it is engraved on your pupils forever. No matter where you hide, her face is visible across the thickest concrete. No matter if you run, her voice sounds as if she were breathing on your neck, holding you with a sorrowful embrace that will make you suffer the loneliest loneliness." Reinhard became lost in his thoughts, beholding his blood-stained leather glove. "I'm just human, after all… bound to mortality. Unlike the bornless."

"That's what you are to me, a devil! A monster!" I squeezed a fistful of dirt, spotting my children lying wounded from the crash. "You're the worst. You're wicked and cruel, and a despicable human being!" Breathless, I tried to get back on my feet, aware I could not win this fight but rejecting surrender. *You must finish it, Emma.*

Reinhard pondered for a moment. "We are all somebody else's monster. Who do you think is the monster to the families of the soldiers you've just slain?"

Dozens had died during the explosions and derailment I'd provoked. Despite being Nazi soldiers, they were still human beings. My face contorted in anger. "It was you! Everything is your fault! They're all dead because of you! I-I didn't want any of this! I was innocent!"

"I know how it feels." Reinhard pulled a tin box from his jacket pocket. "I was not born a monster, I was raised by one. I was innocent like you." From the box, he extracted a syringe and drew the contents of a vial. "But I became responsible by feeding the monster with my fear, anger, and hate, reinforcing her dominion over me."

Ghislain's eyelids cracked open. His irises scanned the surroundings until he found me, granting me relief. He extended his arm slowly, to avoid calling Reinhard's attention. An iron rod was lying within his reach. Figuring out his intentions, I forced my eyes to meet Reinhard's, to avoid unintentionally revealing Ghislain's plan.

"Feelings turn us into victims, prey for monsters." Reinhard hooked the syringe into his track-marked elbow and injected. "But we can stop the suffering… if we can…"—the empty syringe fell from his shaking fingers—"stop feeling at all…" He shivered as if suffering hypothermia. Blood vessels popped up over his skin like forking rivers, conveying the substance into his entire body. Clots formed in his wounds, stopping his bleeding without the need of sutures or bandages. This explained how he had recovered so quickly from the gunshot received during my escape from the hotel in Hamm. Reinhard's muscles tensed and bulked as his vascular arms flexed. His troubled face turned impassive, his eyes cold and lifeless. All trace of emotion previously displayed was gone. Reinhard had turned himself into an automaton.

"Only we can eradicate the suffering of the world. Only we can guide the underman to become the Overman." Reinhard unsheathed a knife from his belt and pointed it at me. "This is bigger than you and me, Fräulein Niemeyer. More important than your dead parents and even larger than this war. It's about stealing the fire from the gods to give it to mankind, as Prometheus fooled Zeus and stole fire to give to humanity. The gods' secrets remain locked within the genes of these children. I'm going to harvest those genes so the *Übermensch* can thrive, even if as punishment a Reichsadler will devour my liver for eternity," he declared, referring to both the Imperial Eagle standing over the swastika and the eternal punishment imposed by Zeus upon Prometheus.

"You have certainly given fire to humanity… and by doing so, you set everything ablaze." I engaged in his argument to provide more time to Ghislain. "In my wanderings from Wewelsburg to here, I saw nothing but suffering and desolation. You Nazis didn't save German folk. You offered up humanity as a sacrifice to trick the gods."

"You're just a simpleminded woman, incapable of understanding."

"No. You gave me the fire, Reinhard. In that dungeon, you sparked an ember within me that burns with the flames of justice and will not extinguish until it devours those who have hurt us." I drew strength from the memory of the charred remains of my parents to push myself up to my knees. "This is a tale in which the monster burns at the end."

"I admire your bravado, but I won't falter, even if I have to squeeze the remaining life out of you, Cockroach."

"I dare to object…" Ghislain had risen behind Reinhard, wielding the iron rod. "Gruppenführer."

Reinhard revolved and Ghislain swung double-handed, like a baseball player trying to hit a home run. The rod hit Reinhard's neck—and bounced. Ghislain gaped in awe; the impact had barely shaken Reinhard, despite him using all his strength.

Reinhard snorted like a raging bull, clutching his knife. "Poor judgment, soldat."

Ghislain swiped again, this time aiming for the head, but Reinhard ducked and slashed horizontally, drawing a blood line across Ghislain's thighs. Ghislain stumbled back, incredulous.

"Ungrateful!" Reinhard kicked Ghislain's chest.

Ghislain fell but dragged himself away, still facing Reinhard.

"The Reich gave you everything, and you dared to betray us? All you had to do was pull the damn trigger!"

Ghislain grunted and released another blow from the ground, but Reinhard parried it with a kick. The rod flew out of Ghislain's hands, landing yards away. Now off guard, Ghislain received a kick with such strength it flattened him against the ground.

"Wolfrick did not ask you to think!" Reinhard viciously trampled Ghislain, who threw up his arms to shield himself. "It was a goddamned order!" Reinhard pulled back his arm in preparation to thrust the knife into Ghislain's chest.

I gathered my remaining strength and charged against Reinhard's back. My head whipped and my spine compressed at the impact. But despite my effort, Reinhard only staggered a few steps forward.

"You bitch!" He turned, landing a backhanded blow on my face.

The wooden haft of the knife cracked my cheekbone. I fell on all fours, spitting blood, with a skull-splitting pain numbing my thoughts. Reinhard stomped on my back, and my limbs surrendered.

"Are you so eager to crawl beneath my boot, Cockroach?" His heel crushed my vertebrae amid my sobs of pain. "Shut up, for once!"

"Let her go, monster!" My children came to my rescue. The smaller hooked themselves to Reinhard's legs and the older jumped over his back, joining efforts to subdue him.

"Children! No!" I crawled toward them, in spite of the acute pain in my back pinning me down.

"Vermin!" Reinhard mercilessly punched and kicked his way out of entrapment, hurling my children through the air. "Unwanted by your families! Rejected by society! We offered you redemption! To give a purpose to your"—once freed, Reinhard inhaled and exhaled soundly—"pointless lives." Those last words triggered something in Reinhard's head. He spat, combed back the tufts of his hair using his hand, and his haughty face craned over the desolated landscape. Then he looked at me askance, as if I truly were a cockroach. "But you… all you had to do was be kind… but you had to be so mean. Of the entire world, you were the one who had no right treating me like that."

Reinhard's words triggered the repressed memories of my rape, when he'd addressed me as if I were somebody else. *"Don't you love me?… Why have you chained me?"* he had reproached me with a childish voice back then.

"All I wanted was to feel your arms around me… even if you had to pretend you loved me." Reinhard's eyes filled with tears as he battled to restrain his emotions. He had become the Crying Man, as my children had nicknamed him. "But I didn't deserve even that… Mama." Reinhard shook his head, as if he wanted to get rid of the thoughts controlling him.

Finally, the hideous realization struck me that the person he was seeing in me was none other than his own mother. I could barely imagine the horrors his mother had subjected him to, to turn him into such a monster.

"But even if before your eyes, I'm unworthy… I'll show you how I'll carve my name into the annals of history in flesh and blood." Reinhard laughed edgily as he approached me, his eyes alight with determination to take revenge on his mother, embodied in me.

But before he could stab me, gunshots resounded.

Reinhard lurched a couple of steps before collapsing. A final mouthful of air escaped his lungs as he went motionless, only blood kept spilling from two bullet holes on his back.

Standing behind him was Bill, his face covered in dried blood and mud, as if he had just crawled out of his tomb. Bill's arm dangled loosely, holding the murderous pistol. "We disembarked on these shores to *prevent* a madman from writing history." Bill staggered to me. "It's over, Peach… He's dead now."

Dead? Is Reinhard finally dead? I could not conceive it after everything my children and I had gone through. *Is Edelweiss's death finally avenged?* I remembered holding his inert body in my arms while his spirit held Sidney's hand… *Sidney… Where is Sidney?* I looked around, distracted. If Reinhard had truly died, the second sight would have allowed me to see Sidney reaping his soul… *But I didn't…* and the only explanation would be that… *Reinhard is still alive!*

"Bill, he's not dead yet! Look out!" I screamed.

Before Bill could react, Reinhard stabbed his calf. Bill shrieked and aimed feebly, searching the ground, but Reinhard was already standing by his side. Bill witnessed in awe as the undead towered over him, brought back to life by the drug's regenerative powers.

"Amused?… *Ami.*" Reinhard smiled viciously and plunged the knife into Bill's chest.

"Nooooooooo!" I cried as Bill collapsed.

Amid my consternation, Ghislain surprised Reinhard from behind, wrapping his arms around his neck, and choked him. Reinhard twisted and turned like a raging bull trying to buck him off.

"Let-me-go!" Reinhard gasped, stabbing Ghislain's thigh and flank, gushes of blood spouting at each thrust.

"Ne-never!" Ghislain replied through clenched teeth.

Horrified, I got to my feet to help him, but somebody was already heading toward them.

Breaking through the flaming debris with firm strides, Sidney lurked behind the two men like a hungry wolf stalking its prey. *But whose life will he take?* That was the question, as the scales were tipping in favor of Reinhard. Exhausted and lacerated, Ghislain could no longer sustain the pressure needed to asphyxiate Reinhard. Aware of his unfavorable situation, Ghislain reached for his utility belt with his right hand for a last resource—a stick grenade.

"You will pay for what you did to her!"

"Let me go! That's an order!" Reinhard insisted.

"No, no, no!" I limped with trembling legs, like a toddler learning to walk, afflicted, considering the only thing I was good at in life was running. "Sidney, no!" I screamed out in despair. "Ghislain, don't!" But despite my words, Ghislain uncorked the cap of the grenade with his mouth and secured the cap in his left hand, still hooked around Reinhard's neck.

"Release me! That's a damned order!" Reinhard begged as he realized Ghislain's intentions of blowing himself up and carrying him along.

"*Nein!*" Ghislain pulled the grenade cord, extending it until it triggered the detonation.

In the remaining fleeting seconds, I forced my legs to run a race against Death, as prophesied by Renenet. Ghislain's sterling-gray eyes rested on me one last time and his troubled expression eased. As I ran, I extended my arm to reach him, in hopes I could anchor him to this existence.

"*Lebend,*" Ghislain said with a melancholic smile.

Sidney's raven wings extended, and he embraced Ghislain, his life extinguishing in the explosion.

Live, was Ghislain's last word for me, when all this time I had been rushing toward my encounter with Death.

CHAPTER 48

"FROM WHOM ARE YOU RUNNING AWAY?" Ghislain asked me, just like the first time we met.

"From... destiny?" I said, unsure.

Ghislain's hand caressed my face with ice-cold fingers. "Run no more..." he whispered.

I regained consciousness and peeled my eyes open. Dusky cumulus clouds upholstered the sky, sprinkling snowflakes. It had not been Ghislain's icy fingers in my dreams, just snow. *Snow in September?* I wondered, oblivious to my reality. I caught a snowflake with my numb hand, but when I unfolded my fingers, the beautiful geometric figure made of ice had melted.

I sat upright, still disoriented from the grenade blast that had thrown me back. The battlefield was glazed in cotton white, fires extinguished; only columns of smoke remained. A body lay by my side and I realized with dread it was Reinhard's—or what remained of him. It was only his upper torso, with head and left arm still attached. My stomach churned as my eyes followed the trail of blood and entrails to the site of the explosion. Reinhard had used his last breath to... *creep toward me?* The thought sickened me. As he finally lay cold on the ground, I waited for the stream of relief to come. But it didn't matter how hard I forced the gleeful thoughts, my heart remained hollow, my tearful eyes battling the urge to seek Ghislain. I wouldn't bear the shock of finding him like this or even worse. It was better for me to believe he had vanished entirely from this world, just like the snowflake in my hand. Consumed by the explosion… or rather by my thirst for vengeance.

Ghislain's words, uttered last night, echoed in my head. *"I can't hold a beautiful flower in my hands without withering it."* Maybe I was cursed, just like my children… *my children?*

"Children?" I scanned the snowy landscape.

Boots trampled on the debris behind me, and I turned to find myself surrounded by SS soldiers.

"Hands up!" a soldier instructed, pointing at me with his rifle.

But my sore limbs refused to comply, or maybe I really didn't care what could happen to me anymore.

"Do it now!" he threatened.

An officer in a trench coat broke through the line of the squad and tapped the soldier's shoulder, ordering him to lower his weapon. The officer walked to me and removed his cap. Otto. He adjusted his spectacles as he gazed at Reinhard's remains.

"He—he is finally dead," I muttered.

Otto extended his hand toward me, but I flinched. "I won't harm you." He stroked my blood-smeared hair. "You're in shock. It's normal. You'll be all right."

But deep down, I knew I could never be all right again. I scowled at him. "Where are my children?"

Otto motioned his head toward an arched metal piece of the locomotive acting as a canopy, protecting my huddled children from the snow. Three soldiers guarded them.

My heart palpitated and my breath shortened at the thought of them being taken back to that horrid place. I attempted to crawl to them, but Otto held me.

"Calm down. You're wounded. You'll hurt yourself."

I struggled to free myself, but I didn't have the strength.

"Everything will be all right. Please…" Otto appeased me.

"What—what are you… doing with them… with me?" I dared to ask, confused about what his intentions really were. After all, Otto had known my plan when we met in the pantry at Wewelsburg, yet he'd allowed it, and even started the fire that served as a distraction for our escape. He'd acted as if he wanted me to take the children with me. But why?

"First, we need to tend your wounds. Medic!" Otto ordered, and a soldier carrying a leather medic's bag approached. "Where is Ghislain?"

"He—he…" I gulped. "…dead." My flooded eyes betrayed me as I glanced toward the site of the explosion.

Otto pressed his lips together in a grim expression.

"Are you in pain?" The field medic checked my vitals and continued the medical interrogation as he tended my wounds, but his questions fell on deaf ears. My gaze wandered with Otto, who searched the battlefield for Ghislain until he found him draped beneath a white sheet of snow. Otto beheld his friend with an afflicted countenance and rested a caring hand on his chest, noticing a bulge in the pocket. He pulled out a small book from inside Ghislain's jacket and browsed through the pages, reading here and there until he shut it. He stroked Ghislain's face, closing the eyelids, and placed the heel of his hand on his friend's forehead, uttering some words. Otto got back on his feet and straightened his spine. He clicked his heels and extended his arm, saluting his friend and brother-in-arms for the last time.

"You should read this." Otto deposited the book between my shaky hands upon his return. "He…" He went short of words. It was the notebook Ghislain had found in the house that he'd used *"to jot down recipes, lists of ingredients, and things of the sort,"* but which oddly he had guarded too jealously for it to be a simple recipe book. I was about to open it, guided by the red-ribbon bookmark, when a soldier interrupted us.

"Sir, the Ami is alive."

"Bring him," Otto instructed.

Bill? My troubled soul sighed, relieved of the weighty blame of his death.

Two soldiers carried Bill in their arms and lowered him by my side.

"You're alive!" I wailed, tears of happiness this time.

"Still… or so it seems." Bill grunted in pain as the medic sterilized and sutured the knife wounds.

"You will make it," Otto addressed Bill in English. He lit a cigarette, drew a mouthful of smoke, and offered it to Bill. "Smoke," he offered with a hoarse voice, making it sound more like an order.

Bill breathed in but coughed the cigarette away. "I'm—I'm sorry. I don't smoke."

Otto chuckled. "What boys do where you live, if not smoking?"

"They do smoke in Wisconsin… just… not me."

"Wisconsin? Next to the Great Lakes?" Otto asked, carefree, as if Bill were a stranger he had bumped into while crossing the street. "I visited Niagara Falls once. *Ameizingggggg!*" Otto drew from the cigarette again. "Were you at Camp Edwards?"

"No, Camp Blanding."

"You held yourself bravely on the train. I saw you from the rearguard." Otto had probably been leading the Kettenkrad group that stayed behind.

"Thank—thank you… sir," Bill said, visibly uncomfortable with how to address the amicable politeness of this battlefield rival.

Otto dropped the cigarette and pointed to the horizon. "The border should be some five kilometers heading west. Don't stop until you cross the Meuse River. You will reunite with your menfolk there."

"Am I free to go?" Bill asked dubiously. "Or are you going to shoot me once I turn my back on you?"

"Not today… but I can't vouch for tomorrow. Once you have crossed that river… then we can resume our enmity."

"What about her? Is she free to go as well?" Bill nodded at me.

Otto glanced over and knelt before me. "You fought like Valkyrie, Fräulein Niemeyer." He yanked the Iron Cross hanging from his neck. "The Führer should award you the Gold Cross of Honor of the German Mother," he said, referring to the topic we had discussed on our way to Wewelsburg Castle. "But these are wartimes." He gave me his cross. "I wish my mother had had half the courage you showed today." He half smiled. "One of my men will take you home. The fatherland needs strong women like you to rebuild once the war ends." He stood.

Home? Did I have a home, after everything that had happened? Could I return to an empty house? Everybody I loved was dead. The only thing keeping me clinging to life at that moment was… "Can I take my children with me?"

Otto pondered for a moment. "You can go, but not the children."

Giving up on them now would render all my sacrifices meaningless. "I don't need your pity or your recognition! I want my children!" I tossed the Iron Cross onto the snow.

"That's impossible," Otto said solemnly.

"What will you do? Lock them back in a cage? Subject them to more laboratory tests? Is that what those children are to you? Animals?" I was infuriated, but Otto remained placid. "Answer me!"

Otto cast his eyes down and pulled out a golden chain, fishing his gilded watch from his pocket. He knocked three times on the lid embossed with the Black Sun as if it were a door. He opened it and observed the tiny clock attentively, as if the time provided by the hands would reveal the answer he sought. After a moment, Otto closed the lid with determination and issued an order. "Line them up!"

CHAPTER 49

THE GUARDS TOOK MY CHILDREN OUT of the canopy and led them into the open field, followed by all the soldiers of the squad.

"What are you going to do?" I bawled, but everybody ignored me. "Otto, please! Please!"

Otto glanced back at me. "What is meant to be," he resolved with a stern look.

What is meant to be? I wondered. *Fate. What is fated! My children's fate!* I freaked out in terror, remembering Renenet's words. *"Why are you so willing to spoil your life for the sake of those children, not born from your own flesh and blood, whose fate has been already decided?... Nothing you do could change their fortune... How much more blood needs to be shed for you to realize these children are going to die no matter what you do?"*

"Otto, please, don't do it! It doesn't need to be this way... Please, please, reconsider, you have the power to decide otherwise... My children... they don't have to die."

"There is but one fate for the Children of the Damned," he said, referring to descendants of the Grigori. "Only death can atone the sins of the Fallen, and nothing we do can alter the wishes of the High Ones."

"No! I refuse to abide! Damn the High Ones!"

"A drop of fresh water doesn't sweeten an ocean. The tears you shed will be a cruel reminder that only suffering waits for those who dare to challenge destiny," Otto said with disillusionment, as if he were the prey of destiny himself. "Your role here is complete now, girl. Leave without looking back. *Auf Wiedersehen!*" Otto donned his cap, flashing the *Totenkopf* insignia, the skull and crossbones, and joined his squadron. The soldiers had formed a line in front of my children, who hugged each other, glancing with fearful eyes at the firing squad before them.

"I will not allow it… even if it's the last thing I do." I stood with effort.

Bill held my arm. "Peach, there's nothing you can do—there's nothing we can do!" he corrected himself, the bitterness of defeat dressing his voice. He was right, yet I pulled free from his arm and continued on. "Don't you fear death?"

I turned back. "I should be dead now, but I'm not because of them. They showed me that despite the horrors I've endured, there is still a purpose for me. If they face death, the least I can do is stand by their side."

"You may turn around if you wish… It will make it easier for you." Otto addressed the children as if speaking to grown-up soldiers charged with treason. But the truth was, it would only make things easier for the soldiers—pulling the trigger would be easier without having the children's innocent eyes upon them.

"Why would we turn our eyes away from our own demise?" Valeska said, fearless, stepping forward. "By knowing when our life ends, the remaining breaths become even more precious."

Otto stared at her with awe, probably from hearing her speak for the first time.

"Don't pity us for leaving this existence. Feel compassion for yourselves, who waste the here and now, and your descendants, who will yearn to squeeze the hours out of the seconds." Her words infused her brothers with courage, and they faced the squad with heads held high and linked hands. "We know where we're heading… I hope you do as well."

The soldiers of the firing squad exchanged worried glances.

"Enough!" Otto called. "Squadron ready!"

The soldiers straightened their backs and presented their rifles.

I limped, dragging my feet across the snowy field, aware these could be my last steps.

"Aim!" The rifles and machine guns targeted them, but my children didn't cower.

Breathless, I interposed myself between the firing squad and my children, arms wide open. "If you want to shoot my children, your bullets will need to pass through me first!"

The squadron waited, immobile, for the brigadeführer's instruction.

"Step aside, girl!" Otto warned.

"No, I will not!"

"Peach, you've done enough. They want us, not you. Please step aside," Jov said. "We love you, no matter what."

"No, it's not enough… It will never be enough," I said, battling my tears.

"Step aside, girl!" Otto screamed, red-faced and infuriated. "I'll not repeat myself."

What can I do? How can I save my children? Damn it! My mind revolved, elucubrating, despite knowing no answer could solve my predicament. I was on the brink of the waterfall, and the sole outcome was to go over.

"On the count of three!" Otto said as ultimatum, offering me a last chance to reconsider.

Amid my excruciating wait, the Harbinger of Death made his appearance. Sidney promenaded behind the firing squad, expectant of his cue to pace onto the stage for the finale of this play—this Greek tragedy. *There must be a way*, I thought, recalling it had been Sidney who had guided my way safely through an entanglement of bullets when I boarded the train. Sidney had the power to turn things around. He had the power to prevent my children from dying. After all, he was Death itself.

"One!" Otto started the count.

"Please… Sidney… I know you can prevent this… please!" I begged, but he remained silent. Expectant. Impassive.

"Two!"

"Please!"

"Three!"

I drew a last breath of air and squeezed my eyes shut instinctively. The rifles clattered until magazines emptied. My ears buzzed as the stream of bullets swooshed by. Then, there was only silence.

Am I dead? I cracked my eyelids open and peeked at the soldiers staring at me in disbelief. I was alive, unhurt despite the dozens of bullets. *Sidney?* Had he done something? But he had disappeared.

"Witch!" a soldier broke the silence. "She is in cahoots with the devil!" Fearful of those words, the soldiers backed off, as if they were facing a massive army. It was not men but the dread of Death they faced. I knew it better than them, as the silence behind me amassed, whispering to my soul what my mind refused to accept. Until I gathered courage enough to turn and confront the grim face of Death.

Sidney was standing among the riddled bodies of my children.

I fell on my knees with an overwhelming pressure in my chest that almost stopped my heart. I crawled, wheezing with unvoiced screams, "Please wake up…" My hands covered in blood, I tried to arrange their limbs back together with the despair of a toddler who broke her Christmas toy, hoping if I did, they would open their eyes again… but they didn't. "Why?" I wailed, heartbroken. "They were… only children!"

"Children of the Damned, descendants of the Grigori," Sidney clarified.

"No! They were my children!" I hammered my chest. "*Meine Kinder!* And nobody else's." I caressed their heads as I pulled their lifeless bodies against me.

"They were nobody's children, but you took them in like your own. You fulfilled their wishes of being truly loved for once." But Sidney's words offered no solace for my broken heart.

"I-I tried to protect them… to shield them from the bullets with my body… but… they died and not me," I babbled, unable to explain what had happened. "But you could have helped them… You had the power to save them!" I turned to Sidney, enraged.

"It's forbidden for me to alter the course of a human life."

I stood and faced him. "But you helped me! You showed me the way to avoid the bullets! You saved my life!"

Sidney shook his head slightly. "It was never me. Even if I had forewarned you about the trajectory of the bullets, you could never have reacted fast enough to dodge them. I did not save you… They did." Sidney's eyes glanced at my children lying at his feet. "You were protected by an invisible barrier—electromagnetism, as your scientists call it—capable of altering the trajectory of a bullet. A field created by your children. A skill inherited from the Grigori."

Von Schroeder's words about the Overman, mentioned during our dinner in Wewelsburg, became vivid. "*A being with superior strength and reflexes, with outstanding psychic abilities, capable of bending the trajectory of a bullet in battle.*" And as proof, I had the soldier who'd shot me twice in the control car of the train. Shots impossible to miss, which he ended up failing... *No! My children made him fail!*

"I've witnessed a person twisting the trajectory of a bullet at will, whimsically, as if the bullet had a will of its own," Sidney continued. "But your children were too young yet to discover the true power of their abilities. They couldn't have protected you, standing on the roof of the train, while they remained locked in the cell. I had to let them know where you were. That's the reason I created a tunnel, to funnel their abilities, like sonar pinpointing the position of a battleship. All that time I was not guiding you; I guided them."

"But why me? You should have helped them instead of me!"

"Because they asked me to. You just witnessed it yourself. They could have created the electromagnetic field to protect themselves, but with the immeasurable love they had for you, they shielded you instead. As the water of a river is parted by a stone and converges afterward, the bullets bypassed you and continued toward the intended direction—your children. Your children saved you at the cost of their lives. They wished nothing else but your well-being."

"But why?" I kept asking, believing all this time it had been me who was sacrificing for them.

"Maybe because despite your intention to end your life, you deserve to live until you uncover the beauty and happiness of living," Sidney said, all-knowing.

"You knew this would happen, yet you allowed it?"

"You were informed as well—"

"But I don't have the—the... the powers you have!" I stood to look Sidney in the eye. "You could have saved them if you had wanted! But you just stood there and watched them die!"

"It's forbidden to me to alter the course—" Sidney started reciting the same line.

"*Scheisse!*" I ranted, pouring all my frustration out on him. "I don't care about anyone's rules! You had to do it! What were you risking if you broke those rules? Your life? Would Death reap his own life? Goddammit!" My tears rushed uncontrollably. "Are you telling me you could not put something on the line for these children, when I sacrificed everything I had? My family, my friends... my love... my own life... I lost everything. So don't tell me that crap, that you could not break the rules!"

Sidney stared at me, unmoved, even-tempered, his green eyes peaceful as a lake I could not disturb, no matter how many rocks I threw. After all, he was the Harbinger of Death; maybe it was within his nature to have the inability of experiencing sorrow. Or perhaps he had grown numb after carrying so many souls to the hereafter.

"Have you ever harbored a feeling in that ice heart of yours?" I dared to ask, but his lips remained pursed. "In your coming and going around the world, have you ever stopped to observe how a gesture as simple as giving a flower can outshine the gloominess in the heart of a person? The stirring sensation caused by a poem, dancing goofily until you burst into peals of laughter, or the shuddering sensation of kissing for the first time. Have you?"

"I have wondered…" Sidney said, with traces of melancholy in his voice, "…how it feels."

"Well, you still have time to find out… but them." I gestured to my dead children with bloodstained hands. "They will not have the chance to uncover the beauty and happiness of life, just because someone up in the sky, who hasn't experienced life himself, thought 'it was time' for them to leave. The sole person in this world who could have interposed against such egoistic Will was you. But you lacked the empathy and the courage to rebel against the orders given to you… My children are dead because of you. You robbed them of the possibility of growing old."

"I'm… sorry." Sidney's left eye rim reddened.

"I thought of my ability to peek into the hereafter, this second sight, as a curse. But now I look around and can't tell the difference. There's only death surrounding me. I hope you feel accomplished in that."

"Emma—"

"Go away! Leave me alone! I'm sure somewhere else somebody is eager to die."

But despite my harsh words, Sidney stood before me until tears sprouted from his left eye. He ran his fingers across his cheek and examined his moistened fingers as if he had never shed tears before. His nostrils flared as his breathing turned agitated, puffs condensing in the cold air. Sidney's ever-impassive face lost its composure. The muscles in his jaw tensed and he bared his teeth. His fingers curled into a trembling fist, bulging the arteries and poking out his knuckles. Amid his rage, Sidney uttered words I could not understand, and then he sprinted, fast as a cheetah trying to catch its prey, until his silhouette was lost on the orange-tinted horizon, leaving behind a trail of footprints on the snow.

Once alone, I lay down beside my children. "Don't miss me… I'm coming," I whispered, and closed my eyes, wishing next time I opened them, I could be with them.

CHAPTER 50

BILL SHOOK ME AWAKE. "We need to leave. More soldiers will come." He pulled at me to get me back on my feet.

"You go," I protested without flexing a muscle. "Go back home... Return to your brother."

"Peach, please! I'm not leaving without you!" Bill struggled to drag me across the snowy soil with a single arm, the other still immobilized in a sling. "Even if I have to haul you to the border."

"Bill, let go of me. I'm ripped apart. No red thread could stitch me back together." I felt hollower than his teddy bear.

"I'll make sure you have the chance to uncover the beauty and happiness of life," Bill quoted my words, admitting he had eavesdropped on my discussion with Sidney. But before his ordinary eyes, I should have seemed like a crazy woman ranting to the wind. "I'll make sure... you die so old... that there's nothing else left for you to accomplish in life," Bill said, breathless.

It was unfair of him.

In the end, Bill's stubbornness finally pulled me out of my lethargic state and reignited my survival instinct. I got back on my feet, and with arms entwined across shoulders, we lumbered west, holding each other during our moments of frailty.

I left without looking back, knowing if I dared, I would crum-

ble.

We hobbled without stopping. As it got darker, the temperature dropped. With our wounds and the cold, if we halted to rest, we might never make it back on our feet. We had to keep ourselves in motion. We descried farmhouses along our way. Our feet begged to knock on the doors, asking for a place to rest while our mouths implored a glass of water. But as painfully excruciating as our tramping was, we refrained ourselves from doing it. We had to abandon this land as fast as we could. This was no longer my country. I had become an outsider.

The clouds parted and the moon peeked out, lighting our path through the woodland, making it less terrifying. But the moon also brought the howling. A deep howl like that of a wolf resounded amid the cacophony of artillery from the battlefield. We came across a trail of paw prints in the snow. The enormous claws of the animal had sunk until reaching the layer of mud below.

"These huge paws belong to the howling wolf?" I asked, fearful it could still be marauding the surroundings.

"More bear-size than wolf," Bill mused with a worried expression. "But the prints are indeed canine: four-fingered with a rhombic shape, as opposed to the five-fingered, pentagonal-shaped paws of bears."

Ahead, the paw prints turned bloody. As we advanced, the feeling we were approaching a battlefield circled in my head. *Maybe the wolf just scavenged meat from the cadavers,* I tried to convince myself. But my hand flew to my mouth at the sight of the massacred bodies covering the field, with wounds not produced by bullets but carved by claws. As I navigated through the corpses, I recognized their uniforms; they were SS. "Otto's unit," I babbled upon finding Otto's inert body, eyes lost, staring at the sky through broken, blood-flecked spectacles.

"The entire squadron… butchered." Bill gesticulated, looking green. "Despite their armaments and training, they were incapable of resistance. Who or what did this to them?"

A golden chain dribbled from Otto's clenched fist resting over his chest. I uncurled his fingers, revealing his gilded watch. I ran my thumb over the engraving. "The Black Sun," I whispered, and knocked three times before opening it, as Von Schroeder and Otto had.

The clock's hands were fixed at 1:30; who knew since when. I discarded the possibility of a hit during their ambush being responsible for the malfunction. No scratches were visible. It seemed Otto had treasured it, given it was the watch and not his gun he held devotedly during his last moments, with pistol still sheathed in his belt.

The watch had a tiny mirror placed on the interior face of the lid, instead of the usual photo of relatives. Weird; Otto had never seemed like a vain person to me. I brought the watch close to my face and looked at myself in the mirror with bewilderment, not from my haggard reflection, but because the shadowy face of a woman with piercing eyes poked over my left shoulder, as if she were behind me. She placed her elongated, knobby finger over her carmine lips and shushed me.

A shriek of horror escaped me. I shut the gilded watch and turned back, startled, but there was nothing in sight.

No woman or footprints to confirm she had been there.

"Peach! Are you okay?" Bill came to my aid wielding a firearm he had collected from the bodies.

"I-I-I'm fine," I said, trying to convince myself the image had been just a byproduct of my altered nerves or conjured up by my second sight. "It was nothing. Just a figure formed by darkness."

CHAPTER 51

WE ROAMED UNTIL WE ARRIVED at the Meuse River and crossed it near Knikkerdorp. Soon after, we were spotted by a reconnaissance company, and they transported us to a partially destroyed Eindhoven—recently secured by Allied forces. A medic inspected Bill while I recounted the happenings to a lieutenant of the 101st Airborne Division, Irwin Lovelock, who listened attentively with probing eyes, circling a cigar around his mouth skeptically. Not a surprise, considering I was wearing the uniform of his enemies.

It was difficult to tell things as had happened, not because I was ashamed, but because it was too painful, so I edited my story. I removed my parents and brother, my rape and torture, Sidney and the stuff beyond belief, from my telling. And without the proofs of the experiments my children had been subjected to, I could only narrate the horrors endured, not just by them, but by all the Jews and the German detractors of the Nazis detained in the concentration camps. I vindicated Ghislain by saying it had been him who had helped me, rescuing my children from a concentration camp—true in part. It was easier that way. Simpler.

When I finished, Lieutenant Lovelock approached me.

"I'm sorry for your loss, kid," he said solemnly. "But I'm thankful to you for rescuing Corporal Hurlbart and for your aid in our fight against the Nazis. Brave youngsters like you, not brainwashed by propaganda, are the only hope for this world." He squeezed my shoulder. "Rest now. You're safe here."

Safe? I wondered. "I-I—" I could not articulate the words.

"Don't worry," Lieutenant Lovelock reassured me. "Tomorrow a transport will take you to a hospital for proper attention."

"Thank you."

Lieutenant Lovelock grinned and marched away.

Bill staggered to me. "You have nothing to worry about, Peach."

Being homeless, friendless, and without family, I had everything to worry about. But somehow, the burden on my shoulders had eased. Maybe I didn't care anymore what could happen to me tomorrow, in an hour, or even the very next minute. Or it could be simply a side effect of losing everything. Having no attachments to anything in life, I became free. Fearless.

"Once I get better, I'll need to rejoin my unit," Bill explained. "But when the war is over, I'll come back for you."

I didn't know what to say.

"I'll leave you to rest," Bill said amid an uncomfortable silence.

"You need to rest too."

Bill nodded and left the room.

I sighed and collapsed onto the stiff mattress, feeling neither alive nor dead, physically and mentally numb, breathing by inertia. My mind had adapted to the physical pain of my wounds, but an emotional, unstoppable ache gnawed at my heart. I pulled Ghislain's notebook from my pocket and opened it to the red-ribbon bookmark.

"Epithalamium," I read at the top of the page under the dim light, remembering its meaning was a poem written by a groom in dedication to the bride, like the one declaimed by Bruno to Gerda during their wedding.

> "Crossroad without names,
> A crystal birdcage for the volition.
> Crossroad without fates,
> Allow the wind to blow me into fruition.
>
> Life roads without senses,
> In your crossing I was neglected.
> Across darkness I ambled aimless,

Believing I could never be loved.

Crossroad of bone and blood,
Eyes lost under the hood of persuasion,
Shackled to a yoke labeled brotherhood,
It showed me the sole way was sedition.

Crossroad where my hopes converged,
Skies listened to my midnight prayers.
Heaven sent me the angel for whom my heart yearned,
Her smile prettier than blooming flowers.

Even lost in the journey to nowhere,
Among all stars, your eyes shone the brightest.
Your velvet voice guided me ashore,
Making my ancient heart feel the youngest.

But of attaining your love I am unworthy,
Your heart crowning the highest mountain
Where the peaks caress the sky.
Of having wings, my thoughts entertain.

High roads toward the world's end,
No matter how far and remote,
For holding your hand, to God I supplicate;
Seeking after you, my entire life I would spend.

If my dream life could fulfill,
Always by your side I would be.
Emma, your happiness as creed I ascribe,
And if for you my life I need to give,
Worry not; do this I happily will.
Because without your love,
For living I would lose the thrill.

Crossroad without names,
For flying high, you gave me the intuition.
Crossroad without fates,
For conquering Emma's love, grant me redemption.

And in life let me never walk astray
From Emma's side until my dying day."

I squeezed the notebook against my chest, as if the poem were the missing half of my broken heart, hoping if I kept it always close, it would weld back together.

CHAPTER 52

THE NIGHT OF OUR ARRIVAL AT THE HOSPITAL, I fled without letting Bill know. I was not fully recovered yet, but I had become acquainted with pain. It became a sort of atonement.

I headed southwest, and with the aid of Good Samaritans who offered a lift across some parts of my journey, a roof to spend the night under, and a bowl of hot soup, after a couple of days, I arrived in Paris. Even while the havoc of war was still visible, the streets were alive and swarming with people. I visited the places Anton had described in his letters; the thought of walking the same streets my brother had and imagining my young parents enjoying their most lovely times in this city provided me crumbs of solace.

I got a job as a waitress in a coffee shop from where I could see the Eiffel Tower, and I worked there until news of the end of the war broke across Europe.

One day, a family visited the cafe, and the daughter recognized me. It was the family of Jews I had come across during my escape in the city of Hamm. The husband fell to his knees, asking my forgiveness for pushing me out of their hideout. Although my children did not survive, I didn't hold a grudge against him. If he had allowed me in, they would have ended up in a concentration camp. The family invited me to break bread at their house as a token of gratitude, and after a recount of our traumatic experiences, they asked me about my plans. I had none.

Many nights I had thought about visiting my mother's sister in the UK, but I was terrified of answering the questions about the whereabouts of my family that I knew would come. So, every time a glimpse of enthusiasm for reconnecting with my past flourished, it sublimated away.

"We will immigrate to the United States," the husband explained. "You can come with us, if you wish."

"I really appreciate your generosity, but I'm a ghost. Today I go by the name of Emma, tomorrow perhaps I'll be Mildred… War snatched everything from me. Even my identity."

"A friend of mine can forge you a new identity, you see? That way you can truly leave everything behind and start anew."

"Please, Emma, come with us!" the daughter, who had grown fond of me, gushed. "We're going to visit Liberty Statue."

"The Statue of Liberty, honey," her mother amended.

Liberty? I pondered for a moment. *Could I really be free there?*

The urge to distance myself from the memories linked to this land made me accept the proposal. From that day on, I was reborn as Emma Blum, daughter of Abigail and Esau, sister of Ilana. And as wise Renenet had foreseen, Emma Niemeyer became just another dead girl who'd burned alive along with her parents inside a country house in the marshes. Their remains were lost among the millions of nameless lives consumed by war.

Migrating to the United States provided me with an opportunity to rebuild my life: continue my studies, make new friends, and within time, even give myself the opportunity to rediscover love. However, despite crossing the Atlantic to leave my painful memories behind, I always carried with me an ominous reminder of my past.

Sometimes, as I walked the streets, I recognized him among the crowd. Sidney, the Harbinger of Death, doing his errands. I always switched sidewalks and pretended not to notice him, as if by doing so I was avoiding the spell of death. Even the few times we stumbled into one another, he didn't utter a word. His olive-green eyes stared at me, glowing with the fondness of a long-unseen relative. But I always continued my journey without looking back at him.

Until the day he paid me a visit.

"Honey, I'm home!" I shouldered the door open, juggling the Moses basket in one hand and a grocery bag in another. I rested the Moses on the coffee table in the living room and tickled baby Luvena, who waved her tiny hands and kicked out of excitement, baring her toothless gums with an ample smile. "What a gorgeous smile, my dear! Who's hungry? Who's hungry? Now, Mommy is going to prepare you the vegetable porridge you love so much!" I emptied the contents of the brown bag over the kitchen bar, carried the vegetables to the sink, and washed them. "Hon? Are you hungry? Or can you wait until supper?" I called to my husband, who was resting on the bed upstairs. He had skipped lunch due to a stomachache. Footfalls sounded behind me and I turned, startled. "Hon?"

Sidney was standing by the coffee table, his hand extended over Luvena, who babbled, her tiny fingers trying to grab his hand. "She reminds me of you," he said with a soothing voice and turned to me. "She inherited your vibrant eyes."

"Not so lively anymore..." I said, nostalgic, considering that over three decades had passed since we first met, yet Sidney looked like it had been yesterday. "I grew old."

"I see you the same through the waves of time." Sidney half smiled and returned his attention to Luvena.

My heart pounded at the thought he could be here to harm my daughter. "What do you want?" I searched with one hand for the knife resting in the sink behind me.

"I miss speaking with you."

"What did you expect? Friendship? After all the misery you brought to my life?"

Sidney stared at me, speechless for a moment. "I also... wish things were different... I'm sorry." He said this with disappointment, before heading to the door and vanishing.

I sighed, dropping the knife, and rushed to secure Luvena in my arms. "Everything is okay now, my dear. Don't be scared," I lulled her, but it was me who needed to be reassured.

After my nerves calmed, I gasped. "Hon?" I yelled, but got no reply, so I rushed upstairs to materialize my fears. My husband lay sprawled on the bathroom floor. Unresponsive. Lifeless.

EPILOGUE

"'IN THAT MOMENT, MAIA DEAR,'" I continued reading the last words my gran had written for me, "'I understood there is no running away from the past. I had to embrace it. To be resilient. I promised myself to endure the harshness of my curse for the rest of my life. But unfortunately, in the same way my children had inherited an ill fate from their forefathers, the Grigori, I transmitted mine to my offspring as well. Ruddy Bear, when Dr. Emmerich shared the dreadful diagnosis of your cancer, you were just a child, admiring the goldfish in the fish tank at the reception counter, heedless about your fate. But I knew. My cursed eyes could see the Harbinger of Death standing by your side. I could not bear witnessing such an image, so I covered my face and cried, ashamed of the fate to which I have subjected you.

"'While you struggled between life and death in that hospital bed, destiny reunited me with Bill, who had suffered a cardiac arrest. During his stay, we caught up on the last decades of our lives, and after he was discharged, he returned the documents I had trusted him to deliver to the American Army back in the war—he had hidden them before being captured by the SS. The documents include this book you hold in your hands. I reused its endless blank pages to avow my guilt, and as testament of the past I could not rewrite, no matter how many pages I tore away.

"'I'm sorry for not having the courage to tell you this personally, Maia, but despite my cowardice, you have the right to know that the ghosts of my past will come back to haunt your future. You need to be resilient, my Ruddy Bear, to be brave on your own, because I won't be there for you anymore. It breaks my heart, not being by your side when you will need me the most, but if Death could concede me an additional breath of life, I would devote it entirely to you. My love forever. Your grandmother, Peach.'"

My tears fell, moistening the page by her signature. I shut the book and ran my fingers over the knife marks on the cover forming the word *Resilience*, which I read with trembling voice, remembering the misfortunes recounted by my gran: she'd survived sexual assault, lost the children she fought so hard to save, outlived her first love, who sacrificed himself for her, and even watched her parents—my biological great-grandparents—get murdered before her eyes. Too much suffering for one life.

I limped to the draped piano, where the family portraits rested.

"And above all, you still sacrificed for me?" I asked her, holding the photo where she and my grandfather held my baby mother in their arms. I had been my gran's last sacrifice. It hurt me deeply to be the reason she was no longer with me. *If only I had been healthy! If only I had been strong!* I slammed the dusty fallboard of the piano.

"Resilience… resilience…" I repeated, remembering her last words. "I can't be as resilient as you were… I'm not that strong! Not when you're not here with me!" But I had no right to ask for a peaceful life. Not when my gran's life had been a constant struggle.

I had to be like the woman of unwavering will and a heart of gold who gave everything for those she loved. My heroine. My grandmother.

I curled my fingers, leaving tracks across the film of dust on the board. My piano, one of the earliest and fondest memories I had of my gran. She'd bought it for me when I turned five, and I'd played it every single day until I received my cancer diagnosis two years later. Then it became just another piece of furniture in the house. Although the piano was valuable, and she had serious economic difficulties with my treatment, my gran never sold it. She always harbored the hope that one day, I would play it again…

I pulled the stool and sat carefully, considering my wounded leg. I uncovered the keys and positioned my fingers across, with my healthy foot on the pedals. My rusty fingers stumbled over each other, trying to keep the pace of my commands after a decade of abandonment. But I didn't care if it sounded sloppy and out of tune, *Bahiti's Sonata* transported me to the ballroom of my dreams, where I waltzed endlessly over the sleek marble floor, guided by Sidney.

The uncanny being more dream than man.

The Harbinger who confronted Death to save me, sacrificing his eternal life.

The Man with a Thousand Names, of which I call him only one…

My destiny.

ACKNOWLEDGMENTS

I want to give my most sincere recognition to my mother: her resilience before the vicissitudes of life and relentlessness to provide her children with the best she could despite her circumstances, which not only shaped the men my brother and I became but also influenced this tale. A tale of feminine fortitude being written across generations by all the brave women in my family. The selfless foremothers who sacrificed themselves to provide for their children and who became the pillars of their families, giving meaning to the place we call *home*.

My dearest appreciation to my brother, family, and close friends who have cheered me through my publishing journey and provided the words of encouragement that have helped me to overcome my moments of doubt.

My heartfelt thanks to my developmental editor, Kelly Schaub, not only for helping me shape this novel to life, but also for mentoring my writing skills and showing me that I still have plenty to learn about the writing craft.

Special thanks to Lara Kennedy, my copy editor and proofreader, your keen eye helped me polishing every detail to get this manuscript in the best shape possible.

And especially, my sincere appreciation to all of you, my readers, who have joined me in this creative endeavor. With your aid, you are proving that a nontypical fantasy series like *Vandella* can thrive in the overcrowded book market. Your continuous support is what fuels my creative engine to complete the telling of this story and materialize this dream I had, and slowly, *Vandella* is becoming yours as well.

ABOUT THE AUTHOR

M. CH. LANDA is a longtime blogger and author of *Vandella* and *Vandella's Chronicles* series. Death and the hereafter play a key role in the legends and traditions within the folklore of Mexico, where he was born. From a young age, he took *fabulism* to heart, endowing his stories with the duality of reality and magic. When he is not writing, you can find him watching a movie (his first passion), working out in the gym, reading a book from his endless list while he tastes a wine, cooking a new recipe, or hanging out with family and friends.

For more information, please visit:
www.mchlanda.com

Or follow him on Social Networks:
Facebook—M. Ch. Landa
Twitter—@MChLanda
Instagram—@m_ch_landa
Goodreads—m_ch_landa
TikTok—@m_ch_landa